Pavel Kornev

THE DORMANT

*thank you for being
my Reader!
without you Books
are nothing!
PAVEL KORNEV*

SUBLIME ELECTRICITY
Book Four

Magic Dome Books

The Dormant
(The Sublime Electricity Book #4)
Copyright © Pavel Kornev 2018
Cover Art © Vladimir Manyukhin 2018
Translator © Andrew Schmitt 2018
Editor: Barbara D. Jenkins
Published by Magic Dome Books, 2018
All Rights Reserved
ISBN: 978-80-88231-60-8

TABLE OF CONTENTS:

NEW BABYLON is the capital of the mighty Second Empire. Dirigibles drift over the city, steam trains race down its tracks, and the factory chimneys never stop billowing smoke. The hegemory of science is unquestioned, and yet magic hasn't disappeared from the world entirely. It remains dissolved in the blood of those who are called illustrious. Hardline reductionists find that hard to accept, but it is not in their power to change the longstanding status quo.

Everything threatens to change with the death of the widowed Empress, and Leopold Orso, an illustrious gentleman, can sense the looming changes clearer than most.

He feels the draw of far-away lands, but a gloomy past holds him in place like a deadly snare. Will the whirlpool of coming events pull our troubled illustrious hero to the very bottom or throw him up to unimaginable heights? And will anything remain to throw him up to? It's impossible to say. After all, there are highly placed conspirators willing to do whatever it takes just to get what's theirs.

Bullets from hired killers, anarchists' bombs, blood magic of Aztec priests and electroshock therapy in a psychiatric clinic. Leopold will have a difficult time overcoming everything fate has in store for him and remaining himself through it all.

"A HEART PRESERVED IN A TIN CAN
BEGINS TO BEAT AGAIN."

Steamphonia (Russian Steampunk Band)
Song Title: *Heart*

PART ONE

TARGET

Silver Bullets and a Smokescreen

1

ANY RAZOR, in its essence, is akin to the ritual sickle of the Celtic druids on the holy day of the renewal of nature. A pull of the hand and the skin becomes clean, while the face grows younger as if the weight of many days is hewn away together with the stubble.

I appraised my reflection in the mirror and nodded, agreeing with my judgement. After that, I shook the foam from the razor into the basin of warm water, led the blade along my soaped-up cheek, and again - a strip of clean.

For the last week, I hadn't bothered with shaving, so it was as if the sharpened metal was carrying away time itself. I was growing younger right before my very eyes.

By the way, there's a good reason people say razors are dangerous: if you get distracted, you're sure to cut yourself.

I didn't get distracted. Someone distracted me.

"My dear!" I heard from the bedroom. "Have you given any thought to our wedding day?"

My arm quavered, and the blade painlessly slit my skin with ease. A droplet of blood leaked out. With a condemned sigh, I stuck a little piece of paper over the cut and continued getting myself in order. After that, I spritzed my hands with cologne, clapped them on my cheeks, then left the bathroom in no rush whatsoever.

"Did you say something, my dear?" I addressed

Liliana with all possible tranquility. She was lying on the bed with a ladies' magazine in her hands.

She tore herself from her reading and repeated the question:

"Have you given any thought to our wedding day?"

"Are you in the family way?"

"Oh, Leo!" my girlfriend rolled her eyes. "You're just like my mom! She asks about that incessantly!"

"And are you...? "

"No, I'm not pregnant!" Lily snorted indignantly. "Where do such thoughts even come from?"

"Well, where do your questions about marriage come from?" I parried.

"You don't want to take me as your wife?"

I did want that. And who in their right mind wouldn't desire to legally marry such a girl, who was pretty, smart and the heiress to a considerable fortune?

Admittedly, I was rich enough not to take such factors into account. I simply enjoyed the company of the only daughter of the Marquess Montague regardless of mercantile considerations.

Liliana tossed a black lock off her face and grabbed my attention, losing patience:

"Leo!"

"I do want to!" I shuddered. "Of course I do. As a matter of fact, I was just thinking about that momentous date..."

"You little liar!" Lily easily sussed out my

cleverness.

"In fact, I'm simply lost in admiration for you."

And now that was the purest truth. Liliana and I had been together for three months, and my feelings for her only grew stronger every day.

Sounds like something from a romance novel? Maybe so, but I really did... love her? Probably. The most important thing was that, when I saw Liliana, my soul felt warm, and the rest meant nothing. No matter what anyone said...

Liliana caught a pensive gaze from me and adjusted her peignoir, slightly covering her bare legs with the long skirt.

"Leo, don't get distracted!" she demanded.

I took a seat on the bed next to her and gave her a kiss.

"Leo, no!" Lily laughed, moving away. "Not now! My mom keeps saying I'm riding you too hard!"

"She keeps saying that?" I asked, so dumbfounded that I even stopped stroking her lithe feminine leg.

"Well, not to me..." Liliana said in embarrassment. "To my dad. I heard it by accident."

"You were eavesdropping."

"Leo, you're avoiding the topic!"

I tousled a lock of Lily's black hair, admired her beauty and classical profile, then admitted with a smile:

"Yes, I've lost weight. And what of it?"

Over the summer, I really had lost fifteen kilograms, but I wasn't even close to my former sickly emaciation and was still quite large and powerful. I hadn't become slim, but lean. And our amorous liaison had absolutely zero relationship to these changes. A somewhat larger role was played by the fresh air of the mountain resort town, dumb-bell workouts and proper nutrition.

And also, I stopped being a werebeast.

Yes, the family curse had left me in that ill-fated basement in Montecalida, and my shaving cuts now healed just as slowly as they did for everyone else.

To be honest, I had long since grown accustomed to my new reality.

"Leo!" Liliana waved her hand before my face. "Leo, your head is in the clouds!"

"Yes, my dear?"

"We weren't talking about your weight, but our wedding day!"

I got up from the bed and walked over to the window. The hotel Benjamin Franklin was situated atop a promontory and, from its fourth floor, the view over the historical part of town was amazing. To be more accurate, there would have been a great view, if there wasn't a damp haze hanging over the city. The nasty September weather and the capital's usual smog enshrouded the building like a wet towel, so I could see only the silhouettes of roofs and the high spires of palaces.

"Our wedding day?" I drew out my words in thought. "You want to know the exact day?"

Liliana swished through the pages of the

magazine.

"It says here that Duke Logrin announced the engagement of his eldest daughter to Baron Alston. The wedding will be on the twentieth of October, Emperor Clement Remembrance Day. A very symbolic date, Leo, don't you find?"

I shrugged my shoulders.

"I'm ok with any day."

"Is that so?"

"Yes. But not here, not in New Babylon. Tomorrow, we're flying to the continent, did you forget? We could stop for a week in Madrid, and head to Barcelona from there. How do you like that idea?"

"It's an amazing idea!" Liliana smiled, but then wrinkled her forehead. "Wait, Leo! Did you say tomorrow? Will I have time to see my parents?"

"The flight is scheduled for five thirty in the evening," I reassured her and turned away from the window. "Do they even know we're leaving?"

"There hasn't been a good time to tell them," Lily answered frivolously. "We'll tell them tomorrow. You are coming with me, after all, right?"

"If need be..."

"Leo, don't worry! Mom and dad are crazy about you. They won't lock me up at home!"

"I greatly hope so," I snickered.

"Although..." Liliana sighed. "Are you sure you don't want to stay in New Babylon for a bit?"

I did not want that. In the capital, it was far too easy to have a chance encounter with an old acquaintance, and I really didn't want to fall back into the field of view of Department Three or, even worse, people from her Majesty's inner circle. So, I answered with one short categorical word:

"No!"

Liliana could perfectly hear the note of annoyance that slipped through in my voice and jerked her head up.

"Leo, is something the matter?"

I sighed. I really should have told Lily some of the secrets of my past a long time ago, but I simply hadn't had the spirit for it. I was afraid. I was afraid to scare her, afraid to push her away. So, I kept silent.

I didn't reveal the true reasons for my worrying now, either. I turned away to the window and looked at the gray city then, with a heavy sigh, I said:

"In the papers, they're writing that the Empress will meet her maker any day now. The heiress's health isn't so very strong either. Laborers are striking. Socialists are demanding the dissolution of the Imperial council and the establishment of an elected senate. Some anarchist threw a bomb at the Minister of Justice, and only a miracle kept him from dying. There were shots fired at a Justice of the High Imperial Court. Bottles of kerosene were thrown at the military recruitment station. And every day it goes on like this. I want to be as far from here as possible when everything goes south."

"If you say so, my dear. If you say so."

I bowed down to kiss Liliana and warned her:

"I'll be back in two hours."

"I'll be waiting," she sighed, laying the

magazine open and suddenly wondering: "Do you remember the first time we stayed here, in June?"

"Yes. And what of it?"

"At that time, I was lying in bed waiting for you to knock on my door. But I didn't wait long enough and fell asleep."

"I could knock right now," I offered with a smile.

"No!" Lily did not agree. "Go about your business. And I'll be languishing and waiting for a knock. You will knock this time, right?"

"Most assuredly," I promised, kissing the girl again and going into my adjoining room.

I didn't wait around there for long. I just changed into a new shirt, tied on a neckerchief and put on a jacket. I didn't take an umbrella or a raincoat. Although it was cloudy outside, it was dry. The season of autumn rains hadn't yet arrived.

Pulling out the upper drawer of my writing desk, I got my passport, wallet and Cerberus from it, placed them in my pockets and went on my way.

"Leo!" Liliana called out to me.

"Yes?" I glanced into the door of the adjoining room.

"Come back soon. And don't forget, we were invited this evening to Albert and Elizabeth-Maria's!"

"Don't you worry, I'm not planning to take long," I calmly assured Liliana, although the dinner invitation had entirely flown out of my head.

After the triumphant performance in Montecalida, which had ended in fainting spells and mass hallucinations, Albert Brandt had acquired a scandalous fame as a true wizard of words and become a desired guest at New-Babylon society functions. Instead of heading to the New World, he had rented a place not far from the academy and was preparing to stage a play of his own authorship in the Imperial Theater.

Ignoring the poet's invitation would be at the very least impolite on my part. Who could say when the chance to return to New Babylon would come again? And all that remained was to hope that Albert didn't have all the local Bohemians coming over tonight as well.

I took my derby cap from the shelf and went into the hallway. I decided not to use the elevator, instead heading to the stairs and thinking about what little bauble to give Albert as a souvenir.

Passing by the bell-boy's table, I greeted the sleepy clerk with an impolite nod, went down to the first floor and headed to the receptionist's stand, but I was cut off by a sprightly gentleman of middling years, quite gaunt and red of hair.

"I'm here to see Mr. Witstein," he said with a clear Irish accent and, when the receptionist opened his journal, he introduced himself: "Lynch. Sean Lynch."

The clerk looked for the last name in the guest list and pointed to the elevator in silence then, with an attentive smile, he turned to me:

"How may I be of service, Mr. Shatunov?"

I caught myself on the fact that I had been

looking just too stubbornly at the redheaded Irishman as he walked away, shuddered and set my room key on the table.

"I just wanted to leave my key!"

"Any special requests?"

"No, nothing," I shook my head and, nervously waving my hand, stepped through the vestibule.

Hearing that family name knocked me off track. After all, he had clearly been speaking about Abraham Witstein, Vice President of the banking house that carried his family name. A chance meeting with him in the hotel vestibule threatened to quickly and definitively upend my anonymity.

Devil! I shouldn't have given in to Liliana and stayed in the Benjamin Franklin again. Devil take this sentimentality!

I winced, threw open the door with a nervous shove and walked outside up to a porter in livery with a flowery pattern. In reply to his business-like grin, I smiled no less formally, threw a quick gaze over Emperor's Square, packed with frolicking public, and clipped my dark glasses on my nose.

I got distracted for an instant, but that short moment decided everything.

"Don't move! Hands up!" sounded out from behind me, and I froze at half step.

My hand jumped to my jacket's side pocket all on its own, and I was barely able to jerk it away before the strong uniformed men all around me opened fire. They were holding their revolvers at the ready, fingers frozen on the triggers.

The investigator behind me gave another order without delay:

"On your knees! Hands behind your head!"

I hesitated, but immediately decided that not wanting to dirty my pants on the paving stones was hardly an adequate reason to experience the effects of an electric discharge device. All I allowed myself was to get down on my knees unhurriedly, in a vain attempt to maintain the remnants of my dignity.

Somewhere nearby, a powder engine barked out in rage, and a sluggish police armored car rolled out abruptly onto the square from an alley. Gawkers just gushed in from all sides, and a paper boy was nearly caught under the wheel, hurrying to roll his hand-cart out of the way.

The investigator approached from the back, put my hands behind me, clinked some steel cuffs onto my wrists and, with a bit of gravity in his voice, announced:

"Leopold Orso! You're under arrest for murder!"

I breathed out a silent curse.

My past had finally caught up to me. And, as is typical, it caught me at the very worst moment.

"On your feet!"

Ungracefully, due to my hands being bound behind my back, I stood from my knees and clarified:

"And who did I kill?"

"You can ask the investigator about that!" came the laconic reply, and I was shoved into the dark innards of the armored vehicle.

2

AN ARRESTEE is a creature without rights. From the moment of detention and until someone of the legal persuasion comes to the prison, they simply disappear, and absolutely anything could happen. Right up to falling off a bridge into the cloudy waters of the Yarden. And just about every other arrestee is subjected to arm twisting, kidney punches and strangling.

But not in my case. The uniformed investigators who'd shoved me into the armored vehicle didn't ask me a single question over the whole ride, just held me in the sights of their revolvers. It was as if they were afraid I would break the handcuff chain and throw myself at them with fists.

Fear. I could sense their fear.

There were six guards against one of me, but they were clearly afraid, and that was truly strange.

Had they heard about my *talent*? I doubted that greatly...

Be that as it may, I didn't make even the slightest attempt to draw the investigators into conversation and figure out what I'd been accused of. I just sat in silence on the bench. I simply didn't want to give the nervous boys a reason to shoot me full of holes. I knew for certain that they would fire to kill without the slightest hesitation.

THE POWDER ENGINE of the armored vehicle was

sneezing measuredly, its powerful wheels cushioning the uneven spots in the paving stones. It only really shook when hitting very severe potholes, careening on the bench from one guard to the other. And then the light of day went dark, the gray of the sullen sky beyond the side window grates changed into the gloom of a garage, and the heavy self-propelled carriage came to a stop.

The armored vehicle led me into the garage of the metropolitan police headquarters. In the jargon of the New Babylon's jailbirds, this was called "getting checked into the Box."

The investigator to my right unclipped the chain holding my handcuffs to the floor. The investigator to my left threw open the side door.

"To the exit!" The policeman opposite me ordered.

Whew, so many men just for little old me...

But from there, it only got worse. In the spacious garage, I was awaited by constables armed with semi-automatic carbines and four-barreled luparas. My ankles were immediately clinked into shackles and, to the jingling of a steel chain, I started to amble down the corridor like an especially dangerous recidivist.

The police administration building, huge and monumental, occupied a whole block and even went a few stories under the earth. A random person might get lost for hours in its confusing nooks and crannies, searching for the right door. In my days as a constable, I'd heard plenty of frightening stories about coworkers who disappeared without a trace simply by turning down the wrong corridor.

To be honest, I was seriously afraid of sharing their fate but, just a couple minutes later, I was led into a small windowless room flooded with the blinding light of electric lamps.

The search didn't take much time, if what they did could even be called a search. I had to simply remove all my clothes and, in exchange, pull on the striped uniform of an arrestee. My personal effects were placed into a canvas bag without a glance, and it was stamped with red wax seal.

Our next stop was in the photo room. There, I was sat in a wooden chair adorned with a plethora of clamps and fasteners, which bore a certain resemblance to an electric chair. The phlegmatic photographer clamped my head in a vice to take a full-face photograph, followed by a profile shot. After that, the photographer captured all my tattoos, and the police clerk took my finger prints, smearing my hands in black ink and forcing me to place them against a sheet of thick yellowish paper.

What followed was a total bore, measuring height and composing a list of distinguishing features. But it took no less than an hour. It became clear that, unlike my previous arrests, this was completely serious, as I was being processed in full accordance with protocol.

What the devil?!

And although I was still shaking in nervous agitation, I was in no hurry to set upon my former colleagues with questions. Soon. Everything would become clear soon. And, perhaps, I would even have pity for the fact I hadn't remained in blissful ignorance.

But one thing was already clear: this arrest had nothing to do with my troubles this summer in Montecalida, because Thomas Smith had managed to quash all the accusations of my involvement in the murder of the Indian bartender, while the death of the Tacinis was blamed on an accident all the way back at the preliminary stage of the investigation. The coroner's report contained nary a word about suicide or bullet holes. It just mentioned the many wounds sustained in the collapse of the ancient building's floor.

My tremors passed, and my fears flooded me with a grievous weight. It was taking me more and more effort to hold back the shaking, but I clenched my teeth stubbornly and started waiting for the end of the formal procedures. One thing was clear, that was totally certain: this was an official arrest, and not done at the behest of her Majesty's inner circle.

This wasn't the Imperial Guard, and that left a decent chance this would end in my favor. And it didn't matter how serious the charges were –the wealthy were treated differently. I was no longer a moneyless ragamuffin, I could afford to hire the most famous lawyers in New Babylon. In the worst case, the trial would draw on for years but, in the best, I could be set free tonight.

I really wanted to believe that...

— The Dormant —

AFTER PROCESSING, to the measured clop of my shackled boots, the guards took me into the interrogation room.

The lightbulbs under the ceiling were shining right into my eyes, but there was really no reason to look at anything here. The walls were thick and had damp, cracking plaster. The floor was dusty, and the furniture was all worn. Discounting the electric lighting, a criminal could have been interrogated in an identical room one or even two hundred years ago.

The only other thing that stood out was the phonograph machine in the far corner. It was totally inappropriate for the cell.

FOR SOME TIME, I SQUINTED, trying to get a better look at the sound recording device, then I sat back in the uncomfortable chair and closed my eyes. I didn't open them even when, to the creak of rusty hinges, the door flew open.

There was simply no need. I recognized the man who entered even with my lids shut. The aroma of his cologne and the subtle scent of expensive cigarettes was just too characteristic, instantly breaking up the musty damp of the chamber.

"It's been so long since we've seen each other, inspector!" I chuckled to my old acquaintance.

"Senior inspector!" Moran corrected me, throwing a fat folder of documents in front of him on the edge of the table. "Senior inspector, Mr. Orso. Senior. Don't you know the difference?"

Bastian Moran hadn't changed one bit since

our last meeting. His gaunt face was still marked by an aristocratic pallor, while his pomaded hair, sharply curved brows and thin lips made him look more like a decadent dandy than a policeman. His well-kept hands fully conformed with this, and his stylish suit and expensive vest with diamond buttons didn't let me down one bit. But it was all spoiled by the cold gray eyes of a hardened taker of souls.

A cop, that's what he was. That wasn't meant as an insult. It was more like a prisoner's brand. Work makes its impression on us all.

"Everything is ready!" the assistant declared, a new roller now in the phonograph.

"Begin the recording!" Moran commanded.

The police clerk started the device and, to a quiet bassy hum, it started to softly quiver and creak. The light in the cell flickered a few times but, to my greatest disappointment, the electric system was fairly resilient and there were no power failures.

The assistant left the chamber and I, perfectly aware that every word I said would reach the report, couldn't hold back a barb:

"You just keep grabbing respectable subjects of her majesty on the street. That's a quick path to a demotion... senior inspector."

Bastian Moran arched a crooked brow in muted amazement.

"Respectable?" he asked with mock surprise in his voice. "There is only one respectable subject of her majesty in this room, and you are not it, Leopold Orso. Or should I say Lev Shatunov?"

The senior inspector asked, taking my new passport from the folder and throwing it onto the table with a contemptuous snort. In reply, I just shrugged my shoulders calmly.

"However you want to call me."

But my calm demeanor hardly made any impression on Moran. He curved his thin lips up into an acrid smile and declared:

"A respectable man has no need for forged documents."

"So, was I cuffed just for that?" I asked, clanking the steel chain. "Shall I remind you of the Imperial law on national passports? Don't forget, senior inspector, my grandfather was Russian. He took the last name Orso on his induction into the nobility..."

And now, I wasn't bluffing one bit. Documents under the name Lev Borisovich Shatunov had been passed through all Imperial registries and, as a result, it wasn't particularly difficult for my attorney to draw up an official petition for a new passport and get it attached to the file backdated.

It cost a small fortune, but it was worth it.

I couldn't say that Bastian Moran's faced changed at these words, but he did take on a rarely confused appearance.

"Leopold, are you aware that this statement is extremely easy to check?" the senior inspector asked.

"The sooner you send a telegram to Petrograd, the sooner you'll have your answer," I answered calmly. "And the lower will be my restitution for illegal detention. I have quite a talented attorney, you know."

Moran got up from the table and left the cell but returned very soon, most likely having given his assistant the mission of sending a telegram to Petrograd. He didn't get right back to questioning. Instead, he took a pack of Chesterfields from his pocket, lit one up and exhaled a stream of fragrant smoke at the ceiling.

I winced for show.

The senior inspector didn't pay any attention to my grimace, tapped the ash onto the floor, sat at the table again and started leafing through the file of documents, as if wanting to refresh his memory on the case materials. The ease with which his first charge was overturned was an unpleasant surprise for him.

The tobacco smoke started making my throat itch but, when Bastian Moran put his cigarette out, I wasn't glad at all. With a very sharp and decisive movement, he pressed the butt into the edge of the ashtray, the surface of which was already stained with many dark spots.

"So then, let's get down to business!" the senior inspector declared. "Are you ready, Leopold?"

"Always," I smiled in reply, but my smile was crooked, masking nervousness with irony. In fact, I had shivers running up my spine.

"Where were you the seventeenth of June this year?" the senior inspector asked and even leaned forward, as if trying to catch me off guard with an unexpected question.

And he did. I snorted in reply, totally sincerely:

"I have no idea. Do you remember where you were?"

"I do," Moran confirmed. "Thanks to you, I don't have the most pleasant memories of that day. And, considering my lengthy service, that is no trivial matter."

"You must be confused. We haven't seen one another for more than a year."

"Where were you on June seventeenth?" the senior inspector repeated his strange question.

I moved my gaze away and started looking at the uneven cracking plaster on the walls, remembering the events of last summer. June? Where was I on June seventeenth?

It was surprising but, as soon as I thought about it, the event of three months earlier rushed back into my memory. It wasn't so simple to forget being strangled around the neck by a garotte and falling into the abyss of unconsciousness.

"No, I don't remember," I shook my head a little while later.

"But you were in New Babylon on that day?"

"That may well be."

"You were," Bastian Moran declared confidently, and took the guest register from the Benjamin Franklin from the folder, with an official stamp from the hotel manager. "Here is indisputable proof of that fact."

"May I?"

"Please," the senior inspector pushed the sheet

of paper to me.

Next to the manager's signature was today's date, and that made me think for a long time. The arrest suddenly stopped seeming like the end of a prolonged search operation; more likely, I had merely fallen into the field of view of an old acquaintance.

"I hope you will not claim that you were not yet Lev Shatunov then," Moran chuckled, taking a new cigarette from the pack.

"You smoke too much," I warned him. "It's bad for the lungs."

"Answer the question!"

"In the middle of June, I did spend a few days in the capital, and it was at the Benjamin Franklin. Was that precisely the seventeenth? I can't say I remember, but I have no reason to disbelieve the register. Let's suppose that, on that day, I was in New Babylon. What next?"

Not showing any kind of satisfaction with my answer, the senior inspector took a deep draw on his cigarette, then put it out on the tabletop and calmly stated:

"Your fingerprints were discovered at the scene of a crime."

"Sure they were!" I laughed. "You're playing with me!"

"Not at all."

"I don't understand what you're talking about. This must be a misunderstanding."

Bastian Moran was onto my game without a doubt but, because I was not denying or disavowing my presence in New Babylon, I had forced him to lay his last trump card on the table, whether he wanted to or not. To be more accurate, it was a pack of trump cards in the form of many spent pistol casings, photocopies of fingerprints from my dossier and expert reports, reaffirmed by several blue stamps.

"These casings were discovered at the scene of the crime," the senior inspector began laying out his version of events, 'and the fingerprints taken from them matched yours, which we have on file. We have an expert report fully confirming that as well as a repeat investigation from today. And what, Leopold, do you have to say to that?"

Sweat washed over me. It took considerable effort to hold a composed expression on my face. And did I even manage? I was sure Bastian could see straight through me.

Wanting to draw out my time, I extended a hand for the photographs, but the chain was too short, stopping me from reaching them.

"May I?" I then asked the senior inspector.

Bastian Moran slid the stack of pictures over and shot me a relaxed smile.

"No tricks, Leopold! And I'm sure that you will know even without my reminding you, that a full confession will lessen your punishment. Think about it! Think well!"

I didn't answer at all, quickly looking at the pictures and moving my gaze to the Senior Inspector, but he had already returned the expert conclusions to the folder, not letting me familiarize myself with them.

And that was truly strange: without expert testimony, all these photographs were a simple collection of unconnected shots. So, why then didn't Moran want to hammer the last nail into the top of my coffin?

I was almost certain I knew the answer, and still my throat went dry, while my soul was pierced by a sharp attack of fear. My ears started ringing. Yes, I was afraid. And who could maintain their presence of spirit in my place? Life at a labor camp was not sweet, and the difference between being sent to harvest timber in snowy Siberia and being shipped somewhere nearer-by for hellish rock-breaking was not large. In any case, I would hardly be able to survive until the end of the term they'd give me for killing six people, even if they were Hindoos. It would not be too easy to prove that they were all Kali Stranglers and had attacked me first...

Devil!

Devil! Devil! Devil!

Gathering my willpower, I suppressed the panic, turned my gaze away from Bastian Moran's satisfied countenance and stared at a spot of falling plaster. The phonograph in the corner was humming measuredly as before, so I was in no rush to explain, carefully choosing the right words.

"Leopold," Bastian Moran sighed, having caught the doubts coming over me. "I'll be as frank as possible: I don't fully understand what happened there. I suspect it may have been self-defense. And if you tell me honestly, this case really doesn't have to reach formal charges. Perhaps you were bewildered by the circumstances of the arrest, but we acted strictly according to protocol. Nothing personal, after all. You've been in such situations before, isn't that right?" the senior inspector reminded me with a conciliatory smile. 'Judge for yourself: the deceased were suspected of membership in the illegal thuggee cult, and clues found at the scene confirm that fully. There isn't a single judge that would sentence you..."

There was a certain rationality to his words, but I knew the inner workings of the Newton-Markt too well to accept the senior inspector's admonitions at face value. When they first tried hard to back someone into a corner, then suddenly opened a path to safety, every door left obligingly ajar could only lead to a more cramped cell.

And so, I preferred to remain secretive and put on a surprised look.

"Thugees? What are you talking about? I don't have anything to do with the Kali Stranglers!"

"Leopold!" Bastian Moran frowned in annoyance. "Let's not play these games! This case is hanging around my neck like a stone.' The senior inspector even placed a sleek hand on the collar of my shirt. "And I need to close it no matter what. The inspector general is huffing and puffing! Help me, and I promise there won't be a criminal investigation."

"I'm always glad to help an investigation," I said, still looking past the man at a spot of falling plaster, carefully choosing my words. "But it wouldn't be right for me to take the blame for a crime I didn't commit. I mean, I could do that for you but, if I did, the true killer would avoid punishment, and that goes against my principles. Remember that rule, senior inspector."

"Fingerprints!" Moran reminded me.

"What about fingerprints?"

"Your fingerprints were found at the scene of the crime on the round casings, Leopold. It is senseless to deny that. If you refuse to work with the investigation, this will draw on for months, and you'll have to be under guard that whole time. Do you really want that? I know I am not burning with desire to see your sour countenance every work day for the next year, or maybe even two. I'm sure talking with me won't bring you any particular pleasure either. So, let's help each other out. I won't demand anything supernatural from you. Just tell me what exactly happened!"

The senior inspector's offer to choose the lesser of two evils was definitely not an ad lib; that was exactly what he was hoping for when he ordered me arrested and brought to the Newton-Markt with all the prescribed formalities. The shackles and prison clothes were supposed to show how a refusal to work together would end. But excessive openness had never led me to anything good before.

That was for certain, so I made a suggestion:

"Let's return to the fingerprints. How confident was the expert report?"

"An error would be impossible!"

"Well, of course!" I couldn't hold back a flagrant chuckle. "After all, it's business as usual to find a distinct fingerprint on a spent round casing! And I'm not talking about the effects of powder residue and high temperature, just a casing all on its own... it isn't very large, and the contact area with a finger would be even smaller. An error would be impossible? Come now, Bastian!"

"And nevertheless, it is true," Moran answered calmly. "The dermal ridge patterns all correspond with yours."

"The patterns you managed to find, senior inspector. As far as I remember, criminal scientists refuse to take partial prints into consideration, isn't that so?"

"I insisted on a dactylographic report, and it was undertaken in accordance with all requirements."

I screwed up my face.

"I'm not sure the court will take those results into account."

"There's no need to take this case to court."

"Good!" I relented. "I fully allow that those could be my fingerprints. Around that time, I went looking for a new pistol, and visited several gun stores. I looked over a number of models and, naturally, loaded and unloaded them. Most likely, that explains the fingerprint match... – no! – resemblance."

After finishing my version of events, I moved my gaze off the spot of falling plaster and looked at Moran. He looked like a gourmand who'd just taken a sip of a refined vintage wine with a sour apple flavor.

"Nice try," the senior inspector smiled

skeptically "But forgive me if I question your words."

"Doubt them as long as you want. The issue is whether a jury will buy them. When I was arrested, I had a Cerberus confiscated from me. You can check in the sales records from a shop called the *Golden Bullet*. I bought it there, on one of those days."

"Leopold!" Bastian Moran clapped a palm on the table. "Enough of the lies! The model of pistol the shots were fired from has not been released for public sale! The whole shipment was sent directly to the New World! You simply never could have found such a pistol in a shop!"

"And what about the weapons market on Piazza Archimedes?" I squinted. "I recall that, once, during a raid there, we confiscated a high-caliber Gatling gun stolen during the repair of an army dirigible!"

The senior inspector took a loud sigh and started drumming his fingers on the table. Now, I could read open hatred in his gaze. And that was no small wonder. The weapons bazaar I had just mentioned had long been a headache for the metropolitan police and, if some pistols had disappeared on their way to the New World, that is certainly where they'd have turned up.

"So then, you were at the market..." Bastian Moran said a bit later, drawing out his words. "But naturally, you don't remember which stall might have shown you the pistol?"

"I don't even know exactly what kind of pistol you're talking about. I spent a few hours wandering around there."

— The Dormant —

Moran suddenly jumped sharply at me and said:

"Leopold, I know it was you!"

"Juries don't normally treat police intuition with the same level of trust," I answered calmly, even though my heart was still skipping beats, and my back had begun to perspire. "And as for the police having a bias against arrestees, it's quite the opposite. They believe that extremely easily. You are biased against me, senior inspector. And now that is established in your recording."

"Balderdash!" Bastian Moran shot out shortly and slammed his palm down on the table again. "You killed the Hindoos. I know that for certain. And I have the clues to prove it!"

I sat back in my chair and tried to cross my arms on my chest, but was prevented by the handcuff chain, stretched to its limit.

"Allow me to doubt your words. You've forwarded baseless accusations against me before, senior inspector. Isn't that right?"

My words hit square in their target. Bastian Moran went red in rage, but still held back and didn't give me an open-palm slap, which he would have done to a normal arrestee as a matter of course.

"My accusations, Leopold Orso," he said in an official tone, " were not baseless then, and they are not baseless now!"

"Are you serious?" I asked, startled. "You still suspect me in the murder of Levinson?"

The manager of the New Babylon branch of the

Witstein Banking House had been torn to shreds by a werebeast, and Bastian Moran had initially suspected it was my handiwork. Even my iron-clad alibi hadn't been enough to convince the senior inspector otherwise. Only a blood test performed by a police doctor had made him refuse to charge me officially.

Back then I was still not a full werebeast, as I also was not now. And no analysis could show otherwise. Even if some things were retained, like an instinctive ability to dodge silver, that noble metal was no longer able to poison my body. My blood would not react to it.

Bastian Moran pursed his lips but still gave a direct answer to the question.

"Yes, Viscount. I still suspect you of involvement in Levinson's murder!" he declared after a brief pause.

"But I was the one who shot his murderer! Me!"

"In interrogation, the werebeast may have told us the true motives for his crime, but you killed him. Very convenient, don't you think?"

"His true motives? Did Procrustes ever need a motive?"

"Come off it, Leopold!" Bastian Moran waved it off. "We established the identity of the werebeast you shot and, at the time of several of Procrustes' crimes, he was awaiting the death penalty in Kilmainham gaol. He only managed to escape after!"

"What do you want from me, Senior inspector?" I asked directly.

"The truth!"

"You heard it."

Moran opened the folder and carelessly tossed me one of the photographs laying there. I glanced at the picture and gave an involuntary shudder. The dead black eyes of the Hindoo were staring back at me from the paper. But that wasn't what spooked me. I was beside myself from seeing the dead man's crushed larynx. Crushed by my very hand.

"And who might that unfortunate be?" I asked, suppressing a nervous shudder.

"That is one of the bodies, next to which we discovered the round casings with your fingerprints," Bastian Moran explained.

"Partial fingerprints," I spat out mechanically, but the senior inspector let my remark go in one ear and out the other.

"While this picture," Moran set forth the next photograph, "was taken in Levinson's home. As you can see, the character of the wounds on the deceased Hindoo in June and the banker's guard are very similar. What's more, I took some shots of Procrustes' victims from the archive..."

"Enough!" I couldn't hold back. "What do you want from me? Tell me straight!"

"The truth!"

"I've told you everything."

"I know this was you," Moran declared directly. "It was you, Leopold Orso, who killed the Hindoos and you, without a doubt, were involved in the murder of Levinson. I don't know why or how, but you can be sure, it's just a matter of time. I'll stop you no matter what it costs me!"

"I need a lawyer."

"A lawyer won't help you now!" the senior inspector waved it off. "You'll never be set free, and you can believe that. I'll make sure of it!"

A vile sour taste appeared in my mouth, but I overcame myself and, with the power of my will, drove off the approaching wave of panic.

"You have no clues, and the fingerprint matching was not done by the books. No court will accept this. The tooth imprint of the werebeast I killed lined up with one of the wounds on Levinson's servant girl. And what's more, if you think I am a werebeast, let's take the simplest route and do a blood test. Last time, it didn't show anything!"

"Everything in its time," Bastian Moran frowned. "We'll do tests as well. I'll personally cut you into little pieces, if that's what it takes, but I will get the truth."

"That sounds like a threat."

The senior inspector got up from the table, turned off the phonograph and took the roller from it.

"You don't say?" he turned to me with a foul smirk. "What led you to that conclusion?"

I didn't have time to answer. With a sharp burst, the door flew open and, in an instant, it became cramped and unbearably sultry in the cell, although just one person had joined us.

The inspector general of the metropolitan police, Friedrich von Nalz, was old and his face resembled a pagan idol, carved from the rootstock of an ancient pine. The reflection of his colorless eyes was unmistakable even in the bright light of the electric bulbs, while the ghostly heat emanating from the old man made the air oscillate around him like a red-hot blaze.

However, it just seemed that way. Fear has big eyes, and I was afraid of the inspector general much more than all of Moran's threats taken together. If von Nalz decided to beat the truth out of me, no lawyers would be able to stand in his way, not even the High Imperial Court.

The inspector general's *talent* could burn a person in a few seconds but, fortunately, the old man wasn't even paying attention to me.

"Bastian!" von Nalz addressed the senior inspector. "What is going on here?!"

"An investigation," he answered with a composed look, raising a brow. "And what of it?"

"I beg your pardon, Leopold," Friedrich von Nalz sighed and called Moran into the corridor. "Just a minute, Bastian..."

I started feeling very apprehensive, because the inspector general was perfectly aware of my blood relationship with the Imperial family. Although my mother was not the legal daughter of the Grand Duke of Arabia, Emperor Clement's brother, blood was thicker than water. Von Nalz considered my status sufficient to intervene in my fate and, the last time, his intervention had ended in me getting my heart cut out.

How it would end now was frightening to even

imagine.

3

THE CONVERSATION in the hallway went on for no less than a quarter of an hour, and that was surprising for the simple reason that no one from the metropolitan police could stand up to the inspector general for that long.

As a matter of fact, I thought the police administration had decided to continue the conversation in von Nalz's office, but then the door flew open, and Bastian Moran walked into the cell, his face petrified, yet pale in rage.

If the senior inspector were *illustrious*, and had a gaze that could kill, my heart would have stopped at that very moment. As it was, I had shivers running down my spine.

But I made it.

"Leopold Orso, you're free to go!" Bastian Moran declared in a voice ringing in agitation, turned around and left the cell, stomping his shoe soles on the stone floor of the cellar unnaturally distinctly.

The constable who came to take his place unlocked my handcuffs and took off the shackles, then the unfamiliar detective sergeant set a whole stack of documents on the table. I was required to sign a box on each of them saying I was familiar with its contents.

Among them was one telling me not to leave town, together with a requirement to inform the police if I changed my residence and to appear at the Newton-Markt if requested, which was the very least they could saddle me with in this situation. I wasn't upset.

Devil! I mean, I was practically in seventh heaven!

I WAS LED OUT of the interrogation cell into a changing room with scratched-up cabinets, damp humid air and faucets that ran with rusty water. I tried to wash the fingerprinting ink off my hands, but I just used up the last of a bar of soap and ruined a handkerchief. The skin on my palms was still bluish-gray.

But that didn't really bother me. They gave me back my clothing, and I got dressed, throwing the striped prison clothes on a bench. I went out into the hallway, already feeling like a free man but, instead of the exit, the mustached sergeant led me somewhere deeper in the Newton-Markt.

"Excuse me, my good sir..." I said, getting on guard. "The exit is the other way!"

"The inspector general would like to see you," the police-man said and threw open the door to the stairs. "Follow me."

Refusing the order wouldn't have made even the slightest bit of sense so, with a fateful sigh, I started my way up and out of the basement. The sergeant was walking in front. Behind me there wheezed two strong constables.

I was surrounded...

IN THE INSPECTOR GENERAL'S reception room, an adjunct, fairly intrigued with the proceedings, made me sign for my effects, which had been confiscated on my detention, gave me time to distribute them in my pockets and, only after that, informed von Nalz of my arrival.

"Come in, the inspector general is ready to see you now," he declared, setting the telephone receiver back on the hook.

In some situations, "ready to see you now" was in no way different from "needs to speak with you immediately," so I suppressed a fated sigh and decisively threw open the heavy oak door.

The Cerberus in my jacket pocket gave me a certain confidence, but there was more significance in the very fact that I actually had the weapon than any benefit I might gain from actually using it.

Gloom reigned in the office of the head of the metropolitan police. The windows were covered with a thick curtain, concealing what little light the already cloudy September day had to offer. A dull flame was dancing on the logs in the fireplace, and gas lamps on the wall burned with a muted light. The lamp on the table, which was inundated with newspapers and correspondence, was not turned on and, on the backdrop of the utterly gray space, the only bright light was the luster of the inspector general's eyes.

"You surprise me, Leopold," von Nalz said

morosely, without even offering me a seat. "Do you understand that your behavior discredits the memory of your great forbearer?"

"I haven't done anything reprehensible, inspector general."

Friedrich von Nalz winced and asked:

"Why did you get a second passport?"

"I wanted to start a new life," I answered with basically the pure truth. "Is that not allowed? The passport is authentic."

"If it had been forged, I wouldn't have intervened," the old man declared directly. "But the accusations forwarded against you are impossibly..."

"Contrived," I offered.

"Doubtful," the inspector general finished his own thought. "And in that the clues are all of a tangential nature, I don't see any basis to detain you for the duration of the investigation. I hope you won't make me regret that decision."

The fiery gaze of his colorless eyes burned with a fell flame but here, fortunately, the inspector general got distracted by the ringing of his telephone, and I caught my breath with relief.

"Have them wait, I'll be down in a moment," Friedrich von Nalz answered shortly after picking up the phone and threw it back on the hook with annoyance. He spent a few seconds sitting, staring forward in agitation, then decisively got up from the table, walked up to me and slapped my back with his palm, which was thin and hard as a board.

"Leopold! My advice to you: stay out of trouble.

After all, you aren't just any old citizen. Your reputation must remain flawless for the sake of the memory of your grandfather, the most important political actor of the epoch of the Empire's foundation!"

I fitfully swallowed and managed to squeeze out only a none-too-intelligible:

"This is all some kind of misunderstanding..."

"I hope that's true."

Von Nalz's cold tone scared me so bad I started hiccupping. But I still overcame my hesitation and asked a favor:

"Inspector general! Please don't tell my... relatives. I want to solve my own problems. On my own, do you see?"

"That merits respect," Friedrich von Nalz nodded. "I don't think there's any need to tell them. Her Majesty's health leaves a lot to be desired. She certainly doesn't need any more reason to worry."

"I thank you," I caught my breath with untold relief.

The inspector general smiled.

"I hope, Leopold, that our next meeting will be under somewhat less disreputable circumstances."

I gave a short burst of quick nods. I was now ready to agree with the inspector general about anything, and I hurried to slip out into the reception. The adjunct, when he saw me, tore himself from the typing machine and asked:

"Should I call a constable?"

"No, I can find the exit," I refused. "Do I need

any kind of pass?'

"Just go. I'll call the guard desk."

"Thank you!"

With a sense of unbelievable relief, I left the reception room and, first of all, pulled a handkerchief out of my jacket pocket, but it was all covered in black and blue ink blotches, so I couldn't wipe the sweat from my face. My heart was beating very unevenly so, on the second floor, acting on an old memory, I ducked into the men's lavatory, washed up and stared at my reflection in the blurry and cracked mirror over the sink.

My reflection looked haggard and fearful.

Curses! I looked squeezed out like a lemon and terrified, like a tiny shepherd boy sitting at a little dying fire surrounded by hungry wolves.

Bastian Moran would not back down. Devil! He would be certain to take the investigation to the end and dig up all the background information. And the problem wasn't a personal dislike or desire to restore justice – devil, I had killed the Thugees! – the senior inspector had some kind of personal interest in this case.

Maybe a promotion? Friedrich von Nalz was old, he couldn't stay in the post of inspector general for long, but how would my case help Moran move up the ranks? And also, why was he so driven to uncover a crime, if society was sure that the thugees had been shot by police?

I didn't understand...

AT THE GUARD POST, no one even glanced at me. A shift change was underway. Some constables were hurrying to work, others were already on their way to the exit, all in civilian clothing. In all the helter-skelter, I calmly strolled out of the Newton-Markt.

But when I entered the colonnade-lined portico of the police administration's internal yard, I was surprised to discover a fairly large crowd on the stairs. It didn't look much like a demonstration: there was a thin chain of police easily holding back the large number of fancily-clad gentlemen, who were armed not with placards and sticks, but notepads, pencils and cameras.

"Newspapermen!" I realized, donning my derby cap. I was already on my way to a side arch when, from behind I heard:

"Lev! Lev, wait!"

I almost had a seizure! Mechanically, and not considering my actions, I stuck my hand into my jacket pocket. But, at the last moment, I came to my senses and turned around. A black-haired thin young man in an ill-fitting suit and a rumpled gray cap was hurrying after me.

"Lev, I really wasn't expecting to see you here!" laughed Thomas Eliot Smith, the investigator from the Pinkerton Detective Agency.

I unclenched my fingers from the handle of the Cerberus with relief and, removing my hand from my pocket, extended it to Smith.

"And I was not expecting to meet you, Thomas!" I smiled. We exchanged hand-shakes and, clipping my dark glasses on my nose, I asked: "After all, you were preparing to return to the New World isn't that right? What winds blew you to the capital?"

"It's all blasted work!" the investigator told me with histrionic pity, stroking his black mustache in a habitual motion and asking: "And what led you to this bastion of law and order? Not more problems with the law I hope?"

"A small misunderstanding," I frowned. "Nothing serious."

"Can I help?"

"No, it's all been solved to the best effect."

Professional mistrust flickered in the investigator's dark eyes. I knew, however, that they only seemed dark because of colored glass lenses. Thomas Smith was *illustrious* but hid that fact very artfully.

Wanting to distract the investigator from the reason for my visit to the Newton-Markt, I hurried to ask:

"I suppose something extreme must have shaken out, if you were sent across the Atlantic again."

"Lev, I did such a good job this summer, that they decided to have me stay in the Old World!" the investigator laughed. "Now, I am a mobile agent-consultant with a zone of responsibility encompassing half of Europe! Paris, London, Lisbon and Madrid. Where haven't I been this summer! Now something's afoot in New Babylon..."

I had the words "travelling salesman" turning

on the tip of my tongue, but I didn't want to offend the man. I also didn't fish out the details of his new assignment, instead pointing at the crowd.

"I don't suppose you know what all this is about? What's going on? Yet another sabotage at a weapons factory or a flash anarchist operation?"

A barely visible grimace slid over Smith's face, as if the topic was unpleasant. Instead of answering, he slipped me the morning edition of the *Capital Times* with a yard-long headline reading:

"Bloody Ritual on Faraday Boulevard!"

"More gossip?" I clarified, skimming the article.

"No," the investigator shook his head. "I'm afraid it's all real."

"Is that so?" I asked in surprise, because the headline was about a crime that was extreme even by the ghoulish standards of New Babylon. Murder was no rarity in our guest houses but, this time, the victim was a young unmarried lady of light scruples, and the murderer had pulled out her eyes and cut out her heart. The police were called by the apartment tenant a floor below after blood started dripping from his ceiling. A theory was put forward that malefics were mixed up in the case, but there wasn't any evidence of that. The police had announced a search for her procurer.

At that moment, two constables with red department-official bands of on their arms threw open the doors and, just to make sure, propped them with iron stoppers. The newspapermen moved forward, and the police had to expend a reasonable amount of force to hold them behind the perimeter at the columns.

"Is the inspector general going to make an announcement?" I guessed.

"That's right," Thomas Smith confirmed. "And here he is now...'

Friedrich von Nalz came out to the press conference in a ceremonial uniform; his adjunct had a folder in his hands and was following the head of the police at some distance. The constables straightened up and started pushing even harder on the now silent newspapermen, but they were holding dead tight on the steps. They only managed to reconquer the first two or three highest rows.

"I suppose I'll be going," I decided. "Glad to see you..."

Thomas Smith extended a hand to say farewell and, at that moment, a disheveled young man managed to jump past the perimeter.

"Die, bloodthirsty satrap!" he shouted and, before any of the policemen managed to get moving, caught off guard by the unexpected attack, he threw up his pistol. "Freedom to prisoners of conscience!"

He should have just shot but, for such individuals, political slogans always came first, so the anarchist first shouted, then fired. To be more accurate, he tried to fire, but didn't find much success: his pistol simply exploded.

Fragments of the weapon flew in all directions as red-hot shrapnel. Fortunately, no one was seriously hurt by that, and the unsuccessful murderer was instantly dog-piled on the ground by quick-moving constables. Now, he was no threat to anyone and, what was more, he needed emergency aid himself: blood was spurting out of the stump of his mangled arm.

"Doctor!" one of the newspapermen began to wail, but the person who helped the anarchist was no police medic.

Von Nalz decisively pushed away the constables surrounding him and approached the wounded man. I sensed a burning echo of his *illustrious talent*, then the frightening wound hissed and instantly stopped bleeding. The wounded boy immediately stopped struggling and went limp in the constables' arms. Then, in a senseless state, he was carried inside the Newton-Markt.

"The press conference is postponed!" the inspector general's chalk-white adjunct shouted.

Thomas Smith immediately realized how problematic it would be if we got stuck here and pulled me to the side exit.

"Let's go! Otherwise we'll be stranded here until evening!"

By some miracle, we managed to leave the yard of the Newton-Markt before the arch was blocked by quick-moving constables. Then, on the street, Thomas Smith immediately turned down a side passage where, in front of a grocer's shop, he was awaited by a self-propelled carriage – the very same Ford Model-T.

"What was that, devil take me?!" the investigator turned to me, firing up the steam boiler. "Lev, do you have any idea?"

"What's to understand?" I snorted. "That was either an anarchist, or a gunman from yet another underground socialist cell. Perhaps he was also a Christian, but that is hardly likely. They tend to use different slogans."

"Not that!" Smith turned sharply. "Why did the pistol blow up?!"

"The inspector general is *illustrious*. He has a very... inflammatory *talent*."

"Ah, so that was it!" the investigator drew out his words, pulled on his driving gloves and asked: "Do you need a ride?"

I considered it for a moment, then clarified:

"Can you drop me off on Mendeleev Avenue?"

"Where is that?"

"Not far. I'll show you."

"You'll show me? Then let's go!"

I sat down next to Thomas and the self-propelled carriage started off, bouncing on the uneven paving stones of the alleyway. Then, a few minutes later, we came out at the service door of the nearest underground station.

"Take a right here," I said at an intersection, and he turned the wheel sharply, nearly hitting an old lady standing on the sidewalk.

Curses followed after us, but Smith didn't even cock an ear. He increased his speed, drove around a cart and jumped before the very nose of a police armored vehicle. Then, he pulled out onto Mendeleev Avenue with such confidence it seemed he had been driving a self-propelled carriage down the confusing alleyways of New Babylon his whole life.

However, success soon left him. Not risking flying over the rails at full speed, Thomas slowed to a crawl, then the Ford Model-T cut into a dense traffic jam and, from there, we had to dawdle at a turtle's pace.

There was no wind. The streets were filled with smog. The unpleasant aroma caused a tickling in my throat. My dark glasses did a piss-poor job of protecting my eyes from dust, so I was plainly envious of the investigator, who had clip-on goggles that held tight against his face.

"This is my first day in the capital," Thomas Smith told me. "You wouldn't happen to know a quiet and calm hotel near the Central Train Station, would you? Just so I don't get caught with my pants down."

"I'm afraid I don't."

"I was recommended the *Heinrich Hertz.*"

"I'm sorry, I've never heard of it."

At an intersection, a cart laden with empty barrels had lost a wheel, and it was blocking off half the street. The driver and a few volunteers were trying to either smooth out the situation or clear the roadway, but they weren't making any progress. There was a long file of coaches, carts and self-propelled carriages waiting to pass through the still-open lanes and, as is usual in such situations, the cabbies and drivers were whistling cursing and promising to tear off one another's heads, if they weren't immediately allowed to pass. Two constables were observing the pandemonium from the sidewalk with the calm of philosophers, in no hurry to do anything.

Thomas Smith didn't waste his nerves on empty cursing, pulling a map of New Babylon out of a map case, unfolding it and asking me to show him where we were.

"Aha," the investigator lit up. "Lev, if I let you out near Brown Bridge, would that be alright? I'm thinking of taking it to the other side of the Yarden."

I gave a cursory glance at the map and agreed.

"Alright."

And here, my attention was drawn by a pencil mark at the very border of the Old City. Just a fat dot on one of the residential neighborhoods, but that was enough.

"Were you on Faraday Boulevard?" I guessed.

Thomas Smith started folding up the map with a rustling sound.

"Where'd you get that from?" he asked, looking at me sidelong.

"Just a guess. Is the agency looking into that case?"

Just then, the cart was finally rolled off the roadway, and traffic started flowing. I decided that I wouldn't be getting an answer to that question now, but the investigator eventually satisfied my curiosity.

"Yes, you're right. I was assigned this investigation," he said with a sigh after a theatrical pause. "But don't go blabbing about that, alright? The agency doesn't bear windbags. It could give me problems."

"Well, you know I'm not a big talker," I

answered with no false modesty.

"I'm very much counting on that," the investigator sighed and turned toward the sidewalk in hopes of driving around a cart, which was dragging along uncommonly slowly. He didn't gain anything with that maneuver, though, because there was a sluggish steam truck in the far lane.

At this rate, it would take us at least ten minutes to get to Brown Bridge, and I decided to continue my line of questioning.

"So then, if you were brought in, this was no simple murder. Either this involves a malefic known to the Pinkerton Agency, or..."

"Or," the investigator interrupted me. "You've got the right idea."

I whistled. Aztec priests were known for the lovely habit of cutting out their victims' hearts. But only truly extreme circumstances could drive such savages this far from their homeland.

"Is this the start of something serious?" I asked.

"I don't know," Smith answered. "No one does."

"But you're here. And you came to the capital before it all started."

"You know how it normally goes," Thomas snorted. "Someone spilled the beans to someone else, but the ends cannot be found, so I was sent to figure it all out. It's business as usual. This time, though, the rumors were confirmed. There really are Aztecs in the city."

I nodded, totally allowing that the investigator

was being completely open with me. Any policeman knew perfectly well just how difficult it could be to track a rumor to its source.

Just then, Brown Bridge came into view before us; Thomas Smith turned onto it and stopped the self-propelled carriage, letting me out onto the sidewalk.

"Thank you!" I said, giving the investigator a salute.

He threw his hand up over his head in a parting gesture, and the Model-T rolled away.

I didn't tarry on the bridge either, running across the street and jumping onto the back of a steam tram crawling slowly up the hill. I rode it to the nearest underground station, transferred and headed to the factory outskirts. I needed to immediately have a discussion with Ramon Miro and figure out what exactly he had done with the rest of the stolen pistols. There was too much riding on this horse to just let the chips fall or trust a telephone call...

4

RAMON AND I SET OFF back toward our respective homes. The constable left his lupara in his work locker and was now empty-handed, but he walked with such gloomy focus that it seemed he had a heavy pack on his back. I had no doubt that he was now tormented by doubts on the reason for the inspector's order. We couldn't discuss it though, as questioning orders from the higher-ups was something this hulk was not planning to do.

And neither was I.

Now perhaps Ramon, ignorant of the real facts, was filled with lingering doubts. I though, on the other hand, knew too much. And the fact that lots of knowledge can bring lots of sorrow is something that smart people noticed a long time ago.

I wasn't feeling any less sick either, so we walked in silence.

Right after the Dürer-Platz, the constable took a left and trod down the hill to Little Catalonia; I was going in the opposite direction. Up the winding slope of the hill, the street began rising to Calvary. The dense urban development was soon behind me. Mountainous fences now extended along the road, hiding the estates of retired army officers, diplomats and ministerial civil servants from the immodest gazes of passers-by.

The city had long surrounded Calvary on all sides but, for some reason, Calvary had never expanded vertically, with the exception of the two-hundred-and-two-meter-high open-work iron tower erected on the very peak of the hill a few years before the overthrow of *the fallen*. At night, its signal light was turned on, and lighting often struck it, not only during thunderstorms, but also in clear skies.

When Gustav Eiffel saw this rusted monstrosity, he became obsessed with the idea of outdoing it and, by some unfathomable miracle, not only received his monarch's approval, but also sold the design to the Paris city council. Admittedly, he must be given his dues for his talent as an architect – the new three-hundred-meter tower, based on post cards I'd seen, looked somewhat more elegant than its predecessor.

Roads had only started being built up the hill a quarter century ago, which is when one of the plots ended up in my grandfather's possession. Not Court Kósice, who never even had enough to rub two sticks together his whole life, but retired Imperial Army Colonel Peter Orso, my grandfather on my father's side.

Our property was located on the outskirts. It was truncated on two sides by steep slopes, and the third was lined with the rustling leaves of a small thicket. I can't say for sure if my grandfather chose such a secluded place on purpose or not, but we weren't often pestered by our neighbors. No one came around at all, to be honest; even tax inspectors just looked the other way.

They had for the last sixteen years in any case...

WHEN I BEGAN TO HEAR the gurgling of a fast stream in front of me, I turned toward the curb to face a small pile of stones, taking the one on top. After that, I walked up the steep bridge and sent a heavy stone flying at full speed into an eye that was shining back at me from beneath it with a fell light.

The beast roared up, and quieted down, then

the pair of eyes retreated.

I have no idea what kind of creature lived down there, but it wasn't fond of this kind of treatment.

It would have been wise to solve the problem once and for all, but the retirees who lived around here had long since lost their former influence, and all their complaints usually slipped past the ears of the city government unnoticed. None of the clerks were too eager to be the one to pursue an unknown creature at night, and even those local inhabitants who loved boasting of their African safaris did nothing but give mere promises to dig their old weapons out of their closets. And they were right: it wasn't yet clear who would be hunting whom.

What was more, the unknown creature hadn't actually caused any problems. At least, that's the opinion our community treasurers were inclined toward after familiarizing themselves with a few estimates from professional exterminators.

Past the bridge, the road began twisting up to the top of the hill, and a few turns later, you could already see a stone fence with denuded blackening tree branches behind it.

That was my destination.

The oil lamp near the gate, as usual, wasn't lit, but you could still clearly make out a black square containing a diagonal crimson cross on the doors – the quarantine symbol of the Diabolic Plague, discolored and flaking.

Without pulling the bell cord, I moved the iron hasp from in front of the key hole, and opened the lock with my key. The gate swung open. To the screech of its rusty hinges, I clapped it shut behind me and headed for the night-darkened giant of my three-story manor straight through my dead garden.

The dried-out trees surged up to the sky, their twisted branches and black leaves stretching out in all directions. Dried grass stuck up from the earth in brittle gray spears.

The manor itself looked just as dead as the garden. There were no lights on, and no smoke coming from the pipes. Not a single sound could be heard. When I was five years old, one horrible night, death had visited our estate. Everything had died. Only my father and I had survived. Though, as for my father, his survival had only been partial; something cracked inside him and burned out forever. He could no longer stay for long in one place, and didn't allow himself to accrue possessions or personal attachments. And, like a shark, he stayed in constant motion. In his head, not moving was equivalent to death.

And, when the inspector asked what the devil had made me seek employment with the police, I hadn't been totally frank with him. I mean, I really did have to pay bills, but the true reason was my aspiration to discover those who had cursed this place and all its inhabitants. And it had been done so artfully that the curse could still kill sixteen years later.

Curses...

I sighed and threw my head back to the sky.

There were dull stars shining back like pieces of worn glass. The curse usually pricked the back of my head with an uncomfortable cold, weighed down on my heart, and ran up my spine, but did no actual harm to me.

Why? I do not know. Despite how much I had racked my brains over the topic, I still hadn't figured it out. And figuring out what had attracted this sorrow to my home in the first place had also come to naught; even having access to the police archive, which I had received with the rank detective constable, hadn't helped at all. There simply wasn't even a shred of information in the investigation reports; and there hadn't been any real evidence as such, either.

Diabolic Plague, they said, and that was that.

And I retreated; I had no time to waste on stirring up the past. I simply waited until I came of age, comforting myself with the fact that my family's money would allow me to not work and dedicate myself to seeking the truth.

But now I do not know, oh I do not know...

I shrugged my shoulders, walked onto the porch and swung open the unlocked door. I threw my derby hat on a rack in the entryway. The small flame of a kerosene lamp flickered in the dark corridor.

"Is everything alright, Viscount?" wondered a lank middle-aged man in an old-fashioned frock coat.

"Completely, Theodor," I laughed. "Couldn't be better."

Theodor Barnes was my butler. He had served

the Kósice family for his entire life, as his father and grandfather had served my ancestors before him. He was even present for some of the first memories I had.

"Is there anything you require?"

"No, thank you," I shook my head, but immediately snapped my fingers and corrected myself: "No, wait! Prepare the room on the third floor. We're expecting guests. A guest..."

Theodor was a butler by family trade; he could bite the bullet like no other, and usually didn't allow himself any expressions of strong emotion, but this time had gotten to him.

"What, excuse me?" Barnes clarified, not able to hide his amazement. "But, how do you mean...?"

I gave my servant a reassuring clap on the shoulder, throwing out frivolously:

"Just trust me," and headed for my bedroom.

I immediately turned the gas fixture there on, took off my jacket, pants and shirt, put them in the wardrobe, and unloaded my Roth-Steyr. But the Cerberus I did not unload, placing it near my wrist chronometer on the bedside table.

Then, I lit the night light, checked to see if the blinds were shut and, only after that, put out the gas light.

Funny?

I do not know, I do not know.

Life had taught me not to ignore my fears, no matter how contrived they may have seemed.

The night light must be on, the blinds must be closed, and a loaded pistol must be lying on my bedside table.

Period.

A RESTLESS BEAM OF SUN, having discovered a crack in my aging blinds, stole into my bedroom and went straight into my eyes, heralding the morning.

I turned over on my other side, but immediately got myself together and, unlike before, didn't keep snoozing. I splashed along the cold floor with my bare feet, swung open the windows one after the other and, just in case, took a persnickety look at the thickened boards of the blinds for fresh scratches.

But no – new ones hadn't appeared.

Morning freshness frolicked into the room, filling it completely; I went back to throw on a robe, then turned to a window facing East. From the hillock, an indescribable view of the old neighborhoods of the city was revealed, showing a plethora of steeple-roofs, gilded towers, palaces and gardens. Much farther away loomed the grayness of the factory outskirts; there were a great many smokestacks stretching out toward the sky there and freight dirigibles drifted lazily in the black clouds of smoke they expelled.

They say, once, in clear weather, you could see the ocean from the top of Calvary. But now, clear days in New Babylon were harder to come by than pearls in a cesspool. Smoke, char and smog rolled over the city from all sides.

No matter! I shrugged my shoulders and walked away to the bedside table. I snapped the chronometer bracelet to my wrist and set about getting dressed. In my head, though, like a broken gramophone record, one word kept turning over, again and again: 'Sunday. Sunday. Sunday!"

Ball!

At four o'clock P.M., the ball would start, and if something went wrong there...

I didn't even want to think what could happen.

Straining my will, I forced myself to forget the ominous presentiments and headed for the bathroom.

"Is the room ready?" I asked Theodor who happened to be going the opposite direction.

"Yes sir, Viscount," the butler confirmed, slickening down his pitch black mutton chops. "What is the news from the New World?"

"Same as before," I said. "Houston is embattled. There is currently trench warfare raging on all fronts."

"The Aztecs just won't settle down, eh?" Theodor shook his head and hazarded: "Would you like to take a look at the guest room?"

"That won't be necessary," I refused and went down to the first floor.

My gut was crying out in hunger, but I wasn't in the habit of eating breakfast at home. On weekends, I usually dropped into the Italian taverna close by, where I had a line of credit. And, in that my normal order of the day had already gone down the drain, all that was left was to swallow my spit in expectation of this evening's reception.

I took a vexed look at my timepiece and, there in the entryway, the bell clanged.

"Oh!" My butler said pointedly, not taking even one step back.

The news of the guest arriving simply knocked the man sideways. However, it also set my nerves indescribably more on edge. In much knowledge, there was much sorrow, that was true.

Nevertheless, I did nothing to display my agitation.

"Leave that to me, Theodor," I said, calling off my servant. I then left the house and hurried to the gates. As I walked, I clipped my glasses to my nose. The dark round eyepieces returned my confidence in my own abilities to me all at once.

The doubts left me; I swung the door open decisively and smiled to a young girl with fire-red hair, proper features on her pretty round face and the colorless-glowing eyes of the *illustrious*. The guest's figure was covered up by a long cloak, but I still knew that the body beneath it could teach a lesson to Aphrodite herself. She had taught thighs, an hourglass figure and a high chest...

"Elizabeth-Maria!" I smiled with all the cordiality I could muster, driving away the vision rising up before my eyes. "Words cannot express how glad I am that you found it possible to accept my invitation..."

"Leopold, you were extremely convincing," the girl burst out laughing, handing me her voluminous traveling bag. "You simply gave me no choice!"

"I hope I haven't spoiled your plans..."

"Not at all, I assure you!"

Her snow-white teeth flashed a smile and, with a certain share of deprivation, I decided that only her thin pale lips were keeping Elizabeth-Maria from being counted among the city's great beauties. But I didn't stress my attention on that and hurriedly stepped back to the side, letting my guest enter:

"Come in, I beg you!"

The girl stepped past the fence, cast her gaze on the dead garden and couldn't resist a bemused observation:

"How sweet..."

In the morning sun, the black trees didn't look nearly as ominous as they did in the dead of night, but I still thought it necessary to correct my guest:

"Original. Unusual. Provocative. But in no way sweet."

Elizabeth-Maria cast her attentive gaze on me and nodded slowly:

"As you say, Leopold."

We walked up onto the porch and entered the house. There, I handed her traveling bag to my butler and introduced my guest to my servant.

"This is Theodor, if you have any questions, you need only ask him. Unfortunately, I must take my leave. It's time for work."

"I am at your service, madam," my butler announced ceremoniously, accepting the girl's cloak.

Elizabeth-Maria smiled favorably in reply, removed her hat, and shook out a thick shock of hair.

"Leopold, you can't tell me you plan on leaving me alone so soon, right?" she cooed. "We could..."

I swallowed nervously and hurried to take the situation under control, or more accurately, took the girl under the arm and led her to the guest room.

"The ball is at four," I reminded my guest. "I need to go pick up my suit from the tailor's. And your evening dress..."

"Don't worry about that, dear," the girl answered and stopped opposite the fireplace, her attention caught by a saber hanging on the wall.

"To Captain Orso for personal valor. Zuid-India, October thirtieth, eighteen thirty-seven from K. N." Elizabeth-Maria looked closely at the engraving on the blade. "Is this your father's weapon?" she turned to me.

"My grandfather's," I shook my head. "He distinguished himself in the assault of Batavia. He was given the rank of captain there and made a hereditary noble."

"Yes, that's right!" the girl realized. "Year thirteen after the founding of the Second Empire! Forty years ago. That's a long time."

"My grandfather retired at the rank of colonel. He's the one who built this house..."

But Elizabeth-Maria wasn't interested in the history of my estate. With acute fascination, she continued to look at the saber and, as she did it, something uncharacteristically inappropriate was throbbing in her shimmering maidenly eyes.

"Blood," she whispered. "This saber has taken a rich harvest..."

"My grandfather was the best saber-man in his

regiment," I told her. Then I was shaken by an inexplicably returning lack of confidence, and said: "Theodor will show you to your room. I will see you at lunch."

"As you say, Leopold," the girl nodded and unexpectedly asked: "Is the saber sharpened?"

"It would assume so," I sighed and turned away to my butler who was standing in the door watching us with unhidden amazement. "Theodor!" I raised my voice, attracting the attention of my servant who had grown unaccustomed to having guests in recent years.

He shuddered, lifted the traveling bag and turned to the girl, saying:

"Follow me, madam."

Elizabeth-Maria walked into the guest room; on the stairs, she slightly lifted the skirts of her dress, looking uncharacteristically elegant.

My heart clenched up. A chill rolled over me; a strange mixture of desire, relief, fear and contempt filled my soul. But I did not indulge the self-flagellation, instead grabbing my derby hat from the rack and jumping headlong away from my house.

While I was walking to the gates, I saw the rusted top of the tower looming on the summit of the hill. Now, you couldn't see the blinking navigation signal on top of the rusty finger cascading up into the sky, causing mixed feelings. Its sheer decrepitude was impressive, but it simultaneously weighed on you with its power. Like something forgotten, something from an entirely different era. And I couldn't even say if it was from the past or the future...

It would seem that I should have grown accustomed to this view long ago, but no – I still felt ants on my skin for what must have been the thousandth time.

When the gate swung open, an envelope that had been stuffed into the crack fell under my feet. There were no stamps on it, and it had nothing written on the outside. I looked quizzically at the desolate street, picked it up and folded the titanium blade out of my jackknife. I cut open the seal, familiarized myself with the laconic missive and cursed fatefully.

Inspector White had set our meeting for midday, and I wasn't at all sure that I would be available by that time. And what was more, I wasn't sure that I wanted to see the inspector today anyway.

I cursed out again, this time louder and started walking down the hillock. Crossing the bridge, I couldn't resist looking down, but there was nothing there, just water babbling and jumping between the rocks.

I LEFT THE TAILOR'S WITH A RENTED three-piece suit, unbearably fashionable and just as unbearably gaudy. Unfortunately, I also left with an empty wallet. I didn't have any money left, even for lunch, but that fact was no longer capable of spoiling my mood.

If something went wrong this evening, hopelessness would be the least of my problems. To be more accurate, it wouldn't even have been a problem.

And in fact, what does a corpse need money for, anyway?

Also, there was still the inspector. What the devil did he need from me on the weekend?!

Having shifted the bag containing my old suit into my left hand, I clinked two coins together, slipped the shimmering change back into my pocket and walked over to the Yarden Embankment. This Sunday morning, it turned out to be impossible to even elbow your way through the loitering city-dwellers, and I soon grew sick of intercepting the gazes of people whose eyes I'd caught: chic ladies, their no-less-gauche gentlemen and the street traders. Then I turned down Des Cartes street, and miscalculated once again: the normally empty little street was plugged up by a motley public, sorrowful and quiet. And only the whooping of the boy handing out leaflets carried over the crowd, flying out like the screeching of a seagull over a desolate sea coast.

"Six-blade shoe polisher here! Patented design!" chirruped the grimy little boy, sticking his advertising in the faces of passers-by. "Just one turn of the handle! Shine guaranteed! Easier than ever before!"

I took the rumpled paper and held it up to the boy.

"What is the meaning of this public demonstration?" I asked him.

"Some famous conductor is being buried," he answered airily. "He lost his favorite baton and the freak popped his neck in a noose."

People began staring at us, but that didn't embarrass the boy whatsoever.

"Choked with a rope, the dummy," he continued, sharply throwing his thumb upward. "His head popped off."

"I see," I nodded and stepped out of the way.

From behind, I was overtaken by a scream:

"Steam iron! Lighten your wife's load! Gets rid of wrinkles fast!"

And the quiet hum of the honorable public, which slowly moved to the Imperial Theater, covered up the rage-filled squabbling of the two boys competing for territory.

And that scene encompassed New Babylon: another's death here wasn't even worth a minute of silence.

Nothing was, for that matter.

And it never had been.

I threw the advertisement into the first trash-can I came across, turned down the neighboring street, looked at my watch and increased my pace.

The Imperial Theater was hidden from view, and the street curved in an arc, taking me to a stone-block paved square. In the middle of it, there was a pigeon-shit covered monument of the great trinity – Ampère, Ohm, and Volt.

But then, the lyceum of the Sublime Electricity, rushing up to the heavens in two steel masts, was a place those flying vandals kept a wide berth from. And it was no wonder. Around the huge copper balls, which crowned the elegant constructions, there were wavering halos of electric current. From time to time, they lit up in blinding sparks, which caused a distinctive clicking to ring out over the square, but only those who were visiting from the provinces tucked their heads between their shoulders in fear. City-dwellers sitting on the open verandas of the many cafes didn t even look away from their newspapers.

The huge Nicola Tesla coil must have used a simply monstrous amount of energy, which was always a riddle to me: why would these learned men waste electricity so wantonly day after day, and month after month? Simply to demonstrate their greatness? And only now, when the manmade lightning was circling directly over my head, did I truly feel the power of science in full measure.

Immeasurable power was the true thing that Nicola Tesla's creation embodied.

Power and safety.

The energy bubbling around could blow any infernal creature to smithereens, and dissolve its remains into ash. Any, even the most powerful demon, would burn here in a few short seconds' time in the blessed flame of electrical discharge; it wouldn't be some mere dash into the underworld with a slightly singed pelt, this creature would be annihilated once and for all.

There is no protection from electricity. Electricity is stronger than magic!

The sett tiles under my feet were slightly

trembling, shaking in time with the powerful steam generator in the lyceum's basement. In a strange way, that shivering gave me confidence. I removed my derby cap from my head, went into the complex and took a look around the room, which was filled with bright electric light. The inspector didn't catch my eye. To the sound of the lecture coming over the loudspeaker plates, I had to set out in search of a boss I wasn't even sure had been here today.

I found him in the western wing of the complex. With one leg thrown carelessly over the other, Robert White was sitting back in a wooden bench and, with a helpless look, gazing into a battle painting titled "The Great Maxwell kills a *Fallen One*." I did nothing to distract the inspector from his thoughts, taking a seat next to him in silence and listening to the lecture.

"We all live in a surprising time. A time of change!" Carried out from the slightly creaking speakers. "The old world is in its death throes. The era of steam is coming to an end, and the era of electricity will soon be upon is! But, as man came to this earth writhing and screaming, so the labor pains of progress are rattling the present, giving birth to conflicts. The greatest minds of our time, Nicola Tesla and Thomas Edison have disputes on the course of electricity's development. But don't believe the sensationalist newspapermen smacking their lips, and writing in words the average person doesn't know. The truth is born in disputes! Remember! Direct current or alternating, it doesn't matter. It's all electricity! Sublime Electricity! Knowledge in its purest form!"

Here the inspector turned to me and asked:

"You do know the story of Maxwell, right Leopold?"

"Who hasn't heard of the great Maxwell and the demon?!" I grew surprised.

"The *fallen one*," my boss corrected me. "Maxwell made his *fallen one* obey."

"And what of it?"

"I mean that I do not want to spend my whole life stagnating in anonymity!" Robert White's eyes glimmered in rage. "I don't want the next quarter century to be spent busting my butt, just to make it to senior inspector. And that's the best case scenario! That's if some greenhorn with a high-ranked friend doesn't get it before me! And now, a chance to blow that endless circle up has presented itself, see?"

"I'm afraid I don't," I replied with a confused tone.

But I did understand. I understood it all. And I could feel that understanding jabbing into my chest like a jagged shard of ice. But I didn't want to hear what else the inspector had to say.

The inspector, though, wasn't at all stopped by that.

"The *fallen one* in that basement," he said slowly, looking at his right palm, "he was real and everything you said was true. I sensed his heartbeat. I felt a living heart in a marble sculpture!"

"And what of it?"

"If he escapes..." Robert White whispered, but

immediately corrected himself: "If you free him, we could both become powerful beyond our wildest dreams!"

"No! He would simply turn us to ash on the spot!" I objected, not having tried to persuade the man that I was incapable of freeing the *fallen one* from its stone prison.

Robert White just broke into laughter.

"*The fallen* have long lost their power," he declared flippantly. "For the first thousand years, their rule was undivided and unchallenged but, the longer they went, the more they lost their rage. *The fallen* ceased to be Divine Retribution, and got carried away playing ruler. Some considered themselves leaders of the world, and some thought themselves anchorites. Finally, they became nothing more than a shadow of their former selves. Our fathers and grandfathers on the Night of the Titanium Blades poured their blood over the entirety of Atlantis and another half the world as well, so you can't seriously think that we won't be able to handle one lone *fallen one*, right?"

"Sure, we'll handle it, but what then?" I grimaced. "We will control the *fallen one* jointly, and make it obey us. But just think, how will society look on this? Well, I can tell you! The Empress will order us skinned alive, quartered and roasted over a low flame, and that, they say, is extremely unpleasant!"

"I'm glad to see you've retained your sense of humor, Leo," the inspector glanced at me unkindly with his colorless eyes. "As for that old nag, you don't need to worry. She's just the Emperor's widow, and the Crown Princess is a constantly ill little girl. People need a strong hand! The old aristocracy spent centuries licking the paws of *the fallen*, they'll have to obey – servility is in their blood."

I didn't share my boss's confidence on that. When, sixteen years ago, after the Emperor's death, his own brother, the great Duke of Arabia stopped short in his claim to the throne, he and all his close relatives were cut down at once by a flu from Africa. Few doubted that her Imperial Majesty's hand was mixed up in such a sudden end.

After all, he was her brother-in-law! But us? The inspector and I were simply dust under her feet!

For that reason, I said with as much confidence as I could muster:

"The old aristocracy has long lacked any influence."

"That is precisely why they will support us!" Robert White gave his answer with fanatical confidence. "I'm not such an idiot that I would start an open rebellion, but the power of even one *fallen one* would be enough to change the balance!"

"I don't like that," I admitted honestly.

"Me neither," nodded the inspector appeasingly. "But we can't just let this chance slip through our fingers." He shook his head and again started staring at his open palm. "I felt his heart beating. They turned him into stone, but they couldn't kill him. I sensed his power, I touched it..."

"If your right hand tempts you, cut it off," I said

in a detached manner, looking at Maxwell lashing a *fallen one* with an electric whip; sputtering fire was shooting off in all directions, as well as pieces of snow-white feathers. "The *fallen one* is tempting you, inspector."

"Hold your tongue!" Robert White threw in sharply. "It wasn't for nothing that I set our meeting here precisely! My mind is free. Spells and curses cannot touch us in this place!"

"As you say."

"So, are you gonna help or not?"

"I don't like this," I repeated stubbornly.

"You prefer to vegetate on twenty thousand a year in income when you could be rising to the very top?"

"Rising to heaven, more like," I snorted. "But we don't believe in such fairy tales, do we? Though we do have firm evidence that hell exists. And that's exactly where we'll be going if you don't smarten up."

"Nonsense!" The inspector cut me off. "So, yes or no?"

"I need to think about it."

"Make the right choice," Robert White made a wry face, stood up from the bench and stepped off toward the exit; his cane was quivering in his hand like the tail of a disgruntled cat.

I picked up the newspaper he'd left behind, and shuffled off after him on my wobbly legs. I came out of the gates of the lyceum. In a stand on the corner I bought a gas water with raspberry syrup. I sucked down the cup in one gulp, and only then somewhat came to my senses.

To say that my boss's unexpected proposition had knocked me off course is to say nothing. In fact, it scared me. It scared me so bad I was hiccupping. After all, these were in no way empty fantasies, no – Robert White made a habit of getting what he wanted. Also, he could hardly have invented a crazier plot than returning a *fallen one* to life and forcing it to serve him. Even in stone statue form, that *fallen one* weighed down with its power. But if all its energy were to escape...

I shrugged my shoulders and continued into a cafe, its overhang lit up with the uneven flickering of fifty electric bulbs. The cafe was even named for it – *The Bulb*.

Inside, it was absolutely packed with adepts of the Sublime Electricity; the reductionists were having lunch, leafing through thick scientific almanacs, arguing until hoarse, and discussing the latest scientific trends, but I was able to get through into a relatively quiet corner, under a comfortable and not quite so bright bulb.

Basically, the place was quiet, but only relatively.

Yablochkov! Lodygin! Tesla! Edison!

Amperes, volts, generators, circuits, charges!

Electricity!!!

I had already looked everywhere for a somewhat calmer place to sit. Oh well. Just then, a waiter walked up to my table.

"I'll have a scoop of ice cream," I asked,

remembering my empty wallet just in time.

"Anything else?"

"No thank you," I refused, putting up the newspaper as a shield.

As luck would have it, the front page was "decorated" with a photograph of a lank old lady with two light-struck eyes – the photographic film had proven incapable of containing the gaze of her Imperial Majesty – Empress Victoria.

I gave a shudder. That sweet old aunty wouldn't even hesitate to feed to her hunting hounds whatever remained of me after the interrogation. That was precisely how this all would end, there wasn't even the slightest doubt. And that was if the *fallen one* didn't eat my soul first!

Did I even have to say that I didn't consider the inspector's proposal seriously, and wasn't preparing to? I only had to come up with a way to refuse my boss and not make a deadly enemy in the process.

Should I tell Department Three?

I knew quite a few people who hated snitches deep down, and even announced that for all to hear but, thanks to their opportunistic interests, would denounce their colleagues or acquaintances at the first chance. I was not preparing to snitch myself, though.

Snitching is like the boomerang used by the aboriginals of Zuid-India; you wouldn't have time to come to your senses before it comes back and smacks you in the head. It would be one man's word against another's, and who would be believed in the end: the inspector or the detective constable? No, the balance of power was definitely not in my favor.

"Your order!" The waiter announced and placed a little dish of ice cream before me. He did not hurry on further.

I dug a few fifty-centime coins from my pocket, tossed them on the table and dived back into reading, trying to come away from these unhappy thoughts with something.

But I didn't.

Would Empress Victoria be finishing her visit to Paris, restored after last winter's flooding, and returning to New Babylon? On the landing pad, would her Imperial Highness Crown Princess Anna be there to meet her grandmother? Was the fifteenth birthday of the heir to the throne coming up?

And what did I care?

I was only concerned with the inspector's request and... the ball.

I scooped a bit of the vanilla ice cream into my dessert spoon and nodded.

Right, the ball!

Problems must be dealt with in order of their significance. And, if Inspector General von Nalz roasts a certain detective constable over a low flame, Robert White's intention to get the same one involved in unpleasant business would already have utterly no meaning.

Do I have to answer the inspector?

Curses! I'll have to worry about that this evening!

I glanced at my watch, set the newspaper down, shoveled down my ice cream in double time, and stood up from the table. I grabbed the bag with my old suit and, with relief, left the overly noisy institution.

Amperes, volts, lumens...

Phooey!

I HAD TO BORROW SOME MONEY from Ramon Miro for a cab; luckily, he wasn't so small-minded as to refuse his colleague, just asking with a smirk:

"I wonder if your yearly salary will cover your debts, or not?"

"I'll dig you up a tenner somehow," I answered, hiding the pair of rumpled bank notes in my wallet. I said nothing of the fact that, with interest, my debts had already piled up to thirty thousand francs.

"You can take it from your advance," the constable reminded me.

"I can take it from my advance." I agreed and set off to find a carriage suitable for my next appearance.

My income from the inheritance fund would be going in its entirety to paying back debts for the first year or two, so the perspective of losing my detective constable's salary had pushed me into a very natural depression. But not going because of that would be playing right into the inspector's hand! Life is more valuable...

I ROLLED HOME in an open carriage. It was nothing luxurious, but completely appropriate to the occasion.

The cabby's livery was decked out in shining laces cleaner than a general's uniform.

"Wait here," I ordered him, opened the gate and went into my home. And there, I whistled in surprise, having discovered Elizabeth-Maria in a pink satin dress, draped in lace, beads and sequins.

"Is it time yet?" The girl wondered, trying on a hat in the mirror. Her miniature reticule was waiting on the rack.

"It's time," I affirmed.

My guest walked up to me and took me by the arm.

"Then let's go!"

I slid my glasses down to the very tip of my nose and looked at the girl above their dark lenses. While I'd been gone, she had applied subtle make-up and, now, with lipstick, her lips no longer seemed withered and thin.

"Is something the matter, Leopold?" Elizabeth-Maria smiled charmingly, doubtlessly satisfied with the effect she'd achieved.

"You are simply charming," I answered, returning my glasses to their place.

We came down from the porch and walked through the dead black garden to the gates.

"How romantic!" Unexpectedly, the girl began laughing uncontrollably, plucking a blackened carnation from its stalk, dead like everything else around. Her graceful fingers nimbly broke the brittle stem off and stuck the flower into the buttonhole of my jacket. "There. Now that's much better!"

I sighed hopelessly and requested:

"Don't do that anymore."

"Why not?"

"They don't grow back."

"Oh, Leo!" my guest shook her head. "Do you also find dead flowers beautiful? You and I are so alike..."

I swung open the gate, helped the girl into the carriage and, only after we'd pulled away, expressed:

"That is not the issue. I simply remember when these flowers were still alive. Their value to me is as mementos, and not in their, as you put it, 'beauty...'"

"You must value what you have, not look into the past," Elizabeth-Maria reproached me. "I advise you to live in the present day, dear..."

"As you say."

"Or has this house made its mark on you?" the girl continued cooing. "Your butler is also strange. It's simply impressive, his composure. I've never seen the like."

"He's just old school," I once again let out a couple words, not wishing to speak about Theodor.

"Is something bothering you, Leopold?" Elizabeth-Maria took a closer look at me.

"What do you think?" I looked gloomily at her through the dark lenses of my glasses.

The girl only started laughing carelessly.

"Everything will be alright!"

"Let's hope so," I snorted, not sharing anything on the inspector's request.

I didn't even want to think about that, to say

nothing of actually discussing it.

Soon, the narrow little streets of the old town were behind us, and our wheels stopped bouncing around on the uneven tiles. But the jostling was replaced by smog that stretched out over the street. The smoke from the factory outskirts made my throat itch. Elizabeth-Maria just kept silent, covering her face with a perfumed kerchief.

It grew easier only when the carriage turned onto Newtonstraat and the colossus of the police headquarters was looming in front of us. There was a whole file of carriages lined up in front of the central entrance; cabbies were dropping off passengers and immediately leaving, so I came to an agreement with our driver on where exactly he would be meeting us after the end of the reception, jumped out onto the sidewalk and pulled my companion after me by the arm. And when she stepped down from the running board, I pushed down the last remnants of doubt and led Elizabeth-Maria down to the flung-wide doors of the Newton-Markt.

The dress shirt on my back was soaked through with sweat. My mouth had gone dry, and the little hammers of an approaching headache were starting to pound in my temples. But I just smiled and looked around imperturbably. I handed my invitation to the steward standing in the doorway with a look of complete and total carelessness; I simply handed him the triangle of chalk paper and headed directly into the room where we normally held our staff meetings.

Now I could hear snippets of music coming from it, and Elizabeth-Maria slightly shifted her pace to fit the rhythm of the joyful melody. I couldn't even dream of such grace, so I simply walked through the corridor and greeted my acquaintances, who I came across from time to time. I didn't converse with anyone. The most I did was trade a few meaningless sentences for a few seconds.

I saw the inspector general standing near the entrance. The old bobby was busy speaking with a tall fat man and a doughy young boy in a shamelessly fancy suit but, when I approached, he immediately left the Minister of Justice and his nephew and made way for us.

"Viscount!" he faded into a smile. "Won't you introduce me to your companion?"

I swallowed nervously and smiled with great difficulty:

"Inspector general, my bride the *Illustrious* Elizabeth-Maria Nickley. Elizabeth-Maria, the head of the metropolitan police, Inspector General von Nalz."

"Viscount!" Friedrich von Nalz erupted into laughter, his eyes glimmering with colorless flame. "No need for such pomp! Everyone here today is a friend or sympathizer. No titles!"

"As you say... Friedrich," I bowed my head slightly.

"Come on in! Come on!" the inspector general allowed, then and returned to the conversation I'd interrupted. And I led Elizabeth-Maria into the room.

"That was the meeting you were so

apprehensive about?" She whispered to me.

"Apprehensive? Me? Where'd you get that from?"

Then the girl got up on tip-toe and very quietly exhaled into my ear:

"I could smell your fear, Leo. And I still can. Why?"

"Nothing to be surprised at," I smiled light-heartedly. "He's just an overly talkative person by nature, and that makes me devilishly uncomfortable. I cannot bear being the center of attention."

"As you say," smiled Elizabeth-Maria craftily, not continuing to insist

I simply shrugged my shoulders and sent the girl to the buffet table at the far wall.

"Would you like to dance?" Elizabeth-Maria asked in surprise. 'Listen, such music!"

"I can't hear. A bear stepped on my ear," I got out of it with a saying that I had heard quite often from my father.

"You're just..."

"And I didn't have time to eat lunch."

"Now that's a good reason!" the girl laughed uncontrollably.

In the end, before all the formal pandemonium began at the tables, I managed to scarf down my tenth canape, then sauntered around the room holding a glass of soda water. Elizabeth-Maria limited herself to a glass of cherry juice.

"Pretty much the same as blood," she told me

"Only sour."

"I meant color-wise."

"Arterial is brighter, and venous is darker."

"You're unbearable!"

"Nerves," I sighed and, as Elizabeth-Maria was becoming an object of discussion, I began introducing the girl to my colleagues. And it would've all been hollow interaction, but then Inspector White appeared.

"Leopold!" He smiled as if nothing had happened. "Let me steal your treasure away for a few dances!"

"Naturally, inspector!" I allowed without the slightest hesitation.

I wasn't planning on dancing today in any case.

At that moment, the orchestra on the improvised stage began playing a new melody. Robert and Elizabeth-Maria joined the dancing couples, and I headed back for the buffet tables, making an effort to avoid running into anyone I knew.

It's nothing! But I couldn't hide.

"She is pretty, though," rang out from behind my back. "And, they say, she looks somewhat like me."

I turned sharply and found myself face to face with the inspector general's daughter. Elizabeth-Maria von Nalz noticeably surpassed my companion in height, so our eyes were hardly on the same level. Mine, colorless-light, and hers light-gray, with blindingly orange sparkles. They were the kind of eyes one wanted to look into until the end of time.

"Few could compare with your beauty, my

illustrious lady," I answered with an awkward compliment. Not having mastered my temptation, I pulled off my dark glasses.

According to rumor, the *Illustrious* Ms. von Nalz's talent was the ability to bewitch people with a glance, but I wasn't at all worried by that now.

"What a flatterer you are, Viscount!" the inspector general's daughter shook her head.

"I may be a flatterer," I shrugged my shoulders, "but not in this case. And, as the chance has presented itself, I would like to offer you my most sincere apology for the deplorable incident with the paper. Believe me, I had no idea that poets could be so unrestrained."

The daughter of the inspector general just laughed uncontrollably.

"Think nothing of it!" she declared, twirling a reddish lock of hair around her finger. "I even found it flattering, being the main character in a story in the society pages. And it was so fun to see daddy get mad..."

Fun? Not so much for me.

I smiled sourly:

"I'm glad everything worked itself out."

"I'm sure that tomorrow, this misunderstanding will be the farthest thing from anyone's mind," the girl noted frivolously and got curious: "Viscount, do you really know Albert Brandt? He is called the most mysterious poet in modern times! How did you ever make his acquaintance?"

"The thing is..." I faltered, not able to keep my

gaze from her dazzling feminine eyes and, much to my own surprise, answered with the pure truth: "It was in Athens, if memory serves..."

"In Athens?"

The pressure in my temples became unbearable. I replied:

"Yes," but immediately found the power to correct myself: "Or in Angora, I don't remember for certain. Albert got into a difficult position, and I did him a small service. And, since then, we talk."

"How interesting!" the inspector general's daughter gasped. "Have you done a lot of traveling?"

Instead of answering, I suggested:

"Elizabeth-Maria, why don't we continue this discussion over a dance? Maybe. You know, now that it wouldn't cause idle gossip..." and was struck by my own bravery in waiting for an answer.

"Naturally, Viscount!"

We joined the spinning couples in a waltz. I began leading the girl and immediately realized that Elizabeth-Maria danced incomparably better than me and, in order not to fall face-first into the mud once and for all, I would have to distract my partner with conversation.

And not step on her feet. Just make sure not to step on her feet...

"My mother died when I was five," I told the girl, "and that nearly killed my father."

"I'm very sorry..."

"I cannot recollect exactly, but I seem to remember us spending a certain period of time going from place to place after that. Around six months."

"Surely, you toured the whole Empire in that time!"

"No, not the whole Empire," I laughed uncontrollably, masking my nervousness. "But I did get to see quite a lot."

"And where did you like it most?"

I answered without hesitation:

"New Babylon, the heart of the Empire."

I did not share my impression that it was an ulcer eating the Empire from the inside, though.

"And your friend, Albert?" Elizabeth-Maria wondered. "Is he really as strange as they say?"

"No stranger than the other bohemians," I answered with a meaningful and even mysterious air. "Have you read about the conductor who took his own life after losing his wand?"

"Yes, simply horrible!"

At that moment, the music went silent, and I had to step back from the girl.

"It was nice to meet you, Viscount," Elizabeth-Maria smiled goodbye, walking away with the light step of a dancer.

Her breathtaking eyes paused on me, leaving me stunned, and I squeezed out:

"You too. You too..."

It grew dry in my mouth. I wanted to wet my throat unbearably, but before I'd had time to reach the buffet tables, I was grabbed by Robert White.

"Have you thought over my proposal?" asked my boss.

"No."

"You still haven't?"

"No, inspector," I shook my head and put my dark glasses on. "And I will not."

"As you say," Robert White shrugged his shoulders with surprising nonchalance and did not try to convince me. "But let's talk tomorrow when our minds are fresh. Promise me you'll think about it."

"I will," I promised.

"Don't come to work. I'll come to meet you," the inspector warned, giving a salute with his glass and heading back homeward.

Curses! His last remark had hit me right in the Achilles' heel. If the inspector doesn't have a change of heart about firing me, I'd be just as likely to see my advance as my own ears. After all, he definitely wouldn't change his mind...

I cursed silently once again and someone took me by the elbow.

"Leopold, is everything quite alright?" asked Elizabeth-Maria, *my* Elizabeth-Maria.

"Yes."

"You're breathing like a spooked horse."

"It's stuffy in here," I said, looking all around absent-mindedly. "Let's go get some fresh air."

The girl, after dancing, wasn't panting in the slightest. The blue vein on her neck didn't even start beating more rapidly, but I was obviously not doing well. My heart was pounding, and for some reason, it was uneven.

"You wanted to suck all the life out of the

party?"

"Not a bad idea, don't you think?"

"If you're already finished..."

"Yes, we can leave."

We headed for the exit, but in the door we were intercepted once again by the inspector general.

"My *Illustrious* Mademoiselle," the ghastly old man smiled, "allow me to have a brief word with your handsome cavalier..."

Friedrich von Nalz and I walked over to a flung-open window and there the inspector general spent some time in silence looking at the row of electric torches illuminating the night outside.

"I am impressed, Viscount," he said some time later. "You are quite the shrewd young man."

"Thank you..."

"But!" The inspector general turned unexpectedly sharply, and I felt like I'd been doused in boiling water from head to toe. "In the future, keep your distance from my daughter! Get that straight!"

"There's no need for this warning whatsoever," I assured the man, making an effort to stop myself from taking a step back.

"Wonderful..." the old man uttered with detachment. His eyes gradually grew dim. He nodded a few times, as if agreeing with his own thoughts, and returned to the ball room.

I followed him with a steadfast gaze, then extended my hand to the approaching Elizabeth-Maria and, with her in tow, headed for the exit.

"What did he want from you?" the girl wondered when we'd gone out onto the street.

"Not going into particulars," I chuckled, "the inspector general told me that I'm lucky to have you."

"Can't argue with that!" Elizabeth-Maria laughed uncontrollably, sincerely and rollickingly.

I wiped off the perspiration that had started forming on my forehead and led the girl down the electric-light-ensconced sidewalk. We found our cabby waiting just where we'd left him. Together with the shadows, an uncomfortable chill had swept in, and Elizabeth-Maria, sensitive to the cold, wrapped herself in a weightless mantle.

"Will you stay with me for a few days?" I asked, helping the girl into the carriage.

The question cheered her up, and she laughed uncontrollably again:

"Naturally, dear. I am yours to command."

"That is excellent."

I threw myself into the back of the seat and closed my eyes. The future, as before, was making me weary. It was too indistinct. And though now I didn't have to be afraid of the inspector general's wrath, the threat of losing my soul scared me no less.

The reductionists were free to sound off on the Sublime Electricity and push their pens in libraries, trying to acquire their sacral *knowledge*, but I wasn't so naive. The underworld existed, I didn't have to doubt that, and I absolutely did not want to take up residence there. But now, everything in my life was leading to that.

And losing my salary, when compared with that, somehow didn t seem so worrying.

Some things cannot be bought with money.

WHEN WE GOT HOME, night had already fallen completely over the city. Walking among the houses, it was mute and inky black but, from the hill, one could see just how spotty the night's hold over this city really was. Part of New Babylon, had in fact capitulated without a fight and would be immersed in darkness until the very morning, but other neighborhoods were yellow with the uneven light of gas torches and, over the very center, the light was silver with the luster of electric bulbs. And everywhere around, there were the flashing spots of navigation signals when you looked up.

"What a breath-taking place," Elizabeth-Maria said, lifting herself up on my hand and getting out of the carriage. "From up here, you can see the evanescence of being perfectly."

I didn't respond to her remark in any way, and led the girl into my house. I handed my guest over to the butler who'd come out to meet us, myself going up into my bedroom. Once there, I untied my neckerchief with relief.

And that was how that crazy day ended. Just like that...

I folded my jacket, vest and pants carefully, stored them in their bag and placed the bag by the door so I could have it back to the tailor's first thing tomorrow. After that, I shed my dress shirt, stood next to the full-length mirror and took a skeptical look at my reflection.

The first thing that caught my eye was that I was thin. Thin and lanky like a pole.

There was no challenge at all in counting my ribs.

Gangly? No, just thin. And though my father never stopped harping on about how "if bones remain, flesh will grow," I still didn't believe that in the slightest. I was a thin person, period.

And also, just not a very handsome man. The lines of my face were too sharp. My nose was overly long; my uneven teeth did nothing to add to my attractiveness, either.

But in general, there was nothing special. Just an ordinary young man twenty-one years from birth. Although, no, not ordinary. I would be ordinary if not for my eyes.

The piercing gaze of my withered-light *illustrious* eyes caused fear, at times even in me.

No one could grant the title of *illustrious*. You could only be born *illustrious*, or become *illustrious*. To be more accurate, you used to be able to become *illustrious*. All *the fallen* have long been destroyed, and no one will ever again have the chance to bathe themselves in their cursed blood.

But had they really all been destroyed? I remembered the underground chapel in the Judean Quarter, and my mood instantly went sour like milk over a flame. It would have seemed worse, but it would have been naive to suppose that I had truly reached the very bottom. An infernal, bottomless abyss.

The inspector would never let up...

"That's the ticket!" whistled out suddenly from behind my back.

I turned to Elizabeth-Maria, who was frozen in the doorway with an irritated frown on her face.

Curses! There didn't used to be any reason to lock the bedroom at all...

But the girl had already stepped foot into my room, not at all embarrassed that I was standing in front of the mirror wearing nothing but underwear.

"A blank cross!" she whispered dumbfounded. Her thin small fingers slid along my spinal column. "Down your whole back. Did it hurt to get the tattoo?"

"Go away," I snapped, but it was in vain.

Elizabeth-Maria stepped away from the mirror and took an evaluating look at my nearly-naked form before her.

"An eight-pointed star on your heart, a fish to the right," she continued enumerating my tattoos, "a chain around the neck, and a Chi Rho on your spine, on your arm, though..." She took a closer look at what was written. The tattoo wrapped around my right bicep a few times, but the letters were too small for her to really make sense of. "Is that Latin?" she then asked.

"Pater Noster," I clued her in, and the girl involuntarily took a step back.

"Leopold, you're just full of

surprises!" Elizabeth-Maria shook her head. "But by the fires of hell, why? Why'd you get more inked up than an Egyptian sailor?"

"My dad didn't always explain the reasons for his actions," I answered calmly and took the robe thrown on the bed.

"Original," the girl noted, frustrated. "It can't be that you never asked him about it, right?"

"He didn't want to talk about it."

"You didn't argue?"

"That wouldn't have been too smart."

"Surprising!" the girl shook her head, then tossed a red lock of hair from her face and said with a thoughtful smile: "But you know, there's something of a lack of symmetry with the left arm."

"My dad had some plans for it," I confirmed, pulling on the belt of the robe. "And now, if you're not opposed, I would like to get some sleep."

Elizabeth-Maria got closer and whispered:

"Shall I stay?"

"No!" I cut her off very sharply, but did not apologize. "Please don't."

"Not today," the girl agreed and finally left me in peace.

I locked the door, lit my night light and checked all the shutters. After that, I put out the gas lamps and lay down in my bed. I began mentally sorting through the events of the past day, trying to restore in my memory the face of the inspector general's daughter, but all that remained of her image were orange sparks in a pair of gray eyes and the light aroma of perfume. And her voice.

To its captivating sounds, I slipped into a restless slumber.

PART TWO

PATIENT

Hereditary Pathology And Electroshock Therapy

1

BELLS. When I woke up, bells were ringing. Ringing ceaselessly. The sound would get stronger, totally filling my head, then quiet down as if it were coming from somewhere far away, just barely at the edge of audibility.

But the sound never dissipated entirely, even for a second, or an instant, just rang and rang and rang.

Bing! Bing! Bo-o-ong!

Sometimes the sound drifted, sometimes it was drowned out by ambient noise, but I heard only the ringing as if there was a bell slaving away inside my head. Perhaps that was what called me back to life? I didn't know. I was drifting in a boundless blackness, not feeling my own body, not able to move my arms, or my legs. All I could do was listen. All my life was one constant ringing.

Bing! Bing! Bo-o-ong!

Then my sense of smell returned. Through the delirium of nothingness, there came the sharp odor of smelling salts, and then all the other aromas rolled back in as well. It smelled of medicines and antiseptics. Stacked on that was the stink of human excrement and rotting flesh.

A hospital?!

The smells awoke my memory; I was reminded of what had happened on the Roman Bridge. Someone had sunk bullet after bullet into me. Immediately, I was filled with vertigo. Vertigo? Oh no! My whole being was spinning! Spinning and being pulled into silence and darkness.

For a moment, even the unchanging bell sound disappeared, but then I realized that my sense of smell had not left me in full measure. The sharp smacks on my face came through, even with the numbness of unconsciousness.

"No! No! No!" I heard from somewhere in the limitless distance. "Don't you leave us! This frail world is not yet ready to bid you farewell!"

And again, I was struck in the nose by an acrid stink of smelling salts. I inhaled shortly, then started coughing and breathing.

Oh devil! I was under anesthesia!

Morphine? Looked like it...

And the bells immediately stopped ringing. Instead, I smelled cheap tobacco and booze breath.

"Hey, they finally shut up!" someone nearby said in an unsatisfied tone. "That lousy peal was making my head split!"

I still couldn't feel my own body. My consciousness was lightly swaying in the limitless black, and I didn't even want to think about what would happen to me when the anesthesia passed.

How many times had I been shot? Three, four? After all, I also fell off the bridge...

"The main thing is why they were ringing!" the invisible complainer broke the silence once again.

"Easy!" a rude and unkind voice rebuffed him. "It isn't every day that Empresses die."

"The devils in hell have been waiting a long time for that old bat."

"Easy, I said!"

I seemed to feel a light rocking then a landing, as if I was being transferred from a gurney to a hospital bed. The orderlies left, and I was left in silence and darkness, all alone. But not for long.

My hearing had almost totally returned, and I heard the creak of the door, and the tapping of shoe soles on a stone floor.

"Well, what do we have here?" someone asked a few seconds later, drawing out their words at a sloth-like pace.

"An *illustrious* man," came back the quick answer with light notes of ingratiation. "Delivered without documents, hasn't yet come to. The gunshot wounds in his forearm, and thigh are perforating. We removed one bullet from his innards, and another is still lodged in his spine."

The man I took to be a professor snorted and asked with incomprehension:

"Why did you think this case would interest me?"

And again, the attending doctor answered without the slightest hesitation:

"He's *illustrious* and a Christian. You'll like this, professor."

"How do you know that, if he hasn't yet come to? Was he talking while anesthetized?"

"See for yourself, Dr. Berliger."

I seemed to feel a gust of air, as if the blanket was jerked off me, then the professor drew out his words in confusion:

"Yes, that explains a lot."

"As soon as I saw these tattoos I thought of you, Dr. Berliger."

"But this *illustrious* man is half dead, even if he is a Christian..."

"The patient's condition is stable," the doctor assured him.

"And the bullet in his spine?"

The question caught the doctor off guard, and he faltered.

"I won't hide it – the wound is serious. I suspect the bullet is stuck in his spine. I cannot do such a complicated operation, but you and your assistant can work real miracles!"

"No need for all the praise," Berliger replied with slight notes of disgust. "Totally unnecessary."

"Your assistant is the best surgeon I know!"

I got an unbearable desire to have such an experienced physician working on me but, no matter how I tried, I couldn't squeeze a single word out.

Curses! Ahh, what bad luck!

The professor, meanwhile, was clearly in doubt about whether he should take my case.

"I don't even know," he drew out his words in thought. "Even if we have operated on difficult patients before, there's no guarantee that we'll be able to get him to the clinic alive."

"But this is a unique case!"

"And how is it unique? *Illustrious* Christians are not such a rarity."

"Well, look!" the doctor said mysteriously, and I

heard a strange ringing as if a piece of metal was clinking on the sides of a glass jar. "This is the bullet I removed from the patient's stomach cavity."

"Silver?" The professor was dumbstruck. "They tried to shoot him with a silver bullet?!"

"See, I knew this would interest you!"

"Now there you were clearly right!" Mr. Berliger admitted. "So, you say he didn't have any documents with him?"

"None."

"And relatives?"

"What does that have to do with it?" the doctor snorted. "Look at what is on his palms."

"What is that?"

"Traces of fingerprinting ink. This man must be an inveterate criminal. No one will come looking for him."

"And again, your logic is flawless, colleague," the professor agreed with the medic and swished through some bank notes. Meanwhile, a wave of horror swept through the cottony apathy of my anesthesia.

What was happening?! Why wouldn't anyone be looking for me?!

Who was this Professor Berliger?!

"But first, a little check," the professor declared. Then, my eyelid was raised, and the blinding beam of a pocket torch struck my vision. "Excellent! His pupil reacts to light. I'll take him."

"Shall we make an additional injection of

morphine?"

"If you'd be so kind. We have quite a long way to go..."

2

THE BAD PART about being treated with morphine is the lack of choice.

At first, you have that junk injected to stop the pain, but very soon pain becomes an excuse for another injection. And no self-control can help. The addiction is too strong. Physiology and psychology join forces into a slipknot, which a normal person cannot easily remove.

The *illustrious* cannot either. Especially me.

The morphine affected my *talent* directly, forcing me to see things that weren't really there, and confuse reality with narcotic lunqdy. And it wasn't as if I was dreaming of the pastures of heaven! My visions were coming one worse than the last, as if on purpose. Under the effects of morphine, strange and frightening episodes from my past were sparking up in my memory. I had lived through those ghastly moments many times before, only now they were one hundred times more real and vivid than reality.

I would have ignored the pain and demanded they stop injecting me with narcotics, but I couldn't get a single word out. My body no longer obeyed me.

BASICALLY, FIRST THING'S FIRST. First, there was darkness, nothing, emptiness.

For how long I do not know, because there was also no time. At the very least, not for me.

And did I even exist? I wasn't sure. Not at all...

Too vague? Well, how else can one be after first being dosed with morphine, then returning to consciousness in a room with white walls and a garland of bulbs under the ceiling. Naked, I was lying on my back and trying to remember where I was and how I'd gotten here. I tried and couldn't.

"Operation room!" I suddenly realized.

But then, where were the doctors? Why had I been thrown on the operating table alone?

Then I heard the clanging of a little box of tools and the cold scraping of metal on a metal scalpel. The surgeon leaned over me, and I recognized him. I recognized the doctor and immediately remembered the operation room. I gave a jerk, but it was in vain. My arms and legs were tied down to the table with tough leather straps.

"No!" I shouted. "You're dead! I killed you!"

"Codswallop!" Maestro Marlini answered with a cold smile, sticking the scalpel's sharp edge into my chest. As soon as he split my skin, the cut filled with a burning liquid flame!

"Just like the blood of a *fallen one*..." flickered a frightening thought, then the wound exploded in unbearable pain, and I was thrown out of the nightmare into impenetrable blackness.

I WAS AWOKEN AGAIN but not as quickly and much more painfully.

I was lying on an ironclad bed in a little room I couldn't even get a good view of. Before my eyes, everything was floating. My body was being gnawed at by pain. I was nauseous. And although I was lying totally motionless, I was being rocked as if I was on a ship at sea.

On a chair pushed up to the bed, someone was sitting in a white robe. I licked my lips and exhaled hoarsely:

"What's wrong with me, doctor?"

"Everything is just fine with you, Leopold. Just great. For now."

The doctor leaned over me, and I could see dark-blue hand marks on his neck. The marks of my very own hands!

Maestro Marlini jerked the pillow out from under my head, covered my face with it and leaned into me with his whole weight. It was torturously painful to start breathing again.

MY CONSCIOUSNESS RETURNED to total darkness. And I wasn't lying down. I was standing and afraid to move. Because there was someone with me in the dark. Someone big and scary. And he was looking for me.

Someone? Oh no! I knew perfectly well who. And so, I was standing motionless, not daring to even sigh. My legs were buried up to my knees in ice, which was crumbling and rustling, giving away my presence. Then, the flame of a lighter flickered in the darkness. The uneven reflection lit up the basement of my family manor and a dark figure with a carving knife in hand. But it was not the right figure, not at all the person I was afraid to see.

"Very interesting..." Maestro Marlini drew cut his words in thought, and the nightmare, deprived of the last traces of logic, started to dissolve like a house of cards brought down by a slight breeze.

I was pulled under the ice, which peeled back my flesh to the bones.

Just another death.

Abominable.

HAVE YOU EVER THIRSTED to kill someone?

Striven just to take and strangle a person with your own hands, not for any tangible benefit but, simply because the wind blew the wrong direction?

If you have, without a doubt, you know how wrong it is. Passion leaves a gap in the soul, changes you and makes you a different person. It pulls you to the bottom of that gap and never lets you go.

I knew that for certain, because I hadn't merely wanted to kill, I had done so. And I was about to kill again! My hands clenched the neck of Maestro Marlini, and my fingers were shivering in desire to squeeze and strangle the hypnotist, who didn't leave me in peace even after death. His own death, naturally. Not mine.

The hypnotist, tied down to the middle of a wide queen-sized bed, had no fear in his eyes. Before, he didn't believe I had the determination to send him to the other side but now he knew it all in advance. so he wasn't even remotely afraid of the conclusion. The dead are fearless bastards. Worse has happened to them. Or so they think.

"You're dead!" I growled.

"Am I?" the hypnotist asked in surprise and would have laughed, but I clenched my fingers, not allowing him to do so.

"You're dead! I killed you! Dead!"

And I did it again, this time entirely crushing his unyielding throat to make sure. I was out of practice, so it was rough going, but I had plenty of experience in such matters.

The bones cracked, and the summer day was immediately filled with heat. The air from outside heaved with the fire of the underworld, unbearably reeking of brimstone. I turned to the window and hurriedly covered my face with my hand. A flame-enshrouded figure, indistinct and blindingly white, stepped into the room and, after it, a fiery rain tore into the dream. A raging flame devoured my nightmare in an instant and, scorched to the bone, I plummeted like a fiery comet into the bottomless abyss, a circle of darkness spreading out around me.

Probably, the pain from the burns tore me from unconsciousness.

Yes, I woke up. And I cannot say that the nightmares were so totally bad compared to reality...

IT WAS UNPLEASANT to admit, but our reality could be incomparably worse than any nightmare, even the ghastliest. Dreams usually expand on one of the edges of existence, lead it to the absurd and thus bring their victim to a catatonic state. Reality, meanwhile, is frightening by its very wide grasp on all manner of nasty things.

The sound of heavy breathing and distant shouts, fearful and doomed.

An acrid reek of piss and the suffocating smell of chlorine.

An aching pain in the whole body then serenity, brought on by an injection of morphine.

Gradually, it all came together into a unified whole, and I performed a conscious action for the first time in a long while: I opened my eyes.

The soft gloom of the hospital room initially blinded me with unbearable luster and, although I hurried to squint, fragments of details of my circumstances were burned dead into my mind: the white silhouette of a closed door, gray walls, the hook of an unmounted gas bulb. Dim beams of autumn sun made a checkered rectangle on the floor, but the window itself was outside my field of vision.

I wanted to turn my head toward it, but I couldn't. I couldn't do anything. All I could do was lick my dried-out lips and blink.

What was happening?!

A barely audible croak tore itself from my mouth, but no one heard me. And no one could hear me: the bed at the opposite wall was unoccupied.

In an attempt to suppress a panic attack, I took a few deep breaths. My head immediately started spinning and my ears started ringing. For some time,

I managed to balance on the very edge of consciousness, but not too long. Another wave of stupor swept over me...

THE NEXT TIME I AWOKE, there was a breeze of fresh air.

Having left the door wide open, a muscular orderly in an unbuttoned white smock changed the bedpan under my bed and started for the exit.

"Wait!" I rasped out after him.

"Woah!" the boy was surprised, his muscular hairy forearms sticking out of his rolled-back smock sleeves. "He snapped out of it!"

"Wait!" I demanded, but the orderly had already gone out into the corridor and slammed the door behind him, then I heard the scraping of a key turning in an obtuse hole.

I cursed soundlessly and tried to get up but couldn't even move. And the problem wasn't even that my wrists were held to the bed with cloth straps – even a child could get out of such frivolous tethers – my body simply refused to obey me. I couldn't force myself to sit up or bend my legs. I couldn't even give my fingers an elementary wiggle.

The only thing holding me back from panic was the morphine-induced tranquility. I was lying, looking dully at the ceiling and waiting indifferently for things to develop further.

Now, someone would surely come and explain everything, so there was no need to worry. Everything would solve itself soon. As for the strange weakness, there was nothing unusual in that. Just evidence of the wounds, prolonged immobility, and a morphine drip. My muscles had just atrophied, nothing more. I could feel my body: even a horse-sized dose of narcotics wouldn't be able to fully extinguish the pain tearing at my nerves.

Everything would be fine. Everything would definitely be fine.

Curses! Everything was already fine! For a person who'd taken four bullets, just being alive was worth quite a bit. I was alive, and that was what mattered!

But actually, I was just calming myself down with these thoughts, and I was fully aware of that. But what else was there for a person who couldn't move their arms or legs. Just remain calm and hope for the best. Hope for them all to be blown to bits...

THE DOCTOR APPEARED when I was totally convinced that the orderly had just ignored my waking up. The physician was young and disheveled; from under his wide-open smock, I could see a cheap suit, dappled with dark spots, as if the doctor had recently been caught in the rain. He smelled of bad fall weather, cigarette smoke and medicine.

"Excellent!" he announced from the doorway. "You're awake, that's just excellent!"

"Where am I?" I exhaled hoarsely.

Confusion was reflected on the doctor's plain pitted face. He pulled at his gold tie clip and inquired:

"Do you know what happened to you? What's

the last thing you remember?"

"I was shot."

"And your name? Tell it to me!"

I thought for a long time about how exactly to introduce myself, then said:

"My name is Lev Shatunov."

"Russian?" the doctor clarified, taking a wrinkled notepad from his frock pocket.

"Yes."

The doctor took down my name and thoughtfully stroked his big nose with the end of his pencil.

"Where am I?" I repeated.

"What?" the medic shuddered. "Ah! You're in a hospital."

I took a heavy sigh and stared at the ceiling.

"What's wrong with me, doctor?" I asked, expecting to hear some kind of indigestible medical terminology, but instead, the doctor asked:

"Can you move your arms or legs?"

"No."

The medic cast his eyes down nervously.

"One of the bullets hit you in the spine. Most likely, your spinal column was damaged, and you will be paralyzed for the rest of your life."

"Nonsense!" I exploded and started sizzling from the pain beginning to heave in my head.

"Remain calm!" the doctor demanded. "That is not yet a final diagnosis!"

"I have to get in touch with my attorney. I am fairly well-heeled and can afford the best specialists!"

"You'll have to talk with the professor about that."

"You must send a message to my attorney!"

"The only thing I must do," the doctor threw out, "is tend to your wounds and oversee your recovery. That is all! For the rest, you're going to have to come to an agreement with the head of the department!"

"Then call him!" I burst into a scream.

"The professor will take a look at you as soon as he has time," the doctor declared and threw open the door, allowing the orderly to roll a cart into the room with surgical implements, little bottles of healing ointments and rolls of bandages.

"I want to see the professor immediately!" I demanded, tearing into a scream. "Right now! Is that clear?!"

"Everything in its time," he shot back, taking an iron mug and placing it to my lips: "Drink! You must drink this!"

"What is that?"

"Drink!"

It's hard to resist when you cannot feel your own body. The orderly slightly raised my head and, whether I wanted to or not, I had to swallow the bitter concoction. I didn't spit it out or choke the desire to show my own independence. I just felt an inhuman sorrow that I had lost the ability to turn into a beast.

However, in that case, the silver bullets would have ended me right there on the bridge...

It was a medicinal beverage containing some

kind of narcotic: very soon, a feeling of cottony torpor rolled over me and I wanted unbearably to sleep. Probably, that was for the best: the orderly didn't take the pains to soak the bandages for long and, if I had remained conscious, the reapplication would have been pure torture...

I WOKE UP WITH A HEADACHE and feverish heartbeat. My mouth was so dry that my swollen tongue could barely move. And, adding to all that, I woke up totally disoriented in space and time.

I didn't know where, and I had no idea when.

What kind of hospital was this, and how long had I been here?

There was no one to ask. And could I even squeeze a word out?

What if the paralysis had spread higher and reached my voice box?!

That thought pierced me with a deadly horror. I took a deep breath, then melted into a mechanical smile and felt my dried lips cracking.

Quite the meager reassurance but, at the very least, I could still control my own face.

After that, I tried to bend the fingers of my right hand and managed to do so with unexpected ease.

I raised my head in astonishment, looked at my hand and cursed in vexation: each and every one of my fingers was unclenched. And, no matter how I tried to move them, nothing came of it.

Another wave of viscous prickly fear swept over me.

Helplessness is horrible. You're totally and completely dependent on other people, and you never know how they'll might treat you.

I was shaken and immediately heard a slight rustling, as if someone was slightly scratching at the door. Someone with long and sharp claws who was very, very hungry. The door gave a shudder, creaked and suddenly flew open with a shove.

My heart seized up. My temples began to sweat but, just a moment later, a wave of untold relief came over me. It was not my *illustrious talent* gone off the chain. The time had simply come to put on new bandages. It was the orderlies.

This time there were two: the muscle-head I'd already seen with ape-like long arms and a new one – his hair was carrot red, his face was pimply and his head was shaped like a coconut.

My lips were wetted, and I was allowed to drink, then they picked me up together and confidently transferred from the bed onto a gurney.

"He's heavy!" the redhead said in surprise.

"He'll shrink up," the muscle head answered, clearly familiar with such matters.

These words frankly reeled me.

"Where?" I asked. "Where are you taking me?!"

"To see the boss," the orderly answered, most likely meaning the professor.

The boys rolled the gurney, with a godlessly squeaking wheel, to the long dark corridor, and I raised my head, wanting to see what was going on, but there was nothing to see. Bare plaster on the walls, locked doors, barred windows under the ceiling.

Total uncertainty.

But it was no problem – I'd have a talk with the professor and everything would be just fine.

Would it, though? I just couldn't shake the feeling that I was in a prison. There were bars everywhere and the doorframes were reinforced with iron. Why have such precautionary measures in a normal hospital? I mean, really, why?

And still, I was being rolled down a hospital corridor, no two ways about it. The key was the smell: anyone who had been in a hospital before would recognize it immediately. Stinking medicines, acrid disinfectants, and something else indistinguishable. The smell of disease. And not some banal fall cough, but a drawn-out soul-sucking ailment in the final stages, when there's no longer any cause to expect recovery and the only thing that awaits is pure agony.

That smell scared me. I was finally beside myself. I would certainly have hopped off the gurney and done something dumb, if only I could have.

But I couldn't, and I was devilishly upset by that.

THE ORDERLIES STOPPED THE GURNEY before an office with a plaque reading "Professor Karl T. M. Berliger." The name of his department was not indicated; while the boys were waiting for an answer to a knock at the door, I was staring at that inscription and the neighboring doors.

"Come in!" came a voice after a fairly long

delay, and the orderlies deftly wheeled the gurney through the narrow doorway and froze to wait for further orders.

"Place him against the wall!" ordered the middle-aged gentleman with the gaunt and smart face of a man of good lineage. His jacket was hanging on a coatrack, and he was at his desk wearing a white frock with starched collar, ironed dark blue pants with a crease sharp enough to cut paper, and black leather shoes polished to a shine.

Just one word came to mind: "dandy."

But I noticed all that only after the orderlies had moved the gurney to the far wall and left the office. First of all, my attention was drawn by the only window of the office, which was adorned with bars, as is done in prison hospitals. That gave me some food for thought, but I didn't rush to any conclusions for the simple reason that there was nothing unusual in the rest of it: the table, cabinet and writing desk. On the wall, there was a portrait of her Majesty the Empress Victoria with a ribbon of mourning in the corner.

I couldn't understand so quickly if this was a private clinic or a government hospital.

The professor, meanwhile, took his telephone receiver off the hook and said:

"Doctor Ergant, come to my office. Yes, this is about our new patient."

Returning the receiver to its place, he walked past the gurney and couldn't resist a grimace of disgust. I did smell, and not the best, but I didn't feel any embarrassment and immediately took the bull by the horns:

"Where am I right now?"

"In a hospital," Professor Berliger answered calmly and smiled. "Isn't that obvious?"

"But what hospital exactly?"

"Better you tell me how you're feeling," the professor dodged. "Are you experiencing any pain or vertigo?"

"I am," I confirmed, because my well-being really did leave something to be desired. My thoughts were confused. I just couldn't concentrate on any one thing; my soul was being eaten at by atrophying fear.

"Dryness in your mouth? Do you need water?"

The last thing I wanted was to take such handouts, but I had to put my pride aside for my throat's sake.

"Please!"

The professor filled a glass from a decanter, poured it into my mouth and enquired:

"Can you feel your body below the neck?"

"Doesn't matter!" I bristled, raising my head from the gurney and demanding: "I need to speak with my attorney!"

Berliger set the empty glass on the window sill and spread his arms.

"I'm afraid I cannot allow that."

"What do you mean, you cannot?" I asked, startled.

"The rules of this establishment forbid patients from talking with the outside world."

"To hell with your rules! Call my attorney at once!"

"I won't even think of it."

"You don't have the right to detain me without my consent!"

"Now there you are mistaken!" the professor answered, taking a paper from the table with a blue heraldic stamp and holding it up to my face. "By order of the Coulomb district court, you have been sentenced to forced medical treatment in connection with severe critical thinking disorder, which presents a danger to those around you."

The lines of text danced and melted before my eyes, and I just exhaled:

"What nonsense is this?!"

"I quote: 'while in an unconscious state, the patient made threats and insults directed at her Imperial Majesty, along with extremist declarations of a religious character.'"

"No!" I barked. "None of that happened I remember you, you paid someone to take me here!"

"Your wounds caused a paranoid disorder."

"Allow me to call my attorney!"

"You will be in our clinic until you are fully recovered."

"You listen!" I bared my teeth. "If you don't allow me to make this call, I will kill you!"

The professor looked at me with unhidden contempt.

"Threats won't help you."

"Please," I smiled, and blood started dribbling

from my split lip again. "This isn't a threat."

"Then what is it?"

"A promise, professor. A simple promise."

I pulled at the edge of the fear that started stirring in Berliger's soul, but there was a lot of morphine in my blood and I wasn't able to focus on the professor's phobias. My vertigo gave way to a sharp headache, and I had to bite my lip and squint.

"This will be added to your disease history," Berliger promised and, at that moment, the doctor who had looked at me earlier came into the office without knocking.

"Give the patient a sedative," the professor commanded.

Doctor Ergant didn't ask why, just pulled out a leather travelling bag, placed a new needle into the glass syringe and filled it with morphine.

"Stop it!" I demanded, but to no avail. "Stop this at once!"

The doctor performed the injection and turned to the professor.

"What else, professor?" he asked.

"Do you think the patient is ready for the procedures?"

"He has a surprisingly strong body," Doctor Ergant avoided a direct answer. "His wounds heal extremely fast. There's nothing supernatural in that, but this is the first time I've seen such powerful regeneration."

"Yes or no?" the professor asked point blank.

"Oh,   sorry!" the   doctor   said   in

embarrassment. "I got distracted. Yes. Beyond all doubt, yes. We can begin"

I had to ask exactly what we could begin. I was simply obligated to do it, but I couldn't.

The morphine reached my blood in an instant and the walls of the office disappeared. The ceiling bent in and turned into the dome of sky, gray with a layer of smoke. As far as the eye could see, the earth was burnt out, baked and covered in ash. In places, puddles of burning sludge spit fire. The suffocating smell of brimstone was everywhere, yet I found it surprisingly easy to breathe. I couldn't really feel the heat at all, and my eyes were not tearing up from the acrid smoke.

But everything was still in front of me: I simply hadn't yet fallen all the way into the vision; somewhere in the distance, I could still hear doctors' voices. I could make out a bright triangle of window through the gray haze.

"Did you really kill him?"

I turned sharply and quickly covered my eyes, blocking the unbearable luster. The silhouette of the man was blindingly white, as if the sun cut right through his heart in my dream.

"So, did you kill him?" The strange voice seemed to be sounding out right in my head.

"Who exactly?" I answered with a question. "I've killed many people..."

The dose of morphine and unreality of it all untied my tongue, and really what of it? There was no court in the land that would admit what I said under these circumstances as evidence.

Under these circumstances? I only now realized that I was standing totally naked in the middle of a steppe scorched by fiery rain. My bare feet were crinkling through crumbly burning ash, and I didn't feel hot at all. The luster of the strange man even stopped cutting into the eyes.

This was my dream, and I liked it here.

Devil! My body was obeying me again, just like before!

Why couldn't morphine solve all my problems in real life?!

"You've killed many?" The man's silhouette gave a slightly noticeable shiver. "And how many of them have you strangled? Did many of them have their hands bound when you did it?"

"What are you, my conscience?" I bared me teeth and instantly took a slap.

A moment later, another blow followed, then the narcotic vision fell to pieces, and I was in the professor's office once again.

"You really gave us a scare there, Lev," Doctor Ergant exhaled loudly and wiped the sweat from his forehead with a dirty handkerchief.

"If the patient is recovering as quickly as you say, there's no need for furthermorphine injections," Berliger decided, filing his ideally even nails.

"Noted, professor," said the doctor, not disputing that decision. He then threw open the office door. "Lucien, Jack! Move the patient to room three."

The orderlies exchanged glances, and the

stronger one confirmed:

"Three? Are you sure, doctor?"

"Yes, Lucien, I am."

"If you say so, doctor."

I was taken out of the professor's office and rolled down the corridor, but very soon the gurney was turned down a side passage and stopped before a closed door. Lucien unclipped a keyring from his belt and undid the lock, then the redheaded Jack steered me down a ramp.

"Ugh, why doesn't the elevator go to the basement?" he hissed, holding the cart back from a rapid descent with strain.

Lucien jabbed him in the ribs with a smile and the redheaded orderly unclenched his hands in surprise. The gurney started off rapidly into the basement, and they barely managed to catch it before I collided with a railing blocking off the passage.

"Having fun?" a guard wearing a gray uniform and a police baton on his belt shook his head and unlocked the door.

"Look who's talking!" Lucien snorted and clapped his partner on the back. "Roll, Jack. Roll!"

And the gurney was pushed under the stone vaulting of a ghastly basement.

The squeaking wheel was really belting it out, but its shrieking howl was not enough to cover up the dull thuds on the doors we passed. The orderlies didn't pay any mind to the staggered clop; patients behaving this way was clearly business as usual. As were piercing screams. And not even so much screams as they were endless mournful wails, all stretching on and on at the same note. On the backdrop of this wailing, I was somehow not afraid of the sharp cries and occasional inarticulate exclamations.

Powerful electric bulbs under the ceiling blinded the eyes. Their color added an additional reality to what was happening, not allowing the ghastly details to be written off, like the badly cleaned streaks of reddish brown on one of the walls, unduly acting on my imagination.

And the smell. Here it smelled not of illness, but of madness in pure, if not to say distilled form.

I had never before found myself in a psychiatric clinic, but I had no doubt that I now found myself in precisely such a terrifying institution. Where else could they put a person with my diagnosis?

When I heard a broken recitative plea for a speedy death from behind one of the doors, I couldn't hold back and turned to the orderlies.

"Boys, how does a hundred a piece sound to you?" I asked them, wanting to test the waters. "Just give news to my people. They'll pay. And as soon as I'm dragged out of here, you'll get a thousand. How does that sound, huh? That's a whole a heap of money!"

"When you're dragged out of here?" redheaded Jack cracked up. "Freak, this is Gottlieb Burckhardt, no one is gonna drag you out of here! People only leave here in body bags!"

That struck me. When it had been built, this

clinic had been euphemistically described by the press as the height of humanism. After all, in many private hospitals of the time, the mentally ill were subjected to truly monstrous conditions. Any murderer would be glad to go to the work camp, because being sent to forced treatment was, at its very basis, a veiled death sentence.

It was thought that the Gottlieb Burckhardt Psychiatric Hospital would be lacking the egregious flaws of such facilities but, in the end, it became the culmination of them all. At the very least, this place had a certain infamy. And that was in no small measure because of how harsh the staff was.

After casting off the consternation brought on by the unpleasant news, I spent some time gathering my decisiveness, then said penetratingly:

"I have connections. I will be helped. And you'll get..."

"Shut your mouth!" Lucien demanded quietly and even somewhat languidly, but it was such that I instantly stopped wanting to contradict him. "Shut up or I'll shut you up. And believe me, you aren't gonna like it. I have a lot of practice!"

I believed him and went silent.

I had no way of resisting the raw power of the orderlies, while my intuition, common sense, life experience and ability to understand people, which I had perfected over my years with the police, were now saying all together: "This man is not joking, and you should not joke with him."

So, I didn't try to rush things, deciding instead

of artless and direct bribery to try and find a weak link among the staff. People everywhere are the same. Sooner or later, success would smile on me. As long as I wasn't the weak link myself...

THE NEW ROOM – or maybe cell? – was smaller than the last and reminded me of an elongated pencil case with bare stone walls. The orderlies pushed the gurney into the narrow door, totally blocking off passage to the second patient's bed and set me on a bed at the side wall, not forgetting to place a bedpan under it.

As soon as the orderlies appeared, my neighbor jumped up from the bed, cowered in the corner and started whispering something disconnected under his breath. He was hiding his face in his hands, all that was visible was his shaved head.

"Don't be afraid, he's quiet," redheaded Jack laughed, patting me on the cheek and following his partner out into the hallway. The door slammed shut, the lock clanked.

I was left one on one with a psycho, but I wasn't exactly troubled by that, because my neighbor's ankle was attached to the wall with a steel chain, which looked strong and short.

He could never get to me, and that was nice. As soon as the orderlies left the room, his whispering became louder and started forming totally distinct words:

"Electricity is the devil. Electricity is the devil. Electricity is the devil."

And so on without end, not shutting up for a minute or even a second.

The skin on his cleanshaven head was covered with inflamed scabs, and his hospital robe looked dirty and worn. And it smelled. It smelled disgusting in this cell, and I was not at all sure that the only source of the reek was the open sewer drain.

My neighbor, meanwhile, wouldn't calm down and just kept muttering:

"Electricity is the devil..."

The measured recitative was keeping me from calming down or falling asleep: I couldn't hold back and cursed out in a fit of anger:

"Just shut up!"

Then the psycho took his hands from his pale and sunken face and looked at me as if he was seeing me for the first time. He looked at me, and I at him. He immediately turned away, but all it took was that short moment for shivers to run across my skin.

The problem was his eyes. His eyes were totally transparent, as if they were carved from two identical pieces of glass. It seemed, when looking at them, I could see straight into his brain.

That was wrong. Totally wrong. The *illustrious* have colorless gray eyes that sometimes glow slightly in the dark, but I had never before seen such crystal-clear pupils, lacking even a hint of coloration.

I didn't know if this deformity was from his mental disorder or had arisen during treatment, and I could only hope that such a thing wouldn't happen to me.

Quite a meager hope...

3

IN THE MORNING, the orderlies woke me up. To be more accurate, they didn't even wake me up, they just grabbed me by the arms and legs and moved me from the bed onto the gurney. The redhead was clenching my wrist so hard that his fingers left bruises on my skin.

It wasn't painful. I could actually barely feel my body, so I didn't protest. As I didn't repeat my attempt to bribe the orderlies like yesterday. That no longer seemed like a good idea.

"Where are you taking me?" I asked instead.

"Where you need to go," Lucien threw out shortly, locking the cell door.

"You'll like it," redheaded Jack asserted, assuring me of the opposite with an unkind smile.

This time, the cart was rolled not into Professor Berliger's office, but in the opposite direction. Soon, the corridor led to a small hall with a few tables and benches screwed into the floor. There was either a hired worker or a patient in there sweeping up dust. I couldn't see. The orderlies were pushing the gurney too hard, not at all worried that any random collision would certainly turn it on its side.

The silence of the clinic was suddenly cut through by a prolonged shriek, but no one paid any mind to the rebellious patient's screams. Jack calmly threw open a door with a plaque reading "Laboratory," while Lucien pushed the gurney into a room flooded with the bright luster of electric bulbs and asked:

"Where should we put him, doctor?"

"Right next to the generator," Ergant pointed at the massive device in the corner of the room. "And strap the patient down."

The orderlies complied and left the laboratory, then the doctor approached the gurney and shook his head with a heavy sigh.

"Bribing the staff, that is bad, very bad," he said judgmentally.

"Bad?" I bared my teeth. "I just want to get in touch with my relatives! Is that not allowed?"

"Communication with the outside world is possible only with the sanction of department administrator, but Professor Berliger thinks that would not be to your benefit now."

"Complete nonsense!"

"Rules are rules. Next time, it won't be limited to a simple warning."

I chuckled.

"And what will you do? Make me skip dessert?"

"We don't have such a tolerant view on breaking discipline!" Doctor Ergant answered weightily and filled a chipped-enameled iron mug with a sharply anise-scented liquid. "You need to take this medicine!"

"What is that trash?" I asked, but the doctor didn't consider it necessary to answer.

With a calculated movement, he poured the

contents of the mug into my mouth, and I nearly choked swallowing the bitter liquid.

Then Doctor Ergant glanced at the watch he took from his pocket, walked away to the table and started writing something. Clearly, he was filling out a medical chart.

"Why did you restrain me?" I shouted out to him. "I mean, I'm paralyzed!"

"Everything in its time," the doctor answered, not looking away from his activity, and not saying anything more. He was in no mood to converse with a patient.

Slightly raising my head, I started looking at the equipment-filled laboratory, and my eyes immediately caught on jars of formaldehyde and internal organs on the shelves and a surgeon's table in the corner with glazed-tile walls and floor. For a second, it seemed I had landed in the lair of some crazed vivisectionists from a pulp novel but no, this laboratory was not the lair of mad scientists. This was Gottlieb Burckhardt.

The windowless room was lit by electric bulbs. That concoction was causing a buzz in my head and, the noisier it grew, the brighter and more piercing the luster of the bulbs became. I squinted, trying to look at the implements on the opposite wall, but the unmoving arrows behind glass, many switches, coils of cable and circuits of electric jars didn't tell me anything.

Then the door flew open and we were joined by Professor Berliger.

"Is the patient ready?" he asked in the doorway.

"Yes, professor."

"Has he been given the formula?"

Doctor Ergant glanced at his watch and said: "Four minutes ago. Orally."

"On an empty stomach? Then, let's not waste time!"

Professor Berliger removed his jacket and hung it on a hook, throwing a white frock over his shoulders in its place. After that, he cracked the bones of his long thin fingers and finally, addressed me:

"You must be horribly afraid right now, but I assure you, there's really nothing to fear. This treatment is in your best interest."

I went silent. I had great doubts in the professor's sincerity.

He was entirely fine with my silence.

"You are deeply ill," he said, continuing his monolog. "You have been ill since your very birth, but you weren't aware of it, and you still aren't fully. Your consciousness has been infected with a severe mental disorder, and it is my duty to restore your clarity of thought and sobriety of mind. Not only yours, but those of all *the illustrious*!"

"What are you talking about?!" I asked, startled.

"It is traditionally thought that the root of the *illustrious'* troubles lies in their blood. As if there is a poison dissolved in it that gives people unnatural abilities. However, that is not the case! There have been experiments that completely replaced the blood of *illustrious* individuals with that of normal people, and they have not met with success. Just as the reverse procedure has not led to any results. And there isn't a single laboratory, nor a single naturalist that has yet managed to detect any unique component in the blood of the *illustrious*! And why is that? The answer is simple: that is just not the issue!"

The professor's cheeks went red, making him look like a university teacher yearning for lectures. And Berliger was saying unthinkable, simply outrageous things, yet he wasn't in the least bit embarrassed at how mad his words sounded.

"But if not blood, then what?" the professor continued. "The answer can only be one thing: the brain! It is rooted in the human brain, that depository of all the most unbelievable riddles! That is precisely where the curse of the *illustrious* is hidden!"

Here I couldn't resist, slightly lifted my head and broke off his diabolic monolog:

"It is no curse! Leave me in peace!"

Doctor Ergant took the watch off the edge of the table and made a laconic note in the medical chart.

Professor Berliger just shook his head.

"You are damaged and don't even know it. The *illustrious* are a rudiment of a bygone era, the quintessence of everything antiscientific in this world. The *illustrious* poison our society and slow our march toward progress. Just the fact of their existence confuses weak minds and pushes them down the path of mysticism."

"If it got out you were saying things like that, you wouldn't even stay long in prison. Department Three..."

"All people with common sense share these views on one level or another!" the professor cut me off sharply. "We have plenty of likeminded individuals even in the police! And there's no reason to threaten me with Department Three. Unlike many others, I am categorically opposed to the idea of exterminating the *illustrious*. And it isn't some false humanism, but recognizing the necessity of finding a scientific way to solve this problem. Killing is easy. But killing won t help us find the truth, nor give us the key to the mysteries of creation! It is primitive, at the end of the day!" Berliger pulled on his rubber gloves and sighed. "Your role in my scientific works will one day be judged worthy, no doubt about that. That must flatter you. When I m given the Nobel Prize for this research, you can be sure that I will not forget to mention your name from the high podium."

"Go to hell!"

The professor covered his polished face with a gauze wrap and gave a quiet laugh.

"That was a joke. But you have nothing to worry about. My goal is to heal, not to harm."

"Find other guinea pigs!"

"In your case, I'd say rats!" Berliger threw out sharply in response. "Just what's got you so alarmed? You believe in the immortality of the soul, after all, isn't that right?"

"I do," I confirmed, overcoming the sudden onset of sleepiness.

"Then what do you care about mortal flesh? Your fabled soul won't be harmed by electromagnetic radiation, isn't that right?"

"It's hard to harm that which doesn't exist," Doctor Ergant smiled unpleasantly, getting up from the table.

The Professor threatened him with a finger and turned back to me:

"Do you also believe in the Creator? Heaven and Hell? The heavenly angels and the Savior?"

"I do," I answered stubbornly.

"What an untroubled conscience!" Berliger shook his head and warned his colleague: "You must note this in your medical chart. We must evaluate how quickly the treatment effects a patient with such a grave critical thinking disorder."

"I'll note it right away, professor," the doctor promised, taking a comb and scissors and starting to cut my hair.

"What the devil are you doing?!" I objected, but my shout was simply ignored.

"What method will we use this time, professor?" Ergant enquired.

Berliger stopped fidgeting with elastic cords with iron contacts attached by long rolls of isolated wire to a generator, thought briefly and decided:

"Electric stimulation doesn't give the proper effect, let's try magnetic radiation this time."

"Shall we concentrate on the back part of the midfrontal cortex, as before?"

"Yes, let's see what results are given by suppressing activity in that section in a patient with more severe medical issues."

My eyes stuck together. The laboratory started vibrating and was drowned in a gray haze but, before sinking into a deep sleep, I could feel the contraption of elastic bands and iron plates being clipped onto my head.

A moment later, I fell into a dream and suddenly found myself in the middle of a steppe burned by sulfur rain once again. The familiar faceless silhouette appeared nearby, as the reality of the dream grew jerky, rolling up and turning into a void of electric shocks.

They were curing me of my very self...

I WOKE UP TO THE SQUEAKING of the broken hospital gurney wheel. But it wasn't that nasty sound that woke me up, it was a strong shiver. While I had been unconscious, they'd tried to wash me, and now the hospital shirt was sticking to my wet body. It was cold and unpleasant.

What exactly had served as the reason for the washing procedures, I did not know, but electric shocks could easily cause evacuation of the bladder or colon.

Shocks! I remembered the compulsory treatment and gave a loud exhale. Devil in hell!

Devil! Devil! Devil!

I would be cured to death if this went on too long! And if not to death, they certainly wouldn't let me out of the clinic, regardless of whether the mad professor's experiment ended successfully or not.

I needed to do something. I had to...

But for now, all I could do was lie on the gurney. I could also breathe and blink, speak and listen. Think. What I couldn't do was stand up and walk. And I wasn't even in the right state to use my own *talent*: the morphine and other medicine deprived me of clarity of thought. It was as if there was a dense fog hanging in my head.

In the room, the orderlies picked me up to set me on the bed as usual but, this time, Jack's fingers suddenly unclenched, and my back and head slammed down on the stone floor at full speed. It wasn't painful, but air expelled noisily from my lungs.

Lucien let go of my legs in a fit of anger and stared gloomily at his redheaded partner.

"Stop messing around!" he demanded.

"What?"

"Don't involve me. Got it?"

"If you say so..."

The orderlies picked me up by the arms and legs again and set me on the bed, then pushed the gurney into the corridor and moved to the second patient.

"No!" he screamed, jumping out of bed, cowering in the far corner and covering himself with his hands. "No! Electricity is the devil!"

The boys easily pinned the nut-job on the floor,

packed him into a straightjacket and, only after that, removed his ankle shackles. My roommate resisted desperately, but he didn't stand a single chance against the two brawny orderlies, and soon he was dragged to the exit.

And then I noticed something I hadn't seen before: there were metallic electrodes implanted in the poor bastard's shaved head. The skin around them was red and festering.

"Electricity is the devil!" strained out the psycho, who had once been *illustrious*, and I understood with a shudder that he was not really so far from the truth.

In my case, there was no sense in waiting for mercy from electricity.

Sublime? More like divine retribution...

The door slammed shut, the lock clanked, and I was left all alone. A bulb under the ceiling, covered with a cage, suddenly started to flicker, as if the electric system was overloaded by something very powerful. The electric demon must have reached my neighbor as well...

THE NEXT DAY, I woke up with a humming head, a ghastly pain in my whole body and a no less ghastly hunger. I woke up not from my neighbor's already usual muttering, but from the stinking smoke of a papirosa cigarette.

"Here's some smoke for our man with ties," redheaded Jack smiled kind-heartedly, but his eyes remained evil and cold. "It's time for breakfast."

The orderly began to feed me with a spoon so unskillfully, that my pillow was soon soaked through from the gruel that fell outside my mouth. Yesterday's fall hadn't been a mere coincidence. This degenerate just liked to mess with me. But... my ghastly headache was stopping me from reaching out to his fears!

After breakfast, I was brought back to the laboratory. It was just like yesterday, but now the room was filled with patients. The other nut-jobs were gulping down their hospital food in complete silence. Most of them had bandaged heads.

And then I realized, sooner or later, the professor would trepan my skull as well.

That realization made a lump of nausea roll up my throat, while my heart started beating faster and faster. It just kept pounding like a madman's the whole way to the laboratory. My feverish heartbeat only settled when Doctor Ergant attached a huge leather strap and metal plate contraption to my head. They weren't going to drill my skull now.

But I didn't know how long the professor would wait to perform a lobotomy, and I could never know. And the unknown scared me. There was a lot that scared me in this cursed place.

"The straps," Professor Berliger reminded his assistant, when he attached the wires to the electric generator.

The doctor thought better and deftly lashed down my wrists and ankles with firm knots. Then I saw the bruises.

They weren't making the straps too tight; just they alone couldn't be making marks on my skin in any way, which meant I must have been twitching. I was twitching from the electric current, as if I was not paralyzed...

I didn't manage to finish that thought, though: Doctor Ergant poured the same medicine from yesterday down my throat. My thoughts immediately began to get confused and my eyes started closing. Today, the concoction worked much faster than yesterday.

"Do you believe in the resurrection of the dead?" Professor Berliger asked with an unhidden smirk.

"With all my heart," I answered in spite, drifting into narcotic unconsciousness.

"Doctor Ergant, turn it on..." I heard from an unfathomable distance, and my dream was instantly filled with blinding flashes of lightning.

4

I WAS TAKEN IN for procedures twice a day, once in the morning and once in the evening. I was stuffed with medicines; my head was held down with leather straps and metal plates and they were given electric charge. My skull, unlike that of my poor neighbor, was still intact for now, and it had only come to burns a few times. I suppose that happened when the professor lost patience and ordered his assistant to increase the voltage to the limit.

Every time during the electroshock therapy, my muscles twitched and shook to the point that there were bruises and abrasions left on my wrists and ankles from the straps. The seizures usually lasted some time after the diabolic procedures. Then, I managed to clench and straighten out the pinky of my left hand.

Clench and straighten. Clench and straighten. Clench and straighten.

Soon, I could do it even after the seizures ended, and I spent the long and sleepless nights restoring my control over my own body.

Rinky, ring finger, middle.

Pointer and thumb.

Wrist.

Bit by bit, I managed to restore movement to my whole left arm, but progress was slow, and I didn't have any certainty that I would manage to finish my plan before I went mad or finally disappointed the professor. But I tried. I tried, tried and tried.

All the rest was bad. My innards were being gnawed away in pain. I totally lost the ability to sleep, and my soul was sorrowful and nasty. The redheaded orderly who'd chosen me as his victim was always thinking up new tricks, and I'm sure that only the professor's interest in me stopped Jack from giving me a thrashing. For now, it was limited to humiliating pinches and slaps. Also, that asshole would give me my pills not one at a time, but all at once, watching with a satisfied smile as I fitfully attempted to swallow them.

The worst was yet to come, I knew that for certain. Some people simply cannot stop themselves before it gets bad. As soon as they feel power over someone, they just push and push until they've destroyed their victim, crushed them and turned them to dust. Or they take a shank to the side but, in my case, the conclusion was obvious.

Not long ago, I would have easily broken all this scoundrel's bones and dug into his most hidden fears and crushed him morally but, to my horror, the professor's treatment was bearing more and more fruit. I could no longer control my *illustrious talent* and couldn't even feel it. What was worse, I was becoming someone else bit by bit.

When a person loses faith, they don't go out into a crowded intersection and shout to the Creator that he doesn't exist. They simply begin to think how dumb and pointless it is for an enlightened man to believe in something that cannot be detected either by the newest measuring instruments or human sense organs.

Thomas the Apostle couldn't stick his fingers in Christ's wounds and still overcame his doubts. But *the fallen* once darkened the skies up above him with their wings. I meanwhile, had nothing but childhood memories.

And they did help me hold out on the very edge. My grandfather and father had read me the New and Old Testaments, told me the stories, explained me their example of what is good and what is bad. If I were to deny my faith, would that not be a kind of betrayal?

I did not want to be a traitor.

And that tiny factor stopped me from falling into despair. The tinder of old memories lit the fire of my faith time and again. And so I would go away from the edge of the abyss but, after the electroshock therapy, I would find myself standing in the same place every time, staring into the chasm.

I was sure that my eyes had also become totally transparent like those of my neighbor, that prisoner of the electric devil. There just was no mirror to make certain of that.

That said, my roommate had given in quicker than me. I do not know what experiments the professor had conducted on him but, with time, all that was left of the poor man was a bone frame covered with skin.

"Electricity is the devil!" he would repeat over and over, as if the electrodes implanted in his head didn't allow him to think about anything else.

I tried not to draw his attention. Meanwhile, when I forgot myself and started saying something aloud, the nutjob would fly into a rage and flail in hysterics. Just like he flailed in hysterics any time the orderlies dragged him off for procedures.

One day I asked him:

"What color is electricity?"

"Devil!" the nutjob called back habitually.

"Color! Did you see its color?"

"Devil! Devil! Devil!"

And although my *illustrious talent* had left me, I could sense my roommate's phobia.

"Did you see lightning flashing in the sky? Bright flourishes on a dark background? Lightning is electricity. Electricity is the color of lightning," I said penetratingly. "It's fiery yellow, amber red. Electricity has the luster of molten copper. That's its color."

"Devil..." the nutjob exhaled quietly.

Ever since then, I told him about electricity every night.

I had almost stopped sleeping. I couldn't even drift off into a half-dream for more than a couple minutes, so I normally spent all the time until morning moving my left arm, which was obeying me more and more, and also talking with my cellmate. Soon, he would know for certain what his devil looked like. I was totally fine with that.

IT WAS HARDEST OF ALL to not give myself up to the orderlies. Not moving when you're unceremoniously heaved onto a gurney, not grabbing the bed as you fall to the floor yet again, and not wrenching your hand to protect yourself from the strong stream of cold water.

But I managed. I was not planning to die in Gottlieb Burckhardt.

I had great things ahead of me. I believed in that with all my willpower.

And I still remembered Liliana and guessed how she had taken my disappearance. She may have decided I had left her and run away from our marriage. Or had she understood that something bad had happened? I was hoping for the second option. Sometimes, sorrow poured down with such a force that my heart stopped but, time and again, it started back up and, every time, it seemed it was precisely Liliana's faith that was supporting my life force.

And that's probably what was happening...

SUCCESS SMILED TOTALLY at random. That day began even worse than the rest – around morning, I was drifting in a half-sleep, then I couldn't understand for a long time who I was or where. My heart was beating with long breaks. It seemed as if the left side of my chest under my ribs had nothing in it but emptiness. And even the light touch of Liliana's faith could no longer warm me.

"Our man with ties is all burned out," redheaded Jack said, noting my state.

"Easier for us," was all Lucien could snort out.

Together, they set me on the cart and, as soon as they rolled me out of the cell, the basement was filled with the metallic clang of an alarm. Squeezing their electric clubs in their hands, two guardsmen walked past us but, almost immediately, they came back unhurriedly.

"Everything is fine," one of them told Lucien. "You can go."

I was rolled into the laboratory and, very soon, saw unfamiliar orderlies, who were dragging a gurney with a body covered by a sheet. The unevenly slashed wrist peeking out from under the material gave a lifeless wag every step they took.

Someone had kicked the bucket...

In the end, we were late to the procedure, and Professor Berliger didn't fail to give the orderlies a tongue lashing. They jumped out into the corridor like they'd been scalded.

"No responsibility!" the head of the department was outraged, directing the beam of his electric torch into my eyes.

Doctor Ergant, reading a newspaper, uttered out an incomprehensible agreement, then said:

"Ever since her Highness fainted during a reception two weeks ago, she hasn't been seen in public. There are rumors that the Princess is still in an unconscious state."

"Yes, her Highness's health leaves something to be desired," the Professor confirmed.

"Coma?"

"Most likely. But I'll refrain from making any diagnoses on the basis of newspaper articles and untested rumors. And I'd like you to do the same."

"Naturally, Professor. Naturally," Doctor Ergant was embarrassed.

If someone had asked me, I'd have said this was no coma at all, that the heart transplanted into the Princess had stopped beating. My imaginary heart.

Due to the electroshock therapy, my *illustrious talent* was impossibly weak, and I no longer had the ability to manifest things from my head in reality with the power of my imagination. And so, those who depended entirely on me, would now have some fearsome things happen to them. Crown Princess Anna, Elizabeth-Maria, that leprechaun...

"We need a regent, a new government, changes! The Empire only stands to gain from this!" the professor declared weightily, turning to me and smiling, but not nicely, skeptically and with an unpleasant smirk. "And you? Do you still believe in those Judean fairy-tales?"

I kept silent, but Berliger didn't need any answers. At each of our meetings, the first thing he did was evaluate the state of my eyes and take down the results in his notepad.

I could retain my faith out of pure stubbornness, but it was not in my power to continue being *illustrious*. The electroshock therapy was turning me day by day into a normal person, and there was nothing to be done with that.

"We need to increase the active ingredient content! The additional effect on his brain will eliminate his natural defenses and speed up the electromagnetic treatment," the professor declared and looked at his assistant, distracted with reading. "Doctor Ergant, where is the medicine? Have you prepared it?"

The doctor hurriedly set the newspaper aside, and embarrassment flickered up on his broad face.

"Yes-yes, right away..."

But Professor Berliger was a man of action, and the delay made him lose his mind. With a vexed snort, he grabbed a glass cup from the table and started measuring some powders in it by hand. After that, he poured water from a decanter, dripped in some opium infusion and started fervently mixing the resulting suspension with a measuring spoon. The solution quickly turned light, acquiring its usual transparency.

All that time, Doctor Ergant was watching his manipulations with the look of a beaten dog. He didn't even have to tell the professor that he was using his glass to prepare the formula. The doctor himself always used an iron mug.

After evaluating the transparency of the mixture, Berliger threw the measuring spoon on the table and leaned over the gurney.

"The taste might seem a bit unusual," he warned, placing the cup to my lips.

And it really was. The sharp bitterness burned my tongue and the roof of my mouth, and I didn't even have to fake the attack of nausea. My teeth gritted all on their own. The thin glass crunched and broke to pieces. The professor pulled back his hand, but it was too late: my mouth was already full of sharp glass. Lifting my head, I coughed and spit the shards onto my chest; a spot of bloody spit spread out on my hospital gown.

"Ergant!" the professor turned to his assistant and that short minute of general confusion was enough for me to pull my hand from the wide leather strap, hide the largest piece of glass between my fingers and return my hand to its place.

The bloodied glass pieces quickly were swept onto the floor and down the sewer drain with a bucket of water, then my mouth was carefully checked, and they dressed my lacerated lip. After that, a new dose of the concoction was prepared, and everything took its turn, with one small exception: my fingers were clenching a piece of glass. And that fact changed everything. Or to be more accurate, it would.

LAST NIGHT, I had sat up in bed for the first time. Not all the way, just braced with my left hand behind my back, applied some force and pushed myself up. And even though I immediately fell onto my side and hit my shoulder on the cold stone wall, that didn't darken my joy one bit. Not too long ago, I couldn't even do something that small. However, now, it was as if my body was made of cotton. My legs wouldn't obey, and my right hand could just barely move.

"Devil..." I heard from my cellmate.

My lips started to bleed. I spit the red saliva on the floor and exhaled loudly.

"Yes! Today I'll tell you about the devil. About the devil and how to kill him..."

At night, the electricity in the rooms was turned off, and the only lighting we had was a very narrow little strip that came in from the corridor under the door. In my former days, that would have been more than enough, but I didn't see very well in the dark anymore, so I spent a long time leading my fingers along the wooden side of the bed, searching for an appropriate crack.

"Devil!" my neighbor reminded me of his presence.

"Yes, yes!" I reassured him. "Soon!"

I started digging the piece of glass into the wood and widened the hole until I could grab a sharp ten-centimeter long splinter from the bed and pull it out. Any nervous twitch of the glass could cut me, so I had to maintain the greatest caution, and work was going slowly. But I had the whole night ahead of me. The whole night and a conversation about the devil.

THE NEXT DAY passed as usual. Procedure in the morning, incomprehensible drudgery until the evening's electroshock therapy, then lockdown.

Breakfast, lunch, dinner.

Pills. Bedpan gets removed.

Disgust.

And in the evening, when the light was shut off, I couldn't force myself out of bed, even though I was intending to test my strength before my final burst. I was just lying with my eyes open and staring into the darkness without a thought in my head.

Depression and melancholy is normal. Any person will fall into a depressed state of mind sooner or later, and most overcome such a state without any help from someone else.

Another matter entirely is apathy, when one doesn't simply not want to do anything, but one cannot see any reason to even move from place, and just lies around waiting for God knows what. And doesn't even think. The thoughts just spin about in your head all on their own.

Tomorrow will be just another day, in no way

different from today. And the day after tomorrow. And the day after the day after tomorrow. And so on. And so on. And then you die, and you're not around anymore. Not in the slightest.

So then, why all the fuss?

It's very scary to just not want anything at all. It's somewhat worse than when one cannot get what one wants. That's a short path to madness.

Or is that getting better and becoming normal?

Believing only in things one can touch and submitting one's self to the primacy of science?

Is that really so bad in the end?

"Devil!" my mad roommate said. "Devil! Devil! Devil!"

I kept silent. I was in no mood to talk about the devil tonight. And there really wasn't anything to talk about.

"The devil got to you," my cellmate suddenly shot out a surprisingly connected sentence.

And that really was true. The devil had gotten to me.

Electricity is the devil!

I laughed so hard from that thought that my ribs contracted in pain.

It's often said that madness is catching, but losing faith doesn't make a person better, just makes room for more phobias and fears.

"A holy place is never empty," as my father had taught me, and he knew the truth in such matters.

I didn't want to lose my mind, nor become a puppet in another's hands. I wasn't intending to be burned up in the crematorium of the Gottlieb Burckhardt. The simple thought that my brain would be placed in a vat of formaldehyde and displayed to students gave me a wave of truly authentic rage.

And it wasn t a desire to achieve something that made me move, but elementary stubbornness. Sometimes that is enough.

"Devil!" I said, getting up from the bed. "The devil dies tomorrow..."

5

ALL NIGHT, I didn't shut my eyes.

And the problem wasn't my misgivings that I might lose my nerve and again give in to apathy, I simply couldn't fall asleep. I don't know what exactly served as the reason for the punishing insomnia – the effect of electroshock therapy on my brain or the narcotic component in my medicine but, since the very beginning of treatment, I was able to fall asleep only at procedures. At night, I would most often drift into an unquiet half-sleep, so I was madly tired all the time, but I couldn't do anything with that.

Anyway, on that night, I didn't sleep. I felt like a criminal sentenced to death by hanging, guessing whether the rope would hold my weight or snap. Whether they d hang me a second time if I got lucky – that was the question.

And in the morning, the lock clanked, the

doors flew open and redheaded Jack entered the room. As usual, his knobby face was twisted up into an unkind smirk. Lucien pushed the gurney in after his partner and had already grabbed me by the elbows when my mad roommate gave a start.

"Devil!" he shouted out, throwing a pillow at the redheaded orderly. "Electricity is the devil!"

Jack picked up the pillow, but didn't throw it back and, instead of that, walked up to the nutjob and laid him out on the bed with a strong crack.

I raised my head and asked Lucien:

"What day is it today?"

"The twenty-fifth," he answered mechanically.

The orderly led his gaze away from his partner only for a moment but, at that precise instant, Jack gave a hoarse exhale:

"Ah-h-h!"

The redhead didn't have a single chance. The psycho, under the sway of the electric devil, waited until the orderly turned his back and threw himself on his back. Jack tried to get out, but the patient was clutching his frock with a dead man's grasp.

Stab! Stab! Stab! he started going at the neck of his victim fitfully with the sharpened splinter, and streaks of red flew throughout the cell.

Lucien ran to his partner's aid, but the passage was blocked by the gurney, and the strong man had to squeeze between that and my bed. I grabbed him by the collar and pulled him toward me. In surprise, the orderly took a step back, then I cut his throat confidently and harshly with the piece of Bohemian glass.

I cut him just once, but true: in the side of his throat, where the main blood-carrying arteries pass, splitting the skin and flesh in one go. A taut stream of crimson sputtered out of the split artery.

Not losing time, I threw away the piece of glass and jerked the unbuttoned frock off the orderly as he lost consciousness. The white fabric had just a few red spots on it, but that didn't upset me one bit.

I was upset just as little as by the double murder. They should never have backed me into a corner, and that was that.

Pulling the frock on my body, I got off the bed and removed the keyring from Lucien's belt. I then pulled a handkerchief from his pocket and tied it on my head in order to at least somewhat hide my uneven haircut. The dead man's boots were quite large, but I didn't waste any time lacing them up – the fingers of my right hand couldn't really move properly. In any case, I would just be wasting time. And time was of the essence.

My cellmate was still madly beating his lifeless victim with the broken splinter. I, meanwhile, grabbed the gurney, gathered my strength and fell down chest-first on it but, even so, I nearly fell back onto the floor.

Gathering my strength, I pushed the cart into the corridor and slammed the door behind me, starting to hobble toward the basement exit. My knees were giving out, and I couldn't feel my ankles or feet at all, but still I managed to push the gurney down the corridor without hitting a single stone wall or locked door.

The vile squeal of the broken wheel was screeching in front of me and cutting into my hearing like an emery board. My back was wet with sweat, and my heart was beating like a madman's and not one iota out of worry, though, just because my strength was all going toward keeping up my intended tempo.

Push. Push. Push.

The whole way, I was half-lying on the gurney and forced myself to straighten up only at the finish line, though I did lower my head at that, hiding my face.

The guard who looked out of his booth at the creak of the wheel didn't suspect anything at first. He just stuck his hand to his side and was about to make a joke to the orderly, who had already been tormented by work since morning. He was going to let me pass but, by the time he changed his mind, it was too late. Before he managed to swing his club, I had sent the gurney at him, pinning him to the wall.

The strong old man didn't lose consciousness, but the strong blow to the stomach made him double over and drop his weapon. The guard quickly pushed the gurney away, straightened up and peeled himself off the wall but, by that time, I had already fallen on my knees and grabbed the rubber-coated handle of the police club.

"Drop it!" the old man ordered. Instead, I jabbed the club into his groin.

An electric charge cracked. The guardsman's eyes rolled back, and he crawled down the wall onto the floor. I dragged him back into his booth and, removing the kerchief from my head, clipped on his gray cap with the clinic's emblem. I didn't take his pea coat, though: the orderly's frock covered my naked legs, while the jacket would have been too short.

Returning to the corridor, I threw the club on the gurney and rolled it up the steep ramp, getting out of the basement. But as soon as I unlocked the door and pushed the cart into the wide first-floor corridor, I heard a surprised exclamation.

"Where are you going?!" a guard barked, not fooled by my masquerade.

He slammed down on the alarm handle, and a frightening wail blasted out. I tried to repeat my trick and knock the boy off his feet with the gurney, but the distance between us was too great, and the guard pushed the cart away with a sharp kick, turning it on its side. I fell on the floor along with it and immediately waved the club, counting on not so much hitting my enemy as driving him back, but I missed again. The man sniffed out the simple trap, waited for the right moment and slammed his club down on my head at full speed.

The blow made contact with the crown of my head, and consciousness left me even before the electric shocks started...

I WOKE UP in a solitary cell with the floor and walls covered in a thick layer of white padding. I tried to move but couldn't and got dead scared that the paralysis was back, only to realize that I had simply been squeezed into a straightjacket. My whole body was numb, my head was splitting in pain, and my right eye was swollen and wouldn't open, but I was alive nevertheless.

Surprising? Considering the orderlies I killed in my escape attempt, yes.

The taste of blood was still fresh in my dried-out throat. I wanted devilishly to drink. To drink and to breathe. I had no way to take in a full chest of air: either my ribs were broken, or the straps of the straight jacket were too tight.

But still, I didn't have any regrets.

None...

Then the doors flew open, and two unfamiliar orderlies walked into my cell. One had an electric club squeezed in his hand, and the second was grasping a glass syringe in his thick short fingers.

I tried to hit the club-wielding boy in the ankle with my foot, but he easily dodged and body-slammed me, pinning me to the ground. His partner used the syringe and the white walls immediately began spinning, melting into a kaleidoscope of mad visions.

I could feel sharp blows to my kidneys, already drifting into unconsciousness.

"Bastard!" one of the orderlies cursed out, but it might have just seemed that way.

By that time, there was already a white abyss spread out around me. I was hovering in it, hovering and hovering. I became the center of creation. There

was only me, everything else had lost all meaning
Damned morphine...

Then I was pulled down and fell to earth, as if
repeating my long-ago jump from the burning
dirigible. Only now I was racing, striving to gain speed
right until the very end, and the blow was so strong
that clods of dirt flew for hundreds of meters around
the steppe, which was scorched by a fiery rain.

"You again!" rang out the faceless voice in my
head.

I got out of the huge pit with unexpected ease,
looked around and, not far away, saw a familiar white
silhouette.

"How are you doing that?" a new question
followed. "How are you entering my dreams?"

"This is my dream," I objected, starting an
argument with my own subconscious with a certain
shock.

"Not at all," the silhouette objected, leading a
fleshless hand from left to right and, at that very
instant, grass began growing up through the scorched
surface of the earth.

I didn't manage to even blink before everything
around turned into a green meadow.

"This is my dream," the silhouette said, but I
just shook my head.

The grass went black, the flowers dried out and
the trees began swishing their brittle leaves.

Night fell.

Now we were in the cursed garden of my family
manor, and the only light spot around us was the

silhouette of my unknown conversation partner, foreign to this vision.

"Devilry!" he whistled.

And so much surprise sounded through in his voice, that I couldn't hold back and asked:

"Who are you?"

"The Dreamer," his quick answer followed. "And who, devil take me, might you be?"

I chuckled. It was funny to me.

Morphine and an *illustrious* imagination make for a killer combination.

"The man dreaming this dream," I answered, wanting to make him mad.

"No!" He refused to believe me. "I can only go into the dreams of people I know!"

"That means we know each other, no more no less."

The silhouette didn't answer, touching the branch of a dead tree. One black leaf instantly filled with a young greenness.

"We know each other?" the Dreamer asked slowly. "That's impossible. I don't have a very wide social circle and I know all of their nightmares by heart."

I looked around the imaginary garden and laughed.

"Well this is no nightmare. Do you know the word: nostalgia?"

"Yes, it is too calm here to be a nightmare," the silhouette admitted. "And I no longer feel pain. I am at ease. Nothing hurts. Surprising..."

"That's the morphine," I said, watching lighting flashes bloom in the black sky in the distance.

"Narcotics rot the brain, they are pure evil. But sometimes, the pain can be simply unbearable. I might visit your dreams sometimes, alright?"

"Visit?" I asked, and suddenly his answers came together into a unified whole like the pieces of a mosaic. "Are you *illustrious*?" I groaned. "And going into dreams is your *talent*?"

"What a good guesser!" the Dreamer laughed.

"Curses!" I exhaled, not able to believe my own luck but, before I managed to ask for more, a strong wind blew into the garden. It tore the black leaves from the trees, spun them around me with a whirlwind of electric shocks, and the dream started dissolving into little pieces.

"No, wait!" I shouted, but I had already been cast out.

The electroshock therapy session had begun.

WHEN THE PROCEDURE was over, and I was fed broth degradingly through a tube, then was returned to solitary. I was just thrown inside from the doorway, a knee jabbed into my ass for good measure.

And I stayed there, lying on the soft padded floor. I was being torn apart. My mouth was full of the bitter taste of bile. Enraged at my escape attempt, the professor had decided to increase the duration of the electroshock therapy to the limit, and that had borne fruit.

I didn't care at all. I didn't want to move,

breathe, live... So, I just lied there. Lied there and waited for evening. To be more accurate, I waited for the unchanging injection of morphine.

A dose of morphine was simply necessary.

And I got it.

I WAS STANDING on the top of Calvary, looking down on an unfamiliar city from the top of the hill.

It was not New Babylon and, behind my back, there was not a rusty steel tower. In this dream, the hill was only topped by three wooden crosses. All that remained was the smog. Squat stone buildings were drowned in a gray haze, as if the waters of the Yarden were overflowing its banks.

"You're back?" the Dreamer was surprised. "Already?"

"As you see."

"Alright. It's too bad though. You're about to die."

That put me beside myself.

"Why do you say that?" I objected, although I was preparing to ask something else entirely. "Why must I die?"

"How much morphine do you take every day?"

I shrugged my shoulders.

"Doesn't matter! Could you do something for me?"

The white silhouette stood next to me and glanced at the city. I supposed his eyes saw a totally different picture. The illusions brought on by the narcotic were extremely... erratic.

"Are you asking for a favor? In a dream?"

"Yes, I am. Is that strange?"

"Unusual."

"Can you help?"

"What do you want?"

"Send news to a friend of mine," I explained and asked as my heart skipped a beat: "Can you co that?"

"It won't work," the Dreamer shook his head. "I cannot go into the dream of a person I do not know personally. That would be impossible."

"Devil!" I swore. "Forget about dreams! I want to you to send a telegram! I'll go gaga if I'm not dragged out of here soon!"

"Out of where?" the silhouette wondered. "Where do you need to be dragged out of?"

I hesitated, but still answered:

"Do the words Gottlieb Burckhardt mean anything to you?"

The Dreamer laughed.

"The psychiatric clinic? I've heard of people going gaga in the walls of that institution before. But many have their sanity restored there as well."

"Do it," I asked. "Do it, I'll pay you. Name your price!"

I heard laughter again.

"Where is this world headed! A psychopathic murderer is offering me money! What devilish irony! Money is the last thing I need!"

"Then I'll owe you a service."

This time the Dreamer didn't rush to answer.

But, in the end, he just shook his head.

"Hrmph," he said with unhidden pity. "I cannot help you. I cannot wake up. Dreams do not leave me. We're both in a trap, my mad friend."

"You don't have to wake up! Just ask someone to send a telegram. After all, you're the Dreamer! You can go into someone else's dream!"

The silhouette slowly nodded.

"I can," he admitted. "And, if I do that, you will owe me a service."

I cast my gaze at the far-off lightning flares and quickly said:

"Anything!"

"Anything? Even if you have to kill someone?"

I hesitated, and the Dreamer hurried me on:

"Well? Decide! Yes or no?"

"Yes, devil!" I exclaimed. "I'll kill if need be! I'll kill!"

"Swear it!"

The figure extended me his glowing hand. I accepted it and said:

"I swear!"

And immediately, I felt a shiver pierce through the dream.

"You cannot change your mind."

"Curses! I swore!"

"You swore," the Dreamer confirmed and, to the hum of an incoming hurricane, asked: "Who should I inform?"

"His name is Ramon Miro," I answered and dictated my former partner's address by memory. "He will get fifty thousand as long as he drags me out of here!"

"What is your name?"

"Lev. Tell him it's Lev!"

Blinding shocks of lightning started tearing down from the sky. I shouted:

"Gottlieb Burckhardt, Berliger basement!" Then the earth underfoot dissipated, and I began to fall endlessly into an abyss.

6

DO YOU THINK DESPERATION and hopelessness lead to madness? Nothing of the sort. Desperation leads to desperate actions, and hopelessness gives them a suicidal character.

Uncertainty leads to madness. When nothing remains certain, one begins to doubt everything, even one's own mind.

"Was the Dreamer real, or was I just conversing with my own hallucination?" Now, locked in solitary once again after another electroshock therapy session, that question was all I could think about.

Had I finally gone mad from the massive doses of morphine, or had I really made a deal with an *illustrious* person? That question was just turning over and over in my head and, as soon as I assured myself it was all real, doubts flooded me with a renewed force. They destroyed my concentration and pushed me into a vortex of uncertainty. I was just one tiny step away from madness.

Gathering my strength, I got up to my feet and started pacing in the stiff straightjacket from one corner of the cell to the other. My body was numb from the overtight garment. I hadn't felt my arms in a while and, no matter how I tried to spread my shoulders, trying to loosen the straps, my attempts didn't lead to anything. It didn't help that the pain of fresh blows and old wounds had started penetrating the narcotic haze.

Very soon, my knees started giving out in exhaustion, and I fell down on the padding. I closed my eyes and tried to sleep, but I couldn't even drift off. My consciousness had been too strongly reshaped by Professor Berliger's experiments, I been injected with too much morphine too frequently in the last few days.

My bones were twisting, my joints breaking. I wanted unbearably to drink. The straightjacket was soaked through with salty sweat. My breathing became choppy and uneven. And my head was splitting hellishly. Now, I would easily have refused anything for a glass of water and a few gulps of an opium infusion, but no one was preparing to persuade me of anything.

Do you know why the devil doesn't try to buy human souls? He doesn't need to! They fall at his feet like overripe apples! We are our own worst enemies. And we are also our own best tempters. There's nothing so vile as the justifications a person can think up.

Sensing madness taking control of my consciousness, I turned onto my side, leaned my forehead on the wall, and got up to my knees. I quickly vomited. My ribs seized in pain, but that did make my head slightly clearer. I moved away from the puke, which had also spattered on my straightjacket, and kept kneeling. I was just kneeling, not praying, no.

It wasn't that I'd finally lost faith. That's not why I wasn't praying; it's just that one needs to pray out of an earnest yearning of the soul. It would be stupid to ask for a miracle in a situation with no way out. There are no miracles. I knew that for certain.

"There are no miracles," is what I was thinking when, in the corridor, I heard alarmed voices. Then, the door of my cell flew open with a clank and I was blinded by the beam of a powerful electric torch.

But I didn't change my opinion. I didn't believe in miracles. I believed in deals.

I only hoped this was not a deal with the devil...

"There he is!" Doctor Ergant declared. "But we cannot give him to you. He might be a criminal, but he's here on court order."

A moment later, Ramon Miro, decked out in a police uniform, kicked the doctor in the back, pushing him into the cell, and aimed a revolver he pulled from his holster at the orderly accompanying him.

"Get in! If you so much as twitch the wrong way, I'll shoot!"

The boy obeyed.

"Up against the wall!" Ramon ordered, and the workers of the psychiatric hospital hurriedly retreated to the back of my cell.

The automatic four-hundred-fifty-five caliber Webley-Fosbery revolver, massive and bulky, could convince anyone to behave.

"Can you walk?" Ramon asked me, not taking an eye off his captives.

"No," I admitted.

"Tito, help him up!"

A boy in a uniform cloak and peaked cap with police emblem took a step into the room and I lurched forward, getting up off my knees. I stumbled and could barely stand, but Ramon's nephew grabbed me in good time and pulled me out into the corridor, where he then left me lying on the floor.

"Remove the straightjacket!" I demanded. "Faster! I can't feel my arms!"

Tito loosened the straps. Sensitivity started to return to my tightly clenched hands and I began to groan through my teeth, gritted in pain.

"Pull it off!" I repeated.

"We still have to accompany you past the guards!" Ramon announced and returned his revolver to the holster. "We'll take it off outside!"

"Accompany? Who is gonna let us out?! We're gonna have to fight our way out!" Not listening, I kept trying to shake the hated garment off my body.

"Damned stubborn bastard!" Miro cursed out. "Tito, come on, help him out!"

Ramon's nephew pulled the straight jacket off me, grabbed me by the shoulders and set me on my feet. Then, with a moan, I leaned against the wall, although I knew perfectly well that time was slipping through our fingers like water.

"We need a gurney," I said, not feeling strong enough to move. "Gurney! Find a gurney!"

Ramon looked at me angrily, but immediately snapped his fingers.

"That's right, a gurney! Tito, do you remember? We saw one in the corridor. Run!"

The hulking man's nephew ran off, the soles of his uniform boots thundering, and I walked along the wall to the door of my cell, opened the viewing window and glanced inside.

"Leo, what are you doing?!" Ramon asked in alarm.

"Stay back!" I waved him off and smiled at the prisoners. "Do you know what I'm about to do, doctor? I'm looking for kerosene and matches. And I'll be back. I'm not sure if this padding is flammable, but it's sure to go up a treat with kerosene! I'm gonna burn you all! This whole den of snakes!"

The orderly gave a slight whimper of fear, while Doctor Ergant went white as a sheet, but I couldn't fully enjoy their horror. There wasn't time. Ramon pulled me away from the door and slammed the window shut.

"Leo, tell me you were joking!" the hulking man barked out, his face gone crimson in anger. "We didn't sign up for that!'

I wasn't joking. I was scaring them. But I didn't delve into details and crawled down the wall onto the stone floor.

"Ramon, what kerosene? Get real! We have to get out of here!"

Miro nodded, but kept looking at me with unhidden suspicion.

He didn't trust me.

Just then, I heard the wail of the broken gurney wheel come down the corridor, and Tito pushed it into our corner. My rescuers lifted me together and set me on the familiar mode of transportation, then threw a none-too-clean sheet over top of me.

"What the devil?" I asked, startled.

"Easy!" the hulking man ordered. "Just play dead for a second, it won't do you any harm!"

And we headed off on our way. If any of the orderlies and doctors we came across on our way did notice the constables, who must have forgotten something in the clinic, they didn't interrogate the guardians of order one bit. And only the guard watching over the exit asked anything:

"Now what's this?"

"One of your rebellious souls," Ramon yawned. "He cut down two orderlies."

"That one?" the guard asked, disgruntled. "What happened to that degenerate now?"

"He was trying to get out of his straightjacket, and got strangled," my former partner informed him tranquilly.

"Or someone helped him," his nephew added. "You didn't happen to see anything suspicious last night, hm? We've got this guy on some serious charges. If you could help out, we could..."

"I just got to work!" the old man answered quickly and clanked his keys, unlocking the door, but doubted: "How're you gonna take him without documents?"

"We're going now to draw some up," Ramon Miro quickly twisted out of it. "The department administrator is already at work. He can do everything."

"Professor Berliger?" the guard drew out. "Ah, that's right. Who if not him..."

The gurney gave a jolt when crossing the high lip of the ramp, and I jerked the sheet off my face.

"What now?" Ramon whispered, setting it back. "And?"

"They won't let us out the door without documents. It's a dead duck."

"There's three hardheads there." Tito reminded him. "All with revolvers."

Miro cursed out soundlessly and stopped at Berliger's office door. There was a thin strip of light coming out from under it.

"Fifty thousand francs or five years hard labor. The choice is yours," I reminded them, and my former colleague, casting off his doubts, broke into the professor's office.

"How can I help?" asked the department

administrator, standing in front of the coatrack with a long cloak in his hands.

Before the professor managed to raise the alarm, Ramon and his nephew tied him up, tore off a strip of white fabric from his frock and stuck it in his mouth. And although Berliger was wailing desperately, my straightjacket was pulled deftly onto him and he was left to lie on the floor.

After that, Tito returned to the corridor and, not without difficulty, pushed the gurney into the office.

"What now?" he asked his uncle, who was tearing through the professor's card cabinet.

"Stand watch," Ramon ordered.

Soon, the hulking man had found my hospital chart and, setting a pile of some forms on the table, started forging the signature of the department administrator with confident strokes of a feather quill.

I couldn't bear it and leaned over the gurney toward Berliger. His left eye was twitching.

"Do you know what I want, Professor?" I asked. "I want to kill you. But that would be wrong. You aren't a threat to me now..."

"Leo!" Ramon called out.

"We're just talking!" I waved off my former partner and turned back to the professor: "But revenge is not such a great motive. After all, you cured me. Although it wasn't your goal, the electroshock therapy helped me overcome my paralysis. And I'm thankful for that. Which is why I won't kill you... yet. But one day, when you are monkeying with your implements, I'll come up behind you and stick one of the wires in your left ear, and another in your right. And don't you worry, you won t die instantly. I'll do my due diligence and figure out what voltage is needed to fry brains... low and slow. Oh, it will be a wonderful experiment!"

Tito chuckled, and his uncle threw out angrily from the desk:

"Quiet, you!"

"Professor, remember this conversation. One day, you will turn around and..."

"Just shut up!" Ramon said, enraged. "Shut up! Don't make any noise!"

I stayed quiet but didn't deny myself the pleasure of a characteristic gesture, leading a finger across my throat. The professor's face turned the shade of fresh-fallen snow, but a bit green. He believed me, and that slight echo of another's fear set my soul at ease for the moment, as if my *illustrious talent* had woken up again.

But no, it didn't wake up.

Devil! Who was I now?!

"Let's get out of here!" Ramon commanded, getting up from the table. He brought my medical chart with him, along with a forged patient release form indicating my death by natural causes.

Tito covered me with the sheet again and rolled me out into the hallway, while Ramon Miro locked the professor's office and, breaking the key in the hole, followed after us with a business-like demeanor.

NONE OF THE ORDERLIES or cleaners suspected anything. Sure, they stared, but they didn't come at us with interrogations and, what was more, didn't try to stop us. The senior guard expressed barely more interest in the corpse and, when Ramon extended him my papers, gave them nothing more than a cursory glance.

"And where is Doctor Ergant?" is all he asked, not detecting any forgery in the signature of the department administrator.

"Doing his morning rounds," Miro didn't miss a beat.

The hospital guard couldn't find any more questions. Tito rolled me outside and off the porch down a narrow ramp.

"Faster!" Ramon whispered and waved his hand at yet another false policeman parked at the exit in an armored vehicle. He quickly jumped to the side door and threw it wide open.

A gust of wind ripped off the sheet, but Tito didn't pay that any mind, just hurried up, pushing the gurney with all his might toward the self-propelled carriage. The yard flickered by, surrounded by a high fence, then the gloomy hulk of the main building of the psychiatric hospital. Then Miro grabbed me by the armpits and dragged me into the trunk. Tito jumped in after me, and the armored car started off to the sharp claps of the powder engine, quickly gaining speed and driving out of the yard of the psychiatric clinic.

A moment later, we were rolling away through

the city, stretched over by a morning fog.

"Ugh!" Ramon then exhaled loudly and unbuttoned the stiff collar of his uniform. "Leo, old buddy, this is none of my business, but how'd you end up in Gottlieb Burckhardt? Problems with your head?"

"A simple misunderstanding," I said, not wanting to reveal too much. "I'll smooth it all over."

"I don't doubt it," my former partner laughed. "Where should I drop you off?"

"Where can you take me looking like this?" I answered, collapsing on the side bench, all my energy sapped.

Ramon cringed in disgust and admitted:

"Yes, you don't smell too great."

"You're tact in human form"

"Believe me, Leo, I am being very tactful. You should see yourself!"

I just sighed.

"Take me to your office. And find out where Albert Brandt is living these days."

"What about the fifty thousand?"

"I'll pay you as soon as I meet with my attorney."

"Tell me, Leo, was that court order authentic?" Ramon suddenly asked. "Does Moran have something to do with this? Should I start working on an alibi?"

"Forget about it," I waved it off. "Moran has nothing to do with this."

"Gottlieb Burckhardt!" the hulking man shook

his head. "Just think!"

I didn't answer. The armored car went very smoothly down the asphalted road, lulling me to sleep. But my eyes didn't close, just went blurry. When the wheels started shaking on paving stones, and then started falling into potholes on the alleys of the factory outskirts, it got easier to stay awake. But it still turned me inside out just to get out of the trunk into the back yard of Miro's office.

"Water!" I rasped out, straightening up.

"Here," Ramon extended me a bulbous flask.

I spent a long time sucking away at it. I poured the remnants of the water on my head.

"Brr!" I shivered from the morning chill. "It seems cold for September!"

"Leo," Ramon looked at me somehow strangely, taking the flask, "it's the end of October."

"Bugger!" I unwillingly spat out my imaginary friend's favorite word and asked: "Can you heat up a couple buckets of water?"

"Whatever you want for that money!" the hulking man laughed and asked: "The boy you sent to me, do you know him well?"

"Someone came to you?" I asked in surprise. "It wasn't a telegram?"

"No, it wasn't a telegram. So, do you know him?"

"No. And?"

"I didn't like the look of him. He was from the nobility. I always expect problems from those types."

"Too bad," I muttered. "I owe him a service."

"I don't want to know anything," my former partner waved it off and went off to heat water, I meanwhile crawled up onto the lower step of the porch. It was chilly, but the fresh air cleared my head and chased off the nausea. It got easier.

Devil, it was as if I'd been reborn!

I HAD TO WAIT a little less than a quarter hour for the water and, although I caught quite a chill during that time, I pulled off my hospital gown without hesitation and threw it in disgust on a pile of trash. And then, despite the brownish marks of fresh bruises, I started going mad, rubbing myself down with a piece of cruce soap. Ramon poured hot water on me.

"They really beat the shit out of you. And you're thin. It hurts to look at you," he noted after I had dried myself with a coarse towel. I put on some pants and a shirt, which had been washed to an even shade of gray and were too short for me. Then he asked, "do you want to eat?"

"No. Have you got vodka?"

"Only rum."

"Let me have some. And bring two glasses."

"I don't drink rum."

"And you won't have to. Find out where Brandt lives."

Ramon helped me get up onto the porch and led me inside. There, he placed a bulbous bottle of dark glass on the table and brought two faceted cups, then set out to find out the poet's address.

"If you need anything, ask Tito," he warned me

before leaving.

"Alright," I nodded, leaning heavily on the wash basin.

It took me a long time to build up the courage to look into the mirror over the wash basin. When I finally overcame my indecision and glanced at my reflection, without any surprise, I met with water-clear eyes. Not colorless-gray, as before, but simply glass.

The professor had worked me over well. Too well even. I should have strangled him while I had the chance.

I flicked the light switch, and the room was immersed in gloom. The headache somewhat abated. My legs ached madly and could barely move. I sat down at the table heavily, filled a faceted glass from the liter bottle and started drinking it, getting the rum into my system gulp by gulp. It took some effort to keep the strong sharp alcoholic beverage down, but it was worth it. Very soon, the tension retreated, the pain in my beaten body quieted down, and my head was filled with a light fog.

I took another gulp now without any disgust and didn't even collapse but melted behind the table. After that, I filled another glass to the rim, and immediately saw a massive figure stand up in the corner of the room, immersed in gloom. It was wrapped head to toe in a long flowing robe. The newcomer's face was hidden by the shadow of a deep hood. Only two burning dots could be seen, its eyes.

Its angular fingers pawed at the glass, and the

glass gave a plaintive creak at the squeeze of its deformed claws. After that, the monster poured rum down its throat and loudly slammed the glass on the tabletop.

"Bugger, that s good stuff!" my imaginary friend exhaled and nabbed the bottle from the table. "Alright, boy. Let's drink to commemorate our reunion!"

PART THREE

ORACLE

Dreams and the Dreamer

1

PEOPLE CHANGE. First, they become mature, then old. On the way, they might grow fat, skinny, gray, or bald. It's normal business.

But such metamorphoses are only normal for normal people.

Imaginary friends don't change. They simply are not capable of such things. An imaginary friend exists exclusively in one's head. It is the fruit of an overly vivid imagination, and nothing more. That isn't what changes. What changes is one's consciousness.

And if my white-haired leprechaun pipsqueak had turned into a ghastly chimera with claws that could easily scratch a glass cup, I must have had serious problems with my head. To put it more simply, I'd lost my marbles. Gone loco. Bats in the belfry. Out of my mind.

That's what I was thinking when I saw my old friend throw back the hood, but I didn't make any comments. Instead, I asked:

"What happened to the top hat?"

The albino showed me his middle finger in a familiar gesture, with its ghastly looking claw, and drained the glass of rum in one swig.

"Bu-u-uger!" he shook his powerful head, then looked at me with his eyes half closed and melted into an acrid smile. "And why did you change your haircut?"

I lead my hand over my unevenly cut crown, took the glass, but didnk and looked above it at the leprechaun. He caught my gaze and melted into a somewhat scary smile.

"And how do you like me?"

"You were an ugly creature, and you still are," I answered, bending the truth a fair amount.

Although the leprechaun couldn't have been called a looker before, in his former body, he wouldn't have scared anybody. But now, one look at him made my knees shiver and I wanted to press my back up against the wall.

His eyes, burning with a ghostly fire, were hidden behind massive curved brows; his teeth, it seemed, could not all fit in his wide frog's mouth. His thin lips were stretched tight over them, leaving long fangs to stick out. His sharply pointed ears were tightly pressed against his head, while his flat nose looked absolutely inhuman, and his short bristles of white hair looked like the rough fur of an animal.

However, the albino was not a disgusting monster. It was as if he had taken in a share of the unearthly beauty of the *fallen one* whose heart he had eaten. That internal luster smoothed over his rough features, mitigated them and turned his frightening countenance into a template which a skilled sculptor could easily form into the face of Apollo.

I took a sip of rum and shook my head.

"Come on, it's nothing..."

"Look at yourself!" the albino got offended, placing a cigar on the table and cutting the tip with a confident swipe of his claw. A deep scratch was left on the wooden tabletop.

Squeezing the cigar between his thick fingers,

the Beast started smoking and breathed a stream of stinky smoke in my direction. It was not a cheap cigar.

"You don't want to ask what's wrong with me?" the albino finally broke the prolonged silence.

"Chicken pox?" I joked.

"Bugger!" the Beast cursed out and leaned over the table. "In the madhouse, they scrubbed your brains clean, boy! You stopped believing. You stopped believing in me, that's what's wrong with me!"

The tobacco smoke made my eyes tear up; I pushed the cigar out of my imaginary friend's fingers and threw it in the tiny bit of rum at the bottom of the glass. It gave a hiss and went out.

"When I was five, I completely forgot you existed and didn't remember until I was a legal adult! What's changed now?"

"Power!" the albino barked, jumping off the table, the fringes of his torn jacket shooting upward like ghostly wings. "Everything was changed by that damn power!"

"Power?" I didn't understand.

"The power of the *fallen one*!"

"And why did you eat his heart?"

"Why?" the albino gnashed his teeth. The luster of his sunken eyes filled with a gloomy purple. "Well, do you know any other way to destroy such a monster once and for all?"

I didn't.

"I simply didn't have a choice," the Beast stated dully.

"But you also wanted to devour it."

"I did," the albino admitted and licked his lips with his long pink tongue. "Bugger! If only you knew how nice it is..."

"Get to the point!" I demanded. Due to the rum I drank, I was feeling hazier and hazier, and I had no idea how long I would be able to remain conscious.

The albino pointed a clawed finger at me and demanded:

"Show me some respect! I saved your ass!"

"Get to the point!" I repeated, getting up from the table and stumbling over to the washbasin with the uneven gait of a drunk. "Speak or bugger off!"

However, I already knew. The leprechaun had swallowed too great a piece of power, and that had messed him up.

"The power!" the Beast shouted out. "It burns from the inside! It is changing me! Turning me into something different! But I don't want to change! Do you understand? Bugger! I don't want to change!"

"Does your back itch?" I asked, leaning over the sink.

"Yes, and what of it?" the albino asked in simpleminded confusion.

"You're sprouting wings."

"Bu-u-uger!" the Beast exhaled and, in his exclamation, I heard unhidden fear. He understood everything.

I vomited; I turned on the water and washed up.

"You shouldn't have eaten the *fallen one*'s

heart."

"And you?!" the albino roared. "What about you? You ate one too! That redheaded vixen fed the whole thing to you!"

"I'm a human, a higher being, and you're just a phantom created by my imagination. I stopped thinking about you, and you should have returned to nonexistence. But you couldn't. The strength of the *fallen one* held you on a hook and kept you in reality. Now, it is forming your appearance, not me."

"So, turn it all back! I want to be like I was!" the Beast spoke up. "I don't want to change!"

"No one does. But such is the order of things."

"Put it all back!" the albino demanded. "Or this will not end well! You'll regret it!"

I drank my fill of water, closed the tap and straightened up.

"Look me in the eye," I demanded, touching my temple with my pointer finger. "Look and tell me what you see. Or to be accurate, what you don't see!"

The Beast gave a loud sniff but kept silent.

"*Talent*!" I hinted. "My *talent* was taken from me! And there's nothing to be done."

But the albino didn't think so.

"Find them, find them all," he demanded. "Find them and scare them to death. Or just kill them."

"Do you think that will help?"

"Oh yes!" my imaginary friend melted into a ghastly grin. "Don't you doubt it, boy. That always helps."

"I'm not so sure."

"Not sure?" the albino frowned and suddenly shouted: "Well, check! Try to make me like I was!"

"I'll try."

"Bugger!" the Beast cursed out, grabbing a glass from the table and throwing it full force at the wall. "Help me, Leo," he pleaded. "Help, otherwise I won't last long."

I returned to the table and, without strength, collapsed onto the chair.

"I don't have the power."

The albino just snorted.

"After changing, becoming different, I'll come after you, do you understand that?" he asked.

I nodded.

"Then get your ass out of that chair and start saving us!"

Instead of an answer, I stuck up my middle finger.

"Bugger!" the albino cursed, sharply turning and, in one moment, melting into the shadows, as if he had never been here at all.

And maybe he hadn't, and this had all happened only in my head. I didn't delve too far into the issue. I just fell chest-first on the tabletop placed my hands under my head and closed my eyes.

Did I fall asleep? No, more likely, I simply stopped existing in the here and now...

2

RAMON RATTLED ME when the sun had already begun to shine through the window, which was not totally obscured by its curtain.

"Leo!" he said, grabbing me by the shoulder. "Leo, get up!"

I peeled myself off the table and looked around, not having the strength to realize where I was, or how I'd come to be here.

"Leo!" Ramon shook me again. "Are you alright?"

"No," I answered shortly, getting up from the table and hurrying to the wash basin on my failing legs. I drank right from the tap, washing away the nasty sugarplum flavor, then washed up and looked in the mirror with hope, but there hadn't been a miracle: my eyes were still clear as glass.

"Tito said you were speaking in two voices," Ramon said thoughtfully. "I don't believe in the story of Jekyll and Hyde, but understand what I'm saying: they don't just take any old people off the street and plop them in Gottlieb Burckhardt..."

The hulking man stopped short; I turned and saw that he was looking at a glass with a cigar put out in the rest of some rum.

"What the devil?!" Ramon gasped.

I walked over to him, grabbed him by the shoulder and looked him in the eyes.

"Fifty thousand."

The grandiose sum instantly distracted my friend from all the discord and lunacy. He shook his head, winced in annoyance and pointed to the door.

"Let's go, I found your poet. He lives on Yablochkov Street. It's downtown."

We went outside, and I shivered in the brisk wind. It was chilly. The autumn sun, dimmed by smog, was peeking out in the gap between the dense clouds. And suddenly, I felt unbelievably calm and nice. There were no walls around me, no bars. Sky, fresh air, sun. A godsend. It made my head spin...

"Want a cloak?" Ramon offered, having changed his sergeant's uniform into pants and a jacket of a subdued brown shade.

"Give me a pistol," I asked, coming down from the porch.

Ramon gave a loud sniffle and, I saw doubts roll over his ruddy high-cheekboned face.

"We'll take you there," he reminded me.

"Take me there," I nodded and leaned on the porch railing. "But a pistol still wouldn't hurt."

"I no longer keep an arsenal at home," the hulking man refused and clapped a rumpled cap on the crown of his head. "And I'd imagine you know why, isn't that right?"

Department Three investigators could show up here at any time with a search warrant, and I didn't have to doubt my friend's words, but I also wanted to acquire a firearm and wasn't going to take no for an answer.

"Barrel, Ramon. I need a barrel. I am in no

state to run or fight right now, and I am not going back to Gottlieb Burckhardt. I know for certain that you have something on you..."

"You said it was a misunderstanding!"

"I still need time to smooth over the formalities!"

Ramon rolled his eyes, then pulled the Webley-Fosbery from his belt holster and handed it to me.

"Will this do?"

I agreed without a second thought.

"Perfect!"

"Need a holster?" Miro asked, beginning to undo his belt.

"Keep it," I refused, waggling the gun in my hand. The huge revolver weighed just over a kilogram and, at that, its six-round drum turned automatically after firing, and the hammer also cocked on its own. Four-hundred-fifty-five caliber rounds were distinguished by a respectable stopping power; once upon a time, Ramon had managed to stop a werebeast by filling it with seventeen-gram bullets practically at point blank range. It hadn't stayed down for long, but still. A person would be easily laid low by just one such lead pill.

Miro ran his gaze over the revolver with pity, shook his head and walked to the garage. In its wide-open doors, the mud-streaked nose of the armored car glistened. The investigator's nephew had already poured water into the radiator and was now filling the engine with granulated TNT.

I peeled myself off the porch railing and could

barely stand but my vertigo soon passed, and I had no need for anyone's help.

"Ramon!" I threw out to my friend.

"Yes?" the big man turned around.

"How'd you manage to score a TNT license?"

"I have connections," Miro said, not revealing anything and extending me the hospital chart. "Here, this is yours."

I sat down on the armored vehicle's running board, setting my revolver down next to me and, opening the cardboard cover, started quickly looking through the sheets of paper. I didn't discover anything interesting there, just standard medical records, an invention from the first to the last word. The professor hadn't entrusted his card cabinet with information about the experimental electroshock therapy and must have been keeping the real information some other place.

I remembered his notepad, sighed and asked Ramon:

"You got a light?"

Miro patted down his pockets and pulled out a box of matches. Not waiting for me to ask, he struck the reddish tip on the rough sole of his boot and, with a loud hiss, a smoky fire started in the gloom of the garage. I set the edge of a sheet to it and the flame began to quickly devour the dry paper. A black, weightless ash flew up to the ceiling.

The smoke attracted Tito's attention; he was looking at us with unhidden disapproval, but wasn't sure if he should tell his uncle. Instead, he walked over to the barrels in the corner of the yard and returned with a bucket. When the paper had burned through, the boy carefully poured water on the ash and smoldering cardboard.

"Alright, let's go!" Ramon hurried me along.

With a revolver in my hand, I got into the back and, without strength, fell back on the bench. Tito pulled on the driving gloves, took a seat at the wheel and, in a few turns, maneuvered the awkward armored car out of the garage and into the yard. It took long enough for Ramon to go into the house and return with a semi-automatic rifle in his hands.

"There's always problems with you, Leo," he grumbled, answering my unasked question. He threw a travel bag of extra magazines on the bench.

Ramon Miro was worried about potential problems, but the armored car drove through the gates and calmly rolled down the road between the manufactories, their smokestacks puffing away dismally. No one blocked our way, no one shot at us. and no one tried to make us stop.

Such a start to the trip did nothing to calm Ramon's nerves. He loaded a round and started looking in agitation out the barred side window. I only laughed at his fears.

Professor Berliger was highly unlikely to raise a stink. No board of doctors would pronounce me a madman, no court decision would ever put me back into Gottlieb Burckhardt. What was more, his attempt to turn *the illustrious* into normal people was not some scientifically pioneering research. It was just arrogantly playing god, metaphysics at its most provocative and, beyond that, state treason.

I was also not at all afraid I would be accused of killing the orderlies, because no one had bothered gathering evidence of my guilt. As soon as the case reached court, it would fall to bits like a house of cards. With such process violations, even the craftiest prosecutor couldn't get a guilty verdict.

I was somewhat more worried by the leprechaun's warning. My imaginary friend, who had undergone such a terrifying metamorphosis had not been exaggerating one bit: if the power of the *fallen one* took the reins, we would both be in for some shit.

But how to return the albino pipsqueak his former appearance if my *illustrious talent* would no longer obey me?

A little rain started sprinkling, droplets rustling on the roof. Ramon relaxed somewhat, sat back on the bench and asked:

"How are you planning to pay up?"

"Easily," I laughed, and when I saw veins bulging on my friend's face, I told him the address of my attorney's office.

"And what should I do with that?" Ramon frowned.

"Pick up the maître and take him to Brandt's. We'll fill out a transfer."

"You can just slice off fifty grand no problem?" the hulking man doubted.

"Why the devil did you pull me out of the clinic, if you didn't believe I could pay?"

"I had no doubt, I simply supposed you would ask to pay later. And after all, you and I are friends, right?"

"We are," I confirmed, sensing that my former partner hadn't quite finished his thought. "Something else?"

"No," Ramon shook his head and looked back out the window. "We re almost there."

"What has you worried?"

"Other than raiding a psychiatric clinic?"

"Other than that, yes."

"The guy who came to tell me..."

"As I said, I don't know him!"

"Understand what I'm getting at: there will be more problems with him," Ramon sighed. "And don't ask me to get rid of him, alright?"

"I won't," I groaned, not feeling any certainty in that.

At that moment, the armored car slowed its pace, then came to a complete stop. Ramon threw open the side door and pointed to a tidy two-story house.

"Here's you."

I got out of the armored car onto the uneven paving stone of the sidewalk, and suddenly had an attack of vertigo. I had to sit down on the running board.

"Need help?" Ramon asked.

"No," I refused, looking at the narrow street. Its houses were pressed up one to the next like stray dogs on a cold night. The only difference from one to the next was the darkened copper numbers on the walls and the planters of withered flowers on their windowsills. The pollution and soot of the city didn't leave the plants a single chance to brighten the view of passers-by.

In every other way, the street also looked gray, wet and unremarkable. It didn't look at all like the places the poet had preferred to live before.

"You're sure it's here?" I doubted.

"I inquired with the Imperial Theater," Ramon confirmed.

"Well, if you say so..."

I extended a hand. The hulking man helped me up from the running board and warned:

"We'll wait."

"That's nice," I agreed, even though smoke was coming out of the pipe on the steep tiled roof.

If Albert was not home, I would not be allowed in looking like this. I know I wouldn't listen to a thin barefooted wanderer with long gray stubble and clumps of unevenly cut hair, who was crammed into slightly dirty second-hand clothes that didn't fit right...

But there was nothing to be done. I schlepped myself up the cold stone stairs to the house and gave a few raps of the knocker on its copper plate. At first, nothing happened, then I heard footsteps, the door peeked open and a middle-aged lady in an austere dress and bonnet stared out at me in astonishment.

"We don't give charity!" the housekeeper declared with a clear English accent and tried to close the door, but I managed to block it with my bare foot. It squeezed and hurt.

"Is Albert home?"

The old lady with the prim and proper face of a grandmother hesitated for a moment, then said in annoyance:

"Go away, or I ll call the police!"

In bygone times, Albert Brandt himself would come home looking like this quite often, but I didn't say anything about that, just asked:

"What do you see behind my back?"

Although the armored vehicle Ramon had stolen didn't have any emblems or side numbers, and the Gatling gun had been removed from the tower before its sale, few could distinguish it from a real police self-propelled vehicle on first glance. The lady had her doubts.

"How do you know..." she started, but I immediately heard the fast clacking of heels behind her, as if someone was running down the stairs from the second story.

"Has something happened?" asked a pleasant female voice and, without missing a beat, a joyful cry sounded out: "Leo!"

Liliana jumped out of the house and threw herself around my neck, nearly knocking me off my feet.

"Leo! You came back!" Laughing and overcome with tears at the same time, my girlfriend hung off me. "I knew it! I knew you'd come back!"

It was as if Lily's arrival gave me strength and,

by some miracle, I managed to stay on my feet.

"Let's go inside," I suggested, sensing my knees giving out.

Liliana wasn't listening, and I had to walk in on my own, pulling my girlfriend after me. The housekeeper quickly closed the door behind us, not wanting to attract our neighbors' attention with such a piquant scene and, in that regard, I was in complete agreement.

"Leo, my beloved!" Liliana squeezed herself to me. "I was waiting for you with bated breath, I was so hopeful!"

I kissed her, forcing her to go silent, then quietly whispered in her ear:

"Thank you for believing in me. Without your faith, I'd have never made it."

It was as if Liliana woke up, took a step back and looked at me from the side:

"Oh, Leo!" she gasped. "You look horrid! You're so thin! You need to get in bed right this instant!"

"I'm completely fine!"

"I won't even argue!" Lily cut me off. "When was the last time you had a hot meal? Missus Hardy, cook some..."

"Broth," I asked, because there was nothing more my stomach could take at this point.

"Yes, broth!" Liliana confirmed. "And call the theater, tell Albert that Leopold has returned."

"As you say," Mrs. Hardy took that order with an icy calm.

"Leo, you need to lie in bed!" Lily said, again

showing concern. "I'll call a doctor!"

"No need, my dear," I refused. "I'm completely fine. And, to be honest, before lying down, I would like a bath."

"A bath is the best thing for a cold," Mrs. Hardy approved of that decision, looking expressively at my bare feet.

Liliana pulled me to the stairs; I, meanwhile, pulled an edition of the *Atlantic Telegraph* from the newspaper table and hid my Webley-Fosbery, which had been causing my pants to nearly fall due to the lack of belt. If that happened, my fingers could get hurt or the gun might even go off when hitting the floor.

I went up to the second story almost without losing my breath. Most likely, it was Liliana's *talent* at work. She had believed in me this whole time, but it was hard to believe in the return of a person who had disappeared two months earlier without a trace. But now, Lily had bounced back, and it was as if I was bathing in the warmth she radiated.

The stairs led us to a spacious hall with a fireplace a round table and soft armchairs. Now gloom reigned there. The electric bulbs in the crystal chandelier were off.

"Our bathroom is to the right," Liliana pointed to one of the corridors heading in different directions on the floor.

"Our?" I asked in surprise. "Lily, do you live here?"

There was ample evidence that Albert Brandt

and his wife lived here: the rich assortment of alcoholic beverages and paintings from fashionable expressionists on the walls of the living room, mixed in with canvases of nude models, for example. But Liliana? What was she doing here?

"What else could I do?" my girlfriend sighed. "I was waiting for you to come back day in and day out, not wanting to upset my parents." She smiled. "I had to lie that we were traveling through Europe."

"Oh," I exhaled and slumped down in the nearest chair. It was as if my strength left me all at once. My heart was crushed.

"Don't worry, mom and dad don't suspect a thing. Albert's friends send postcards from the continent from time to time," Lily said and turned away, demonstrating her classical profile.

She couldn't hide the tears welling up in her eyes, and my heart burst in pain.

"That's not what I'm worried about," I admitted. "Not at all."

"What happened, Leopold?" Lily asked, sitting on the arm of the chair and embracing me. "What's the matter, my dear?"

"My past caught up with me," I answered, not getting into the details and leaning my forehead against her feminine shoulder. "It was bad without you."

"For me too," Lily said, lifting my head and kissing me on the lips. "Tell me everything later, alright? Now you need to take a bath and drink broth, and I need to take care of Elizabeth-Maria."

"And what happened to her?" I asked, getting on guard.

"Nervous fever," Liliana told me, getting up from the armchair. "No medicine helps, and she hasn't woken up for two weeks."

A shudder ran over me. Nervous fever? Oh, if only! With her current appearance, Elizabeth-Maria was completely and totally obliged to my imagination, and I could no longer hold that image in my mind.

Now, I had another problem hanging heavily around my neck like a millstone...

"Go take a bath, I'll bring you a robe," Liliana ordered, walking down the corridor.

I admired my girlfriend's lithe figure, her narrow waist and copious black hair, but, when Lily was hidden from view, I didn't go into the bathroom, instead glanced into Elizabeth-Maria's bedroom. Her bedroom met me with gloom, a heavy frankincense aroma and the smell of a body warmed by disease. The windows were covered with a curtain, and there was a table at the wide queen bed with a row of glass bottles of medicines and tablets.

When I walked in, Elizabeth-Maria didn't even stir. The sweat-soaked sheet was just barely heaving from the slow movement of her chest. The pillow gleamed with red locks of her fallen hair. Her face was severely slim and had lost its sweet roundness, becoming harsh and sharp. It hadn't lost its beauty one bit, it was just that the true nature of the succubus had begun to peek out, predatory and pitiless.

I tried to resurrect the image of my imaginary bride in my memory, as I had seen her for the first time but, in my memory, beyond the image of the round-faced pretty girl, there was another one that was no less vivid. It was very difficult to forget the succubus licking blood from steely nails with a split tongue while her eyes burned with the fire of the underworld!

I could no longer count on my own imagination and didn't know the potential consequences of the succubus returning to demonic form so, giving Elizabeth-Maria a heavy slap, I quickly retreated from the bed and said only after that:

"Stand up and walk!"

Elizabeth-Maria's swollen eyes suddenly flew open and she stared at me with an unseeing gaze.

"Scoundrel!" she squeezed out hoarsely, licking her dried lips and groaning out: "You're such an unbearable scoundrel, Leopold Orso! And it was such bad luck for me to cross paths with you!"

Under her heavy gaze, I hobbled to the door.

"Where did you disappear off to?" the succubus whispered, raising up from the pillow.

"Doesn't matter. What matters is that I'm back."

"Make yourself scarce!"

Not wanting to test Elizabeth-Maria's patience, I slipped out the door and only there took the revolver hidden under the newspaper off full cock.

"Leo?" Liliana asked in surprise. "You aren't in the bath yet?"

"No, I decided to visit Elizabeth-Maria," I answered with a careless smile, taking the robe from my girlfriend and walking into the little room. In the middle of it, there was a bulbous copper bathtub on animal feet. There were two pipes leading from it: one with cold water and one with hot.

"I'll bring the broth right away," Liliana warned.But as soon as she entered the corridor, she shouted out excitedly: "Mary? You're awake?!"

After closing the door, I threw off my secondhand clothes right on the tile floor, then plugged the drain and opened both shine-polished copper faucets. I checked the water temperature with my hand, got into the bath and fell down limp, enjoying the heat enveloping me.

After a brief soak, I washed my head, wiped the foam from my short bristle of hair and picked up the newspaper. I felt like a piece had been cut out of me, and I couldn't simply lie in the bath and enjoy the return to normal life. I needed a distraction from the gaping emptiness in my soul.

Something wasn't right with me. And that worried me like finding a chip in my tooth with my tongue but much, much worse. It was as if I had been lobotomized, and I didn't even know it.

"Curses!" I swore aloud, opening the newspaper in a nervous motion.

The front page had a flashy headline: "Has the London Reaper returned?" It was talking about a series of murders of young ladies. At the time of the article's writing, there were already four known victims. Each of them had their heart cut out, and the alarmed public was demanding the police hurry to catch the malefactors. There were even calls for the inspector general to resign, but no one was taking them seriously yet. At the very end, there was a quote from an expert who wished to remain anonymous, expounding at length on a theory that the mysterious murderer had moved to New Babylon after being at work in London almost a quarter century earlier.

Remembering the arrival of the Aztec priests to the metropole, I was in complete and total agreement with the expert. The bloodthirsty pagans were known to cut out hearts by the hundreds on the summits of their baleful step pyramids, why would they change their modus operandi in New Babylon?

"The Pinkerton Detective Agency must not have hit the mark in their investigation," I decided, looking at a note about an explosion in a bullet factory on the margin and getting distracted by the sound of the door opening. Liliana was wheeling a serving table into the bathroom, where there was a plate with a mound of toast next to a mug of chicken broth. Seeing normal food led my stomach to painful convulsions.

"Just eat your breakfast for now," Lily smiled, "I'll be in soon!"

Setting the newspaper on the table, I grabbed the mug of broth with both hands and started taking small cautious sips of the hot aromatic liquid.

Nice...

It really did make me feel nice, but I still didn't touch the toasts, afraid of overburdening my stomach, which was not accustomed to hard food.

After eating my fill, I looked back at the paper. The news didn't inspire particular optimism. The world was going down the tubes. The endless workers' strike was still underway, and army divisions had been brought into the city to storm the factories they'd captured. The socialists had exploded yet another police armored vehicle, and a group of anarchists had attempted to plant a bomb in the High Imperial Court but failed. It ended with a firefight and the arrest of the malefactors. Her Highness the Crown Princess Anna had been in a coma for almost a month and, in that time, the regent Duke Logrin, had yet to form a new government. His influence in the Imperial Council was growing weaker with every day and, based on what I could see, the biggest political crisis this country had seen in half a century was brewing.

I didn't even read the criminal blotter. I simply decided to save my nerves. Even without that, I wanted to get out of the bath and take the first ferry to the continent. Basically, if the Empire was coming to an end, there would simply be no more safe places on the planet. There was no reason to feed empty hopes.

The Princess... I led a finger over a scar on the left side of my chest. It was clean and even, not a jagged crude cut. I considered whether I wanted the death of my crown-bearing cousin. Her life or death was in my hands.

I imagined squeezing a heart in my hand – my very own heart! – and I suddenly felt the elasticity of muscle tissue and a very slight beat like the pulsation of an abscessed finger.

I shuddered in surprise and stared at my sweaty palm with unhidden astonishment.

Had I really managed to sense the beating of a heart that now belonged to another, or had it just seemed that way? And could the remnants of my *talent*, burnt out by electroshock therapy, bring Princess Anna back to life? That little bit was enough for the succubus, would it be enough for the heiress to the throne?

A breeze blew past the back of my head again. I turned in alarm but, when I saw Liliana slipping into the door, I relaxed and went into the soapy water up to my neck.

My girlfriend led her hands behind her head with a crafty smile and, when she lowered them, her dress fell freely to her feet. The only clothing Lily had left was a velvet ribbon on her neck, but everything in me was just stuck inside. My mouth instantly went dry, my heart started beating feverishly, and my ears started ringing as if I was about to slip into unconsciousness.

Not at all embarrassed at having exposed her high breasts and a triangle of curly hair below her stomach, Liliana stepped out of the dress and asked in a languishing voice:

"Won't you please rub my back?"

I just nodded, not feeling capable of removing my gaze from the naked woman's figure.

And then someone knocked on the door.

— The Dormant —

Squealing in surprise, Liliana grabbed her balled-up dress from the floor and squeezed it against herself, covering her nakedness, but Elizabeth-Maria didn't pay any attention to the fact that she'd caught her friend in such a piquant situation.

"Leo, someone's come for you," she said, adding significantly: "It's urgent."

With a sharp wave of my hand, I called for her to close the door. After a barely perceptible delay, that is exactly what the succubus did while Liliana, crimson in embarrassment, started feverishly pulling her dress back on.

"Leo, who is it?" she asked.

I got out of the bathtub and put on the robe, having no doubt in mind that it was Ramon having brought my attorney so I could organize the transfer of the reward I'd promised him. But I didn't tell Lily that and just shrugged my shoulders:

"I have no idea."

"Well, go and find out!" Lily hurried me along, pulling on her dress. "Wait! Here are some slippers!"

I stuck my feet into the home slippers, at the same time hiding a revolver in the spacious pocket of the soft bombazine robe. After that, I threw open the door and, grabbing Liliana at the exit from the bathroom, kissed her on the neck.

"I love you."

"I'll be with Mary," she giggled and started walking down the corridor.

I didn't delay either. I wanted to get the formalities over with as quickly as possible and get back into the warm bath. Or lay around in bed. I still wasn't sure.

3

SHAMBLING DOWN the path of springy carpets in the overly large slippers, I walked to the stairs and had started on my way down when the visitor, already having lost his patience, bolted up to meet me. The presentable looking gentleman in a dark cloak and brown hat stopped half-way and raised his head quickly.

He looked at me, and I at him; we recognized one another simultaneously.

To my credit, in spite of my poor health, I reacted first. I simply threw a foot forward and forced my opponent down the stairs with a kick to the chest.

William Grace, the very same lieutenant of her Majesty's Imperial guard who had accompanied me to the operation to remove the heart, threw up his hands and somersaulted down the stairs. When he fell, he hit his head hard on a planter that housed a ficus. He didn't lose consciousness, though, and immediately turned onto his stomach. I yanked my Webley-Fosbery from my pocket but, much to my bad luck, the huge revolver's hammer got caught on the fabric and, before I managed to free it, a sharp command rang out:

"Stop!"

— The Dormant —

A short woman in a dark gray cape and hat with thick veil, whose legs William Grace had rolled up to, gave the command. Two strong fellows behind her in identical black raincoats had already drawn their unusually short carbines, which had thick wire bundles laced around the barrels and box magazines. The exclamation forced them to freeze in place as well.

Even with such a bad turn of events, I easily could have shot right through the pocket but, instead of that, I obediently unclenched my fingers from the handle of the revolver and held my open hands out in front of me. In such matters, one can never guess who might take a stray bullet...

Lieutenant Grace got up from the floor and stuck his hand under his cloak.

"Enough, William!" the strange lady rebuffed him.

"But that's..." the lieutenant gasped, but the lady cut him off with a sharp wave of her hand.

"I don't want to know!" she threw out and demanded: "Hey, you there! Come down at once!"

"Listen!" William Grace objected, taking a kerchief from his pocket and squeezing his nose, which had broken in the fall. "I'm trying..."

"Be quiet, lieutenant!" her cold reply followed. "Or you'll have to report to me for bad behavior!"

And the lieutenant fell silent, while the strange lady turned her attention back to me.

"Will we have to wait long?" she enquired in annoyance, turning to the guards and pointing first one carbine away from me, then the other. "Yes, put your weapons away, in fact! Well, as much as you can!"

"Put them away," William Grace confirmed the order, and the boys obediently lowered their carbines and even covered them with the tails of their raincoats.

But I still hadn't moved from place, instead demanding explanations:

"What do you want?"

The Imperial Guard lieutenant was still silent, allowing his companion to say her fill.

"You gave your word!" she declared in an icy tone. "You're mistaken if you think you can break it unpunished!"

Gave my word? What the devil?!

I didn't understand a single thing.

At the same time, the extravagant lady, who thought she could give orders to the Imperial Guard lieutenant, turned her attention to the housekeeper frozen against the wall.

"Sweetheart, is there a free room in this building?" she asked.

"You can use the office," Mrs. Hardy said, not looking either dead or alive, terrified by all these new people, who were armed to the teeth.

"Well?" the strange lady stared at me and added acridly: "Or would you rather die of old age on those stairs?"

The mention of death cut my hearing unpleasantly, and I obediently came down to the first floor. Lieutenant Grace's astonishment was just too authentic. He was certainly not expecting to see me here, a living corpse, so why the devil had he come? And who was this lady bossing around the lieutenant of the Imperial Guard like her personal servant?

"Why do you look like that? Who cuts your hair? You need a new barber, because you look like a scarecrow!" the vixen threw out with contemptuous incomprehension and extended a hand: "Your weapon!"

I pulled my Webley-Fosbery out of my robe pocket and set it in her extended palm, covered with a black lacy glove. The stranger weighed the huge revolver in her hand and snorted acridly:

"Compensating for the size of your masculine dignity?"

She then asked the housekeeper: "Show me the way, sweetheart!"

Mrs. Hardy started ambling down the corridor. The lady went after her almost elegantly, but in too dancing of a gait. The housekeeper stopped at the office door, confused by her new order:

"Coffee, sugar, cream and pastries. And make sure the pastries are with cinnamon! On the double!"

After giving such an unexpected order the stranger walked first into Albert Brandt's office. The lieutenant suggested I follow her with a gesture. So, under his stubborn gaze, I walked through the doorway into the spacious room with a desk laden with drafts and leaned my elbows on the high back of a guest chair. The boys in raincoats were left in the corridor, and only William Grace joined us.

"This is Leopold Orso!" he declared as he walked.

"He could be Sacher-Masoch for all I care!" the lady answered, throwing my revolver on an empty divan in a careless motion. After that, she removed her hat and, without the thick black veil, turned out to be a middle-aged brunette with very pretty thin face, the noble features of which could not be hidden even with too much gaudy makeup and bright red lipstick.

And also, she was *illustrious*. In the office, with thick drawn curtains over the windows, gloom reigned, so I could detect a light glow in her colorless gray eyes without effort.

The lady unceremoniously set her hat right on the poet's drafts, placing her cape there as well, leaving her in an elegant dress with open shoulders and a deep neckline. After that, she sat down in an armchair and unbuttoned her bag, but immediately got distracted from its contents and fixed her stubborn gaze back on me.

"Take a seat!" she demanded, fidgeting with a strand of pearl beads. "You're so long and tall. When I look at you, my head spins circles!"

I took a look at the lieutenant, who was left at the door and turned the chair in order to have a view of him, at least from the very corner of my eye. Meanwhile the stranger, with the same tough calm, removed from her bag a glass syringe, a vial plugged with a rubber stopper, and a strap. When I saw these preparations, my heart nearly leapt out of my chest.

I was not about to let myself be pumped full of narcotics but, before I managed to jump out of the chair, the lady pulled off her long black glove and began deftly tying the strap around her own shoulder.

"I am a lady-in-waiting of her late Imperial Majesty the Queen Empress Victoria," she told me, pumping her hand measuredly. "I'm here representing her Highness the Crown Princess Anna. I warn you in advance, in order to avoid misunderstandings."

Then came a cautious knock at the door and, when it opened, one of the curtains gave a slow flutter in time.

A cross-breeze? Very interesting...

"Coffee's ready!" said the guard, who peeked into the office.

"Lieutenant!"

William Grace accepted the tray and brought it to the table. I caught his gaze and gave an involuntary shiver. The lieutenant looked at me like an underworld native.

At the same time, the lady poked the long needle into the rubber stopper of the vial, filled the syringe and gracefully expelled the remaining air from the glass cylinder.

"In the last years of the old lady's life, she saw conspiracies everywhere," the lady-in-waiting said, talking none-too-respectfully about the late Empress and staring stubbornly at Grace. "Lieutenant, why are you sniffling like a dog? Do you want to say something? Well, speak! I beg you, don't be ashamed!"

But the lieutenant preferred to keep silent.

The lady poked the needle into an engorged vein, undid the strap and pushed down on the plunger.

"The old hag pushed all the *illustrious* out of her inner circle, but she didn't dare get rid of me," the maid of honor said with a slightly slurring tongue as she sat back in the chair. "She couldn't get by without me. I'm an oracle."

The *illustrious* woman's eyes closed, and her chest started to heave slowly and measuredly, as if she was immersed in a deep sleep. I even started to doubt that there was a morphine solution in the vial. The drug was working too strongly and unusually.

The back of my head was burning unbearably from the stubborn gaze of the lieutenant, but I forced myself to calm down and even sat back in the chair. In the office, it smelled strongly of fresh baked goods and coffee, but those aromas only emphasized the absurdity of it all.

Suspicion ran down my spine with a light shiver, as if I was still lying in solitary confinement in the psychiatric clinic high on morphine and my escape had only been a narcotic-induced delusion. That put me beside myself; the only thing keeping me from panic was a clear understanding that my nightmares were always somewhat more straightforward and purposeful. The loose-lipped drug addict court lady just didn't fit the bill.

But as for William Grace, he easily could have easily been a problem in my dreams or in reality, so I gave a noticeable tug at my robe belt and tied a knot on one end. Sure, a belt was far from being a Kali Strangler's rumal, but it could do the job.

Suddenly, the lady-in-waiting's back lurched. She exhaled loudly and, with a feverish jerk of her arm, ripped the strand of pearls. But she immediately went limp and fell back motionless in the armchair. The nacreous beads ripped off the string and fell onto the floor one after the next.

My eyes on them, I missed seeing her eyes open again. But now, they weren't her eyes at all. Now, they were shining with a clear light, which instantly drove back the shadows to the corners of the office.

"I can't see..." the woman whispered, holding her hand out in front of her, which froze me in place.

Not only her eyes had changed. Her vocal timbre was also totally different. She now sounded young and sonorous and, to match that, her face grew fresher and the wrinkles at the corners of her eyes smoothed out.

"I can't see..." the lady-in-waiting repeated, and the lieutenant waddled over nervously.

"Faster!" he hissed at me. "Touch her hand!"

I got up from the armchair and, holding the robe closed with my left hand, touched the oracle's palm with my right. Instantly, it was as if I was blasted with an electric shock. My mind was captivated by vibrant and painful images; I stumbled backward, breaking the contact and fell back in the chair but, before my eyes, there was still a vaguely familiar young girl's face, pale and sickly thin.

"What the devil?" I couldn't hold back a curse, kneading my temples with my palms.

"It sometimes happens like that," followed the calm reply. "It will pass shortly."

And in an instant, I was left with no doubt that I was speaking with the Dreamer!

"You were totally different in my dream," the Dreamer said through the oracle's mouth after a brief pause.

Was the Dreamer a woman? In the face of the rejuvenated maid of honor there were clearly new features, but they only reinforced her femininity.

"Who are you?" I exhaled.

"The person you owe a service."

And then William Grace cut into the conversation.

"This is Leopold Orso, your Highness," he said, removing the cap from his head and placing it to his chest.

"Is that name supposed to mean something to me?"

"Leopold Orso!" Grace repeated. "You asked for his papers after the death of her Majesty. This is the man whose heart was transplanted into you!"

The oracle turned the gaze of her radiant eyes and asked in annoyance:

"Have you lost your mind, lieutenant?"

"Not at all, your Highness" Grace answered in a curt military fashion.

I could even feel a bit of empathy for him, but

we were talking about my heart, and I wasn't so deeply moved by humanitarian ideas as to forgive someone who was involved in my murder. Even if it had failed, still...

But what did that mean? The Princess didn't know whose heart had been transplanted into her? She didn't know about me?

The oracle tried to get up from the chair, but her body wasn't obeying her well, and the lady-in-waiting fell back down.

"Lieutenant!" now there was a metallic ring in the voice. "A person cannot live without a heart! Are you aware of that?!"

"Of course, your Highness! But this is him. I'm sure of that."

"How is that possible?"

"I haven't a clue! But may I be so bold as to remind you that the body of Leopold Orso disappeared from the operating room after the removal of his heart and, after that, one of the surgeons was found dead. Perhaps a second transplant was performed..."

The conversation had taken an undesired turn, but I didn't manage to do anything to avoid the catastrophe. The oracle stared at me with her lustrous eyes and asked:

"Is it really you?"

Any attempt to weasel out or dodge would be doomed to failure, so I simply raised my hand and waved.

"Hi, cousin!"

"Cousin..." Princess Anna's consciousness,

possessing the body of the oracle, called back. "So, it's true?"

"Whew..."

"So that's why I could enter your dream!" the heiress to the throne guessed. "I have your heart! But how did you survive? Was there a second operation?"

The question put me in a difficult position – if I told the truth about my gift and the imaginary heart, I would instantly find myself in a comfortable cell with soft padded walls. No one would let a person go free, if their death would cause the heiress to the throne to also die. After all, if I were no more, the Princess's new heart would cease to exist. And the last thing I wanted was to find myself in a lonely cell once again. But I didn't run for a flagrant lie, no matter how great the temptation.

"You haven't been wanting to howl at the moon lately?" I enquired with a smirk. "You don't get goosebumps from silver?"

"Balderdash!" the lieutenant couldn't hold back and even peeled himself from the doorframe but, as soon as the oracle threw up a hand, he immediately went back.

"Are you a werebeast, cousin?" the Princess asked, somehow very easily accepting my words.

I'm sure that I hit the mark on the silver.

"I was," I answered, watching the lieutenant with the corner of my eye. "But, after losing my heart, I was totally cured of the curse."

The oracle wrapped her arms around herself and stayed silent for a long time. Her eyes stopped burning like two lustrous flames. It even seemed that the trance had been broken but, then she opened her mouth again.

"That's impossible!" the Princess declared. "That simply cannot be!"

"If you say so, your Highness," I just laughed in reply.

"You aren't the person you claim to be! How did you get into my dream? What kind of game are you playing? Answer me at once!"

I pulled myself together, but the lieutenant reacted first. I didn't even have time to blink before he had me in the sights of his pocket Browning, hidden under the cap he'd removed from his head.

"No game!" I assured my cousin. "And it was you who entered my dream, not the other way around!"

"I need proof!" Princess Anna announced. "Prove that you are the person you claim to be! Prove that you are my cousin!"

The way she phrased the question dumbfounded me.

"What exactly do you want me to prove? Prove that I am me?"

"Prove that the heart removed from you precisely!"

"Easy for you to say!" I objected, but then I heard the dry click of the pistol being cocked, and I had to grab at the first straw I came across. "Wait! Alright! I can prove it!"

I got up from the chair and threw open the

robe. I left my groin covered with the right half, but exposed my chest with two scars and the eight-sided star opposite my heart without any embarrassment or abashment.

"Oh devil!" the Princess said expressively. "Cover yourself, cousin. And please sit down! Lieutenant, put your weapon away."

William Grace hid his weapon in his cloak pocket with a good degree of pity, while I lowered down in the armchair and asked:

"And what now?"

"I didn't know, cousin. I had no idea it was your heart. My grandmother didn't let me in on such details."

"What now, your Highness?"

The maid of honor went silent, but the silence didn't last long.

"You still owe me," the Princess declared. "And although I am embarrassed and upset at how you were treated, a deal is a deal. You gave your word."

With the corner of my eye, I noticed a curtain flutter at the far wall and clarified without particular interest:

"How can I be of use?"

"You'll find out in due time, cousin. You'll find out everything. I need to think it all over," came her vague answer, then the lady's head fell limply on her chest.

An instant later, the lady seized up with her whole body, straightened out and led her unseeing gaze over the office. Her eyes were no longer beaming with an unearthly light. Now, they were just colorless and gray, with crimson threads of slightly engorged capillaries.

The trance had come to an end.

The maid of honor got up heavily from the chair and walked with the uneven gait of a drug user to the table, picking up a mug from the tray. With a shaky hand, she raised it to her mouth, sipped the cold coffee and looked at the lieutenant.

"I hope that was worth it," the oracle said, now in her normal voice.

"Without a doubt," William Grace assured her. "You did a wonderful job."

"Come now, what are you saying?!" the lady-in-waiting laughed acridly, taking a bun and smiling unkindly. "Well then, dear lieutenant, could you do me a kindness and pick up my pearls from the floor?" And, with sadistic satisfaction, she added: "There are exactly thirty-three."

William Grace looked expressively at me, but I was not about to crawl on the Persian rug in search of the nacreous beads and ignored his hint. The lieutenant had to go down on all fours himself and gather the lost pearls in a kerchief.

To be honest, I still felt an urge to whip my robe belt around his neck and pull the knot. I could barely restrain myself.

"There are only thirty-two pearls here," Grace said some time later. "I don't know where the last one could have rolled off to."

"The last one?" the maid of honor asked in

surprise, chasing the strong sweet coffee with the bun. "For pity's sake, lieutenant, there are only thirty-two!"

William Grace got up from the floor, his cheeks burning in rage. And not for nothing. He had spent a good five minutes crawling on the dusty rug in search of a nonexistent pearl.

"You said thirty-three!"

"Oh, I'm just so scatterbrained today!" the maid of honor laughed, dumping the nacreous beads into her bag, then placing the syringe, vial and strap there as well. "Are we done?"

"Yes!" William Grace snarled and turned to me. "Don't leave town. We'll be in touch!"

I just waved my hand in reply, wanting to be left alone as quickly as possible.

The lady-in-waiting donned her hat, took her cape from the table and filed to the door with her former dancing gait, then turned and sent me an air kiss.

"Pay my respects to your cook! Excellent pastries!"

The lieutenant left the office after the maid of honor, but I was sitting motionless in the chair until I heard a knock at the door. And a moment later, I said:

"Come in!"

The curtain fluttered, and I was joined by Liliana, who was holding a pocket Mauser in her hand. Behind her, the door to an adjoining room, which was behind a curtain, appeared for a moment.

"What is happening, Leo?" the girl asked in alarm. "Who were those people? And why did that lady call you cousin? Are you related?"

"Take a seat," I pointed Liliana to the armchair, feverishly remembering the precise moment in the conversation when the drapes had fluttered a second time. And although that had been at the very end of our conversation, I had no way of imagining what exactly she'd managed to hear.

Lily fell back in the armchair, set the Mauser on the armrest and declared:

"I'm listening, Leo!"

"That woman is an oracle. Such is her *talent*. She fell into a trance and opened her mind for someone else. It's like a kind of wireless telephone, if you will."

"You were speaking with your cousin?" Liliana interrupted me. "Why didn't you tell me you had relatives before?"

"I don't have a relationship with them. I got into a court case with some of them over inheritance, and I've just never talked with the others."

"And some of them send armed people and an oracle to you! And who was that lieutenant? Military?"

Every answer spawned a whole avalanche of new questions, so I tried to give as condensed a version of the story as possible.

"Lily, I landed in some trouble, and was forced to contact distant relatives for help. And now I owe them a service."

"And me?" the girl flared up in rage and

shame. "Why didn't you ask me for help?"

"It wasn't the right situation..."

"My father has high connections, you don't know!"

"I didn't want to involve you or your relatives."

"Empty words!" Liliana exploded, jumping out of the office.

I raised up with a groan from the armchair and hurried after my girlfriend, but she ran quickly up the stairs and I simply didn't have the strength for such a feat.

Anyway, what would I have said to her? The truth?

That thought made ants crawl up my spine and then, as if I didn't have enough to worry about, I got another knock at the door.

4

WITH A MUTED CURSE, I ran back into Albert's office and grabbed the Webley-Fosbery I'd forgotten there. From there, pressing my palm against my mercilessly splitting side, I hobbled to the entry, where I could already hear muted voices. Remembering the recent fiasco, I didn't put the revolver in my robe pocket and, as a result, barely managed to hide the weapon behind my back when my attorney came at me with his arms spread to hug me.

"Viscount!" he was filled with joy. "I'm insanely

glad to see you in good health! You disappeared so suddenly, I was horribly afraid that something bad might have happened! I even paid an advance to a lawyer, so he could get to work without any delay. Was that right?"

"You did everything right, maître." I gave a subdued smile and stared at Ramon with surprise as he dragged a fairly large chest into the house with his nephew.

The lawyer caught my gaze and explained:

"Viscount, these are the effects from your family manor. I took it upon myself to bring them with me..."

I just sighed and looked in confusion at Mrs. Hardy. My title as Viscount had forced the housekeeper to forget the visit of armed people for a time, and she called Ramon after her.

"Bring it into the storeroom!"

Based on the reddened cheeks and aroma of expensive brandy, Mrs. Hardy had taken advantage of Albert's bar to calm her nerves. In her place, I also would have drained a glass or two of the hard stuff.

Remembering the rum I drank this morning, nausea rose up in my throat. I feverishly swallowed and led my attorney to the poet's office, meanwhile sticking the revolver in my robe pocket.

"Gosh, I feel bad distracting you now..." the lawyer started to worry, but I didn't even listen to him and raked Albert's drafts to the edge of the table.

"I need a check drawn up for fifty thousand francs," I asked and fell into the deep armchair. "Made out to cash."

My attorney set a leather briefcase on his knees and even unclipped it, but started doubting and asked:

"Are you sure, Viscount? Fifty thousand made out to cash? That is a massive sum!"

"It's a debt of honor," I answered simply, deciding to avoid endless interrogation that way. And I wasn't wrong: my attorney shook his head, took out a pen with a silver quill and started filling out the check.

"Sign here," he pointed some time later. "And here and here."

I had to get out of the deep and extremely comfortable chair and place signatures where he'd made check marks.

"The money will be in the account tomorrow by the second half of the day. After, that the check can be presented for payment."

"That will do," I nodded and asked: "Do you have any cash?"

My attorney, accustomed to all manner of things, was not the least bit surprised by the unexpected question. He opened his wallet and extended me a thick packet of one-hundred-franc bills and a checkbook.

"Five thousand from your main account."

"What is left there now?"

"Seventeen thousand francs."

"Alright," I calmed down. Then I asked: "While I was... absent did any word come from the police?"

— The Dormant —

"There was one call. They wanted to question you at the Newton-Markt," my attorney confirmed, "but Maître Mogfline is worth every centime. Every last one! He disputed not only the request itself, but also the legality of the investigation as a whole! At present, the police have no questions for you!"

"Excellent!" I smiled with relief. I suspected, however, that such a favorable outcome was explained not only by the talents of my new lawyer, but also by the good will of the inspector general.

Anyway, it didn't matter.

I lead my attorney to the exit, evaluated the store-room filled with my things and looked into the kitchen where Mrs. Hardy, having taken Ramon and his nephew for simple movers, was treating them to some apple pie.

"Even better than aunt Marta's!" Tito said, enthusiastic about the desert.

Ramon, having noticed me, quickly finished his tea, thanked the housekeeper and went out into the hallway.

"Are you alright?" he asked apprehensively, nervously kneading his cap.

"Medium height, gaunt, light haired. In a dark cloak and brown hat," he said, giving a short description of Lieutenant Grace. "He came back to you today, right? Did he ask about my whereabouts?"

Ramon's high-cheekboned face went gloomy.

"Leo, believe me, there was nothing I could do!"

We went into the entryway. I pushed my former partner on the shoulder and laughed.

"Relax. That guy can find whoever he wants. He'd have strangled you, the lowlife..."

"Is it that bad?"

I shook my head.

"No, Ramon. It was bad in Gottlieb Burckhardt. But you helped me out a lot, and I value that. Take this."

The hulking man accepted the check, glanced at the sum and whistled.

"Is it all that easy?" he asked, astonished. "Fifty thousand?"

"Present the check tomorrow at the end of the day," I warned him and advised: "But don't deposit it. Take it out in cash right away and spread it around in different places. The money is clean, I just feel uneasy in my heart. You know how it is..."

"I do," Ramon nodded. "That's what I'll do."

"And be ready for a call."

"Just call."

Just then, Tito walked up to us, happy as a clam, and Ramon and his nephew headed off to the four winds. I closed the door behind them and asked the housekeeper:

"Mrs. Hardy, how are things with the rent?"

"Mr. Brandt and Ms. Montague pay on time."

I took a pack of bills from my pocket and counted out five hundred.

"Take this, it's my contribution for the future."

"There's no need for this at all!"

"Well, I feel that there is."

The proper English lady relented and put the

money in her apron pocket, then enquired:

"And what became of your family manor, Viscount?"

I couldn't think anything up, so I answered with the truth:

"Sold it to cover debts."

"So, you're going to be staying with us?"

"I hope so," I sighed and, heavily leaning on the bannister, went up the stairs to the second floor. I wanted to believe that Liliana wouldn't tell me to get lost, or even worse, would leave herself.

In the hall, my resolve to explain myself left me, and I didn't look for my girlfriend, instead falling back in a comfortable armchair in front of the roaring fireplace. The logs were cracking comfortingly, and I started to feel warm and calm. So, I settled in. I just sat there, looking at the fire. Then a glass of something milk-white was stuck into my hand.

"Sharbat," Albert Brandt told me, sitting in the armchair next to mine. "Just how you like it, with lemon juice and not vodka."

I nodded gratefully and took a small sip, but didn't say anything. Normally, there was no need, because the poet had the custom of talking enough for us both, but now he was also just staring at the fire in silence.

It was so unusual I turned and took a closer look at Albert. He had grown somewhat lean and, a deep wrinkle had set in on his high forehead but, in all other ways, his appearance had not borne any changes. It made little difference that his disheveled hair had been styled to disorder by an expensive barber, or that his sand-colored beard was somewhat more even and groomed than before. His light gray *illustrious* eyes looked at me just as penetratingly as always, as if looking through me.

"I won't ask where you disappeared to for two months," Albert warned with a smirk, "but I can see that this trip wasn't as pleasant as your last one."

"Dante Alighieri ventured to hell on his own will. I was thrown there."

"Very vivid," the poet praised me. "An excellent allegory!"

"Banal hyperbole."

"I can see you're not in the mood, my friend," Albert smiled in understanding, walking to the bar and pouring himself a brandy. With a bulbous glass in hand, he returned but didn't sit in the chair and looked me from top to bottom. "Well, I'm doing just fine. Excellent even! I'm staging my own play in the Imperial Theater. How do you like that? I'm hiring actors, agreeing on a budget, and leading rehearsals." The poet finished the brandy and said with a fastidious grimace: "I've turned from a creator into devil knows what! An administrator! Can you imagine it, Leo? Albert Brandt, an administrator! And half a month ago, my wife fell into a coma. I never would have made it without your Liliana."

"Don't exaggerate," I laughed. "You'd have hired a nurse."

Albert thought it over and nodded.

"Yes, that would have been another way."

"And, in the theater, it's like you're in a raspberry patch," I continued, finishing the sharbat. "The actresses must jump into your bed all on their own, isn't that right?"

The poet snorted in laughter and sat back in his chair.

"Hrmph, my cynical friend. It isn't all puppies and rainbows. I had to become a temporary celibate."

"Oh yeah?"

"Oh, you don't even know these seasoned she-wolves! They're sweet and sympathetic while you're a popular poet but, as soon as it's in your power to give them a part, they'll drink all the juice out of you. Vampires have nothing on them! It's a nightmare!"

I set the glass aside, but not on the arm of the chair, on the floor next to the chair and asked:

"Then why did you agree to the work?"

Albert shrugged his shoulders.

"Interesting experience. New acquaintances. Decent money. And again, it isn't all so great as before with private performances."

"Why's that?" I asked in surprise. "Are you saying the admirers of astonishing wordplay have not yet returned to the capital from vacation?"

"They have, of course! The theater season is in full swing," Albert Brandt confirmed and ran his long thin fingers through his hair. "The problem is the reductionists. Those people have started to interrupt performances of *the illustrious*. There's no way for them to get into the Imperial Theater, but private guards simply don't tangle with them. They say a militant cell of reductionists has sprung up in the capital but, for now, all attacks on the *illustrious* are written off by the police as anarchist crimes."

The news grated on me unpleasantly. It was all wrong. So, I clarified:

"Is this all because of the death of the Empress?"

"Yes, the old bat would quickly bring them all to heel," the poet nodded. "But Duke Logrin is too big a politician for decisive action. He's a proponent of compromises and tries to agree with everyone. However, he only became regent due to compromises. And they say that the coalition providing him the majority of votes in the Imperial Council may collapse at any moment, if it hasn't already."

"That's a bit too complex for me," I sighed.

Would the recovery of Crown Princess Anna be a boon to the Empire, or would it lead to a further growth in tensions? I didn't know and hadn't particularly considered that factor. In any case, none of that depended on me now. I had managed to return Elizabeth-Maria to life, but the succubus possessed her own strength. I just had to give it an initial impulse, kickstart the fly wheel. But handling the Princess's ailment would be incomparably more difficult. There was no way around it without my lost *illustrious talent.*

Albert walked out of the armchair to the divan, lit a hookah and started puffing on the carved elephant-bone mouthpiece.

"Let's not talk of sad things!" he declared,

releasing a long stream of fragrant smoke toward the ceiling. "The health of my dear wife has surprisingly gone on the mend, and she is totally fervent with energy, a font of new ideas!"

I looked at the poet with interest.

"What did I miss?"

"You? Nothing," Albert laughed. "The conversation was *tête-à-tête*. Behind closed doors. And do you know what my better half said at the culmination of our... uhhh... conversation?"

"How would I?"

"She wants to fly!"

"What, excuse me?" I figured I must have misheard.

"She feels drawn to the sky," Brandt declared. "The sky, Leo! Airplanes! Dirigibles, she said, are for boring old men!"

"The result of her fever, must be. It will pass."

"Well, I doubt that. Once she's got something in her head, she won't back down."

"But an airplane? A woman pilot? Balderdash!"

Albert laughed:

"You haven't seen her new hairstyle yet! Now that will be a furor, when she shows herself in public!" He grabbed the hookah mouthpiece, drew on it and exhaled, saying judiciously: "But in light of the premier of my play, a little scandal won't hurt. I should add, you know, some peppercorns..."

"Don't burn yourself," I warned him.

"You're advising me from the heights of your life experience?" the poet cheered up. "Leo, it's already eleven o'clock, allow me an immodest question, why haven't you gone to bed yet? What circumstance darkened the reunion of two loving hearts?"

"I cannot stand," I answered calmly.

"You fought, and now you think Liliana has locked the bedroom door from inside? You're afraid you'll knock, and she won't answer?"

I looked gloomily at my friend, then with a heavy sigh admitted:

"That's exactly right."

"And you're planning to spend the whole night here in hopes that you'll be forgiven and called to her bed?"

"Yes."

"It's time to grow up, Leo," Albert Brandt shook his head. "You need to learn to smooth out discord. Go and ask forgiveness. It doesn't matter what for, it doesn't matter who's at fault. Just make the first move. This chair won't be going anywhere."

I just sighed and wrapped myself tighter in the robe. A chill came over me.

"Are you afraid?" The poet had my number.

I didn't know the answer to his question.

Was I afraid of destroying my relationship with Lily and causing her pain?

I was afraid yes, but now out of habit, without the former sharpness. I mean, Liliana attracted me no less than before, I just couldn't hold back the fear, to the point my hands sweated, my knees shook, and I went mute. It was like I was watching this all from a different perspective.

Before, I had been sold short by a lack of confidence in my own powers and ability to abstract myself but now, I would be happy to put that all back, so I could feel all the fullness of life, but I couldn't.

That damned electroshock therapy...

"Go to bed," Albert advised me.

I got up from the chair with effort and was quickly set upon by vertigo. My legs became cotton, my ears started ringing, and the chill gave way to a fire. Sweat ran down my back. My bones and joints were spinning, my muscles were tearing in pain. And I hadn't the slightest confidence that I would be able to lay down tonight without my already customary injection of morphine.

"Do you need help?" Albert asked compassionately. "You're white as death."

"No need! I just sat for too long," I said with a crooked smile, peeling myself off the back of the chair and heading out of the guest room. "Good night!"

"It's the second door after the bathroom!" the poet told me.

He didn't have to warn me, there was only one room in the corridor with its light on. The uneven luster of its nightlight peeked out into the darkness under the door.

I was leaning heavily on the wall and stood that way for some time, but not too long. My knees were giving out, forcing me to gather my resolve, push the door and walk through. Liliana, having changed her dress for a nighty, was lying in bed and reading a book; the light of the electric lamp over the bed cut painfully into my eyes, which had grown accustomed to the gloom.

"Lily!" I pressed out of myself and licked my dried-out lips, not knowing how to start the conversation.

She set the book on the bedside table and sighed.

"Go to sleep, Leo. You don't have a face on!"

"I can't argue with that," I muttered, walking around the bed and throwing my robe on it, sitting down on the firm mattress with a prolonged moan.

"Good heavens!" Liliana gasped behind me. "That scar wasn't there before!"

"It was, of course," I answered and tried to lie down, but my girlfriend held me back.

"No, not that one! On your spine, a bit above the base!" Liliana looked harder and easily sniffed out my lie. "The wound is still healing! And that is the trace of a bullet wound! Leo, were you shot in the back?"

It would have been stupid to deny the obvious.

"Indeed I was," I sighed and slowly lowered down on my pillow.

"By who?"

"I don't know."

I felt another chill, and pulled the comforter over me, at the same time hiding the bruises on my ribs.

"Leo, what if the bullet had hit you in the heart? You would have died!" Liliana shivered. "And with a damaged spine, you could have been left paralyzed for the rest of your life!"

"I know," I sighed. "I know. But none of it depended on me. It just happened to come together like that. And, as you see, I wasn't paralyzed."

Liliana sat up in bed next to me and asked with reproach:

"Why didn't you send me notice?"

"I couldn't."

"How do you mean?"

I covered the girl's palm with my hand and slightly clenched my fingers.

"Lily, I really couldn't. The wound was too serious, and I still haven't fully recovered."

"I could have helped!"

"I know. But the bullet really did damage my spine. I was paralyzed for some time. I didn't have any documents, no one knew who I was, and I couldn't tell anyone myself."

"Albert went to all the hospitals!"

"He didn't think to go to Gottlieb Burckhardt. And he wouldn't have been let in."

"You were placed in Gottlieb Burckhardt?" Liliana was struck. "But why?!"

"I was sent for forced treatment. As you understand, I couldn't object. But it turned out for the best. The electroshock therapy put me back on my feet. And I came back as soon as I could."

"And your relatives?"

"They helped me get out of the clinic," I answered diffusely, pulling Lily to me and kissing her. "Let's sleep!"

But Liliana wasn't thinking of calming down.

Returning my kiss, she suddenly dove under the comforter and led her hand over my chest. My heart was skipping beats. The girl's fingers were sliding over my skin as if on bare nerves. I was thirsting for it to continue but, at the same time, I was afraid. And that was tearing my soul to pieces.

"I missed you so, Leo!" Liliana whispered and, for a minute I thought her colorless gray eyes were burning brighter than the lamp at the bedside.

"I missed you too, dear."

"But I missed you more..."

Her feminine fingers slid from my chest to my stomach, and I smiled in torment.

"I don't think I'll be able to do much in that regard today."

But Liliana kept kissing my chest, gradually going lower and leading with her hand.

"Please, it's no use!" I gasped out hoarsely, feeling the locks of her black hair tickle my skin.

"Calm down, dear. I know what I'm doing!" Liliana called back and fell silent, not ceasing in her attempts to rouse me. Very soon, I understood that the light finger touches that had seemed to be playing on my bare nerves were nothing in comparison with these new sensations. And now I wanted just one thing: for this to never end. What was more, I was shivering from just the thought of the inevitable finale.

But it wasn't that ambrosial fear that unbound my tongue at all. No, I simply realized that, if I didn't tell Liliana about myself now, I'd never get the chance.

And there's little that kills feeling so quickly as skeletons in the closet.

"You want to know about my relatives, Lily?" I exhaled hoarsely. "Alright then, listen up..."

5

I TOLD HER everything. Everything that was relevant to me.

I didn't consider it proper to reveal other peoples' secrets. Some secrets don't kill relationships, they kill people with loose lips. I didn't tell Liliana anything about the Princess's phantom heart, or about where the scars on my chest had come from. But in every other regard, I was absolutely open with her for the first time since we'd met.

And in the end, I felt at ease. Really.

However, there were also purely physiological reasons for that.

"Now you can sleep," Lily sleepily purred into my ear, embracing me and dozing off before I even managed to answer.

I reached for the switch and turned out the light. My heart was beating unevenly, but the girl's measured breathing had already calmed me down, serving as a metronome and setting a rhythm.

And even so, I couldn't get a wink of sleep. Total nonsense was crawling into my head. Fears stole up imperceptibly at night, undetectable but punishing. I felt sick in my soul and full of sorrow, so I couldn't understand how long I'd busted my brains over this.

After all, everything was alright. Why worry? Could this really all have been from missing a morphine injection?

I didn't tell my girlfriend about the narcotics, supposing that I would manage that pernicious habit without her help. But would I? However, I simply had no other way...

LILIANA WAS BREATHING measuredly in her sleep; I was lying next to her and just couldn't doze off. And only when I heard twelve measured strikes of the clock on the wall, somehow unexpectedly, I fell into a nightmare in one fell swoop.

I didn't drift off, I just fell. I didn't even change positions. As I had been lying on my back, so I continued lying. Only now it wasn't the soft mattress under me, but the harsh surface of the gurney. And my soul was again cut by its squeaky wheel.

Squeak. Squeak. Squeak.

I was led down a hall with closed doors; the face of the man pushing the gurney was lost in darkness. I couldn't see it at all.

And still, I couldn't move or squeeze a single word out. I was paralyzed again. I was back at Gottlieb Burckhardt. The realization of that fact pierced my heart with a red-hot needle, and I would have died on the spot, but the universe had completely different plans for me. Gradually, an orange glow came over the corridor, and its uneven reflection lit up the orderly's face. It was Maestro Marlini, and his eyes were dancing with the fires of the underworld.

"Welcome to hell!" he broke down laughing.

I threw my head back and saw that the corridor ended with a crematorium furnace but, just before the dead hypnotist rolled the cart into the fire, I was thrown out of the nightmare as it tore to pieces.

I WOKE UP and spent some time lying on the bed with my heart beating feverishly, greedily sucking air into my wide-open mouth, but as soon as I started to calm down, I suddenly heard a familiar squeaking sound.

"The dead orderlies have come for my soul!" a maddening thought flickered up, but I immediately threw it out of my head.

The squeaking, meanwhile, didn't go anywhere.

I got out of bed, took the Webley-Fosbery from the pocket of the robe on the chair and listened, but no. The squeaking was real and wasn't just in my head. It seemed like something was squeaking measuredly somewhere on the first floor of the manor.

Burglars?

The weakness that had occupied me all evening left me. My legs were no longer giving out, and my arms were not shivering, so I threw on the robe, pulled on the belt and carefully glanced out into the corridor. After the electroshock therapy, my night vision had grown noticeably weaker, but the streetlights peeking in through the windows were enough to make sure there was no one in the corridor.

Squeezing the revolver under my armpit, I cocked it in a sharp motion, but still the metallic clink sounded out in the silence of the dark house like the striking of a smith's hammer.

Freezing in place for an instant, I overcame my lack of confidence and moved toward the stairs. I should have raised the alarm, but the hubbub that would have caused would most likely allow the unknown malefactor to hide, and I wanted to catch him red handed.

Who was he and why had he come? That was what I intended to find out, carefully going down the steep stairs to the first floor. The strange squeaking led me to a back corridor, I turned the corner and saw the store room door thrown wide-open.

Someone had decided to dig in the things from my family mansion? Not a thieving servant, right? And the squeaking, was that an attempt to break a lock?

That story didn't seem convincing, so I grabbed my revolver with both hands and walked to the door... and turned to stone when I saw eyes shining in the darkness.

"Can't sleep?" the Beast asked and again drew his kitchen knife over a sharpening stone. Sque-e-eak!

I was thrown, while the dark figure in the floor-length cloak stepped into the corridor and showed me his knife:

"Boy, just look what I found!"

I took a step back but not fast enough. A blinding spark tore off the edge of the rusty blade and hit me in the arm. My head started spinning, and I fell down on my knees, feeling my heart quiver in my chest.

"Bugger!" the albino barked, jumping back into the depths of the storeroom.

He melted into a cloud of gray smoke for a moment, and the passing unreality was not at all illusory: the carving knife slipped through his clawed fingers, and the Beast caught it only just above the floor.

"Stay away from me!" I ordered, catching my breath.

"Boy, what is this nonsense happening to you?" the albino was taken aback.

I got up from my knees and leaned heavily on the wall.

"You have too much power in you, and you cannot hold it inside. Don't get close to me anymore! Got it? Stay away!"

"That's it! The power is pulling me toward you! After all, you have also tried the heart of a *fallen one*!" the Beast realized, snapping his clawed fingers. "She recognized you as a family member!"

"Stay away from me!"

The albino melted into a wide smile with his whole toothy maw and made a little step, reducing the distance between us.

"Boy, what if you took the power from me, and

put it into yourself?"

"Back!" I commanded, because I simply was physically unable to equal such a burst of energy.

"Bugger!" the Beast grinned in reply. "Why should I listen to you, Leo?"

"If the power of a *fallen one* eats me, it's the end of you no matter what! So, stop being stupid and let me fix everything. I'll think something up!"

"Tick tock, boy," the albino whispered. "Tick tock! Time is slipping away."

I extended him the revolver.

"Here, blow your own brains out, if you're so impatient."

"Nice try!" the Beast chuckled, wrapping himself in the cloak and walking down the corridor, continuing to sharpen the blade of the carving knife as he went. The very same knife that was used to cut out my heart the first time.

"Wait!" I shouted.

The albino turned.

"Yes?"

"After all, you're just an image from my head," I said. "In reality, you only exist there. Could someone else have gotten into my consciousness?"

"Ah, you've finally gone batty!"

"Long ago. Back when I invented you."

The Beast snorted.

"Who exactly is bothering you, boy?"

I gathered my spirits and admitted:

"Maestro Marlini."

The grimace of disgust turned the already

fearsome countenance of the albino into the grotesque snout of a stone gargoyle.

"You should never have killed him," the Beast announced.

"That's not an answer!"

"Leo, you have such emptiness in your head, that I can hear the wind blowing between your ears. There's a lonely little boy locked in a prison cell in there and no one else. Bugger! Even I ran away as soon as I was able!" the albino threw out and walked away.

"Creep!" I exhaled at his back.

"I heard you!" came a quiet giggle in reply, then the Beast dissolved in the shadows, as if he didn't exist at all.

I put the revolver back in my robe pocket and glanced at the storeroom where the albino had thrown the open boxes and trunks all around. In one of them, there was a silver frame with a photograph of my mother; I felt I should take it with me, but I didn't touch anything else. I just closed the storeroom door and went up to the second floor.

LILIANA WAS SLEEPING soundly. I placed the frame with the photograph on the vanity table, threw the robe on the armchair and carefully got under the comforter, as not to wake Lily. After meeting my imaginary friend, I felt beside myself, but the nervousness didn't stop me from falling asleep. I was no longer afraid of nightmares. In fact, I joyfully took shelter in the gentle embrace of dreams, fleeing the problems and cares of reality, which were quickly piling up.

In my dream, I was standing in the middle of an endless steppe. Everywhere my eye could see, there were red poppies bobbing up and down to the rustling of a light breeze. My head was intoxicated by the thick aroma of the flowers. I wanted to lie on the ground and stare into the endless blue sky but, before I managed to manifest that desire, I heard a woman's voice ring out behind me:

"Pretty, isn't it?"

I turned sharply and found myself face to face with a young girl in a long dress that seemed inappropriate for a walk on the steppe. A certain lack of elegance in her open and pretty face was more than made up for by the charm of youth, but the stranger with beaming bright fiery eyes didn't seem like a beauty to me.

Wait! Stranger?!

I remembered her from the newspapers; I closed my robe a bit tighter and bowed my head.

"Your Highness..."

"Come off it, cousin!" Crown Princess Anna laughed sonorously, fixing her hair which had been disheveled by the wind. "This is just a dream. Leave the etiquette for meetings in the palace."

Remembering how my last invitation had ended, I didn't exactly want to meet the heiress to the throne, but I didn't voice my doubts and stayed silent, waiting to see what would happen.

The maid of honor and oracle had brought us

together, now the Dreamer and I didn't see one another as faceless silhouettes, but the Princess didn't make use of her new ability to look at me. All her attention was drawn by the poppy field. Or did she simply not know how to begin the conversation?

That thought ran down my spine with an unpleasant chill.

My rescue had obligated me to one of the most powerful people on the planet, and the requests of the powerful of were not known to be modest. What service would be demanded of me?

But the crown princess didn't voice any requests. Instead of that she led her hand over the field and repeated her question:

"Pretty, isn't it?"

"Yes," I answered in one word.

"It's from a painting," Anna explained. "I've never left New Babylon and know the world only through photographs and paintings."

"Such is the other side of power."

"Not at all," the Princess disagreed. "It's all the fault of my weak health. And I am immeasurably grateful to you, cousin, for my salvation. I simply cannot voice the shame I feel..."

"No need!" I frowned, trying to end this unpleasant conversation quickly. "What happened wasn't your fault, or mine. Other people made that decision. You have nothing to thank me for or reproach yourself over."

"I do!" Anna objected and, for the first time I heard authoritative intonations cut through in her voice, like one would expect to hear in the voice of the heiress to the Imperial throne.

I should have been expecting that. Even if the Princess's grandfather had named himself Emperor, power changes people somewhat more reliably and quickly than many generations of marriage between close relatives.

Albert Brandt had once said something good about that: "the nobility becomes morally depraved long before they begin to be born physically abominable."

"As you say, your Highness," I bowed my head before the heiress to the throne and, at the same time, turned my back to the wind, which was picking up. The sky went dark. The poppies bent in waves like a stormy red sea.

"I owe you my life, but I still must demand a service from you for breaking you out of the clinic," the Princess continued. "I simply have no one else to turn to. While I have been in this coma, even my most loyal people have not had the determination to act. And if I delay any longer, the Empire will fall apart into separate provinces and a total war of everyone against everyone will begin."

"Duke Logrin cannot manage?"

Anna laughed evilly, and strong emotions formed on the face of my cousin in the most surprising fashion. It became more vibrant, making it uncommonly attractive.

"The Duke can't see beyond his own nose!" the Princess threw out. "He's only concerned with keeping his position and so he'll agree with anyone for anything just to maintain the status-quo! He simply ignores anything that doesn't fit into his worldview! Berlin, Vienna and Rome are making a secret pact, and that is going without consequences! The volume of diplomatic correspondence between the governments of England, France and Russia is growing by many times, but no one is paying any mind to that. The Persians lay claim to Constantinople, the Egyptians to Gibraltar and Arabia! There's unrest in India, the New World is straying further and further from the metropole. Can Duke Logrin manage? The answer to that question is obvious. No, he cannot!"

The agitation that overcame the heiress to the throne rolled through the dream with a heavy wind, nearly knocking me off my feet as leaden clouds raced across the sky with a dizzying speed.

"What do you want from me?!" I shouted, striving to overcome the ghastly howl but then, the sky split in two with a blindingly bright light, as if a gigantic fireball was racing overhead. And silence came over immediately.

"Oh no!" Anna exhaled, jumping over me and hitting me on the cheek. "Wake up, cousin! Wake up at once!"

I simply didn't manage. The divided sky opened wide and a rain of burning sulfur began lashing down on the steppe. The poppies burned up in an instant, and a sea of fire spread out around us. Red-hot air and bitter smoke burned my lungs. My flesh held out against the onslaught of liquid fire a bit longer, but the agony drew on and on while the fire ate through my very consciousness.

The pain knocked me out of the dream; I woke up and launched into a heart-rending coughing fit due to the disgusting stink of burning flesh and sulfur smoke. My pillow and sheet were soaked through with sweat, big drops were rolling down my cheeks and forehead, but I simply didn't have the strength to move and dry them with the edge of the sheet.

Meanwhile, a fragment of the dream was just spinning over and over in my head, like a film clip. It was the blackened burning lips of the Princess forming just one word: "Kill!"

"Kill!" she said soundlessly, then a flame burst from my cousin's wide-open mouth.

The Crown Princess didn't have enough time to say anything else, but that no longer played any role. The name of the victim would have to be voiced in our next meeting, and I didn't see any way to refuse the Princess's request.

I gave my word and was obliged to keep it. Or die. There wasn't a third option.

PART FOUR

ARROW

Lenses And Maxim's Patented Silencer

1

A PERSON CANNOT LIVE without water, air and sleep. That is an objective reality, and nothing can be done with that.

I have known people who were afraid to sleep. Some were tormented by nightmares, others were simply afraid to wake up, but none of them could overcome their nature. Sooner or later, regardless of liters of strong coffee and lines of cocaine, they gave in and fell asleep. Some while walking. Others, forever.

I didn't have a single chance to hold out against sleep forever, and I was perfectly aware of that. The Princess would certainly reach me, if not tonight, then the next but still, from the very morning, I didn't even close my eyes once.

However, that didn't require any particular effort. Whether that was evidence of jitters, morphine withdrawal or electroshock therapy, I could not say but I still didn't feel even the slightest call to drift off. I simply lied there next to Liliana, listening to her measured breathing and trying not to think about new troubles and problems.

It didn't come easily.

Then Lily turned toward me and smiled.

"Your eyes are different, Leo."

I put on a careless look and led my palm over my unevenly cut hair.

"Not only my eyes."

"Well, we can get you a haircut!"

Liliana kissed me, threw on a robe and ran to

the bathroom to get herself in order. I loafed in bed for a bit, then carefully got to my feet and listened to my own feelings. My ribs heart and muscles ached but, other than that, nothing was particularly troubling me. My head wasn't even spinning. And much to my surprise, my appetite was back.

I put on the robe and went after Liliana, but I wasn't able to wash up in peace. My girlfriend told me to get undressed and sit on a stool in the middle of the room, arming herself with a comb and scissors.

"It's easier to go to a barber!" I protested, shivering in cold, but Lily was in no mood to listen.

"It's five minutes' work," she said picking up the comb and starting in on the uneven tufts of hair. "As it is, I cannot look at you without tearing up!"

I just sighed.

Soon, my skin started to itch from the loose hairs, but every little attempt I made to scratch myself, Lily would shush me and demand I sit calmly.

"You know, Leo," she said at the end, "I want to tell my parents, but I'm not sure if it will be a comfortable conversation..."

"Why not?" I didn't understand the reason for her strange indecision.

"You just got back, and they'll probably ask me to stay at home. I'll have to spend a day there, maybe even two."

"Don't worry," I stroked my girlfriend's hand. "If you want, I can go with you, but not over night. I need to get my affairs in order."

"I understand that." Liliana flicked the scissors and suddenly giggled: "You're a man of royal blood, now!"

"Not formally, no," I objected and started slightly regretting my openness last night. "Clement named himself Emperor, and his brother became Duke, he was never part of the Imperial family."

"Doesn't matter to me," Lily smiled, setting aside the scissors and inquiring: "Well, how do you like it?"

I got up from the stool and looked in the mirror to discover that my new haircut made me look like either a new army recruit, or a stevedore. The short bristles rose just a bit from my head, but even the most skilled hair dresser wouldn't have managed to do anything nicer.

"Not bad at all. You have a talent!"

"You flatter me shamelessly," Liliana didn't take the praise seriously. "And grow out your hair before showing yourself to my parents. They're people of severe gaze."

"Especially your mother," I sighed.

"You're biased against her!" my girlfriend reproached me and left the bathroom.

I washed up, brushed my teeth and shaved but, as soon as I went into the corridor, Liliana, who'd managed to get into her dressing gown, pulled me down to the first floor.

"Let's go. Mary is making breakfast, and we shouldn't keep her waiting."

"But..."

"No 'buts,' Leo!" Lily cut me off. "And don't worry, Mrs. Hardy took the weekend off, so there's no one home but us."

I had to walk to the kitchen, where Elizabeth-Maria was holding court in a long skirt with an apron thrown over top of a blouse. There wasn't a trace left of her long locks; the succubus was sporting a short boy's cut, which was surprisingly appropriate for her thin face and sharpened features.

When we entered, Elizabeth-Maria tore herself from the stove and opened her eyes wide.

"Original!" was all she said.

I wanted to advise her to look in the mirror, but I overpowered myself and sat in silence at the table next to the window that went into the closed inner courtyard.

"How do you like Leopold's new haircut, Mary?" Liliana inquired, setting two pieces of white bread in an electric toaster.

"You have a talent," Elizabeth-Maria repeated my words and took a pan of bacon off the fire.

"Come on, you're making fun of me!" Lily was offended.

"Not at all, dear," the succubus smiled softly. "Yesterday, Leo had a horrible nightmare on his head, but now just look at him. He's a respectable person! You'd think he just got typhus..."

The girls broke down laughing, I shook my head.

"And just when did you two get so close?"

Liliana set the plate of omelet and bacon before

me, then brought some pieces of toast and said:

"Well, Mary and I found lots of shared interests."

I looked with doubt at the succubus.

"For example?"

"The cultural heritage of India," Elizabeth-Maria said with a mysterious smile.

"You're interested in Indian culture? Are you serious?" I didn't believe her. "Lily lived in Calcutta but what do you know about India?"

The succubus led her tongue over her upper lip and smiled craftily.

"The Kama Sutra is arguably one of the most ancient tracts about sensual relations between man and woman. Mainly, we discussed that."

"Oh!" is all I could squeeze out of myself. I turned to Liliana.

Under my gaze, my girlfriend grew embarrassed, turned beet red and jumped out of the kitchen.

Elizabeth-Maria laughed uncontrollably.

"It's nice to know that our discussions weren't in vain and found a practical application. You can only be glad, Leo. You're in good... hands."

I looked at my breakfast with doubt and got up from the table.

"Well, at least someone hasn't changed," I muttered, leaving the kitchen.

It was no effort to find Liliana: she was sitting on the bed in the kitchen huffing and puffing.

"What happened, dear?" I asked, sitting next to

her.

"What happened?!" Lily was taken aback and even lost the gift of speech for a moment in indignation. "Look who's asking!"

"What did I say?"

"Not what, but how! You couldn't just keep quiet? Mary understood everything!"

"Understood?" I sighed. "What exactly did she understand?"

"What I did last night!" Liliana faltered, blushed again and begged me: "Leo, please don't make me say it out loud!"

I didn't continue the conversation, just embraced my girlfriend and fell down on the bed.

"Don't! Stop!" Lily tried to escaple my embrace, but immediately giggled: "Leo, didn't you say you were in no state?!"

"That was yesterday!" I parried, covering her feminine neck in kisses. "What's more, you showed me the depths of my confusion clearly."

"Leo!"

"Alright, alright, I won't talk..."

2

WHEN WE WENT BACK down to the kitchen, our breakfast was already cold. Elizabeth-Maria graciously agreed to warm up the eggs and shot us a curious look but held back from acrid remarks.

After that, Lily remembered she'd called a cab and ran off to get her things. I decided not to stop her and stayed where I was, drinking tea.

Elizabeth-Maria poured herself a glass of wine, took a seat at the open window and placed a long cigarette in her holder.

"Yes, I completely forgot!" she shuddered, lighting her cigarette. "Thanks for the gift. I'm touched."

"Gift?" I didn't understand.

"Your grandfather's saber," the succubus explained, shaking off the ash into a porcelain dish and guessing. "Ah! That wasn't you!"

"Nope."

"You want the saber back?"

"Keep it," I said, shaking my head and guessing why the hell my imaginary friend had decided to give the succubus such a strange gift.

Had he just been trying to get under my skin, or was there something bigger hidden behind this gesture?

Anyway, I had more than enough to worry about already, and it was incomparably more important, so I decided to leave well enough alone.

A came at the front door, Elizabeth-Maria extinguished her cigarette and headed into the entryway. I didn't show myself in my housecoat and slippers, and stood behind a partition in the corridor, cocking my revolver just in case. But the weapon was unnecessary – it was just Liliana's cabby.

I helped my girlfriend bring her light little

suitcase down to the first floor and hugged her goodbye.

"See you soon," Lily whispered, then kissed me and ran outside.

Elizabeth-Maria locked the door behind her and looked me carefully from head to toe.

"Shall I tell you about the historic value of the Kama Sutra, or will we go straight to practice?" the succubus enquired.

"I'll refrain."

"Smart boy," Elizabeth-Maria burst out laughing, going up the stairs. "If Albert gets home before me, tell him not to worry. I'm going to the airfield!"

"To the airfield?" I asked, confused. "Are you serious?"

"More than."

With a heavy pant, I went up to the second floor and followed after the succubus.

"But why?"

"Routine kills!" Elizabeth-Maria answered, going through into her bedroom. "Sure, we were deprived of the joy of flight and lost the sky, but its memory lies dormant in my bloodstream. I want to reawaken it. Flying in an airplane – I'm sure that will be something special. Perhaps no worse than pleasures of the flesh. I haven't been feeling enough passion recently. I am a loyal wife, after all, Leo. I do not cheat on Albert."

The succubus unbuttoned her skirt and threw it to her feet, remaining in short panties with lacy fringes, and I went out into the corridor.

"Are you sure that's what you want?" I asked leaning against the wall. "Your lost power cannot be restored!"

"Don't rub salt into the wound!" the succubus called back sharply, hurt to the quick by my reply. "Do you think it was easy to part with such power so soon after acquiring it?"

"Flight will not help you forget about the loss."

"Leo, my dear! Even if I don't like it, the wife of a famous poet doing something so extravagant will certainly not be missed by the society page commentators. Albert could stand a bit of publicity and, if I can seduce one of the production participants, it will end in a duel. Although Albert is praised for the broadness of his worldview, he is in fact ghastly jealous."

"True soulmates," I chuckled and headed into Liliana's bedroom, but immediately turned back: "Who's taking you to the airfield?"

"Leo, you're behind the times!" Elizabeth-Maria laughed on her way into the corridor in a blouse and bicycle pants. In her hands, she was holding a short leather jacket. "Albert's commission for the performance in Montecalida was so shamelessly high, that he sent for a self-propelled steam carriage from the New World. I still haven't had the chance to try it out. Wanna come for a ride?"

"You know how to drive?"

"I'm full of hidden talents. Didn't you know?"

"I need to get dressed. Can you wait?"

"I'll be outside the carriage house. Leave through the back door."

I nodded and walked down the corridor, but as soon as I came up to the thrown-wide door of the bathroom, Elizabeth-Maria called out to me.

"Leo!" she cried.

"Yes?" I turned and, at that very instant, glass shattered, and something thudded dully into the wall at head level.

"Get down!" Elizabeth-Maria threw out abruptly and, as soon as I fell to the floor, I heard another thud.

I rolled away from the door, pressed myself against the wall and pulled the Webley-Fosbery from my robe pocket.

"Stay away from the windows!" I shouted to the succubus after that.

She just frowned and ducked into the bedroom, but immediately came back brandishing the saber.

"Leo, do you want to catch the gunman, or not?" she asked, running down the stairs.

It was a gunman precisely. The bullet holes in the walls didn't leave the slightest doubt.

I shouted a curse but peeled myself off the wall and darted after Elizabeth-Maria. Racing outside, we tore off at full speed toward the building across the street. I threw up my revolver, taking the windows in my sights, but couldn't make out any movement. Finally, under the very roof, I saw a dark spot.

Elizabeth-Maria ran into the mansion with saber drawn and pressed a sickly fellow to the wall midgait.

"Where is he?!" she growled. "Speak!"

"What are you talking about?!" the poor flabbergasted bastard was scared half to death.

I glanced at the board with a list of residents and hinted:

"The tenant from the third floor, windows street-side."

"Well then, of course..."

Confidence began to return to the man, but Elizabeth-Maria instantly cranked up the pressure:

"That pervert was watching me in the bathroom through a telescope. Where is he?!"

The manager froze with his jaw hanging down and I, hiding the revolver in my hand behind me, walked over to the stairs at the far end of the corridor.

"Where is he?" the succubus hissed out again

"He left!" the man came to his senses. And it wasn't even a resident, he just asked to take a look at the apartment!

I glanced at the back yard and hid my revolver in my robe pocket.

"Show us the apartment!" Elizabeth-Maria demanded, and as soon as the man started hesitating, she gave a sweet smile: "After all, you don't want me to make a scene, do you? Will we have to call the police?"

"But your s-saber..."

"That is a theater prop," I smiled. "So, do you want to read about this revolting incident in the papers, or can we smooth it over amicably?"

The last thing the manager wanted was for this to get out; he immediately stopped being stubborn and led us to the third floor. Elizabeth-Maria held me imperceptibly back on the stairway and reminded me:

"I didn't hear any shots."

"Me neither," I nodded, again taking my revolver out and hiding it behind my back.

"And the neighbors are not alarmed..."

"No, they are not."

That really was strange. Someone had been shooting at me, but no one had heard gunshots. How could that have been? I was immediately reminded of Bastian Moran's air rifle, and shivers started crawling up my spine. If the senior inspector had decided to take justice into his own hands, all that remained was to either flee the capital, or get ahead of him. And both options were fraught with utterly unneeded complications.

But as soon as we walked into the apartment, these suspicions dissolved all on their own. In the entryway, I could smell gun-smoke, and in the guest room it got even stronger. After running through all the rooms revolver in hand, I returned to the wide-open window, pressed an imaginary rifle to my shoulder and tried to imagine where the round casings might have flown. There was a sideboard against the wall. To look under it, I had to lie on the floor, but it was worth the bother. Right up against the skirting, I discovered a rifle casing of a very unusual caliber.

Thirty-two-twenty, Winchester. I had never

seen something like this before.

Stashing the bronze cylinder in my pocket, I returned to the manager in the corridor, who had already fully given into the succubus' charms and was barely aware of how loudly we'd broken into the apartment.

"Could you describe the man?" I asked him.

"A normal gentleman, a bit over forty," the geezer answered shortly, but Elizabeth-Maria's upset grimace instantly cleared his memory.

"Average height, gaunt, redheaded," the manager began listing features. "Glasses. He introduced himself as Roy Lloyd. His pronunciation was like an immigrant from the British Isles. Whether he was an Englishman, Scotsman, or Irishman, I cannot say."

"Was he carrying anything?"

"Just a tube case. He said he works as a draughtsman."

"Thank you, my sweet. You're simply a wonder," Elizabeth-Maria melted into a smoldering smile. When we started down the stairs, she asked: "Leo, what have you gotten yourself into this time?"

"Nothing."

"Someone was trying to kill you!"

"I have no idea who or why."

I went outside first, looked around cautiously and ran across the street.

"Your death would cause quite serious changes in my life, dear Leo!" Elizabeth-Maria reminded me, locking the entrance behind us. "So, just tell me what is going on! Please, don't make me figure it out on my own!"

I just shook my head and went up to the second floor. The bullet holes in the wall were barely noticeable, but it would have been simply impossible to not notice the broken window in the bathroom. I picked up a greenish shard from the floor and turned to the succubus.

"How could the gunman even see me?"

"First of all, you shouldn't be thinking about that, but how he even knew you were in this house!"

"True," I nodded, remembering the succubus' cry and asking: "What were you going to say when you called out my name before?"

"Some nonsense," Elizabeth-Maria shrugged her shoulders. "I was either going to hurry you along or tell you to dress in warmer clothes. I don't remember!"

"Your nonsense saved my life."

"And that makes me happy. I'm on your side, Leo."

"If you really want to help, get things in order before Mrs. Hardy comes back."

Elizabeth-Maria rolled her eyes and sighed sorrowfully.

"Come on, please!" I asked.

"Alright!" the succubus submitted. "But the self-propelled carriage is already at full steam, and I won't be myself if I cannot go into town today! Where were you going to go? I'll take you. Or you can clean up here on your own."

I thought over Elizabeth-Maria's ultimatum for a few seconds, then relented and waved a hand.

"Have it your way."

"Go down to the carriage-house. And don't go near the windows!"

"The gunman is already long gone!" I objected, but the first thing I did on walking into Liliana's bedroom was draw the curtains.

I didn't necessarily believe there would be a repeat attempt, but it was ghastly uncomfortable to feel like a target at a shooting range, not knowing if I was in the crosshairs or not.

3

IT DIDN'T TAKE MUCH TIME to get myself together. Liliana had brought my things from the hotel; my evening suit and vest were hanging in the closet, and I found the rest in a suitcase on the shelf. And it would have been nothing, but the light half-boots, so nice in the summer heat, were of little use in rainy October. I didn't have any other clothes, though.

I got dressed and stood next to the mirror, looking at my reflection and first of all decided to buy headwear. My hairstyle could only be described as a spot of bad luck.

I found my sunglasses among the things packed in the suitcase, the very same ones I'd bought once upon a time in the pawnshop, with scratched-up round lenses of dark glass. And although my eyes were no longer cut by the bright light of electric bulbs and there were dense clouds looming in the sky up above, I brought them with me.

And the revolver too. The huge Webley-Fosbery didn't fit in my pocket, and I had to stick it in the back of my pants although, unlike the low-profile government-model Colt, its drum pressed into the small of my back.

But there was no other way, I'd have to bear it.

ELIZABETH-MARIA was waiting for me outside the carriage house. I walked up to her, glanced at the gates and whistled in approval when I saw the low bright-red self-propelled carriage with two leather seats, one for the driver and one for the passenger. The headlights, axles and rims glistened with gilding. The front was adorned with the also gilded word: "Stanley."

"Climb in," Elizabeth-Maria told me, putting on her goggles.

"How well you drive this thing?" I asked in worry, doing as the succubus asked.

"It's much easier than taking out a person's brain without harming the skull," Elizabeth-Maria snorted light mindedly, pulling on the leather driving gloves and getting behind the wheel.

I sat down in the passenger seat, and the carriage-house was instantly filled with smoke, then the squat self-propelled carriage started off and rolled into the yard unexpectedly abruptly.

"Relax, Leo!" Elizabeth-Maria laughed. "Albert insisted I take lessons!"

That didn't calm me down one bit, but it was already too late to back out: the self-propelled carriage had driven out of the yard and was now bouncing on the uneven paving stones. While we were rolling down the deserted narrow alleys, everything was going fine. But after that, the roads were packed to the brim with carriages, carts and huge steam-trams. Elizabeth-Maria tacked between them, constantly lashing out with curses and slamming on the horn in rage. A few times, she only managed to avoid certain collisions at the very last moment. I don't even want to recall the curses that flew after us.

And that was with light rain sprinkling down from the heavens, so the gapers were all at home, and we didn't have to fear hitting pedestrians running across the road!

The weather really did leave something to be desired. The air was burning with a chill that was unusual for October, and the heavy clouds hanging over the city were sprinkling a fine rain. It was surprisingly easy to breathe though: the strong western wind had finally driven the smog from the city, and the drizzle brought the dust down to earth.

"Shall I wait for you?" Elizabeth-Maria inquired after stopping the self-propelled carriage at my attorney's office.

"No!" I refused, getting onto the causeway. "Never again!"

During the trip, I had gotten nauseous, and the earth underfoot was whirling. What was more, the whole way, raindrops had been flying in under the canvas top of the self-propelled carriage, and I had gotten quite soaked. Unlike Elizabeth-Maria, I didn't have a leather jacket.

"Weakling!" the succubus laughed and rolled off at high speed.

I looked at the dark gray sky with disgust and hurried to take shelter from the rain in the manor. As I walked, I waved a hand to the concierge and went up to my attorney's office.

"Viscount?!" he asked in surprise. "Has something happened?"

I walked over to the window, looked at the gray street and shook my head.

"No, everything is in order. I need the travelling bag from the safe."

"Are you certain?"

"Completely."

My attorney obviously hesitated, then suggested:

"Shall I call you a cab?"

"No," I turned away from the window, not having noticed anyone suspicious outside. "I just need the traveling bag."

The lawyer unwillingly unlocked the safe and took out the new leather traveling bag with my rainy-day nest egg – one hundred thousand francs in cash.

"Viscount, are you sure everything is fine?"

"Absolutely," I confirmed. "It's time for me to

go. Urgent meeting."

"At least take an umbrella!"

I didn't refuse the umbrella.

Outside, it was still sprinkling rain, and my light summer shoes would soon soak through, so I had to turn onto a wide boulevard with bright displays in the glass shop windows. I went into the first readymade footwear store I came across, acquired a pair of sturdy autumn boots. In a nearby shop, with diffuse mannequins in the display, I tried to acquire a cloak of light rubberized fabric, but they didn't have any in my size. I ended up having to go with a raglan overcoat, sewn of dense black leather. The Webley-Fosbery fit perfectly in its side pocket.

In the end, I had turned into either a retired military doctor, or a private service courier. My derby hat looked quite awkward with the rest of my style so, I decided I should also pick up a peaked cap.

WHEN THE RAIN FINALLY calmed down, I closed the umbrella and began using it as a cane. There was no affectation in it. Walking all this way had exhausted me beyond all measure.

I was headed to Alexander Dyak's but this time, deciding not to tempt fate, I avoided the Roman Bridge. I walked to Leonardo-da-Vinci-Platz right across a square, where the rain had dispersed the street vendors and students of the Emperor's academy. The wind casually fluttered through the wet branches of its sad trees.

On my way to the inventor's shop, I peeked into

the nearby weapon store and bought a Cerberus, three quick-remove clips and a box of rounds. The assortment of titanium-bladed folding knives, unfortunately, left something to be desired. They couldn't offer me anything appropriate.

After leaving the store, I walked across the square with a monument to Leonardo da Vinci, into the shop Mechanisms and Rarities and pushed on the unlocked door. There were no visitors, though someone's wet footprints were glistening on the floor.

The old inventor gave a squint to focus his poor vision, recognized me and threw up his hands.

"Leopold Borisovich!" he gasped with unhidden astonishment. "I thought I'd totally lost you!"

"You don't object?" I pointed to the door.

"Close it! Of course, close it!"

I bolted the door, shook the raindrops from my peaked cap and placed the leather traveling bag before me on the counter.

"What is that?" Dyak got on guard.

"One hundred thousand francs. Hold them here for now."

"Has something happened? Can I help?"

"Nothing happened, nothing at all. I was just taught not to put all my eggs in one basket. If someone comes and asks about a traveling bag, give it to them. If you need cash, use it as a mutual aid fund."

"Well, my finances aren't so constrained yet! I could even loan you a couple thousand myself!" the old man laughed. "Your comrade Miro recently ordered a shipment of incendiary white phosphorus bombs, which gave me quite a windfall."

"I'm glad for you. But still, keep the possibility in mind."

The shop owner coughed into a kerchief and suggested:

"You want some tea? It's dog's weather outside."

"I'd be very much obliged!" I latched onto his offer not only because of the bad weather, but my banal tiredness.

"Come into my workshop. The tea is already brewed."

In the back room, I put the cloak on the coatrack and sat down on a wooden stool at the workbench, resting my overexerted legs. I was afraid that if I sat in the somewhat softer and more comfortable armchair against the wall, I might not be able to stand back up.

"Alexander, just don't tell me you have abandoned your scientific pursuits!" I remarked in surprise, having noticed a certain desolation in the workshop.

"Not at all!" the old man laughed, setting the teapot on the workbench, along with glasses and a basket of cookies. He went to get some boiling water and gave a conspiratorial wink. "It's just that my research requires quiet and privacy."

"Are you working in the basement?" I guessed, pouring myself some tea. "I hope you haven't dragged another infernal beast here for experiments?"

Alexander Dyak went gloomy.

"Having a creature to experiment on would speed up my research quite a bit," he sighed. "But, no. You're right, it's too dangerous."

"You can say that again..." I shivered when he reminded me of the now long-ago exorcism of the poltergeist.

The inventor smoothed over his gray hair and held tight on the glass of hot tea with his old chilly fingers.

"I'm sure I'm on the threshold of yet another discovery," the old man said, "but I might just not have enough time to finish the work. My health isn't what it used to be."

"Come off it!" I didn't take these words seriously. "It's just a fall cough. What are you working on?"

"Electromagnetic radiation with long waves between the infrared and radio spectra," Alexander Dyak answered none too clearly. "They have a surprising ability to transmit energy to substances composed of bipolar molecules."

I didn't understand a single thing in the inventor's explanation and, in order to hide my confusion, finished my tea and took a shortbread biscuit from the little basket.

"Bipolar molecules?" I asked after that.

Alexander understood the reason for my confusion and explained:

"Water, fats, sugar."

"Very interesting, probably"

"Just not to you!" Dyak laughed.

I nodded, took another sip of tea and enquired:

"Alexander, what do you know about the workings of the human brain?"

The inventor batted his eyelids in surprise.

"I'm afraid that question is outside my competency," he admitted after a brief pause.

I wasn't at all surprised by such an answer, but it upset me quite a bit. I had been nourishing the hope that the inventor could help me uncover the essence of Professor Berliger's experiments. Now those hopes had been dashed.

"Tell me what's bothering you, Leopold Borisovich," Dyak suggested. "Tell me, and, perhaps, I'll be able to recommend a good specialist from the medical faculty of the academy."

I didn't refuse to speak, and briefly told him everything I could remember about the magnetic stimulation of the cortex of my brain, electroshock therapy and the effect of the concoction but, in the end, the inventor just shook his head.

"Medicine's not my cup of tea," Alexander said, taking the electric torch off the shelf and shining it first in one of my eyes, then the other. "A change in pigmentation really has taken place, but I have a hard time answering how that might be connected with your *illustrious talent.*"

"They were talking about magnetic radiation."

"There must be a scientific basis," Dyak threw out. "We cannot afford to act haphazardly in such situations. I could send you to the medical faculty, but I'm not sure any of my acquaintances will be able to get understand the essence of the experiments conducted on you. For that, we need at least laboratory notes. Better speak with the professor. He'll probably agree to work with you. He doesn't need the notoriety."

I finished my tea and threw up my hands.

"That's just what I'll do. Can I call from here, Alexander?"

"Naturally!"

"And hide the money in the safe," I pointed to the traveling bag, getting up from the stool.

"Ah, I've got holes in my head!" Alexander slapped himself on the forehead. "Old age is not a joy!"

"You're being too hard on yourself," I smiled and went into the front room, where there was a telephone on the counter.

I called Ramon. He was at work.

"Is everything in order?" I asked my former partner.

"Well, if you're calling, that must mean no," I heard in reply.

And I couldn't argue with that. I told him about this morning's attempt on me and asked him to send someone to keep watch over my house, and maybe even rent an apartment in the manor opposite for a while.

"Money is no object," I advised Ramon. "And as for something else, I need to get in touch with Professor Berliger. It would be best to do so at his home. Can you do that?"

"Am I to understand you haven't read the morning papers?" Miro sighed. "Read the papers, Leo. And call me after that. If you want."

Ramon hung up, and I placed the telephone back on the hook. My former partner's tone had me extremely on edge. I returned to the back room and picked up the top paper from the stack on the workbench.

"Has something happened?" Alexander Dyak looked at me in worry.

"Don't pay it any mind," I waved it off, smoothing out the yellowing sheets.

It was a *Capital Times* from today, but the first page was totally dedicated to political news, while the second had a huge analysis of the schism in the Sublime Electricity movement. Only when I'd reached the crime blotter did I understand the reason for Ramon Miro's worry.

That column had a report about a fire in one of the buildings of the Gottlieb Burckhardt psychiatric hospital. It reported the death of Doctor Ergant and several orderlies; Professor Berliger's body had not been found by the time of writing, but the search of the collapsed building was still ongoing. Beyond the staff, patients had also suffered in the fire, some of whom had managed to escape, and the police had undertaken immediate measures to search for and detain runaways. There was nothing about the cause of the fire.

"Devil!" I sighed out soundlessly.

I had threatened to burn Doctor Ergant alive, and just a day later there was a fire. I would hardly manage to convince Ramon that this was a mere coincidence. What was more, I personally didn't believe in coincidences. The reason for such a horrible event was absolutely certain to have been my *illustrious talent*. Either Doctor Ergant had gone mad in fear in the solitary cell, or Professor Berliger had decided to cover up the tracks of his unnatural experiments after getting scared by my threats.

I remained as before, that was good. What was bad was that now no one could tell me how to get my brain to function normally again. The scientific approach couldn't help, because there simply wasn't time for prolonged studies. Now I had to count on just myself.

"Is everything in order, Leopold Borisovich?" Dyak inquired.

I threw the newspaper on the workbench and smiled.

"Absolutely, Alexander!"

"You seem anxious. And you've gotten very thin. How is your health?"

"The emaciation is just because of my recent wound, nothing serious."

I took my leather cloak from the rack, clipped the peaked cap on my head and asked:

"May I use the back door?"

"Naturally!" Dyak threw his arms wide and reminded me: "Your umbrella?"

"I'll pick it up next time."

"It's raining."

"I'm not made of sugar, I won't melt," I joked slipping through the cracked-open back yard gate and waving goodbye to the inventor. "Until next time!"

4

I WAS SAVED by the bad weather. If today had been a clear day, there would have been students everywhere, and hawkers to bring customers to the nearby pimps and peddlers. I simply wouldn't have noticed a person following me on the opposite side of the street. The inconspicuous gentleman of average height with a plain little suitcase wouldn't have seemed suspicious even if I were on the lookout.

This could hardly be someone hurrying about on business, right?

And even now, on the deserted street, I found him by coincidence. The pursuer simply didn't guess the right place: he had been looking out for me from a street corner where he could see the entrance to Alexander Dyak's shop. But I turned onto the street from the alley, thus messing up his all his cards.

To get closer to me, the spook had to hop out from under the coffeeshop overhang and fly headlong across an intersection. Although he had wisely chosen the opposite side of the street, I had seen his maneuvers.

To be honest, I was expecting something like

this. The attempt on the Roman Bridge had happened right after a visit to my attorney and, just after the maître visited me in the house on Yablochkov street, the sniper had shown up there. I wasn't inclined to suspect that my lawyer was being followed, but I also couldn't write it all off as coincidence.

And so, I looked back.

The bad weather and haywire nerves had helped me see the pursuer, but how would he react if he was exposed? What were his orders: to disappear in the gray wet streets of New Babylon or attempt to finish the matter with a couple accurate shots?

I was betting on the latter, reasonably imagining that he was not tasked to collect evidence, but to kill. But what I didn't know, and simply couldn't miscalculate on is when he would open fire. How close would he try to get before pulling the trigger? And how long would it take before he got sick of looking for a good place to try and kill me?

I didn't have eyes on the back of my head, and the lack of certainty was just driving me mad.

There was nothing worse than expecting to be shot in the back.

Step - breathe in. Step - breathe out. My fingers, gripping the revolver handle in my pocket, were going numb.

Step - breathe in. Step - breathe out. My boots were sloshing on the wet causeway.

Step - breathe in. Step - breathe out. My heart was pounding like mad.

And before me there was a straight road,

building walls and no people. It was as if the old city was frozen, and I could only see the indistinct silhouette of my pursuer fussing around at the very edge of my vision. Try not to break into a run!

But I couldn't run. If I ran, I would instantly become a target.

Sure, I could easily turn around and open fire first. But I simply wasn't ready to either murder a random passer-by in cold blood based on a hunch or start a firefight with a professional.

I was so sincerely afraid to catch a bullet I was hiccupping and my knees were shaking. And I wasn t at all ashamed of that. A month and a half in a hospital bed and paralysis due to a damaged spine produce a truly astonishing effect on the human psyche.

For that very reason, as soon as such a chance presented itself, I went down a narrow stairway into a random bar. In the small drinking establishment, it was surprisingly crowded and horribly smoky. It immediately became clear where the elated students had gone to wait out the storm. There were forks and knives clacking on plates, dull voices echoing off a vaulted ceiling, and beer mugs clinking on one another.

In the first room, which had a long bar, there were no free tables at all. In the far room, it wasn't so crowded, and the people gathered there were somewhat more sedate. Quieter, that was for sure.

"One cream stout," I said, throwing a rumpled fiver on the bar.

"Any snacks?"

I cast my gaze over the chalkboard and ordered the first dish I saw:

"A large order of Belgian fries, please." Then I pointed to the telephone. "May I make a call?"

The bartender nodded, and I picked up the receiver, sending mental prayers to the Creator that Ramon Miro was in his office.

"You again?" he asked, none too glad to hear my voice.

"I need you to get me out of here!" I whispered, not lowering my gaze from the entrance. "This is a serious matter, and I need help urgently!"

"Where are you?"

"A bar called *Playing Hooky* on..." I looked at the bartender and asked: "What street is this?"

"Curie."

"On Curie street. Do you know where that is?"

"I'll be there in half an hour," Ramon answered and hung up.

I left the telephone, took my beer and sat at a table near a hallway with a view of the front door. I put my wet cloak on the coat rack, and initially covered the revolver with a jacket tail, then set it on my knee. The tabletop did a great job masking it.

No one in their right mind would open fire in front of so many witnesses, but I still couldn't shake the irrational feeling that I wasn't taking some extremely important factor into account. I even got the desire to duck out through the back door, but the corridor was blocked by cleaners, and there simply was no other way out of this basement. Perhaps through the kitchen...

Risk it or wait for Ramon? And how long should I even wait?

I glanced at my left wrist and spit a curse when I remembered I had no watch.

Tossing a couple strips of fried potato into my mouth, I chewed them without any appetite, drank a sip of beer and decided to leave the bar through the back door, if there was such a thing, and not wait for my former partner in the bar. But as soon as I got up from the bench, the entrance was sharply pushed open and a metallic cylinder clanged onto the stone floor, thrown in from outside. And another immediately!

Grenades!

I turned the table on its side, flinging my tableware onto the floor. I was hoping the sturdy boards of the tabletop would cover me from shrapnel. The cylinders weren't grenades at all, though, but smoke bombs. Two claps rang out, and impenetrable black clouds of acrid smoke instantly filled the room. Tears poured from my eyes, and I immediately heard two sharp knocks overhead, as if a couple bullets had slammed into the wall one after the other.

But I didn't hear any shots! I didn't hear anything!

The next bullet hit the edge of the overturned table, then I fired at the entrance door, aiming high so I wouldn't accidentally hit one of the students. Then I jumped up and ran down the side corridor. A bullet clunked into the wall behind me just a bit too late, but I didn't fire in return. I barged into the kitchen, which hadn't yet filled with smoke.

Doubling over in a fit of vexing coughing, I stuck a mop in the door handle, then barely managed to jump aside before the wooden panel spat out splinters as my pursuer opened fire directly through it.

I shot back two times, caught an echo of fear from the room and quickly crouched behind the kitchen stove but, no matter how I turned my head from side to side, I couldn't see a back door. There weren't even windows. Finally, at the far wall, I saw a dumbwaiter for food and beer.

I didn't hesitate for even a moment. Shaking from the cough, I ran for the dumbwaiter, slammed down on the handle and jumped onto its shuddering platform. The steam propulsion gave a heartrending wail, and my pursuer, having heard a suspicious sound, threw all caution to the wind. With a few strong blows, he smashed through the bullet-riddled door and ran inside.

I shot at the figure, enshrouded in wisps of smoke, and missed. The killer meanwhile quickly took cover behind an iron cupboard and opened return fire. By that time, though, the platform had already lifted me out of the basement.

I got away!

I fell out of a hatch into a small courtyard, stood to my feet and started hobbling away, drying my pouring tears with a handkerchief. As ill luck would have it, the passage between the buildings soon took me back to the front of the bar, where terrified students were pouring out of the smoke-filled entrance. I turned around and ran in the opposite direction. As soon as I'd hopped around the corner, I ran into a police armored vehicle lumbering in my direction.

And it would have been nothing, but I still was clenching the revolver in my right hand.

I'd simply forgotten about it. It just flew out of my head! Devil!

I took a step back, but then its doors flew open and Ramon stuck his head out.

"Leo!" he waved. "It's us!"

Wheezing in exhaustion, I ran up to the self-propelled carriage and just fell into the back. Ramon jumped in after me and the side door slammed shut.

"Leo, what's happened to you now?" he demanded an explanation.

"Someone wanted to kill me!"

"And?"

I brought my former partner up to speed, giving the condensed version. After a moment of thought, I sent his nephew into the bar. He'd take a look around and, if possible, grab the peaked cap and cloak I'd left on the coatrack.

"Do you have Webley-Fosbery rounds?" I asked shaking four casings from the revolver. After Ramon took a cardboard box from an iron box under the bench, I added: "I need guards."

"We've already sent someone to your address."

"I need a bodyguard," I corrected myself. "I'll pay five thousand a month."

Ramon just shook his head.

"Sorry, Leo. No dice. I don't want to get involved in your affairs..."

"You're already involved."

"...more than necessary."

I just laughed.

"I'm afraid you have no choice."

Ramon's reddish countenance went dark.

"Is this blackmail?"

"This is a business proposition. Six thousand."

"Leo, you're nothing but trouble!"

"There's no avoiding trouble for us now. I am suggesting we minimize the damage. If I don't get this situation under control, everyone will feel it. This isn't a threat. It's objective reality."

"Curses!" Ramon Miro swore. "Why the devil did I get linked up with you?!"

"You got fifty thousand for two hours work," I reminded him, reloading the revolver. "And you'll get six more."

"Ten," my former partner relented.

"Seven and that's my last word."

"What do you need done?"

"Nothing for now. Just cover me."

Just then, the side door flew open and Tito threw my overcoat and peaked cap into the back.

"Let's get out of here," Ramon ordered and asked me: "Where should I take you, Leo?"

"I don't know yet," I shivered. "But we need to

get out of here before the police start asking about us!"

Tito got behind the wheel and started the powder engine. To its measured chirping, the armored vehicle started from place, shaking on the uneven causeway, and Ramon Miro finally stopped boring into me with his agitated gaze.

"What's it like in the bar?" he asked his nephew, opening the window to the cabin.

"There are no wounded. A few people got smoke poisoning, but they were all given artificial respiration. A couple sentries heard the commotion and ran over. While I was there, they didn't manage to get anything sensible out of the witnesses."

"And the gunman?"

"I didn't see anyone with a little case," Tito answered and sneezed. "And the smoke really was devilishly acrid!"

I cursed in vexation and smoothed out my leather overcoat, intending to put it on, but Ramon didn't let me.

"Was your coat hanging on the coat rack?" he asked and stuck a pointer and middle finger into two bullet holes I hadn't noticed. "Strange..."

"What's strange?" I didn't understand. "Are you suggesting it may not be a coincidence?"

"Judge for yourself. If the smoke hadn't yet filled the bar and the killer could see where he was shooting, why did he make holes in your cloak? But if the gunman couldn't see, how did he manage to shoot two bullets so close together? And most importantly why right in the heart?"

I didn't have any answers to these questions, but I was reminded of the previous attempt and smokescreen over the Roman Bridge. The gunman clearly had a very definite modus operandi.

"Listen, Ramon," I said thoughtfully. "You haven't heard anything about similar occurrences, have you? Smoke and silent shooting, does that say anything to you?"

"No, but I could ask around."

"Ask. And better do so right now."

There was clear annoyance reflected on the hulking man's high-cheekboned face, but he didn't get stubborn. He knocked on the divider, getting his nephew's attention, and asked him to stop at the pharmacy. The armored car jumped over the high curb and froze on the sidewalk, then Ramon Miro threw open the side door and went outside. I also didn't waste any time, found a long needle and rough thread in a toolbox and started sewing up the bullet holes, not especially worrying if my stitches were even.

5

RAMON RETURNED a quarter hour later. Getting into the back, he sat opposite me and drummed his fingers on his knees in thought.

"Well?" I hurried my former partner

along. "What did you find out?"

"There have been a few similar occurrences in the last year, but only one is entirely the same as the attempt on you," Miro said and sighed. "That won't give us anything: there are no suspects in that murder. It was a hired killer. Such cases are only solved if the perp is caught red-handed."

"What about motive? Who was the victim?"

Ramon shrugged his shoulders.

"Some New World immigrant." He threw back the side of the uniform cloak and took a notepad out of the internal pocket. "A man named Michael Smith, probably an assumed identity. He spent two weeks in the Three Little Leaves, where he was shot by an unknown person at the beginning of September."

"What is the Three Little Leaves?"

"A casino on the edge of the Chinese Quarter. They rent rooms on the upper floors."

"He must have seriously pissed someone off," I snorted. "Casinos are always full of people. That and plenty of guards."

"There were a few armed bodyguards with the victim during the murder."

"Very interesting," I snorted and ordered: "Let's go!"

"Where?" Ramon didn't understand.

"To the Three Little Leaves, naturally! We'll interrogate the staff. Smith stayed there for two weeks. He must have talked to someone, or at least used the phone. We'll try to figure out who's shoulder he might have put a chip on."

"Our last trip to a casino wasn't so great," the hulking man reminded me, his face going gloomy again.

"Let's go!" I repeated. "I'm not going to threaten anyone, just pay for answers. Business as usual for such places!"

Ramon gave in and told his nephew to go to Maxwell Street.

"Stop a block away, but not on the Chinese side," he warned. "Don't step foot outside the armored vehicle, sit at the wheel and wait for our signal."

Tito nodded, and the self-propelled carriage started off sharply. Ramon Miro took a sawed-off lever-action shotgun from under the bench with a fated sigh and started thumbing buckshot rounds into its tube magazine.

"My heart is telling me this isn't going to end well," he said unequivocally after catching my confused glance.

"And the heart must be believed," I chuckled. "But let's first try to work with our heads."

"If we work with our heads, we might break our noses," Ramon Miro answered, going tit for tat.

I had nothing to object with.

THE THREE LITTLE LEAVES casino was in a three-story stone manor on the Chinese part of Maxwell Street. The sturdy construction was a bit separate from the neighboring buildings. Its back yard was behind a tall fence with outward curving spikes. The first story windows were covered with grates.

— The Dormant —

On the roadside where Tito let us out there were streams of mud, but the dirty ash-blackened water wasn't high enough to reach the sidewalk; Ramon and I walked from the armored car to the casino without getting our feet wet. The rain was still drizzling, staining the gray walls with streams of soot; I was protected from the drizzle by the leather overcoat, and my partner by a uniform cloak with peeling police patches.

Ramon was a bit behind me, holding his cloak, which was bulging from the sawed-off. I went up onto the high porch of the casino first. Two disinterested muscle-men immediately shot up and stood in our path.

"*Illustrious?*" cringed the enforcer with solidly built knuckles.

"We don't cater to white-eyes around here!" his partner supported him. "Scram!"

I raised my black glasses to my forehead in indescribable astonishment and, from my high vantage point looked at first one bouncer then the other. The stubborn gaze of my transparent eyes forced them to shiver.

"Just a mistake," the first mumbled out.

"Our apologies, my good sir," the second threw his hands wide.

"At ease," I threw out shortly and walked into the casino.

Ramon walked after me and the bewildered guards didn't notice his cloak bulging from the sawed-off.

"I've been meaning to ask, what's with your eyes?" the hulking man asked, pushing me into the corridor.

"Nothing, it'll pass," I waved it off and removed my peaked cap and shook the droplets from it. "They don't let *illustrious* in? Are you serious? What's happening to this world?"

Ramon Miro shrugged his shoulders and suggested:

"Better take off your glasses. After all, we don't need any trouble, right?"

I followed my friend's advice, winced due to the overly bright light of the electric bulbs and pulled in air through my nose.

"Opium?"

"That's the one," Ramon confirmed my guess and pointed at a niche not far from the stairs where there was a massive armchair. "I'll wait for you there."

"Alright," I nodded and headed into the casino.

It was still far from evening, but the establishment was not empty. There were three short Chinese men sitting at the card tables, pompous and important, accompanied by two moors and a few entirely respectable looking Europeans. But as for the roulette table, it was occupied by clear criminals; we heard bursts of laughter and popping of sparkling wine. The girls around the table were wearing vulgar shiny getups.

The ringleader there had the gold teeth and cynical eyes of an inveterate thief. For an instant, he got distracted from counting bills and slipped his attentive gaze over my head, but he didn't leave the game and placed another bet. I didn't stay in the roulette room and headed right into the bar, where I carelessly threw down a couple red tenners bearing a portrait of Leonardo da Vinci for the bartender.

"What would you like?" the young man asked compliantly. He had pomaded hair and a thin strip of mustache on his upper lip.

"That's for you," I answered calmly. "We're just here to talk."

"No thanks. Take the money!" the boy got scared.

"We're just here to talk," I repeated, setting another ten-franc note on the bar. "About the dead guy. This can't hurt any of you, trust me."

"Dead guy?" the bartender went pale. "I don't know nothing about no dead guy!"

"Sure you do. Michael Smith. He was shot here a few months ago."

The boy instantly calmed down and nodded

"Oh yeah. But I don't know nothing about that! The cops interrogated all of us already!"

"I'm not interested in the murder," I said softly, trying to catch the man's gaze, but he was stubbornly looking down at his feet. I had to add another two tenners and push the fat stack of bills across the bar. "Fifty francs for a simple conversation. The choice is yours."

The bartender licked his dried-out lips and stared greedily at the money. I felt like I could physically feel the doubts consuming him. In the end, his greed overcame his fear and the boy whispered out:

"What do you want to know?"

"Who was this Smith and where was he from?"

"He was an Englishman, but he was coming from New York. I saw a sticker on his baggage. And he was afraid of something. He wouldn't go outside, and he came down with guards even to gamble."

"Who did he talk with?" I asked.

"Only other players, I suppose..." the bartender drew out his words unconfidently and slightly leaned over to me across the bar. "Although he did place several calls to a Frank."

"Excuse me?" I didn't understand right away and sensed a clear echo of fear.

The man's pupils went wide, he shot a quick glance at someone behind me. I didn't ignore that hint. I turned around and smiled at two gentlemen of strong constitution in identical gray suits, white vests and caps. And I was at ease: my hand was on the revolver against my thigh, and the pistol was pointed at the strangers. All that remained was to pull down on the trigger. These strange fellows wouldn't even manage to draw their weapons, but that apparently didn't bother them one bit.

"Let's talk like civilized people," one offered, with a thin knife scar on his veiny neck. "Let's just talk, yeah?"

"Hrmph, I'm all out of time. I'm on my way out the door."

"Well, it looks like you'll have to hang back."

The strangers didn't start walking and didn't even move a muscle, but Ramon suddenly shot out of his armchair and pulled the sawed-off from under his cloak.

"We're leaving!" he declared softly. "And if I see either of you twitch, I'll blow both your brains out!"

All conversations in the room cut off, and the chips stopped clopping, as if the players had only now noticed that a gun was drawn. One of the mean-looking fellows slightly turned his head, saw the sawed-off and frowned.

"It's no use," he said shortly, but now his calm was only for show. His smooth-shaven cheek was twitching in a nervous tick.

I didn't join the altercation, just blindly groped for the stack of bills behind me, swept them into my hand and stuck them in my pocket. Charity is not my cup of tea.

Without taking the revolver barrel from the boys, I took a step back from the bar, walked an arc around them and joined my partner.

"Big mistake!" the boy with a scar on his neck warned as soon as we'd started for the exit.

We didn't answer at all. I jumped first onto the porch and clocked one of the muscle-heads with my revolver handle as I walked, and when he squirmed, squeezing the wound, I took the second in my sights.

"No jokes!" I warned him, cocking the gun for show.

Ramon jumped past me and blew into his police whistle with all his might.

The company of young men on the corner turned tail and ran at full speed, while the armored car's motor barked and rolled rapidly down the hill. Near the casino, the heavy self-propelled carriage slid out on the wet road, but Tito got control and Ramon and I hopped into the back. The clumsy monster tore from place at a full clip.

They didn't shoot after us. No one even came off the porch.

"Well, what was that?" Ramon Miro wondered, peeling himself from the back window.

"I have no idea," I admitted honestly.

"Did you find out anything useful?"

"No, but I know who to talk to."

"Are you serious?"

"Yes. Let's go to the *Heinrich Hertz*. It's a hotel near Central Station."

6

TO FIND THE HOTEL, the armored car had to drive down a good number of the confusing streets of the train-station area, but the lost time was worth it: after getting five francs in hand, the porter confirmed that there really was a Thomas Eliot Smith among their guests.

But we hadn't managed to catch the agent in the hotel, and the porter had no idea when he would deign to show himself.

"Sometimes he's gone for a few days at a time," he warned.

I nodded gratefully and went outside.

"And what will we do?" Ramon asked, following after me.

"Wait."

"Then we should get a bite to eat," the hulking man decided, pointing at a bistro called The Sparrow on the opposite side of the street. But as soon as his nephew got out from behind the wheel, he kicked him back into the car. "Where do you think you're going? Drive the armored car around the corner and don't take an eye off it."

"But..."

"You can buy a couple pastries."

"I don't have to eat at all!" Tito was offended.

"If you lose any weight, my sister will get on my case, so buy a couple pastries. Got it?"

The boy slammed the armored cabin door shut and Ramon and I went into The Sparrow. It was a Moravian restaurant. Miro ordered himself fried pork with dumplings and cabbage, while I chose garlic soup with cheese. And we also asked for knedle. How can one get by without them?

"Who are we waiting for?" Ramon asked when we had sat at a table with a view outside. "Who is this Smith fellow?"

"The Smith I want to talk to works for the Pinkerton detective agency. But the Smith who was killed, most likely, was no Smith at all. He fled from New York, but they caught him here. Perhaps he's some famous criminal."

"And the Pinkerton Agent is gonna help you just like that?" Ramon Miro doubted, finishing the light beer.

I took a sip of water and shrugged my shoulders.

"He and I have worked together before. And again, who would say no to fast money?"

"If he knew you better," my former partner laughed, "he'd refuse."

I gave a crooked smile and started pecking at my garlic soup. But as for Ramon, he managed to drain a mug of beer and order a second before his hot meal even arrived. Without any rush, we ate, keeping vigilant watch over the window as we did. Then we spent some time just sitting in silence, enjoying the warmth and full bellies.

"You aren't getting a dessert?" Ramon asked in surprise when I reached for my wallet to pay.

"No," I shook my head and immediately noticed that I really didn't want any sweets.

"Is that you, Leo?" the hulking man laughed uncontrollably. "You're really gonna say no to some chocolate?"

"Do you have any?" I inquired. "A mug of hot chocolate would definitely not hurt right now."

"It might take them until next week."

"If they bring it, I'll take the whole shipment," I declared and got up from the table. "But now, wait here."

"Has your agent shown up?"

"Yes."

And in fact, Thomas Smith had just gotten out of a carriage that pulled up to the hotel with a raised canvas top. He was wearing a heavily dirt-streaked beige cloak.

After taking his pay, the cabby rolled on. And I didn't run across the street with shouts of greeting, just stood on the sidewalk and waved. Smith noticed me and, if he was surprised, he didn't show it. He calmly crossed the road and extended a hand.

"Lev! What fates brought you here?"

Thomas's excessively strong handshake gave away his nerves, so I immediately got to business:

"I'm interested in a New World immigrant. Most likely a criminal. You might have heard about him at work."

Smith stroked his gray mustache in thought, but didn't refuse to help right away and clarified:

"Who exactly are you interested in?"

"Michael Smith, and Englishman. He came from New York in the second half of August. He was shot at the beginning of September."

Thomas shook his head.

"Never heard of him."

"Probably a made-up name."

"All the more so, then."

I was not going to give up so easily, though.

"Smith was shot in the Three Little Leaves casino in the middle of the day, and no one saw the killer. Can you find out anything about it?"

"Why do you care?" Smith winced, adjusting

his derby cap.

"There's a relatively large chance that his murderer has been paid for my head as well."

"I see you're not looking to solve this the easy way," Thomas chuckled, rubbing his chin and asking a reasonable question: "Alright, I see why you're interested. But why should I be?"

"You can count on a service in return. If I am to believe the papers, you have yet to catch your Aztecs. Perhaps I can be of use."

Thomas shot me a sour look.

"Alright!" I sighed. "Will five hundred do?"

"Sure," the investigator then waved a hand, "I'll make a couple calls for an old friend. You can keep the money. I'll be counting on that favor, though."

"Agreed."

"I'll be right back," Thomas Smith warned, walking across the road and ducking into the hotel.

I returned to the bistro, noticed Ramon's curious face in the window and shrugged my shoulders, answering the question I could read clearly in his eyes.

The rain had grown stronger and was causing a light rustle on the causeway and tile roofs. Streams of dirty water were pouring out of the gutters. Bistro overhangs were covering me from the raindrops but, even so, I wore myself out waiting for Smith. It took no less than a half hour before he came back outside.

"Your man was named Michael Link. He was a famous safe cracker."

"A specialist?"

"Yes. In August, he pulled off a bank robbery in New York, opening over a hundred safes. After that, he disappeared and resurfaced in New Babylon. No one can say who might be behind his murder."

I nodded in thought, and clarified just in case:

"And what bank was robbed?"

Thomas Smith took out a notepad and looked for the right page.

"The New York branch of the Witstein Banking House. Does that mean anything to you?"

"No," I lied without blinking.

The investigator just spread his arms.

"That's all there is," he said and got a pencil ready. "Lev, how can I find you, if need be?"

I told him the number of Miro's office from memory.

"Ask for Ramon, that's my business partner. He'll be able to tell you where I am. To be honest, I'm a bit of an Aztec specialist."

Thomas laughed uncontrollably and slapped me on the shoulder with a happy look.

"Don't you worry about the Aztecs. I'm already on their trail. we'll take them if not today then tomorrow. I hope the local police aren't all complete dolts."

"Not complete ones," I smiled, bidding the agent farewell and walking down the street toward the armored vehicle.

Soon, Ramon caught up to me.

"And?" he asked, standing next to me.

I just shrugged my shoulders, thinking over

what I'd heard. And I had quite a bit to think about.

The man who'd robbed the New York branch of the Witstein Banking House was killed on the other side of the Atlantic and, at that same time, the Vice President of that very Banking House had come to the capital. I remembered distinctly hearing the porter say the last name Witstein.

A simple coincidence? That may have been. But it didn't seem like one to me. What was more, when the bartender of the casino had mentioned telephone calls to a "Frank," he must have meant The Benjamin Franklin.

"So, what now?" Ramon nudged me when we'd reached the armored car, parked in the narrow alley. "What are we gonna do?"

"Let's go to Emperor's Square!" I declared, casting off my doubts.

The hulking man glanced into the darkening sky and shook his head. But he didn't try to convince me to put off the investigation until tomorrow. In any case, he'd have to drive through the center of town on his way home.

I GOT SOME REST on the way there. I didn't fall asleep, I just laid back a bit on the bench and lost myself in time and space. Perspiration covered my whole body. My heart started beating like a madman's. Nausea rolled up my throat. I could barely keep from throwing up onto the causeway.

I bore it. Nothing strange, just some nausea.

The armored vehicle really was going at a

totally impossible tempo. It would speed up, then slow down to minimum, sometimes even stopping briefly.

"Devil knows what's happening on the roads!" Ramon Miro said in vexation, glancing out a side window. "It's like the whole city is driving right here!"

I winced in suffering and rubbed my temples, which were sticky with sweat. I was plainly not well. So, when the armored vehicle turned off the road onto the margin and stopped, I caught my breath with relief.

"The road is closed from here," Tito told us.

"I'll be right back," Ramon warned and went out the side door.

I didn't remain in the back either though, climbed out onto the causeway and threw back my head, holding my face under the cold fine rain. Over the building roofs, there was a low sheet of shaggy clouds swirling magnificently. Little spouts of smoke poured into it from the factory smokestacks like streams joining a burgeoning river. Right overhead, there was an army dirigible drifting majestically. At the far end of the street, the spires of the Sublime Electricity lyceum were peeking out between the building roofs. The electric sparks shimmering there left white slowly-fading little devils on my retinas.

And suddenly, I realized that I loved New Babylon with all my heart and would never leave it and, even if I did leave it for a time, I'd be sure to come back. This place was my home, nowhere else.

That flood retreated very quickly, and my head

immediately started to spin. I had to take a seat on the running board. When Ramon returned to the armored car, shaking puddle-water off his boots, the attack of strange weakness had already left me, and I just saw the odd white spot flickering before my eyes.

"The square has been blocked off by police," said the hulking man, vexed at the delay.

"No problem," I said with a crooked smirk, getting up from the running boards and freezing for a moment, waiting for the vertigo to quiet down. "Let's go on foot."

"Where?"

"To The Benjamin Franklin."

Ramon nodded in silence and didn't start interrogating me.

I didn't explain a thing, because I wasn't totally sure this would lead anywhere. The Benjamin Franklin was Abraham Witstein's favorite hotel, but the likelihood that the Judean was in the capital at this precise moment was vanishingly small. The banking house had branches throughout Europe, while its headquarters wasn't even in New Babylon, but in the second greatest financial center of the Empire, London.

And yet, I wasn't going to give up on my idea and went with Ramon Miro down a side alley around the police blockade. The entrance to the square was covered by two armored vehicles at once, and the constables in formation between them in black uniform raincoats turned everyone back with no regard. They didn't let the staff of local establishments through, nor the guests of nearby hotels. Newspapermen either.

"Something serious must have happened," Ramon decided when seeing the magnesium bulb flashes of photo reporters.

I nodded and hurried onward.

Going through the back yards of fancy shops and expensive restaurants, we made our way around the square and at the intersection of two confusing alleys, we hit upon a hotel doorman in a raincoat that was too small for his body. In his hands, he was holding a "Temporary Entrance" plaque.

"Now that's what I call service!" Ramon chuckled.

"I'll do the talking," I warned my partner. "Just support me if it seems necessary. Alright?"

"Alright."

In the vestibule of The Benjamin Franklin, it was uncommonly crowded. The employees were instructing their honored guests how to leave the hotel and get around the police blockade. At the main entrance, instead of doormen in gold-embroidered livery, there were two constables with semi-automatic carbines in horizontal position.

When I showed up, the receptionist behind the counter gave a tortured smile, but then suddenly shuddered and his eyes went wide.

"Mr. Shatunov?!"

"The same," I confirmed, removing my peaked cap. "Health problems forced me to leave your wonderful establishment before I could pay my bills, but now I'm prepared to clear my debts."

The man was probably aware that I had been arrested right in front of the hotel, yet he didn't give that away at all. He just started searching for last month's registration journal.

I set my peaked cap on the counter and took out my wallet, but the receptionist expectedly told me I didn't have any debts.

"How is this possible?" I asked, pretending it was extremely surprising.

"There's a note here saying your bill was paid by a Mademoiselle Montague."

"May I?"

"Here, see for yourself!"

I turned the book around and led my finger down the lines, looking for the name Witstein, knowing he had been in the hotel at the same time as me. I found it and scanned over to the special notes section, where guest visitors were usually recorded. In that box, there was just one name: "S. Lynch," no one else had gone up to the Vice President's suite.

"At the very bottom of the page," the porter told me.

"Yes, I see," I confirmed, taking out the notepad and recording the sum paid for me by Liliana. "Thank you. You've done me a great service."

"Just doing my job," the man smiled meekly.

I bid him farewell and walked away from the counter, but immediately turned back.

"On my last visit, I talked with Abraham Witstein about investments. He was staying in the

Emperor's Suite on the top floor, you don't think you could tell me..."

The receptionist understood me and threw up his hands at half word.

"I'm afraid Mr. Witstein left the hotel soon after you."

"I thank you again," I smiled and headed for the back door. They still weren't letting guests out through the central one.

Ramon Miro caught up to me in the back yard and inquired quietly:

"What did you manage to find out?"

I put on my peaked cap and said:

"Lynch. Does that name sound familiar to you?"

The hulking man thought about it briefly, then shook his head.

"No."

But as for me, I was haunted by the sensation I had heard that name before. And in my mind, it was somehow tied with Abraham Witstein.

But where might I have heard it?

"That's it!" I even snapped my fingers when I stumbled on the memory.

Lynch. Sean Lynch. When I was handing my room key to the receptionist, a redheaded Irishman – and I was sure it was an Irishman, my grandma had the exact same accent – told the receptionist he was there to see Abraham Witstein. That was how I discovered the Judean banker was in the hotel.

"What have you got?" Ramon Miro's interest

was piqued.

"I remembered why that name sounds familiar. But it won't exactly give us anything..." I shook my head and suddenly froze, having had a sudden revelation about the riddle.

The apartment manager had described the runaway gunman to Elizabeth-Maria as a gaunt redheaded native of the British Isles and, as far as I remembered, Abraham Witstein's guest had looked exactly like that.

But Roy Lloyd and Sean Lynch couldn't be the same person, right?

Ramon Miro turned around and tilted his head to the side. In his black eyes, a little fire of interest flickered.

"Based on your long face, Leo, you're under the spell of yet another genius idea," the hulking man guessed with a bit of dread.

I patted him on the shoulder and walked on.

"I think I can get a portrait of the killer."

"A portrait?" Ramon screwed up his face skeptically. "The population of New Babylon is more than ten million! What would a portrait give us?"

"We could have a talk with our friends in the Newton-Markt," I said. "That worked last time."

"Last time, we were looking for a criminal, and he was already in the records."

"Ramon, what are the odds that a well-behaved citizen is in the business of hunting people?"

My friend didn't take that argument to heart.

"The work is too clean for some average

cutthroat," he said, being stubborn. "Looks more like the work of active military."

"So, we should first turn our attention on Irish nationalists and people retired from Britain's colonial armies. Can you set that up? If it doesn't work, we'll have to go around to gun shops. The caliber he uses, to put it lightly, isn't too common in Europe."

"Alright," Ramon sighed. "Where will you get the portrait?"

I glanced at the drizzle coming down from the heavens and decided it was too late to catch Charles Malacarre on the Roman Bridge. The blind illustrator couldn't bear working in this rain.

"Let's go to Balsamo square!" I decided and headed for the armored car.

7

BALSAMO SQUARE was glistening with its ideally even patch of vitrified stone. Now it was not black, but more like dark blue on account of the clouds being reflected in a thin layer of water. But for some reason, that looked even gloomier and more ominous than usual.

Once upon a time, this had been the site of the most famous prison in New Babylon, but *the fallen* leveled it when the prisoners there rebelled. Most historians agreed that this uprising against the sovereigns of the world had been led by the self-appointed Count Cagliostro, a famous adventurer and mystic, who had been transferred here from the Lion's Castle.

I didn't like this place. Something was strange about it, and that bothered me. But sometimes there was just no choice: Charles Malacarre lived in a dark little hovel on the second underground level, which had been formed after the nearby houses were submerged underground.

"Want me to come with?" Ramon asked, standing on a rusty ventilation grate. Down below, the lights of the underground street burned, music played, and people were walking.

"No, I'll be back soon," I refused and headed to the nearest stairs into the underground.

The the stone stairs were fire-polished, and the rain was making my boot soles slip. I had to hold onto iron handrails stuck into the stone masonry.

The first underground level was lit with the odd gas torch. But today, the gloom in the space seemed somewhat thicker than usual. While there was water dripping through the bars in the ceiling, sunlight couldn't even be imagined.

I removed my dark glasses to my pocket and walked a familiar path to the illustrator's residence, not paying any mind to the calls of insolent hawkers. Here, clever cheats competed with unrecognized inventors, but the result of talking with both was totally identical and would end in losing one's wallet. And what if you weren't poisoned with some miracle elixir, or sent to the police station with something stolen from a museum?

Well, you could be stunned and tossed into one of the bottomless local wells simply because someone coveted your new boots.

When I heard sound and cries before me, I walked back to the wall and stuck my hand in my pocket with the revolver, but my alarm was for nothing: there was some local madman strolling through the passage in a dirty shirt with a shock of long unwashed hair.

"*The illustrious* are the essence of the devil's progeny!" he wailed with his whole tinny throat. "The devil dispersed his toxic brood over the earth and raised them to be vile abominations with the dead eyes of killers!"

The psycho went around a corner, and I looked around. With no small measure of surprise, I noticed that none of the locals were the least bit bothered by his seditious cries, as if such talk was business as usual down here. And I was immediately reminded of the bouncers from the casino on Maxwell street.

What was happening to this city? The first *illustrious* were on the front lines against *the fallen* but now, a half century later, their descendants had mud flung on them everywhere. No one had a single issue with that. I was even getting the sense that Professor Berliger was not at all alone in his desire to cut off *the illustrious* at the root. And that even scared me a bit.

I shrugged my shoulders, went down to the next level and found myself in pitch blackness. There was no light down here, and I had to basically navigate by touch. Unlike my previous visits, my eyes had yet to adjust to the dark.

Fortunately, it wasn't very far from the stairs to the blind illustrator's place, so I didn't take any lumps on the outcroppings of the uneven stone walls.

CHARLES MALACARRE took a bit of time to open the door.

"Is that you, Leo?" he asked after my third or fourth knock. "I'm sure I recognize your breathing, but I'd like to clear up my doubts!"

"It's me, Charles. That's right."

The illustrator let me into his home, locked the door and shuffled to the table.

"I'll light a lamp. I'm just not sure if there's kerosene."

I heard a gurgling, then with a long hiss a match was lit. Its smoky little flame gave way to the warm glow of a lamp, hanging down from the ceiling like a bat.

"Where is it?" I asked, looking around.

"What are you talking about, Leo?" the thin old man faked surprise, but he couldn't lead me on so easily.

I stood on my tiptoes, felt the high shelf in the entryway with my hand and, without any surprise, pulled down a two-round percussion musket with a full stock and an extremely short barrel.

"Charles, next time you cock it, clear your throat like this," I said, making a throat-clearing sound, putting on the safety and returning it to place. "And really, what do you need a weapon for?"

The illustrator sat down in a concave armchair and turned his head in the air indistinctly.

"*The illustrious* are not in a good way these days, you know."

"Is it that bad?" I asked in surprise, taking off my overcoat.

"Worse than you know."

I lowered down onto the artist's bed with a nasty grimace, threw myself back on the pillow and immediately felt taught pricks of pain in my shot-through thigh. I really shouldn't have exerted my wounded leg, but I couldn't just sit around without moving. I also had a horrible ache between my shoulders. My neck could hardly turn.

Charles Malacarre got up from the chair and, just as confidently as a seeing person, took a glass of tea from the table and came back.

"Fortunately, few would suspect a blind old man of being *illustrious*," he chuckled.

"When did it start?"

"Did you miss everything?"

"You might say that."

The illustrator gave an understanding chuckle

"I can sense that you've changed, Leo. What garbage are you on, morphine?"

"Morphine," I confirmed.

"Your thoughts are just a ghastly mess. How long has it been since your last injection, a few days?'

"I was never doing the injecting, Charles!"

"And I'm Emperor Clement!" the old man laughed acridly.

" I spent more than a month in a hospital. They gave me morphine to treat the pain."

Charles nodded.

"Then everything is clear." He spent some time in silence, then still decided to answer my question: "It started, Leo, with the death of the Empress. In the *Atlantic Telegraph*, there was an article with the headline *The Last* Illustrious *Lady of the Empire* and, although it was praising Victoria, people got it in their heads that the time of *the illustrious* had passed."

"You can't read the papers."

"I'm blind, not deaf! I can hear everything. Judge for yourself: Clement welcomed *the illustrious*. But while he was ruler, they made a lot of enemies. Victoria escaped her husband's legacy but was a guarantor of stability all on her own. And now well, believe you me, blood will be shed. The old aristocracy hates *the illustrious*. The reductionists consider them a hold-over from the past, while the rest simply want to dip their hands into someone else's pocket."

I got up from the bed, looked around the pitch-black room with shadows playing on the ceiling and suggested:

"You wanna get out of here?"

"No, Leo. I don't," the old man refused. Then he asked: "Why'd you come by? What do you need dragged out of your memory this time?"

"A man."

"Well at least it's just that!" he laughed hoarsely, coughing as he walked over to the easel. "Concentrate, Leo. Today, there isn't even porridge in your brain, but the most natural gelatin."

I laid back on the bed and tried to restore my chance encounter with Sean Lynch in the hotel vestibule. But my head was heavy, my thoughts were confused, and I just couldn't concentrate on the redheaded Irishman's face. There were unfamiliar shapes curling on the edge of my consciousness. Charles swore, tore out some sheets and threw them into the basket.

"Drink some tea, Leo!" he suggested. "It's from my personal collection. You'll like it."

I didn't refuse. The illustrator and I sat and chatted for a bit, then Charles pulled a clean sheet of paper over and tossed a portrait of Lynch on the paper with a couple of sparing strokes.

"Sorry, Leo. This is all I could pull out of your head. Stop taking that morphine."

I lit up the sheet with the kerosene lamp and whistled. This time, the blind illustrator had outdone himself: the sparse pencil lines had surprisingly come together into a familiar face. This was the very man I'd seen at the receptionist counter on that ill-fated day.

"Simply astonishing!" I said, not begrudging him the admiration.

"Your words are a balm for the soul," Charles laughed, going into a dark corner and shuffling through some bags. "I'll give you some tea. Drink it three times a day. Everything will get better."

"Excellent!" I smiled and, trying not to make noise, raised the lamp and put a couple of hundred-franc bills under it. After that, following a certain intuition, I pulled one of the rumpled papers from the garbage.

Eyes, fangs, claws.

Vertical pupils, the acrid curve of a wide smile, the glimmer of curved claws.

The Cheshire Cat. I also recognized him from at first glance, but this ghastly monster didn't look one bit like the kind-hearted creature from John Tenniel's illustrations.

"Here, Leo!"

I accepted a little fabric bag from the illustrator, put it in my pocket, then carefully folded the portrait of the suspect and got up from the table.

"Thank you, Charles."

"Take the money," the artist demanded. "I heard money crinkling."

"You only thought so," I lied without blinking, pulling on my overcoat and walking to the door. "Close it behind me."

"Drink the tea!" Charles Malacarre bid me farewell.

"Without fail."

I left the room and went along the dark passages in search of stairs. The conversation about *the illustrious* left me with a burdensome impression, so I kept my right hand in my pocket with the revolver. But no one even glanced in my direction. Either I looked obviously unfriendly enough, or I simply didn't look much like an *illustrious* gentleman with my clear eyes.

THE ARMORED CAR was waiting where I'd left it. I got into the back and handed the paper to Ramon.

"Here's our man."

Ramon shone an electric torch on the portrait gave an indistinct snort and asked:

"Remind me of his name?"

"Sean Lynch. And also, Roy Lloyd, but that's an alias."

"We'll check," the hulking man nodded, writing the names on the back of the paper in pencil.

"What now?" I asked.

Ramon looked at me in doubt and rubbed his chin.

"It's too late now. I might not catch the right people at work. You want me to take you home?"

I shook my head. Albert certainly hadn't yet returned from his rehearsal, Liliana was at her parents', and I had no desire at all to talk with the succubus.

"No, we better go to the Imperial Theater," I decided.

"Are you serious? To the theater?"

"Mhm. I'll call tomorrow morning and get the news."

"If you say so," Ramon shook his head and told Tito to get moving.

THE IMPERIAL THEATER BUILDING impressed first-time visitors with its monumentality, the muscular atlantes on its portico and the great many marble statues on its gable. In the center of the roof, there was a towering dome with gilded spire which, in clear weather, was visible even from the outskirts of town.

The inhabitants of the capital mostly didn't share in these delights, and disdainfully referred to the theater as "the birdhouse." No one could say for certain why it had been assigned that derogatory nickname, but it must have either been due to the tower being shaped like a bird cage, or because of all the songbirds living inside.

Getting inside was no work at all: Albert Brandt had been given a basement room in a side wing for rehearsals, and the guard thought his main job was to make sure the actors, costume artists and scene workers kept their smoking outdoors. The little fussy old man simply didn't have time to keep track of guests.

All on its own, the practice space seemed spacious to me, but not too well kept. I didn't stick around there for long. I saw a half-naked girl running down the corridor, and I asked her where to find the gentleman poet, then headed where she pointed. The actress, her teeth clacking in the cold, didn't even think to ask who I was.

It was barely warmer in Albert's office than in the corridor. His only privilege was that he could smoke right at his desk: when I walked across the doorstep, there were thick wisps of smoke curling under the ceiling.

"Leo!" the poet said in surprise, rubbing a whitish cream the consistency of petroleum jelly on his face. "I was just..."

"No!" I held out an open palm. "Don't explain a thing. I don't want to know about your bohemian affairs."

"Come now!" Albert laughed. and continued rubbing in the ointment. "This is to protect me from the sun. Without it, I'd never have survived the summer in Montecalida!"

The poet really did have an allergy to the direct rays of the sun, but I just snorted in disbelief.

"It's raining outside, Albert."

"Doesn't matter!" the poet waved it off and pushed its tin container to the edge of the table. Its top was screwed off, and the label had a white-skinned vampire standing in the sun and smiling.

"Science makes miracles," I laughed, sitting in the chair.

Albert wiped off the rest of the ointment with a paper napkin, threw it into the waste basket and asked:

"What fates brought you here?"

"Liliana left to see her parents."

"Oh!" the poet lit up, opening his desk drawer. "That means we don't have a time limit!" He took out a bottle of wine and started cutting the wax. "Leo, what'll you have?"

"And what about the rehearsal?"

"It's already over. But now that my darling wife

is healthy again, I can afford to stay a bit late at work!"

"Did Elizabeth-Maria come during the day?"

"Oh yes!" Albert confirmed. "Her new look caused a true furor! I'm sure they society journalists will write about it in their columns!"

"I'm glad for you."

"Leo, you didn't answer. What will you have to drink?"

I looked around Albert's office. It had a single window just under ceiling and practically no furniture. I asked:

"Can I make some tea here?"

"Tea?" Brandt cringed. "We haven't seen each other in so long, and you're going to drink tea?!"

"It's a medicinal tea. I need to get my nerves in order."

The poet rolled his eyes and left the office. Soon, he was back and placed a tea brewer and pot of hot water on the table.

"Get it from the doorman?" I guessed.

"The night guard," Albert corrected me and threw his arms wide. "Well, what do you expect? Pour your water!"

The poet uncorked his wine. I started brewing my tea. After that, we clinked glasses and conducted an unhurried conversation about everything at once, and nothing in particular. The blind illustrator's tea had a calming effect. All my problems seemed far away and insignificant, but I didn't have any sleep in either eye.

My head was clear, I was feeling sprightly, and I didn't want to get up from the chair. All those feelings combined in a surprising way. Albert was also in full swing today, regaling me with tall tales of his theater life.

When the clock on the wall rang one AM, it caught us by surprise. The poet thoughtfully rubbed the bridge of his nose and enquired:

"Do you think there's any reason to go home?"

"Elizabeth-Maria?" I reminded him.

"She'll huff and puff, but I need to catch my breath. Let's just sit and talk like the good old days! You me and no one else. Family life is just wonderful, but if only you knew how I missed all this!"

Albert Brandt led his hand around the office, and I nodded, letting him know that I understood his mood perfectly. And how else should he be? We're all visited by such thoughts from time to time.

"Shall I give you the tour?" the poet suggested.

"Why not!" I didn't refuse.

In the end, we didn't go home.

8

ALBERT FELL ASLEEP right at the table.

To the poet's credit, he dozed off only around seven AM, and had spent all night babbling away like a wind-up toy.

I got up from the chair slowly and carefully,

grabbing the arms and leaning forward a few times to stretch my legs, then headed to the lavatory. I relieved myself, and on the way back, turned to the guard. I'd seen a telephone on his table yesterday. The little old sentry man's shift hadn't begun yet, while the night guard was sleeping somewhere, so no one could stop me from calling Ramon Miro's office.

And although I didn't have particular hope for success, my partner was already at work.

"Leo, where the devil have you gone?!" he hissed into the receiver. "I found your Lynch yesterday!"

"So soon?" I asked in surprise.

"It's his real name!" Ramon blindsided me.

"Are you sure?"

"My man in the card database brought out his personal record. The photograph coincides with your drawing."

"What did he do?"

"His crimes were political. He's under investigation by Department Three on suspicion of connections with Irish nationalists."

"Address?"

"Got it."

"Can you pick me up from the theater, or should I just get there on my own?"

Ramon considered it for a while, calculating the distance, then admitted grudgingly:

"You'll be there before me. But don't sneak up on him alone, alright?"

"Tell me the address."

"A house with a green dovecote on Hamilton street."

"But specifically?"

"Five Hamilton Street, but there aren't any numbers there. Look for the dovecote. Lynch is renting a basement apartment. There's only one in that building."

"Got it"

"Do you know how to get there? It's the Green Quarter..."

"I know," I cut Ramon off, because I knew exactly where the Irish-populated neighborhood was. It was not far away from the Eastern European one, settled mostly by Poles and Russians. Once upon a time, I had lived there for six months or maybe even a year.

"Wait for us on the street," Ramon demanded. "Don't do anything before we get there. Got it?"

"Agreed," I promised and hung up the receiver.

After that, I quickly returned to the poet's office, took my leather overcoat off the rack, clipped the peaked cap on my head and hurried to the exit. On my way, though, I had a change of heart and ducked into the prop room, which Albert had shown me on yesterday's tour. The door was affixed with an English lock, but I managed to open its simple bolt with a couple of pins.

Yes, I robbed the Imperial Theater without compunction. I made off with a wrinkled woolen overcoat, a shapeless felt hat and a shaggy strap-on beard. I crammed it all into a knapsack with an over-the-shoulder strap, slammed the door and hurried away, mentally vowing that I would return these rags at my first opportunity.

For me, this masquerade was simple necessity. The leather overcoat and peaked cap were perfectly familiar to the killer, and I really didn't want to catch a couple bullets in the back while waiting for Ramon Miro.

THE NEAREST underground station was five minutes' walk from the theater, and that's where I headed. The sky had cleared overnight, and the sidewalk had dried off, but it wasn't hot in the leather cloak. There was a chilly breeze blowing in from the ocean. It blew away the smoke from the smokestacks and rustled the branches of the trees.

My head was very slightly humming after the sleepless night, and my ears were ringing a bit but, overall, my wellbeing didn't worry me. Not paying any mind to the heartrending cries of the newspaper sellers, I joined the stream of city dwellers going down into the underground, paid for passage and started waiting for train.

Soon, a sooty train, shrouded in wisps of steam and smoke, dragged a chain of no-less-blackened cars into the station. I took a seat in the corner and rolled through the outskirts. With every stop, there were less civil servants and clerks. Their fashionable cloaks and smart derby caps were gradually replaced by the well-worn jackets and caps of laborers.

When I left the wagon, there were very few clerk types left. Most likely, they were plant managers. For some reason, they seemed very afraid. They didn't show it externally, but my *talent* suddenly came to life and caught a distinct timidity inside them.

Most likely, it was all to do with the continued strike.

On the platform, I walked to the stairs, but drowsiness immediately poured down on me with a heavy weight. It was as if I was pulled into a dream. My eyes started sagging, and the smoke and steam enshrouding the locomotive came to life, forming a gloomy hooded figure in a cloak.

The apparition didn't last long. My head sharply turned, and I woke up. The train rolled on, leaving gray wisps of smoke behind it, which quickly dispersed. But they did drift in the air for some time, their white ringlets forming a malicious grin. I didn't like that at all.

I turned and ran up the stairs. At first, I jumped two stairs at a time but, very soon, I was left short of breath, and felt an unbearable burning in my shot-through thigh. Then I reduced my pace as I met a throng of city-dwellers, who were in no rush down. I didn't push or elbow.

Leaving the smoke-scented underground station, I frowned at the bright rays of the sun, put on my dark glasses and turned down one of the narrow streets of the neighborhood, which was dominated by three-story buildings. Young men, passing a papirosa cigarette in a circle, led their steadfast gazes over me.

but didn't start anything. Either I looked like a local or didn't seem like easy prey.

I didn't care at all. There's little that can inspire self-confidence like a loaded revolver in one's coat pocket and an intention to use it long before any situation could spin out of control.

Just as predicted, I was significantly in advance of Ramon Miro, so I dropped into a familiar snack shop with red and orange birds painted on the banner. However, what brought me to the Phoenix, which is what the locals called this establishment, was not a desire to reminisce about the good old days, but a banal sleepiness. My eyes were just sticking together.

"Coffee. Strong, black, no sugar." I asked in Russian. Then I started to unbutton my overcoat and clarified: "Got any hot food?"

The waiter stroked behind his ear with a pencil in thought and made a recommendation:

"How about some pelmeni or vareniki?"

"What else you got?"

"We could cook you up an omelet. And we have beef stroganoff. But it's from yesterday."

"Give me the beef stroganoff," I decided, sat at the table and threw the theater bag under my legs, which is where I'd also moved the Webley-Fosbery from my overcoat pocket. "Bring the coffee right away!"

The door flew open, and two disheveled lowlifes walked in, ordered a hundred grams of vodka and just one open-faced herring sandwich for the both of them.

— The Dormant —

They drank down the swill, chased it with the food and headed off on their way.

People like that were how this establishment kept its head above water: the tap vodka was sold at three times normal prices, but alcohol stores opened later, and those suffering from morning hangovers had nowhere else to turn.

The coffee was strong and invigorating. My sleepiness retreated. My head cleared up. I turned to the window and tried to get my thoughts in order. The last few days had brought a whole stream of events. I wasn't planning my actions and hadn't even given them particular thought, just reacted to annoyances. So, I had quite a bit to think about.

The hired killer, losing control over my own gift, and the stubborn attention of my crown-bearing cousin. The harshness of these insurmountable circumstances made me feel tense. But there was no way to cut this Gordian knot with one decisive blow.

All I could do was methodically and circumstantially pull individual threads from the ball. First remove the gunman and his client from the game. Then determine the fate of Professor Berliger. If the department head had survived the fire, seek him out and figure out how to neutralize the effect of the electroconvulsive therapy.

And most importantly, not sleep.

I had no idea what Princess Anna wanted me to do, but I could be sure it wouldn't be easy.

The waiter brought my order, and although the beef in sour-cream sauce had been made the day before, it had a simply superlative flavor. Admittedly, I also ate the watery and gluey mashed potatoes to the last bite.

My strong appetite seemed to be a good sign. I drank the strong coffee in a few gulps and got up from the table.

"I'll be back soon," I warned the waiter, slipping him a bluish fiver.

I didn't take my overcoat from the rack, taking only my knapsack with me. At the exit from the snack shop, I didn't see anyone suspicious and hurried down a little alley that smelled of stale piss. I threw on the woolen coat, smoothed the shaggy beard on my face and pulled the formless hat down to my very eyes. I picked up a heavy knotted stick from the ground nearby to use as a crutch, so I could imitate a limping beggar.

The only thing that spoiled my tramp disguise were the new boots and expensive pants, but it was too late to do anything about that. I just had to hope the locals were unobservant.

IT TOOK ME five minutes to reach Hamilton Street and the same amount of time to come across the house I was seeking. There really were no numbers on the scratched-up walls but, on one of the slate-roofed buildings, I was lucky enough to make out a rusted plaque with the number three. And on the roof of the neighboring home, I discovered a green dovecote.

The front yard past the high stone fence was overgrown with cherry trees. There had once been gates separating the courtyard from the street, but they were long gone now. Next to the entrance was the dilapidated ruin of a guard post, its windows boarded up. Plenty of the house's windows were boards up as well. It, however, was not abandoned. There was clothing drying on lines stretched between the trees. and one of the chimneys had smoke coming out. It smelled of fried fish and slightly burned porridge. I could hear a child crying from one of the apartments.

Tossing my gaze over the empty yard, I immediately took notice of a ramp down into a semi-basement next to the porch of the main entry. I walked straight for it with no fear. I was not afraid of falling into the killer's field of view for the simple reason that all the windows of his dwelling were boarded up. There were scraps of cloth shoved into the cracks between the boards.

The padlock on the basement door was not closed, which meant the tenant was home, but I decided not to be rash and waited for Ramon. I went down to the lowest step of the porch, covering my nice shoes by dropping my knapsack at my feet. I set the crutch on my knees.

The walls and fence kept the wind off me. The sun was shining. I felt warm and comfortable. Drowsiness crept up on me unnoticed. I was yawning recklessly but didn't want to stand to my feet. The building carried on living its own life, and I figured I'd attract less attention just loafing about.

I mean, who would care about some itinerant tramp?

A stout mother, with two snotty kids clenching her skirt, lumbered through the yard. She didn't even glance in my direction. Some ancient old ladies rolled a cart of provisions for two through. They also paid me no mind. The only person who even seemed to see me was an ash-caked chimney-sweep, who asked me for a light before leaving the yard. And hhe was certainly a bit drunk. His gait was just too characteristic, reeling from side to side.

Then the door below gave a metallic clang.

Sean Lynch looked out onto the street and stared at me with surprise. But, fortunately, the killer's colorless gray eyes didn't adapt to the bright sunlight quickly enough, and for the moment, I must have looked like a faceless silhouette cut out of black paper and shadows.

And I didn't miss that moment.

My knapsack hit him right in the bridge of the nose and the redheaded gunman flew back into the doorframe. I quickly jumped from the porch into the basement door. The killer, his nose broken, reached for his pistol but was too late again. The stick smacked him in the head at full speed and broke in two, and the Irishman was laid out on the floor senseless.

Taking a five-round pocket revolver and pen knife from the hired goon, I ran for the knapsack sitting on the steps, at the same time locking the front door. After that, I lit a gas lamp and got up to tear a sheet from his bed into long strips. I used the strips to bind the arms and legs of the Irishman to the armrests and legs of a massive armchair. Then, I really went all out and stuck an improvised gag into his mouth and blindfolded him.

Sean Lynch was *illustrious,* and I was not going to take any risks. Once again, everything went so smoothly that, whether I wanted to or not, a doubt crawled up on me that Ramon might have sent me to the wrong man. I certainly didn't want him to see my face before I was sure.

Taking a glass cup from the table, I placed it against the tip of Lynch's worn shoe, straightened up and took a look around. It was an elongated semi-basement with a vaulted ceiling, reminiscent of a shooting gallery. There were no internal partitions in it, only a door studded with a sheet of iron in the stout stone wall at the far end. It was adorned with a pair of complicated mortise locks.

I certainly didn't have the strength to break such locks, but I also didn't have to. There were keys clanking in Lynch's inner jacket pocket. After unlocking the door, I glanced into the small den with wooden shelves along the walls that were impervious to sound, and immediately saw a tube case stuck in the corner. That was when my last doubts fell away.

I pulled a pump-reloading Colt brand carbine from the blueprint case. The steel barrel had been shortened by hand. On the end, there was a coupler linking it to a strange metallic cylinder. Just in case, I clanked the pump, grabbed the round that flew out off the floor and made certain that the weapon's caliber was right: thirty-two-twenty, Winchester.

Then I returned the carbine to the tube and opened the little case on the shelf. In it, I discovered an angular semi-automatic Webley-Scott 18-76 pistol. A cylinder of the same width as that on the rifle was attached to its barrel. The weapons smelled of powder char.

"What the devil?" I muttered quizzically and suddenly turned my attention to the shelf with the box with a flashy red label reading "Maxim," and a laconic explanation: "Exhaust Fume Silencer." On the iron-lidded cardboard tube I pulled it from, there was an even shorter description: "Maxim Silencer."

Exhaust fume silencer?

I unfolded the instructions, glanced at the description of the device, which was produced by the company of the famous weapons inventor Hiram Maxim, and very quickly figured out the design of the clever little thing. Just as advertised, it was a silencer.

There was nothing to explain the elastic rubber mask with glass eye-holes, a hose of rubberized canvas and tank of compressed air. But I had no doubt it was a breathing apparatus, and that it was what allowed hired goon to avoid discomfort from the acrid smoke. I was intrigued by the complex lens system that allowed a few pieces of glass to be inserted into the eyeholes at once. I placed the mask to my face and looked at the light. Everything looked somehow colorless and dull.

Then I removed the upper bluish gray lens from each eyehole. But before I managed to see if anything changed, I heard the sound of glass clinking from the main room. The Irishman had woken up and, trying to free himself, had unwittingly overturned the cup at his feet.

I walked over, squeezing my Webley-Scott in my left hand, and slammed it full-force into the killer's ear. My overly strong blow caused the goon to lose consciousness for a moment. His head swung down limp at his chest.

A miscalculation. It happens.

Suppressing a heavy sigh, I walked through the room with a rag, wiping down everything I had touched. I had to be sure not to leave fingerprints because I had no doubt that, in the very nearest time, this would be the scene of either mutilation or murder.

After eliminating the clues, I looked with doubt at the basement room and came to the dismal conclusion that it would be far too difficult to carry out a full interrogation here. Meanwhile, dragging Lynch into the armored vehicle was just about the worst idea one could imagine. All his neighbors would surely see.

I looked through Lynch's things and found a pair of canvas gloves and a short crowbar. Then, I got up under the window opposite the entrance and broke the boards and dusty rags out of it. Some of the boards, which were nailed in from outside, were moldering. They were somewhat more difficult, but the result was worth it. Now, I could pull the Irishman out into the front yard at any moment without risking being seen by the other residents. All that remained was to wait for the armored vehicle.

Sean Lynch woke up before that.

He instantly spat out the gag, sniffled his broken nose and asked:

"Who sent you?"

The captive couldn't fully appreciate just how pitiable a situation he had landed himself in, and there was not yet the slightest hint of fear in his muffled voice. Did he want to negotiate?

Well, why not?

Lifting the fallen cup from the floor, I filled it with water and placed it to his lips. He drank his fill and repeated the question:

"Who sent you?"

I just laughed.

"Better you tell me who enlisted you to take out Leopold Orso."

"This must be a mistake!" the Irishman immediately started denying it.

"It's worse than a mistake," I said, enraged and throwing the empty cup full force at the wall. It broke into tiny fragments with a tinkling, and the killer was shaken, as if that sound was the cracking of his very own bones.

And fear. I felt his fear for the first time.

"Who hired you?" I hurried to build on my success, but the Irishman just spat blood under his feet and didn't answer.

Lynch's moment of weakness passed, his self-confidence returned, and an attack of rage rolled over me. It was so strong that I wanted unbearably to grab the killer by his swollen bleeding nose and turn it on its side.

Surprise helped me hold back. The rage was so pure that it filled me all the way to the brim, which hadn't happened for some time. Murdering the orderlies at the psychiatric clinic was objective necessity. I was forced to do it not by personal dislike, but cold calculation. When I had intimidated Professor Berliger, it was without my intrinsic bygone fire. I was just trying to shake my dormant *talent* awake a bit. But now...

Now, my only desire was to grab the Irishman by the Adam's apple and tear the damned thing out with one flick of my hand!

I screwed up my eyes and exhaled slowly. When I opened them again, the shadows in the far corner had grown thicker into a gloomy figure, enshrouded head to toe in an impenetrable robe. All black on black, all I could make out were two familiar eyes under the deep hood flickering with unkind flame.

"Give him to me!" the Beast demanded, standing behind the Irishman.

"I wouldn't think of it," I refused the albino. "There's no reason for you to be here."

"Bugger, Leo!" my imaginary friend got angry. "I'll disembowel him in one fell swoop!"

"Hey!" Sean Lynch was startled and turned his head from side to side. "Who are you talking to?!"

"Shut up!" I demanded and pointed my index finger at the albino. "Beat it! I've got this!"

"Open your eyes, boy!" the Beast shot back. Throwing the hood off his head, he hit me with a ghastly grin. "You don't have this! You're small potatoes! Nada! Without your *talent*, you're no one and nothing!"

I wanted to put a bullet between the eyes of the fanged bastard, but I held back.

"Stay back! I'll find the key to him yet!"

"You haven't got time!"

Sean Lynch laughed.

"I've got it! You're pretending to be a psycho to scare me? Well, it won't work!"

"We haven't even begun," the Beast grinned carnivorously, a rusty butcher's knife appearing in his large clawed hand as he pulled it out of the robe.

"Stay away from me!" I took a step back. The blade of the knife flickered with an electric spark.

The colorless skin of the albino lit up with the power unlocked from inside him, and a barely visible halo quivered around his head, like the corona of a black sun ready to blast out.

"Come now..." Lynch began, but I cut him off with a stinging blow from the back of my hand.

"Shut up!"

"Keep it up!" the Beast supported me. "Just start from the feet and go higher! And don't pussyfoot. Use the hammer!"

"Get lost!"

The albino shrugged his shoulders, walked back to the wall and dissolved in the shadows, just his ghastly grin remaining in the air for a moment.

"Are you mocking me?" I groaned.

The Beast instantly appeared again.

"No, boy. I'm not mocking you," he shook his head. "I'm pulling at the last threads! Tick-tock, Leo, tick-tock! Time is slipping away!"

And again, he disappeared in the shadows, this time for good.

I remembered my mother's favorite book, *Alice's Adventures in Wonderland*. I had also read it several dozen times. I gave a cold-blooded shrug. If my imaginary friend had been making visual reference to the Cheshire Cat, things really were as bad as could be.

But to hell with it! Now, I had to talk with the hired killer, and everything else could wait. I need to follow the plan.

"I need to follow the plan!" I said, voicing the thought and walking over to the stove and turning on the gas.

Sean Lynch grew clearly alarmed, but there was no reason to worry. I had just decided to put on some coffee. I filled a jezve with water, eyeballed a good dose of the black aromatic powder, and returned to my captive.

"Don't worry, Lynch," I smiled, standing opposite him. "I'm in my right mind. I got out of Gottlieb Burckhardt two days ago."

The Irishman just chuckled.

"And do you know how I got into the madhouse?" I asked. "It was all thanks to you, Sean. Do you remember the Roman Bridge? The very beginning of September..."

The killer shook his head.

"I don't remember..."

"You don't remember? Well, alright then!" I chuckled, walking over to the stove and turning off the gas. I poured the coffee into a mug with a chipped rim and paced the basement, looking attentively from side to side. "The thing I want to do now most of all is grab you by the neck and squeeze hard enough to mushroom your throat! It's a hereditary trait for me, you know. But I'm fighting it. After all, you're a simple tool, Lynch, but I need your client. Who is he? Tell me and this will all be over. One of my grandmas was Irish. At the end of the day, we should be on the same side."

The killer's face went pale, but it didn't have any effect on his determination.

"I don't remember!" he said stubbornly.

"Drop it!" I've already found your tool. I'm just deciding the best way to beat out the answers I need.

The killer didn't say a single word.

I finished my hot bitter coffee, placed the mug on the table and walked into the back room, leaving the door wide open. I threw the Webley-Scott and silencer back into the suitcase with the rubber mask, having decided not to rely on an unfamiliar weapon. I pulled the box down from the lower shelf. It was full of smoke bombs. Then I wondered about the case, which was surprisingly heavy. I carried it into the room.

I set the case on the table, broke the lock with my knife, threw back the lid and stared in astonishment at the even rows of lenses. Just on the upper level, there were at the very least three or four hundred of them, but the Irishman seem to be an oculist.

I pulled one of the transparent eyepieces out to try and raised it to my face, discovering that it made everything in the basement blurry. I looked through the next and the picture was the same with just one exception. The Irishman bound to the armchair was suddenly filled with an utterly unreal clarity, while everything else was blurred. My eyes quickly started to ache and fill with tears.

Returning the lens to its place, I saw a note opposite its nest made in faded calligraphic handwriting: "7 ft."

Seven feet? There was approximately two meters between me and the killer; I checked the other lenses from the edge row and discovered that they all gave the ability to focus my gaze on objects a defined distance away.

Most of the glass in the other rows was colored. They muted colors, sometimes to the point the world was turned into a black and white cinema. The purpose of the strange lenses was a mystery to me until I looked through the orange one at the far wall. I realized I could clearly make out the minutest details of its rectangular bricks through the darkness of the basement.

Color filters?!

I continued testing and soon was convinced of my theory. What was more, combinations of glass allowed me to achieve astonishing results!

Everything fell into place. I could now explain Lynch's unbelievable accuracy when he had sunk two bullets into my overcoat on the coat rack. Before going into the bar, he had placed color filters into the eye holes of the rubber mask based on my coat.

One pair of lenses gave the killer unusually sharp vision, and the other gave him the ability to see through the smoke screen, while the third kept the victim from getting out of view. He just had to know in advance what shade of clothing they preferred.

In the bar, I had removed the overcoat, which had saved my life. My blue suit had simply blended in with the surrounding objects, because his color filters had focused in on the leather of the overcoat.

After wiping the tears from my eyes, I tapped the lens on the iron rim of the suitcase in contemplation and noticed Sean Lynch clench his teeth as if that slight jingling did him unbearable harm.

And perhaps it did?

"It must have been hard to get such an expansive collection?" I chuckled. "In this day and age, it can be quite hard to find a skilled alchemist."

The killer stayed silent, but I could still see his jaw bones grinding.

I threw the lens at the wall and it shattered into a few pieces.

A large drop rolled down the gunman's cheek.

"Some of them must be especially valuable, I suppose." I egged him on. "That orange one, for example. What'd it run you?"

The Irishman kept quiet, then I squeezed the little glass in my fingers and broke it in two. One of the halves delaminated, but the thick canvas gloves protected my skin from cuts.

"Enough!" Sean Lynch was pushed to his limit.

I left the suitcase with lenses, picked up the mug of cold coffee from the table, took a long sip and demanded:

"Tell me!"

I had managed to find the key to the killer, and we both knew it, but he just smiled a crooked smile.

"And why do I need that? A rich man cannot take his wealth into the kingdom of heaven."

"You'd do well to also remember the eye of the needle!" I grew angry. "Do not commit murder! There's your commandment!"

"The ends justify the means."

I took another lens from the suitcase, threw it under my foot and crushed it with my heel.

"A dead man has no need for lenses," Lynch exhaled hoarsely, convulsing at the sound of the glass crunching as if I was cleaving the lens of his real eye.

"It would be too bad to be left with a bunch of broken glass if we do manage to agree, though, right?" I chuckled but decided not to push too hard on the killer and waved a hand. "So, tell me your conditions!"

The Irishman sniffled his broken nose and shook his head.

"Come on, what conditions could I possibly

have? You're a funny guy."

I pulled a handful of lenses at random from the suitcase and threw them on the ground, then started breaking them one by one with a little hammer from the back room.

"Enough!" Sean Lynch reached a shout. "Stop it! Stop it now!"

"Then start talking."

"I'm only alive while I keep my tongue behind my teeth!"

I waved the hammer a few times to test him and said:

"You're only alive until I run out of lenses. Because as soon as I get started on your bones, there will be no more reason to keep you alive. Sean, do you know how many bones there are in the human body?"

Lynch did have a pretty good idea. I could tell by how suddenly his face changed.

"And what reason do you have to keep me alive now?"

I sighed.

People need hope. They're glad to deceive, and what is more they ask directly to be deceived, lured by the imaginary possibility of salvation.

The irony of fate was that I truly did have a good reason to spare Lynch, if he gave up his client. And that reason was Princess Anna's mission.

"Kill," she had said. I was not ready to end a person's life just because my crown-bearing cousin asked. And although enlisting Lynch to do it was just the very slightest bit less immoral, that now seemed like an ideal way out of the ethical dead-end.

At the end of the day, if this person had been dumb enough to cross the future Empress, he was the one most at fault in his own sudden death.

Yes, beyond hope, people need justifications for their miserable actions. And I had found justifications for myself.

"Most of all I now want to smash your head with this hammer," I said directly to the Irishman, "but that would be wrong. You're just a tool. And you could be of use to me."

"Excuse me?" Lynch laughed.

"You're too well-prepared to be some madman. That means you're working for money. But you live in a pigsty, so you're clearly not moved by the sin of greed. You're ideological. So, judge for yourself: what benefit can you do for your cause if you get your head smashed in with your own hammer in this basement?"

The killer winced:

"What do you suggest?"

"You tell me who hired you. I'll give you a job, paid in cash."

"That isn't right. I don't work against clients!"

"I'll be dealing with your client myself," I snapped. "I'll tell you the name of your target tomorrow. You'll have to work without preparation."

"So, you'll simply take me at my word? What if I lie, just take a name off the top of my head?"

"There aren't so many people who could wish death on me!" I cut him off. "I will not take you at your word. I'll check. And you'll be watched, don't doubt it."

"Not a very tempting perspective."

I poked the tip of my boot at the lens case in disgust and scratched my face, itching due to the theatrical beard.

"It's better than dying on a heap of broken glass."

"I'll be avenged," Sean Lynch jerked up his head in pride.

"Do you think the fighters for the independence of Ireland have nothing better to do?" I laughed.

He turned gloomy.

"Life and work or pain and death," I said. "The choice is yours."

"Alright," Lynch consented. "It was a cop. Senior Inspector Moran."

"Devil!" I was blown away. "You work for Department Three?!"

"No!" the Irishman shot out quickly. "No, he simply left me with no choice!"

I turned around and whipped the hammer at the wall full force.

Devil! Bastian Moran hadn't been able to get me behind bars and had decided to take justice into his own hands! What a twofaced viper!

And what a fool I was! All this time, the solution was right under my nose, but I didn't put forth enough mental effort to find it! Silver bullets! I was shot with silver bullets, but there weren't very many people who knew or even suspected that I was a werebeast. I could have found who hired me by process of elimination.

I took a few loud sighs, patted my jacket pockets and discovered that the notepad and pencil were still in my overcoat.

"Have you got a pencil and paper?" I asked Lynch.

"Whatever for?" the killer got on guard.

"You're going to write a statement to the inspector general..."

"No!"

I didn't have time to insist: I heard the chirring of a powder engine outside. Ramon's armored car had entered the courtyard, ruining all my plans in an instant. Now, the killer would have to be brought out the main entrance in full view of all his neighbors.

I stood behind Lynch and warned:

"If you so much as twitch, I'll blow your brains out!" After that, I undid his wrists from the armrests and immediately commanded: "Hands! Hands behind your back! And head down! Step to it!"

The killer obediently leaned forward, then I bound his wrists together, trying to tie the knots as tight as I could.

"What are you doing?!" Lynch groaned, already hearing the sound of the nearby armored vehicle just as clearly as me. "I cannot go to the police!"

"That isn't the police!" I reassured the man, freeing his legs with the pen knife. "They came for me. Stand up!"

"Eyes!" the killer reminded me.

I tore the blindfold off his face, threw a jacket on his bound arms and pushed him to the door.

"Walk! And no stupid stuff! I need you, but if you twitch, I'll shoot you through the head!"

To confirm the gravity of my words, I cocked my Webley-Fosbery.

Sean Lynch slumped and walked toward the exit.

"Where are we going?" he asked.

"Somewhere safe," I answered and demanded: "Face to the wall!"

The killer obeyed, then I undid the lock and, throwing open the door, pushed him onto the stairs.

"Out!"

And we walked to the idling armored vehicle.

9

WALKING TEN METERS – what could be easier for a healthy person in the very prime of their life? But while escorting a dangerous recidivist, those very ten meters could become a road to the afterlife. So, when the Irishman suddenly started fumbling on the stairs, I stuck the barrel of my revolver into his lower back and placed my free hand between his shoulder blades.

"Walk!"

Instead of that, Lynch stepped back and gasped:

"What the devil?!"

"Never seen an armored vehicle before?" I barked, looking from behind the killer's shoulder into the yard and instantly losing all my confidence. The barrels of a Gatling gun were spinning with a measured hum on the tower of the self-propelled carriage. It was aimed at the stairs.

Luckily, I was standing lower than Lynch.

The silence of the sleepy little courtyard was blown to smithereens by the sudden thunder of a machine-gun burst. Blood spattered on my face. The Irishman's body, honeycombed by high-caliber bullets, collapsed on me from above and dragged me down with its dead weight. I slithered out from under him like an adder, crawled into the basement, slammed the door and did the lock.

A moment later, the heavy boards exploded into a cloud of splinters! The bullets that pierced them flew around the basement with a hum, ricocheting off the stone floor; I wasn't hit by a single one, but it was just a matter of time.

A light spot of broken window met my eye on the other side of the basement and I pushed off the wall and was already making my first step when I heard an echoing boom on the stairs. An explosion ripped the door off its hinges, and the shockwave slammed into my back, knocking me off my feet. I somersaulted along the floor.

My ear drums popped into a cottony silence and nasty echo, but I didn't lose my consciousness and even managed to stand to my feet. Seeking the revolver that flew out of my hands, I walked to it and, immediately, two hand grenades were thrown into the doorway.

I barely managed to take shelter in the back room before a double explosion thundered out and shrapnel flew into the bare stone walls of the basement.

I was reminded of the albino saying: "You haven't got time!" I spit an oath and yanked the pump rifle from the tube. I stuck it out into the front room and just in the nick of time. In the smoke and dust, I could just barely make out a policeman wearing a hard helmet and armored cuirass.

I shot, aiming for his legs. I just didn't want to commit the sin of killing a former colleague. Also, this caliber wouldn't get through the cuirass...

The constable dropped his semi-automatic rifle and collapsed on the steps, squeezing his thigh wound with his hands. I pumped again and got off another shot. This time, intentionally higher up in an attempt to scare off the others. I heard return fire thunder out from the stairs, then the wounded constable was pulled outside, and another pair of grenades flew in.

In that time, I managed to load rounds into the carbine's magazine. I stuck my head out of the back room right after the explosion, but immediately hid again. The police had broken the boards out of one of the windows and stuck the tube of a Lewis gun into the basement. A nonstop rain of bullets thundered out, putting holes in furniture and breaking rubble out of stone walls.

Under the cover of machine-gun fire, the constables could have thrown grenades at me no problem. But before they managed, my eye caught on the wooden box of smoke grenades. Not wasting time, I picked up the weighty cylinder, pulled the pin and threw it into the basement, then sent another after it.

In an instant, the room was filled with an impenetrable acrid gray smoke. In order not to suffocate, I tore off the blood-spattered fake beard, pulled the rubber mask onto my face and clipped the canvas hose to the tank of compressed air, praying to myself that the Irishman had not used it all up.

I was in luck. The tank was not empty. Sticking it into the knapsack hanging over my shoulder, I gathered some smoke bombs from the killer's suitcase and glanced out the cracked door. The lenses over the normal ones allowed me to see the Webley-Fosbery I'd lost in the fall through the impenetrable smoke. As soon as the Lewis gun finally went silent, I grabbed the revolver and ran as fast as I could to the window opposite the entrance I'd broken out earlier.

Throwing a smoke bomb into the front yard ahead of me, I got up onto the table, which was littered with shards of broken ceramic, then climbed onto the wide window sill. Bashing with the case, I broke out the rest of the boards and crawled into the shallow stone niche. Without delay, I jumped out of it like a spooked rabbit and dashed into the bushes.

The front yard was already fully immersed in acrid gray haze, but a strong wind was dispersing the smoke quickly. So, I first tossed a bomb toward the courtyard exit, then another onto the street. Finally, I rolled over the short fence and dashed toward the building opposite.

It was swelteringly hot in the rubber mask and my breathing seized quickly. The glass eyeholes were covered with perspiration, but the roar of the powder engine gave me speed. I heard a knock, a screech and an echo, as if the driver of the armored vehicle had run into a streetlight pole due to bad visibility, and the machine gun started thundering blindly. Not feeling my legs under me, I ran into the neighboring courtyard, grabbed the last two smoke bombs from the bag and threw them in different directions to confuse my pursuers and, under the cover of the thick dark gray smog, ran up to the fence, took a bit more air into my chest and tore the rubber mask off my face. I stuck the breathing apparatus in the killer's case and threw the canvas gloves in the same place. The blood-soaked woolen coat I simply tossed on a pile of trash.

After that, I crawled over the fence and hurried away, coughing and spitting as I ran.

I got away! I actually got away!

A QUARTER HOUR LATER, when I reached the *Phoenix*, Ramon Miro was sitting calmly at one of the tables and eating beef stroganoff with gusto. Upon hearing the door fly open, he tore himself from the plate for a moment, but immediately returned to his refection.

"A mug of black coffee," I asked the waiter, taking a seat opposite the hulking man and sliding the killer's case under the table.

"I see you couldn't wait and kicked up some noise?" Ramon said, not hiding his dismay.

"You took a long time."

"Traffic," my former partner explained. "When we found the building, there was already machine gun fire. Apologies, Leo, but we were not equipped for a firefight with the police. In any case, I decided to check your favorite snack shop, saw your overcoat and decided to wait. I figured, if you did manage to get your butt out of there, you'd surely come back for the coat."

I nodded.

The waiter placed the coffee before me; I took a sip of the hot drink and didn't taste anything but bitterness. I had been drinking too much coffee all day.

"Sugar and cream, please," I asked. When the waiter had left, I rubbed my temples and asked Ramon: "And how are things there now?"

The hulking man understood before I finished and shrugged his shoulders.

"I don't know. We didn't get too close. What did you do?"

I poured some cream and two lumps of sugar into my mug and started stirring in concentration.

"At first everything was going well," I said after a long silence. "But I miscalculated a bit. Lynch was working for Moran..."

"The senior inspector?!" Ramon shot out.

"Shh!" I shushed. "Yes, senior inspector of

Department Three, Bastian Moran. He somehow found out about your questioning and sent people to cover his tracks. They didn't even ask any questions, just opened fire straight off."

"Did Moran want to kill you?" The hulking man pushed his plate away and got up from the table. "Seriously?!"

"Sit!" I ordered. "Sit and calm down. I'll deal with Moran."

Ramon sat down in his chair and nervously drummed his fingers on the edge of the tabletop. I didn't need to be a great physiognomist to read the obvious mistrust reflected on his face. And fear. The fear overcoming my former partner could be felt without any *illustrious talent*.

"And how will you deal with him, Leo?" Ramon frowned. "Are you planning to kill him?"

"No," I shook my head, intending to appeal to Inspector General von Nalz. "I have connections."

"If you've got connections, why did you need me?"

"I won't be bringing you in to this matter any further," I promised. "Take care of Professor Berliger."

"What do you mean?"

"Figure out if he died in the fire or not."

"And if he's alive?"

"Just find him. I'll talk with him on my own. That is all."

"What if they want to interrogate me about Lynch's case? I blew my cover asking about him, after all! What should I say to the police?"

I just shrugged my shoulders.

"Think of something. And don't forget to burn that drawing."

"Alright," Ramon nodded, taking out his wallet Drawing out his words gloomily, continued: "After all I just wanted to go to the Caribbean..."

"So some voodoo priest can curse you?" I chuckled, getting up from the table.

"What's wrong with that tongue of yours, Leo?"

"Nothing," I answered, taking my overcoat from the rack. "I'm dispelling your illusions."

"Don't waste your energy."

"As you say. Will you take me to Brandt's?"

"I won't go downtown," Ramon refused. "The traffic jams on the road are simply monstrous."

"Then go right to Gottlieb Burckhardt," and let me out near an underground stop.

"I can do that."

Ramon paid for breakfast, got a paper bag of pastries from the waiter for his nephew and threw the front door open.

"Let's go, Leo," he called. "The armored car is in the next alley over.'

I grabbed the case and we headed off on our way.

IN THE VEHICLE, there was constant rumbling on the uneven paving stone. But when I got into the underground, I fell asleep a few times to the clinking of the train wheels. I dozed off and gave a start, scaring those around me with my sharp movements.

A little while later, I did it again.

I walked outside feeling like a boiled vegetable. My head was spinning and my legs were giving out. The back of my shirt was soaked in sweat. But at least I wasn't nauseous...

On the steps of the underground station, a briskly striding boy tried to foist a paper advertisement on me. I waved him off and, nearly hitting a newspaper seller's cart, walked off. My mind was gradually growing clearer in the fresh air. By the time I'd returned to Yablochkov street, I had already come to my senses, although my heartbeat was still somewhat uneven due to all the coffee.

However, I felt a flood of strength and lost all desire to sleep. That pleased me.

It pleased me very much.

Then, much to my surprise, I heard a powder engine chirring unusually softly behind me, and a long self-propelled carriage rolled out of an alley onto the causeway. Its headlights were chromed barrels and its radiator had a fanciful grate design. I pulled my revolver from my belt but I saw William Grace peeking out of the flung-open door. At his side, the oracle was frozen motionless with her eyes closed. This time, she wasn't wearing any veiled hat, and her black hair was falling down freely on her shoulders. Under the seat were her shoes, which she'd thrown off her feet.

"Get in, Leopold!" the Imperial Guard lieutenant demanded. "Come now, faster! Faster!"

I hesitated a bit, but still crawled up onto the

brown velvet seat, put the suitcase under my feet and slammed the door behind me.

William Grace knocked on the divider between the passenger area and driver without delay, and the carriage started off, gradually gaining speed. The lady-in-waiting didn't even give a slight movement. The oracle, beyond all doubt, was in a deep trance. Her fingers, clenching a pearl thread, were white in agitation. I could see her eyeballs darting from side to side under her eyelids, and her chest was heaving ever so slightly under her the deep neckline of her garment.

"Has something happened?" I asked, guessing why the inseparable pair had come around this time.

"You didn't sleep last night!" William Grace said. His tone was such that it seemed was accusing me of state treason.

However, that might as well have been the case: I had stayed awake all night long not at all because of insomnia, but because I wanted to avoid meeting Princess Anna.

"There wasn't time for sleep," I shrugged my shoulders.

"Running from former colleagues?" the lieutenant chuckled.

"What do you mean?"

William Grace looked at me with unhidden incomprehension.

"Leopold, yesterday evening Department Three declared you a wanted man! You didn't know?"

"No," I answered, thunderstruck. "This must be

a misunderstanding. The inspector general assured me..."

"A hand-held bomb was thrown into the inspector general's carriage yesterday," the lieutenant dumbfounded me again. "Friedrich von Nalz is dead. Anarchists have taken credit for the killing."

"Devil!" is all that tore out of me. "Who was appointed in his place?"

"The Minister of Justice, on a personal request from Duke Logrin, has entrusted the temporary leadership of the police to Senior Inspector Moran."

I exhaled loudly and stared point blank at the lieutenant.

"This is all Moran," I declared directly. "Son of a bitch! He wants to kill me!"

"Why does he want that?"

"It's personal. You have to protect me from him!"

William Grace just laughed.

"We will not do that," he cut me off. "The crown doesn't need such a scandal. Wriggle your own way out of it."

"If I'm arrested..."

"Well, don't get arrested!"

"You need to rein in Moran!"

"We are nothing now" William Grace exploded. "There's the heiress to the throne, who's in a coma, a disgraced Imperial Guard lieutenant and a morphine-addicted lady-in-waiting! And no one else! The rest..." The lieutenant calmed his breathing and cracked his knuckles. "Are taking a wait-and-see position. And that's the best-case scenario. Many are plainly working against us."

I sat back in the soft seat and exhaled:

"Bugger!"

At that very moment, the lady-in-waiting unclenched her fingers from the thread of pearls, took her hand off her chest and placed it on the lieutenant's groin.

"My dear Willy," she mewed out softly, not opening her eyes, "you must still be mad at me for that last pearl, but I ask you to please control your language! Those things in your knickers are not mere beads. If they get ripped off, they cannot be sewn back on!"

Her long thin fingers with bright red manicure clearly clenched.

The lieutenant swallowed fitfully, and his broad masculine face turned a lilac crimson.

"I'll take it into account," he squeezed out a promise, pressing himself into the back of the chair.

That was enough for the lady-in-waiting. She returned her hand to her chest, but now her fingers weren't clenching the beads, but constantly letting the individual pearls pass through one after the next, like a rosary.

William Grace cleared his throat, unbuttoned his shirt collar and, looking somewhere to the side, assured me:

"Leopold, after you complete her highness's mission, everything will change for the better. We can protect you from the police, I promise."

"Can her Highness influence the regent in her sleep?" I suggested. "What would it cost her to intervene for a close relative?"

"Her Highness's *talent* is not all powerful. It can be hidden from. The Duke does not maintain a relationship with her Highness."

"I see."

Wanting to think over his words, I slid back the curtain covering the window and looked outside.

We just so happened to be passing Albert Brandt's house. I met eyes with a suspicious looking fellow in a uniform who was pretending to fix a bike chain. As soon as the spook was out of view, a freshly-painted self-propelled carriage turned out of a side passage and started tailing us.

"Are those your people?" I asked, throwing the side of my jacket off the revolver stuck in my belt.

"Calm yourself, Leopold!" the lieutenant hissed at me. "Just in case, we have covered the street from both sides."

I slammed my jacket shut and asked:

"What reason did you have to wait for me here?"

The lady-in-waiting gave a prolonged moan.

"Oh, men! You're always thinking about the wrong thing!"

The lieutenant glanced at his companion, slightly moving away from her to the door and suggesting:

"Get to business."

But I wasn't going to let this topic end so

quickly.

"You were following me, after all, right?"

"What a pain in the butt!" the lady-in-waiting said, drawing out her words and opening her eyes. They were barely shining today and looked reddened. "Leopold, my boy! You thought exactly right. As long as you don't go to sleep, her highness cannot reach you. But the mind cannot get by without rest. You drifted off a few times in the underground, and her Highness informed us of that. But none of that matters. You should be asking a different question."

"And what is that?"

A playful smile slid over the oracle's brightly colored lips. Something foxlike slipped through on her thin face, which made shivers run up my spine.

"Ask: 'What do you want from me?'" the lady-in-waiting demanded and, peeling herself off the back of the seat, shot forward. "Well? Ask! It's just words!"

I lead my gaze away from her deep neck line and asked:

"What am I supposed to do?"

"Oh, nothing particular, my boy! You just need to fall asleep."

"Fall asleep?"

"Hearing problems?" the lady-in-waiting cocked a plucked brow. "Yes, Leopold, just fall asleep. Right now."

William Grace looked at his companion in uncertainty and started doubting:

"Is that really necessary?"

The lady-in-waiting turned with a fated sigh and reminded him:

"What did I say a minute ago about the male mindset, William? You joke about women's logic, but always ask stupid and pointless questions, the answer to which should be obvious even to creatures with such limited intellectual abilities as yourself."

"You didn't manage to get through to her Highness?!"

"Is your full name William Obvious Grace?"

The lieutenant pursed his lips and turned away, the oracle meanwhile turned back to me:

"You'll have to fall asleep, Leopold."

Now, nothing depended on me, so I didn't protest. Instead, I fell back in the seat with a smirk and kicked out my legs.

"I can try. To be honest, I recently drank a half liter of coffee, so I'll have to wait for some time."

But the lady-in-waiting was in no mind to wait. She pulled a small glass bottle from her reticule. It was filled to the very cork with small gray tablets.

"Right now means right now, my boy. This will help you fall asleep."

"Are you serious?"

"We've already wasted too much time!" William Grace supported his companion. "We cannot wait any longer. and don't forget: you gave your word."

"Don't be stubborn!" The lady-in-waiting smiled charmingly, twisting off the top of the vial. "Be a good boy, and I'll give you a kiss!"

She shook a tablet out onto her palm, extended

it to me and with a harsh tone that wouldn't bare
objections, demanded:

"Swallow this. Leopold. Now!"

PART FIVE

ANARCHIST

Demons and Bombs

1

NOTHING IS A STRANGE WORD. Nothing means there isn't anything, but is that really possible?

Take away any given thing – emptiness remains. Pump the air out of a laboratory flask, you get a vacuum. Not a single scientific experiment can produce this proverbial nothing. After all, it is a purely philosophical concept, and by no means a physical one.

Nothing useful. Nothing important. Nothing to worry about. All just something that has no importance here or now.

Or so I thought until nothingness spread out around me and swallowed me head and all, dissolving me.

The world ceased to exist, and my thoughts disappeared. My desires and motivations turned to dust. I was nothing and everything at the same time.

It could probably also be called nirvana.

Fading, diminishing, wearing thin, peace.

Death?

No, nothing of the sort. Although I didn't fully understand what it was like to die, I subconsciously expected death to be a fleeting spark of pain, like a cut from a deadly razor, followed by the long icy cold of the grave. Here, there was nothing of the like. Not even close.

With electromagnetic radiation, I pierced the ether, and it was neither cold nor hot. My feelings were left far behind. My body was left in the same place – the back seat of a self-propelled carriage unhurriedly rolling down the narrow alleyways of the Old City.

The lady-in-waiting's tablets were a true wonder.

THEN I WAS BLINDED by the unbearable luster of the sun beating right into my eyes. I raised a hand to cover my eyes and realized with horror that I was floating in the ether amongst an endless cosmic wasteland. Somewhere unbelievably far away, there were huge burning stars but they were simply lost on the backdrop of the orange ball of the sun with its shaggy plasma corona.

"A dream!" I remembered. "This is all just a dream!"

And this dream, beyond all doubt, belonged to someone else.

As if responding to the awakening of my conscious mind, space stirred and, right opposite the blinding ball, there appeared a winged silhouette. The light blinded the eye as before, and I couldn't make out any details. But for some reason, it seemed to me that the silhouette was female.

Using the power of my imagination, I tried to extinguish the shining of the overly bright star, but nothing came of it. I tried to move away but found no success in my attempts once again. This person's dream was unresponsive to my mental orders.

"Cousin!" Princess Anna started with reproach. "You disappoint me!"

With her dreamer *talent*, the heiress to the

throne had given herself an angelic appearance, and so wasn't experiencing any discomfort from being in outer space. I couldn't shake the feeling that I only had to cut an invisible thread and I would immediately fall down and, like a meteor, burn up in the atmosphere of Earth, its blue and green ball hovering right under our feet.

"Cousin!"

I shuddered from the cry but immediately got myself together and chuckled.

"Why all these moral arguments, cousin? Tell me what you need of me, and let's finish this!"

The angel's wings gave a graceful flutter. The Princess came subtly closer but, as before, her figure was an impenetrably black silhouette, as if this had nothing at all to do with the rays of the sun beating at her back.

"You are aware that it is in my power to strand you here forever?" Anna whispered. "Cousin! You cannot hide from me, you gave your word. I can appear in any of your dreams and confine you to whichever dungeon I desire! Continue dodging meetings with me in the future, and I will create the most terrifying nightmare I can find!"

"Get to the point!"

A fierce rage wafted over me, as if I had touched the plasma corona of the sun.

"Cousin, you do not realize the full gravity of the situation!"

"No!" I barked back. "It is you that has ceased to distinguish between dream and reality! If I am killed, I will not complete your mission! Think about that! To save my own life, I had to not sleep, and I did not sleep. One must know how to prioritize!"

"And where among your priorities is the fact you gave me your word?"

I considered how to answer, but not for too long, as not to further aggravate the situation.

"Second. First, as with any other person, is my own life."

"As with any other person!" the Princess grew enraged. "But for me, your delay was akin to death! What do you have to say to that, cousin?!"

I wanted horribly not to explain myself, but the heiress to the throne had spent too much time wandering from dream to dream and wasn't in the best mental state. So, I tried to smooth the situation over.

"You said: 'kill,' but didn't say who."

"We were cut off," the Princess said, now back in her usual tone.

"What was that fiery rain?"

I personally suspected that it was all the fault of the Princess's unstable mind or, perhaps, the effect of my physiotherapy leaking into the dream, but the answer stung me to the depths of my soul.

"Not what, but who."

"There's another dreamer?!"

"More than just a dreamer. The one who lies dormant in our blood, the blood of *the illustrious*," my cousin answered and went silent, but not for long. "I've dreamed of a burning rain cleansing the capital since childhood," she informed me after a pause. "Back then, it was simple nightmares. After the operation on my heart, though, the dreams became indistinguishable from reality. I am ghastly tired of burning alive over and over! If this was the price of curing me, wouldn't it have been better to just calmly live out my time?"

"The price of curing you? What do you mean?" I asked in surprise, rubbing mechanically at the scars splitting my chest.

"My heart was replaced with yours," Princess Anna reminded me. "But our forbearers spilled too much blood of *the fallen*, and you and I have far too much power for just two people. No one was given to hold so much in themselves."

My cousin's words put me in a dead end.

The one who lies dormant in our blood?

What nonsense was this?!

"I don't understand!" I admitted honestly.

Princess Anna broke down laughing and asked:

"Do you know why *the illustrious* were removed from all important posts and assigned to sinecures in the colonies and distant provinces?"

There was no reason to hide my awareness, so I said calmly:

"A conspiracy. After the death of Emperor Clement, some of *the illustrious* decided to support the Duke of Arabia in his claims to the throne."

"That was part of it," the Princess confirmed. "But not all. The true goal was not to allow the emergence of a dynasty of *illustrious*, not to allow all that cursed blood to gather in one person, even if it was many centuries later. That was the very reason I was not allowed *illustrious* suitors."

In any other circumstance, my cousin's words would have seemed foolish enough to make me laugh. But now, under the effect of an unknown drug, I imagined myself drifting between the stars and so, with unexpected calm, I asked:

"And what's the problem with that? What would happen if someone gathered too much power inside them?"

"It would awaken the dormant and curse the apostates. All of us, all humanity."

I chuckled.

"The reductionists invent astonishing fantasies when trying to say whether a higher power exists! We had no choice but to recast the prophecy of the coming of the antichrist in our own image!"

"It is no fantasy!" the Princess shot out sharply. "What do you know about the laws of inheritance? About the accumulation of metals in human organs? About the mutation of living organisms under the influence of various types of radiation? Darwin's theory, in the end?!"

"Empty words!"

"Nothing of the sort! I personally read a report which scientifically established that, if enough nonrelated *illustrious* interbreed, a superhuman would be born."

"A superhuman?"

"Reductionists!" the Princess furrowed her

brow. "They hide from the truth behind numbers and formulas. A curse is dormant in our blood, cousin! Or do you seriously suppose that a *fallen one* can be killed by simply cutting out its heart with a titanium blade?"

"They say the power of *the fallen* carries an imprint of their will," I noted neutrally, thinking of how to draw out time. If the Princess didn't manage to tell me the name of her victim before I woke up, I'd have at least another twelve-hour break.

"*The fallen* are power itself! They didn't die, didn't disappear without a trace, they were simply dissolved in us, in *the illustrious*!"

"All New Babylon was awash in the blood of *the fallen*," I replied, watching the ball of earth, enshrouded in whitish haze. "Tens of thousands bathed in it! Three quarters of them died from the Diabolic Plague in the first months after the overthrow of *the fallen*. How many of them died childless as a result? In the current *illustrious*, there is nothing but a miserable remnant of their bygone power!"

"That isn't the case at all, dear cousin,' Princess Anna objected. "The ones who died are those who were burned by poison, not those left with the power."

"How do you mean?"

"People feared *the fallen* even after they had lost all their abilities. They were afraid of attracting their predeath curse, and titanium blades were few and far between in the capital."

"And what of it?"

"The blood that flooded the streets of New Babylon was human! The old aristocracy defended their sovereigns to the very last. Some garrisons and military divisions also fought on their side. There were battles in the city, but few of *the fallen* were killed in those confrontations. With rare exception, they were not killed, but executed. And there were only a few executioners in the whole city."

I mentally nodded. The squares of New Babylon were red not only from the natural color of granite, but also because of the blood of *the fallen* locked up inside the stone. In my childhood, any old waif knew the execution sites by heart. Tor a half a franc, they would take any curious tourist around to Palace Square, Emperor Clement Square or Brown Bridge. And for more generous compensation they would go to the less famous, but no less bloody ones in the back alleys of the Old City.

"It was the executioners who took the lion's share of the power of *the fallen*," Princess Anna continued. "Some fell to their assistants and guards, but the simple city dwellers raging on the blood-soaked squares got very, very little."

"They were cursed all the same, though," I chuckled unhappily.

"Not cursed, but poisoned," my cousin corrected me. "By the way, we aren't talking about that. My grandfather executed *fallen* on Emperor's square, and his brother in Riverfort."

The Princess was referring to the Duke of Arabia, who had unofficially fathered my mother. That fact gave birth to her fears that there was too much power of *the fallen* in us.

"Nonsense!" I doubted. But I couldn't refute her mad tale so quickly and fell silent, choosing my words more carefully. But after that, a blinding luster came up under my feet, fully drowning out the blaze of the sun and mixing with the darkness, emanating upward around the Princess.

In her dream, my cousin fancied herself a winged woman with immodestly mature forms, but I was not interested in her naked body. My back was pierced by an unbearable pain from God knows where. A huge hump emerged between my shoulders, my skin burst, and two angel wings tore outward. With a light flap, they straightened out. Blood spattered off them and hovered in space as weightless droplets.

I screamed in unbearable torment, but the rays of the sun struck my widely spread wings and pushed them like the wind pushes the sails of a ship. I was spun and cast away, the reality of this dream faded, and I shot downward like a blistering arrow, straight for the earth.

"He awakens!" my cousin shouted, falling next to me.

Her wings folded skillfully, and she tore first into the atmosphere of the planet. I meanwhile, froze in expectation of a forceful impact with the air but instead, I felt a raging fire. In the blink of an eye, the Princess and I raced over Continental Europe, crossed the gulf and plunged down into New Babylon like two fiery comets.

Over the very roofs of the buildings, the Princess spread her wings and evened out her flight. I followed her example and accidentally knocked a tower off a castle but held myself in the air and dashed over the flaming city after my cousin.

Instead of shadows, we left rivers of fire on the earth in our wake...

I SHUDDERED AWAKE on the back seat of a self-propelled carriage which, as before, was driving the forking streets of the Old City.

"Curses!" I exhaled, barely able to turn my dried-out tongue. "Now that's what I call the devil..."

Then I glanced at the seat opposite mine and froze with my mouth open wide. There was a fragile young girl looking at me with clear bright *illustrious* eyes. Her skin was so pale it was as if the rays of the sun had never fallen on it.

"Your Highness..." I hesitated and only then realized I was not truly awake and just had gone from one dream into another.

"Drop the formalities, cousin!" Princess Anna laughed. "You don't object to me spending some time in your dream? Mine smells unbearably of char."

"And sulfur," I said, having caught the familiar scent, and also the reek of burning flesh and something else even more disgusting.

"And sulfur," my cousin confirmed.

"Why all that? Why jump from one dream to another like fleas on stray dogs?"

"You have a rich imagination, cousin. Probably that is what awoke it..."

"Balderdash! It is simply a nightmare that lurks in your subconscious! Phobia. Fear. Insecurity. Get rid of it! Get rid of it and live calmly!"

"We aren't talking about me now!" my cousin grew angry, her pale cheeks tinged by a light feverish blush. "You gave your word..."

"I did."

"...and you must kill Duke Logrin!"

I had to kill the Regent? Did I really have to?!

"You gave your word!" the Princess repeated.

"Bugger!" I exhaled, falling back powerless in the seat and tearing open the collar of my shirt, which had suddenly grown too tight.

I was obliged to fulfill my cousin's request. For *the illustrious*, one's word is not a mere sound. Give an oath, and it becomes an obligation one is forever bound by.

I squeezed my head in my hands, turned my head then shot up and asked:

"Why do you need that?"

"Is the reason so important?"

"What do you think?" I couldn't hold back. "Yes! Naturally it's important!"

The Princess's pale face remained fearless.

"Do you have such a need to feel right all the time?" she inquired with a slight shade of contempt. "The Duke is a usurper. Is that not enough for you?"

"That's just one person's word!"

"It's the word of an heiress to the throne!" My cousin shouted, and her eyes started glimmering with a colorless flame. "Is my word not enough?! Really?"

"No, but..."

The Princess didn't let me finish.

"He won't let my doctors see me!" she announced. "My personal doctors! The quacks the Duke hired don't know anything about operating on hearts, their job is to support me in a stable condition and nothing more. But I don't want to spend the next half century in a coma! I don't!"

"Alright!" I threw my open hands out before me. "You suspect the Duke of betrayal. Why don't you go straight to the Imperial Council?"

"It's all gone too far. I cannot trust anyone."

"But can you trust me?"

"If the Duke finds out about your existence, he will destroy you. You, cousin, I can trust."

I couldn't find the words to answer, just asked:

"And you also have no influence with the police?"

The Princess shook her head.

"Von Nalz was a good man, but the Duke has placed one of his people in that position. Why do you ask?"

"A misunderstanding," I winced and asked: "Do you realize I do not have the slightest chance of success? I cannot simply waltz into the Palace."

"And you will not have to," Princess Anna answered. "Tomorrow at midday, the Duke will visit the Imperial Mint. He will agree with the inspector on designs for memorial coins."

"Is that for certain?"

"The visit was planned last week. I managed to extract this intelligence from the dream of one of his assistants."

"You cannot get into the regent's head?"

My cousin cringed.

"No, the Duke, prudently, does not dream."

"How is this possible?"

"Do you want to know the name of the pills?" Princess Anna smiled. "No, cousin, they will not help an *illustrious* man with an imagination like yours. It would be easier just to sink a bullet right into your skull."

"I may have to do just that if the attempt fails."

"Well, do everything in your power so it doesn't fail!" my cousin threw out. "The Duke's carriage is not armored. You can recognize it by the coat of arms on the doors. How you act is up to you. Just don't forget what's riding on this! You will not get a second chance! If you help me, I will fix all your problems with the police."

"Do you promise?"

"They will no longer bother you."

I nodded, threw open the door of the self-propelled carriage and fell out into soft gray nothingness.

2

IT'S HAPPENED before that I fell asleep under one circumstance, and woke up in another, but my location has never changed while at rest. As a rule, where I fell asleep has always been where I woke up.

But this time, I went down on the luxurious seat of a self-propelled carriage and woke up on a stone embankment under a bridge over the Yarden. My head had been thoughtfully placed on the case I'd stolen from the Irish killer, and my hands were holding the pill-bottle of the lady-in-waiting's fantastically effective tablets.

"Eat me!" said the inscription on the unevenly-adhered piece of paper. It was a woman's handwriting.

I wanted to throw the pill bottle into the river but changed my mind and stuck it in my pocket. After that, I sat up on the cold stones and touched my face; there were traces of bright red lipstick on my fingers. The lady-in-waiting had kept her word.

"May your life be empty!" I cursed mildly, rubbing my cheek with a handkerchief and pulling my revolver from my pocket. I popped it open to make sure all the bullets were in place and hid it back.

There was a ringing emptiness in my head. I don't know how long I sat under the bridge but eventually, I saw two constables looming on the other side of it. I had to stand up and shuffle off down the embankment in the opposite direction.

Fortunately, the police were not interested in

me.

THE LEATHER COAT was not the greatest protection from cold and, after sleeping on the rocks, my body was stiff as a board, and snot was pouring from my nose. So, when I came across a street cafe, I went in and ordered a mug of hot mulled wine. I asked them to bring a couple waffles with whipped cream to go with it then, with a wave of my hand, called over a boy hauling a stack of newspapers on his shoulder. A fresh edition of the *Atlantic Telegraph* ran me ten centimes.

I finishing the warm spiced wine and unfolded the newspaper. Without particular surprise, I saw that the whole first column was dedicated to the murder of Inspector General Friedrich von Nalz.

Somewhere in the depths of my soul, a thought perked up that this news must have come as quite a shock to his poor daughter, but memories of my past love didn't occupy me for long. The further I went, the more my feelings for Elizabeth-Maria von Nalz seemed like just a hellish obsession.

And really what did I have to worry about here? She had a husband and would be fine.

But as for me... I had total uncertainty before me. And the near future didn't seem to promise anything good even in the best-case scenario.

Kill the regent, just think! By the way... what if I did think?

I took a sip of the mulled wine, which was now growing cold, gobbled down a crispy waffle with a surprisingly strong appetite, and started thinking over my cousin's words. She said the regent had designs on the throne. No matter how I wanted to find moral justifications to murder him, I couldn't find any.

Although, as Empress, would it not be in her power to punish and pardon at her own discretion? Princess Anna had told me as much totally unambiguously.

Devil! I was sure the anarchist wasn't troubled by such doubts when he threw a bomb into the carriage of the inspector general. He just threw it and that was that. But as for Dostoevskian moral agony such as, "whether I am a trembling creature, or whether I have the right," that was for those of subtle and sensitive nature like me. Always doubting my thoughts even when right; was that not a refined form of torture? Any other person in my place would take and fulfill the order of the heiress to the throne with a light heart, but I was tormented!

To hell with all that! Anarchists with their fanatical allegiance to idealism had it unspeakably easier...

Stop! Anarchists?

Instantly forgetting the headache, I finished the mulled wine in a few sips and, leaving the second waffle untouched, paid my bills. After that, I crossed the street and bought a tin of orange sugar drops that caught my eye in a pharmacy, meanwhile asking to use the telephone.

A gray-haired old man in a severe frock coat gave a good-natured nod and I took the phone off the hook however, to my greatest pity, Ramon was not in the office; one of his many cousins answered the call.

"Ramon isn't here, and I can't say when he'll be back," he said. "What shall I tell him?"

Considering that Department Three could tap phones, it would have been ridiculously stupid to say where I was, but that didn't change the fact that I urgently needed to meet with my former partner.

"Have him wait for me in the place where we first started our search for Procrustes," I said and added: "And tell him to come alone."

"Alright, I'll tell him," the man answered phlegmatically and hung up.

All that remained was to hope that he wasn't being held in the sights of a Department Three investigator. Although, if that did worsen my position, it wasn't by much. A description of the *illustrious* Leopold Orso had likely already been sent out to all police stations. But arresting a person in the Emperor's Park would necessitate a full-scale raid.

I'd get out of it.

THE EMPEROR'S PARK was a green oasis in the dead kingdom of stone and iron that was New Babylon. That said, it wasn't too green these days. Due to the constant smog and factory emissions, the dry yellowing leaves were covered with a layer of gray. And yet, the trees clung stubbornly to life and, even on the hottest and most windless summer days, the air there was not quite so red-hot and smoky as in the surrounding streets.

On one side, the park was bordered by a train track. The others were crowded with residential buildings. Even the most notorious reductionists wouldn't dream of proposing to build up this piece of free land. And if some innovator was nursing such intentions, he wisely didn't trot them out at public hearings.

I could not claim to know the Emperor's Park like the back of my hand, but I could easily count on crossing it by old memory without getting lost on its shady paths. Then, getting through one of the many holes in its fence onto the tracks and jumping on a passing freight train was no trouble at all.

But I was not considering dirigibles. Airships with their powerful optics and observers could easily surveil the external bounds of the park and send a semaphore to terrestrial units if they saw a runaway from the air.

That came into my head only when I saw an army blimp with the imperial coat of arms and vertical stabilizers drifting slowly overhead. As bad luck would have it, today was a clear and windy day, and the smog was blown off the streets. The only place where the sky remained gray with smoke was the factory outskirts.

Throwing a cabby a two-franc coin, I left the carriage at the park gates and looked thoughtfully into the sky. The dirigible was going unhurriedly toward the Central Train Station. It wasn't after me.

But it wouldn't be wise to write off the possibility.

Paranoia?

Please! For a person officially wanted by Department Three, paranoia is the only allowable form of thought, the only way to avoid being thrown behind bars in the first few hours.

So, I didn't go into the park. Instead, I admired the crowns of the trees and cast-iron fence and bought a glass of carbonated water from a hawker. I finished it and ducked down a side street with a view of the gates where Ramon and I had met last time. On the way, I stopped a grubby boy and told him to keep watch for a red-faced short gentleman in a uniform cloak without patches. I told the boy to send Ramon to the hotel where our first encounter with the werebeast had taken place. I handed the boy two francs and a quarter, and we parted ways, both entirely satisfied with our arrangement.

The boy ran off to wait for Ramon. I meanwhile searched for a free bench, sat down on it and immersed myself in studying the front-page article on yesterday's killing of the inspector general. I was interested in any details of the event gleaned by the savvy newspapermen from their contacts in the police.

I didn't forget to glance at the park gates though, and when my clock struck four thirty, I noticed Ramon Miro walking from the nearest underground station. My messenger immediately hopped out to him then scurried away. His hands were burning with the honestly earned money.

No one followed the boy but, in any case, I walked down a parallel street for a few blocks after

Ramon, then ran off past my former partner and let him pass me, hidden behind a wooden cylinder with theater bulletins tacked to it. Only after that did I whistle and wave my hand.

"What gives?" Ramon frowned, angered by the long walk, but I didn't even listen and dragged him into a small snack shop named Danube Rose with a huge red rose on the banner.

There was no one inside and, with a calm heart, I walked through the small room with wooden tables and a time-darkened bar.

"A bottle of Tokay, if you please," I asked the black-haired swarthy man, taking out my wallet. "And some goulash. You do have goulash, don't you?"

The Magyar sized me up with an attentive gaze, then slowly nodded and walked out into the kitchen without a word. But Ramon couldn't hold back his annoyance.

"Leo!" he hissed, beside himself with rage and nervously puffing out the nostrils of his wide flat nose. "What the devil are you up to?!"

I reclined at the table and smiled:

"Tokay is a white wine, isn't it? What are you so steamed about?"

"I'm not talking about the wine!"

"Sit down," I pointed at the chair opposite mine, "and listen to me. You're already here, so it would be dumb to turn around and leave now, isn't that right?"

After a moment of hesitation, Ramon sat down at the table.

"Speak," he demanded.

"Moran was appointed to von Nalz's position. After all, you did hear about the death of the inspector general, right? Now they're searching for me. That's as short as I can put it."

The Magyar returned from the kitchen and set down plates of goulash, a wooden board of bread and an uncorked bottle of wine with glasses, so Ramon had to hold back. In the end, the hulking man suppressed his rage and, cracking his knuckles, asked:

"What do you want from me, Leo?"

I filled a glass with wine, but didn't drink it myself, instead taking a hunk of bread and dipping it in the goulash. It was hot and spicy.

"Leo!" Ramon started fuming again.

"Drink!" I pointed at the glass, wiping my lips on the edge of the napkin. Then I asked: "What happened to Professor Berliger? Did you find anything out?"

The hulking man took a sip of the wine, gave a nod of approval and turned the bottle's label to face him.

"Berliger is considered missing without a trace after the fire," Miro said after that. "There are more than a dozen bodies still awaiting identification."

"I see," I sighed, but didn't feel particularly at ease after hearing about the now dead-ended investigation. It would be nice to find the professor alive and well, but that could wait. There was simply no possible way to put the Princess's mission on the shelf.

"You asked me here just for that?" Ramon asked, reminding me of his presence and filling his empty glass.

"Hm? No, not just for that," I shook my head and pushed the empty plate away from me. Surprisingly, the portion of satisfying grub didn't dull my hunger one bit. I wanted to eat badly, just as before. "You gonna eat that goulash?"

The hulking man looked strangely at me and pushed his own plate across the table in silence. I, in my turn, pushed him a glass of wine and started going at the food again.

Ugh, I could not even remember the last time I'd had such an appetite!

Ramon sipped from the cup, then wiped his lips with a napkin and demonstratively placed his pocket watch out in front of him.

"Yes, yes!" I nodded several times. "Time is money!"

"And not just a little."

"If you want to talk business, let's get to it! Once upon a time, one could buy anything in Foundry Town with the right connections. Is that still the case?"

"What do you need?"

"A *machine infernale*."

"A bomb?" Ramon's eyes went wide. "You need a bomb?!"

"Shh!" I shushed him. "Not so loud! Can you get one?"

"I can get you grenades."

I shook my head.

"Army weaponry will not do. According to the papers, a homemade bomb was thrown into the carriage of the inspector general."

Ramon Miro exhaled loudly, drank some wine and drummed his fingers on the edge of the table.

"Just don't tell me you want to investigate that case. It isn't our level, Leo. Better stay out of it."

"I'm not investigating that case, and I do not plan on drawing you into it, either," I admitted honestly, and didn't say one more word of truth after that. "I simply need to... frighten someone. If they blame it on anarchists, that would be ideal."

I would have to kill Duke Logrin in any case, so I decided to do everything in my power to set the investigation down the wrong path. The Princess had promised to solve my problems with the police, but I knew I shouldn't rely too much on a person who hadn't come to her senses once in the last two months.

Ramon looked attentively at me, as if he saw my tricks straight through and gave a heavy sigh.

"Alright!" he turned his head decisively and smoothed over his short bristle of coarse black hair. "I'll help."

"Do you have anyone particular in mind?"

"There's a guy who owes me a favor, but you'll have to pay him."

"I need the bomb tomorrow by ten in the morning," I warned.

"Seriously?!" Ramon gasped. "Leo, this isn't just some trip to the grocer's!"

"Tomorrow by ten."

"I'll see what I can do."

Ramon got up from the table, draining the glass in a few gulps and advised: "Call in the morning," then went out the door.

I finished the goulash, asked for a link of salami and bottle of slivovitz to be packed in brown paper. I stuck them in the case, paid up and left the shop.

It was now after six, and autumn's early twilight had begun to gradually creep up. The wind turned freshness into plain chill; I put on my peaked cap, raised the collar of my overcoat and walked to the nearest underground station. I went down and rode to the opposite end of the city, the port area. That neighborhood was not so familiar to me, so I'd need to take a look around when I got there.

Shivering from the gusts of chilly wind, which raced over the cloudy water in high ripples, I stood for some time on the viewing platform. I watched the steam ships and opposite bank, lost in a haze of smoke then, with a heavy sigh, I walked onward.

The street along the river was dammed with carts, but as for the pedestrian part of the embankment, there were few city dwellers; over my whole walk, I saw just a few hurried passers-by, two boys flying a snake kite, and a bearded caretaker sweeping the sidewalk with obvious laziness.

Soon, around a bend in the river, I saw a small

island totally occupied by a tall gloomy building. It had narrow barred loophole slits, sturdy walls of stone masonry, a sharply peaked parapet on a flat roof and towers fitted with machine-gun nests. The spotlights on the corner towers were not yet lit. The posted watchmen were carrying rifles, and the sunlight occasionally flickered off their barrels.

Riverfort, where the Imperial Mint had been located for the last half century, was linked to the shore by an ancient wide arched bridge, but it wasn't used often. Usually, visitors arrived via the dock on the opposite side of the island fort.

After evaluating the arch of the bridge, the slope of the sidewalk and the width of the embankment, I wiped sweat off my forehead and walked onward. The gunshot wound in my thigh was hurting more and more, but I was not so lazy I couldn't make it a few blocks. Then, I turned off the embankment and started back down a parallel street. Here, my interest was piqued by the pass-through courtyards of apartment buildings with sharply peaked tiled roofs, chimney pipes billowing smoke and dormer windows. I was particularly drawn to a shed-covered wasteland between two manors, which just so happened to be opposite the entrance to the mint.

On first glance, this seemed like an easy place to run after throwing a bomb. My plans could only be upset by nosy locals. On the benches in the shady little courtyards, there were gray-haired old ladies drinking beer with men who'd just gotten home from work. On the street there were groups of boys chasing rag-filled balls, and near the fences, younger kids swarmed around heaps of trash.

But this was evening. What about midday?

I had no idea.

3

WHEN A MAN has nowhere to go, where can he spend the night? Should he check into a hotel room, or just loaf around the empty streets until morning?

My experience in the investigative police was telling me that doing such a thing was very unwise indeed. Beyond all doubt, my description had already been sent on to a detective posted at every large hotel, while the little boutique ones would most likely be passed through by investigators in uniform. Being detained for loitering in the city at night was a real hazard as well, though.

Central Train Station? That would be scoured first of all. It would cost nothing to come across a police round-up there today.

The capital was further and further immersed in twilight. In some places, the streets were lit with gas lamps. In others, there was bright electric lighting, both on posts and in glass displays and signs. Their glow stung my eyes and I wanted to clip my dark glasses on my nose, but I refrained. My predilection for black glasses certainly figured into all the lists of my distinguishing features.

After taking an intrigued look, I stood at a wooden column to look at theater bills, but all my thoughts were occupied with where to spend the night. I did not want to crawl into some abandoned building or try and find shelter in a dusty attic.

At that moment a police armored car turned my way from a neighboring street and, to the measured chirring of its engine, rolled unhurriedly along the curb. A constable standing on its running-board was illuminating the faces of passers-by with a swiveling light.

I froze in place for a moment, but immediately cast off my consternation and walked down the sidewalk, feverishly looking down side passages. I felt an increasing urge to speed up, but my maneuvering would attract police attention even without that. If I were to begin making a fuss now, they would certainly decide to detain such a suspicious gentleman to determine his identity.

As bad luck would have it, the buildings on my side of the street were pressed up one against the next, while the rare passages between walls were blocked by high fences. The powder engine rattled behind my back all the more distinctly, then I walked across the road right before the armored car with the confidence of a well-behaved citizen. I didn't stay long on the street and ducked quickly into an establishment with a characteristic name: Cinema.

At the entrance, I had to pay for a ticket, then to the sounds of the dampened melody of the film pianist, I waited for the beginning of the next session in a smoky vestibule. There was no way to leave the building through the back door other than through the auditorium.

Five minutes later, when the film changed over, I walked intentionally nonchalantly intending to slip unnoticed right through the exit. But much to my surprise, I found that I was interested in the title cards and took a seat on the edge of the next-to-last row. The movie was called *La Momie*, and, interestingly, it was in color. Done by hand, I supposed.

The story had just begun to unfold when, behind me I heard the flick of a match, saw the reflection of a flame, and it began to smell tobacco.

"A pitiful spectacle!" came a familiar voice with unhidden judgement. "You can make whole worlds in your head with the strength of your imagination, and you're sitting here staring at these colored pictures. Boy, you disappoint me."

The albino exhaled a stream of thick stinking smoke at the ceiling, and shadows began flickering on the screen. The viewers started stirring and turning around; the ticket checker demanded the cigarette be put out with an angry whisper.

By then, the beast had already dissolved in the darkness, and I showed my empty hands calmly. But my enjoyment was irrevocably spoiled. I didn't stay for the end of the film, walked to the back door and slipped outside. The dark narrow passage led back to the boulevard but, on a habit developed over years of policework, I evened out the edge of my peaked cap and froze in place, as if turned to a pillar of salt.

A carriage rolling up to the cinema, and four strong boys in uniform with revolvers and electric torches hopped out. They ran inside, while the driver stayed on the driving box holding a four-barreled lupara on his knees.

I turned sharply and walked away. As I did, I moved the case to my left hand, and stuck my right into my overcoat pocket for the revolver. But I made it. The darkness of the gloomy alley covered me.

A few minutes later, I jumped onto the back square of a late-coming steam tram and rolled off toward Dürer-Platz. From there, I went on foot to Calvary, which was looming not far away. The hill, surrounded on all sides by the city, was only partially built on; it held the manors of retired army officers, diplomats and ministers hidden from the immodest gazes of the citizenry.

Walking up the path around the slope of the hill, I diligently looked from side to side, but didn't experience particular anxiety. I came to the reasoned conclusion that the investigators wouldn't even think of doing a roundup here. My family mansion had been auctioned off, and no one could know that I had bought it through middlemen.

On the bridge over the gully, I heard the usual grumbling in the dense gloom below, walked another hundred meters and saw some familiar gates with a Diabolic Plague quarantine sign, now finally faded and peeling. The dead trees of the garden had long been felled by wind, and all that remained of the three-story mansion was its foundation. But I still walked through the fence around the ruins right across the lawn, overgrown with tall grass.

The collapsed basement of the mansion seemed like a dark grave, and I didn't even want to look that way, so I didn't. I just stood for a few minutes at one gravestone, then went to another. After that, I walked out past the fence and continued up to the top of the hill where, tossing my head up, I stared at the iron tower that formed its crown. The gigantic tower was no less than two hundred meters high and, rumor had it this had inspired the renowned Gustave Eiffel's design of his even more grandiose building in Paris.

Before my eyes, a blindingly bright zig-zag of lightning came down from the heavens, and the earth shook below my feet. A deafening clap of thunder rolled over the surrounding area.

I smiled at the tower like an old friend – that's just what it was! – and went up to the viewing platform, which had an astonishing view of the city in the evening. New Babylon was already fully immersed in thick twilight; the central streets shone with the nervous luster of electric bulbs and the light glimmer of gas lights, but the further I looked, the more darkened sleeping districts met the eye. On the top of the tower, there were signal lights. There were similar lights blinking in the sky, showing the movement of a great many dirigibles.

The viewing platform was strewn with litter. This place wasn't cleaned all that often, and common people couldn't be bothered to pick it up. I placed a newspaper down on a stone bench, sat down on it giving my tired feet a rest, then opened my suitcase and took out the link of salami. I cut the sausage with my pen knife, weighed the bottle of slivovitz in my hand in thought, but decided not to consume any alcohol.

I simply didn't need to.

Looking over the city from the top of the hill, I took a piece of salami and started chewing it pensively.

When I heard a vile creak of glass, I didn't even cock an ear. The Beast had come out of nowhere and taken the bottle of slivovitz, stuck a fearsome claw into the cork and easily pulled it out of the neck.

"You don't object?" he chuckled, flashing his ghastly smile.

"Drink," I allowed. "Just as I thought, you came to see the lights."

"Have I become predictable?"

"Basically, yeah."

The beast pouted and walked away from me. I was only glad. The white skin of the albino seemed to be glowing from the inside, and having my imaginary friend nearby was making my teeth grind. The power of the *fallen one* was overflowing from the Beast, dissolving and changing his bodily shell. Now, it threatened to break out at any time and engulf me head and all.

The albino overturned the bottle and glugged at it for some time, then gave a burp of satisfaction and wiped his wide maw with the back side of his hand. He went to the very edge of the precipice with the scratched-up bottle and I immediately heard a measured babbling.

"It is pleasant to recognize that there is something unshakable in this life," I noted when the albino had come back.

"You're overintellectualizing, Leo!" the Beast reproached me. After some silence, he added: "Don't be a dweeb!"

"If you say so," I chuckled and started wiping the salami grease off my fingers. I didn't want to eat anymore for some reason.

The albino grabbed a piece of sausage with his claw and sent it into his mouth, then turned back to the city. Lightning flashed overhead. The bench shook palpably, and thunder blasted out. I thought I smelled ozone, and the white hair of the Beast stood on end like the needles of a porcupine.

"What do you think, when did everything go topsy-turvy?" I asked my imaginary friend, knowing perfectly well that I was asking myself.

The Beast took a swig from the bottle, put a clawed finger to his temple and made a screw-loose motion.

"D'you fall off an oak? For you, Leo, everything is great!"

"Are you serious?"

"Bugger, boy! How old are you?"

"Twenty-two."

"That's exactly right!" the albino pointed his

index finger at me. He took a sip of the slivovitz, burped and continued: "You're twenty-two years old, and you're still alive. Not everyone can boast of such things. You know how many die before coming of age, falling under a steam tram, drowning or signing up idiotically for the colonial forces? Or just of hunger, or freezing to death, at the end of the day! Their name is legion. So don't feel bad for yourself. You've had your heart cut out..."

"Twice..."

The Beast nodded.

"You've had your heart cut out twice, and you're still alive! And now you should be afraid of death? You made a deal with a succubus and know exactly what awaits you in the kingdom of the afterlife! An eternity of pain. Bugger! A whole eternity! Leo, you're truly immortal!"

"I'm consoled..."

"But at that, no one will put a paw on your soul while you're alive."

I winced in annoyance.

"I'm more worried about keeping my bodily shell going."

"So, say to hell with it all and run."

"I can't."

The Beast took a kitchen knife he had tucked in his belt and used it to pick between his uneven teeth, cleaning a piece of sausage skin he had stuck in there.

"Do you like feeling like the Empress's chained dog?" he asked with mockery.

"That isn't the issue."

"It is precisely the issue," the albino assured me. "You think they underestimate you. You think that if you complete the mission, you'll be let inside to warm up by the fire. You think they'll give you a little bowl of food and water and lay you out a warm little bed."

"What are you talking about?!"

"What you're thinking! And you're right. They really will let you into the house, pat you on the head and put you to bed. But you aren't gonna wake back up. Never! A gang of hooligans are wanton imps in comparison with your kin!"

"The Princess is strange," I agreed. "I fear the essence of a *fallen one* is dissolved in her blood and one day it might wake up."

The albino took out a cigar and lit it, then looked at me sidelong and snorted.

"I don't even know, Leo. How normal it is to discuss how strange your cousin is with your own imaginary friend?"

"Get bent!" I cursed, though it was without any ill will.

The Beast just started clucking in laughter.

"Chin up! You're the luckiest bloke I've ever met!" he declared, shaking his head. "You're a schizophrenic with split personality, who was smart enough to kick his Mr. Hyde into an imaginary body. Keeps your hands clean!"

"That isn't so!"

"It is!" the Beast barked, and his eyes started

glowing somewhat brighter than the cherry of the cigar squeezed between his teeth. "Have the courage to admit that at least to yourself!"

"Make yourself scarce!" I snarled.

The Beast laughed hard, but I was in no mind to let him have the last word.

"By the way, why couldn't that Irishman in the basement hear you?"

"Sometimes, boy, a man simply speaks with himself."

I didn't get into a senseless conflict with the albino and took out my tin of sugar drops, popping one into my mouth. I rolled it between my tongue and the roof of my mouth, sighed and spit it into the grass. I didn't want sweets.

That was not for me. The Beast instantly nabbed the tin, stuck all the sugar drops into his wide maw at once and crunched them up like candied nuts.

"My advice to you, Leo," he said vaguely, "is to start doing what you do best."

"And just what is that?"

"Fear, boy! Bugger! Naturally, fear!"

I didn't give any answer, and the Beast wasn't counting on one. With a powerful throw, he sent the empty bottle deep into the night and walked to the tower on the top of the hill. I followed him curiously with my gaze, but it was offensively banal. The albino had simply decided to piss on one of the legs of the iron tower.

Lightning flashed over my head once again,

and an arc of electricity sparked up between the tower and dark figure.

"Bugger, that shook me!" I heard a moment later. "Bugger, now that's a shock! A-ha-ha!"

I spat under my feet and returned to the night-enshrouded city. Now, I wanted to just sit in silence.

4

THE DAWN CAUGHT ME on the way down Calvary. I was crossing the bridge over the gully, in fact, when the sun, obscured by cloudy smoke, puffed up over the horizon and started shining impudently right into my eyes. There was a thick shadow in the city below and, for some time, the morning sun and I played tag: I would slip away from its rays, and the aggressive yellow dwarf would go up higher and higher, not wanting to admit defeat.

Then I cheated and ran away from it into the underground.

At such an early hour, nothing in the city was really working yet, but Emperor Clement Square was renowned for its luxurious cafes and shops. It was quite simple to find an open bistro there. It served coffee and pastries at prices unaffordable to mere mortals.

After the restless night on Calvary, where I managed to doze off for just a few hours, I was tortured by yawning and my eyes were sagging. A mug of strong black coffee couldn't fully rectify the situation, but my head grew somewhat clearer. And also, surviving the day seemed more certain, so I was less afraid. I'd force my way through it.

Impressed by my tip, quite sizable even by local standards, the bartender didn't refuse his generous visitor a telephone call, and I made use of a phone sitting on the bar. First of all, I asked the operator to connect me with the residence of the Marquess Montague and ordered the parlor maid who picked up to invite the young lady to the telephone.

"Who shall I say is calling?" the servant inquired.

"Tell her its Lev," I said, giving my newer name.

For a few minutes, the line was dominated by alternating static and silence, then I heard a sonorous woman's voice, and even the bad quality of the line couldn't dull the alarm in it:

"Leo, is that you?! Leo, what is happening?"

"Uh, what *is* happening?" I was struck.

"Mary called yesterday and said the police were looking for you!"

"That's right," I confirmed, trying hard to hold the careless smile on my face. "I've already told you what it's about."

"O-o-oh!" Liliana said, drawing out the word. "Is it all bad?"

"Everything will be alright. Just spend a bit more time at your parents'. I'll call."

"Tell me where you are, and I'll come!"

"Lily..." I sighed. "I'm racing around town like

the White Rabbit! There's so much I need to do, I'm late everywhere by a day or two. I'll call you this evening, alright?"

"Do you promise?"

"I promise. But you have to believe in me, alright?"

"I love you, Leo!"

"I love you too, Lily."

With a sigh of pity, I bid her farewell and called Ramon Miro's office. That conversation was somewhat more business-like and laconic.

"You get it?" I asked my former partner.

"Got it," he confirmed. "We'll meet in two days at my last place of employment. Can you get there?"

"I can."

I placed the receiver back on the hook, thanked the bartender and went outside, not forgetting to take the case sitting at my feet. I didn't leave the square and, in the light gait of a careless ambler, walked to the huge Benjamin Franklin. But I wasn't headed to the hotel, I was drawn by a police barricade nearby. On the reddish granite bridge nearby were black spots of soot and spilled machine grease. The fragments of windshield and blood, if there was any to begin with, were already gone.

Tapping the first piece of a gear I came across with the tip of my shoe, I stopped and looked around. I was looking for possible escape routes the anarchist could have used after throwing the bomb into the inspector general's carriage. As far as I could tell from the newspaper headline, the cops had taken too long to shoot at the runaway, and he managed to hide in a neighboring alleyway. The few eye-witnesses all confirmed that the bomber rode away on a bicycle.

Looking over the scene of yesterday's crime didn't bring anything useful; I lowered my peaked cap onto my forehead and walked away. But then I saw a chubby old man in a gray cloak unlocking the door of a pastry shop with a fanciful inscription reading: "Imperial Blancmange." I followed him into the shop and thoughtfully looked at all the different sweets in the case.

I didn't want any sugar drops. I wanted chocolate, but there wasn't any here and, for obvious reasons, there couldn't be.

While I made my choice, the seller changed his cloak for a clean white robe and sighed bitterly:

"I didn't see anything! And I already told your colleagues yesterday!"

He clearly took me for a cop, and I didn't want to convince him of the opposite, just chuckled:

"My advice to you: never say that you didn't see anything. Sounds too suspicious."

After that, I asked him to weigh me out two hundred grams of cream toffee, paid up and left the pastry shop, leaving the seller finally caught off guard.

The toffee was not bad at all. Working my jaws measuredly, I began throwing one candy into my mouth after the other and suddenly realized what exactly I had been lacking. The sugar drops were too sophisticated and refined; I wanted to act more decisively than simply rolling a wad of melted sugar between my tongue and the roof of my mouth.

I was overtaken by a feverish animation. Invigorated by the caffeine, and all aflutter with the upcoming action, my brain forced my suprarenal gland to release a simply unbelievable amount of adrenaline into my blood, and that made me plainly finicky.

Devil! Had I really taken to the role of the future Empress's chained dog?!

I didn't want to think so; I mentally cursed out the albino and pulled yet another candy from the paper bag. The viscous toffee allowed me, if not to fully overcome my anxiety, then to at least somewhat calm down. So, I went down into the underground now determined and put together.

I went to the port.

At one of the local flea markets, I acquired a pocket chronometer with a timer and a baby carriage with a top that folded back. After not too much negotiation, I bought them both for four and a quarter francs. The facile nature of the roguish salesman was easy to explain: despite its presentable appearance, the carriage had been run ragged, and its wheels not only gave a ghastly whine, but also jammed quite often.

And though the whine didn't have much importance, the latter circumstance was not at all to my liking. I had to buy some oil, rags and a file, then roll my new purchase down a deserted alleyway nearby and make the wheels more functional.

After wiping down the carriage and my hands

with a rag, I pulled on my canvas gloves and headed for the embankment. I walked past Riverfort up the river, stood for a bit on a viewing platform near a parapet and got back on my way. The sidewalk there went down a slope and, when I let go of the carriage handle, bouncing and shaking on the uneven causeway, it rolled to the bridge all on its own.

I didn't stop it, just walked next to it. Only at the way off the street did I grab the handle and hold it, not letting it bounce off the road. It took exactly twelve seconds to go from the nearest street light to the bridge. I just needed to find out how long it took a self-propelled carriage to cross the bridge, and it was all in the bag.

Although I could no longer sense fears in others, I didn't need my *illustrious talent* to know how the driver would react when he got up on the high arc of the bridge and saw the stroller coming down the road. There could be no doubt – he would slam on the brakes. But that wouldn't stop him right away. Inertia would force it to continue moving, then I would enter the game, the Empress's chained dog...

Hrmph, may that white-haired freak blow up! I had taken a shine to this role!

I hid the carriage in some bushes not far from Riverfort and headed out to meet Ramon in the hopes that no squirrely neighborhood boys would find it in my brief absence. Even if they did – it was nothing too bad: the nearest flea market was just five minutes away on foot, and I could find a replacement and come back.

Of course, it was dangerous to hang around so near the scene of my crime, but, if everything blew up, the Princess would find a way to send the investigation in the right direction. The main thing was not leaving any iron-clad clues against me. If I failed, there was no reason to worry about a police investigation.

RAMON AND I agreed to meet not at the Newton-Markt, as it may have seemed from the conversation, but at the coalhouses where he had worked briefly as a guard right after being fired from the metropolitan police. The complex of squat fenced-off coalhouses was located in the midst of a soot-blackened wasteland in behind a boiler house, between a dye shop and some shacks scheduled for demolition.

That was exactly where I came out, carefully looking around. I didn't see any suspicious activity nearby, there were just lorries full of coal coming down the broken road to the main gates. So, throwing off the illusory suspicion, I walked to the warehouse where Ramon and I had once hidden an armored vehicle with weapons I had stolen from *illustrious* conspirators.

I was not mistaken – Ramon's self-propelled carriage, all covered in streaks of dried mud, was right there. Tito was sitting at the wheel watching the road and singing something quietly to himself drumming in time on the dashboard with his fingers. When I approached, he looked out the open door and pointed at the coalhouse.

"Uncle Ramon is inside!" the boy told me, holding a carbine in his hand that was nearly falling out of the cabin.

Crunching the large bits of coal, I walked to the cracked-open gates and glanced inside. In the middle of the pack house, there was a huge inactive steam truck and, in the far corner, there was a wide table. All the rest of the space was filled with heaps of wooden boxes, doubtlessly full of weapons.

Even a complete ignoramus could tell on first glance. And the Maxim machine gun laid out on the table spoke for itself. Ramon and his cousin, both without jackets and with their shirt sleeves rolled up, had just finished assembling it after wiping off the factory grease.

"Going to overthrow the government?" I joked and suddenly turned my attention to a familiar marking on one of the boxes. "Devil, Ramon! You promised!"

"What are you talking about?" the hulking man asked in surprise.

"The Steyr-Hans!" I pointed in accusation at the gun box. "You said you got rid of the pistols!"

"I lied," Ramon Miro admitted calmly, throwing an oily rag underfoot. "Understand me, Leo. There were too many pistols just to get rid of them like that. And don't worry, they won't turn up anywhere! All these weapons," he led his hands over the boxes, "we're bringing with us to the Caribbean."

"We?"

"My squadron."

"You decided to accept the offer?"

"I did. And, as you understand, titanium-slide pistols will come impossibly in handy there."

I nodded, agreeing. The Aztec wizards and voodoo priests could stop a normal weapon with their magic, but titanium served as a decent defense from the infernal attacks of malefics. Science is stronger than magic – that is true.

So, I didn't cause a fuss, just sighed and asked:

"And what's with the machine gun?"

"An opportunity presented itself, and I bought one. Now we're gonna test it," Ramon explained and asked: "Have you got my revolver?"

"Yes," I answered and pulled the Webley-Fosbery from my pocket, extending it to my friend. "Can you give me something in exchange?"

"Take your pick!"

I chose a Steyr-Han. At the same time, I set a belt holster on the table, a few clips and two boxes of rounds. For the first while, that would be enough.

"That'll be five hundred francs," Ramon announced. "And the seven thousand you promised for guard duty."

I pulled a check book from my inner jacket pocket and asked:

"Have you got a quill?"

The hulking man rolled his eyes.

"You're gonna write a check, Leo? Are you serious?"

"You got the money from the last check no

problem, right?"

Ramon Miro exhaled a silent curse, clapped over his pockets and extended an automatic pen with golden quill. I wrote out a check for seven and a half thousand francs, waved it in the air to dry the ink, then handed the paper to my former partner.

"Is everything alright?"

"Give me back the pen," Ramon demanded.

"What about the bomb?"

Instead of an answer, the hulking man placed a bulbous leather traveling bag on the table; I flicked the locks and discovered an iron box inside with an awkwardly welded handle and side lever.

"The case is magnetized, it'll stick dead to a police armored vehicle. I tested it myself. Explosion delay is five seconds. The detonator is electric, exactly as specified."

"Is the electric jar charged?" I clarified, removing the weighty *machine infernale* from the travelling bag.

"It's got a dynamo," Ramon explained. "But keep in mind, it takes some force to get the lever down. There's a good bit of TNT inside, so be careful.'

I clarified just in case:

"How confident are you in the seller?"

Miro threw up his hands.

"As much as one can be with such types."

"Well, let's hope then..." I muttered and set the bomb in my own case. It just barely closed.

"By the way!" Ramon Miro suddenly snapped his fingers. "You're not the only Russian who needed explosives. Someone came to this seller a day before us. But he was interested in dynamite."

"Yeah, to hell with him," I waved it off. "Your man's clients are of no concern to me, I'm concerned with the quality of his goods."

"Take some grenades," the hulking man offered. "I have some white phosphorus ones. I ordered a shipment from your friend Dyak just in case..."

It was a tempting offer, but with a certain share of pity, I had to refuse it. Anarchists had never before made use of such grenades, and I was intending to imitate their modus operandi to a T. Not a single trace could lead back to me.

"No, I don't need anything else," I shook my head, taking the little case and heading for the exit. When I was already in the gateway, I turned back and asked: "No news on Berliger?"

"Nothing," Ramon answered in one word.

"Look for him," I demanded and took out the pocket chronometer. "Is your clock accurate? What time is it?"

"Eleven seventeen."

"Thank you."

I adjusted the arrows, went outside and noticed the case was pulling toward the side of the armored car. As for the magnetized body of the *machine infernale*, my former partner had not been lying.

IT TOOK ME an hour to reach Riverfort at the scheduled time. I didn't walk down the embankment, not wanting to risk attracting the attention of the local beat cops. Instead, I checked the stroller hidden in the bushes and stuffed my leather cloak into it, then ducked into the nearest barber shop for a shave. With the hot towel on my face, sitting in that chair, I even managed to doze off a bit, but the sullen craftsman had no need for sleeping clients, and he pushed me back outside without any respect.

Yawning, I sauntered unhurriedly down the embankment, keeping an eye out for possible escape routes. On first glance, my plan was totally missing even the smallest serious flaw, but I kept turning over the possible ways things could go in my head.

The biggest worry was possible intervention by locals. If someone decided to detain the bomber, I'd have to shoot to kill, but I did not want to cause a bloodbath. Fortunately, the courtyards of the buildings along the embankment faced opposite the river. That simplified things.

At that moment, to the claps of the powder engine, a fine self-propelled carriage turned off the neighboring intersection. It was vaguely reminiscent of the one William Grace had taken me in, although the back was more elongated, and the back doors had no windows. Also, the weight of the carriage was supported by two axles in the back. After it, heavily lumbering on the uneven paving stone, there rolled an unhurried armored vehicle. On its tower, there quivered the barrel block of a high-caliber Gatling gun.

I took out my pocket watch and discovered that

it was just quarter to twelve.

But it was certainly Duke Logrin arriving to the mint. The Imperial coat of arms on the doors left no doubt in that.

The self-propelled carriage rolled swiftly over the bridge and drove into the gates of the fortress, which opened for it obligingly. The armored vehicle made the same trip not nearly as confidently, and its engine was also roaring strangely as it climbed the arc of the stone bridge. It didn't die or skid, though.

Eight seconds for the first and nineteen for the second. That was precisely how long my stopwatch showed.

Taking the first as a basis, I returned to the carriage hidden in the bushes and placed the bomb in it, throwing the case deeper in the thick grass. After that, I donned my leather overcoat, pulled on my canvas gloves and headed out for a walk down the embankment.

Unhurriedly, I strode up the Yarden, stood at a viewing platform and looked carefully around the area. There was something wrong. My intuition told me that clear as day, but I could not say exactly what it was.

It was just... somehow too quiet and calm in the area. And that was no small matter – the de-facto first man in the Empire had deigned to visit the mint, but there weren't even police guarding the nearby intersections. And his only escort was one armored vehicle. No horse guards, no dirigible drifting in the sky. Nothing.

And this was one day after the head of the metropolitan police had been blown to bits?

I mean, such flagrant carelessness by the head of the regent's guard was only to my benefit now, but incompetent people were never elevated to such posts Either the lack of escort was a result of Princess Anna's people interfering, or Duke Logrin had decided not to advertise his visit to the mint for some reason. Neither explanation was a great fit.

But I didn't panic just yet. I tightened my cloak and pulled my head into my shoulders, shivering from the gusts of chilly wind blowing in off the Yarden.

High in the sky, a file of freight dirigibles was lazily drifting toward port, a steam tug was very slowly dragging a barge up river, and the wind was carrying wisps of stinking black smoke over the water. There was no one on the streets. A young couple was walking in the distance. An old man rolled his cart to meet them with an aggravated wheeze. And no one else.

Everything was as usual, everything was as it always was, but the bad presentiment was still making shivers run down my spine.

Butterflies before the main event? Maybe, but I couldn't be sure...

5

I STARTED WALKING from the viewing platform toward the bridge as soon as the thick gate doors began to shudder slowly open. I had already calculated the speed of the regent's carriage in my head and that of the stroller rolling down the hill; all that remained was to walk to the proper section of the embankment and let go. The driver would have to brake before the unexpected obstacle whether he wanted to or not, and the arc of the bridge would cover me from the armored car's machine gun.

"The ideal plan. Nothing to worry about, just nothing," I reassured myself as I walked, biting my lip in worry. Then, naturally, everything went tits up.

The regent's self-propelled carriage raced onto the bridge before the gates managed to fully open. I already had the bomb in my hands by then; I pushed the carriage, and it dashed sharply down the uneven paving stones toward the bridge.

The timing was calculated perfectly. The stroller rolled onto the road right before the front of the car. The driver noticed it too late and could no longer manage to swerve away; all that was left for him to do was slam on the brakes but, instead, he put the pedal to the metal.

The curved fender slammed full speed into the stroller, and the strong blow sent it flying into the middle of the road. The vehicle turned quickly onto the street, grazing a lamp post and raced away, increasing speed further and further.

I was still standing on the sidewalk with a bomb in my hand.

Curses! What was going on here?!

Then, the armored escort vehicle rolled out of the gates. Its powerful powder engine giving a strained roar, it was already atop the arc of the bridge when a wave of darkness followed it out of the fortress. The self-propelled armored carriage flipped into the water as if it weighed nothing. After that, the gate doors flew away with a ghastly thunder, ripped out by an unknown power.

The echo of an infernal splash cut into me, and threw me a few steps away, nearly sweeping me off my feet. But then the embankment shuddered, and a flood of inky blackness gushed out of the fort gates and rolled over the bridge. The further the otherworldly perfect storm came, though, the more it diffused and lost its horrible power. Since ancient times, flowing water was considered a reliable defense against the power of evil. And although few continued to believe in such fairy-tales in our enlightened era, the fact remained – the darkness retreated into the mint, not having the power to overcome the river.

I took a fearful step back but, before I managed to run away, the power that had overtaken the island shot out once again. This time, it took the appearance of an impenetrably black human figure. The moire quivering around it gave off dispersing wisps, but the otherworldly creature didn't slow its pace as it crossed the bridge. But when the faceless monster walked under the electric wires between the lamp posts, a swarm of innumerable gray spots formed around it and flashed up into a heap of sparks, then dispersed without a trace.

A man was armed with a stone knife, covered in blood from head to toe, and coming straight at me; I slammed down on the lever of the *machine infernale* and threw it, but not at the ghastly brute, at the nearest lamp post.

The explosion cast stone fragments in all directions. A buttress blown away by the explosive wave careened and hung on the wires for a moment, but quickly broke them with its weight and fell right at the creature's feet. A blinding shock blasted out, and the hellspawn flew backward. Although it instantly regained balance, there was now a sparking electric wire on the ground between us.

Electricity is stronger than magic!

I believed in the superiority of science over wizardry with my whole soul, and still I turned without delay and ran full speed the opposite direction. After running across the street, I burst into the bushes growing on the side of the road, then scrambled through them into the wasteland. Instantly, two boys in identical black raincoats emerged from the labyrinth of rickety sheds.

The soldiers threw up their short carbines in perfect coordination, and pointed the barrels, wrapped in thick bundles of wire, at me. Right at me, and not at the hellish creature coming after me.

I didn't have time to reach for my pistol, so I just fell to the earth and somersaulted on the grass.

Just then, the air overhead was stitched through with short bursts, and the head of one of the gunmen simply popped, spraying his partner with blood and brains. Another shot thundered, and the second boy collapsed onto the grass. An unknown sniper's bullet had hit him right in the back of the head.

Feeling like a defenseless target, I hopped up and immediately sensed the icy presence of evil. Leaving bloody footprints after him, the tall man with flayed skin tore through the thick bushes. His touch crumbled the leaves to weightless ash and killed the branches, turning them black.

The electromagnetic radiation that penetrated the city finally dispersed the translucent curtain around my pursuer and now I could see him clear as day. His bare flesh oozed blood. I could see his muscles, tendons, veins and arteries, which had not been damaged by the hand of the experienced priest. In the chasms of the dead man's empty eye sockets, an impenetrable blackness curled. The blackness froze me with fierce horror, but that fear just gave me agility. Grabbing the carbine from the ground, I held the stock against my shoulder and pushed down the trigger with my index finger.

I heard the rustle of an electric discharge and smelled ozone. The Gauss caster gave a shake and, with a series of quiet claps, ten bullets flew right at my pursuer. His ghostly defense was broken through by the second or third hit. With a cold calculation surprising for the situation, I started shooting his flayed body.

Burst! Burst! Burst!

The sternum of the corpse was riddled with bullets in the blink of an eye, but the spirit controlling the dead man hadn't left, and I continued shooting, having no idea how quickly the magazine would be empty.

Burst! Another!

The bloodied body stopped running and began walking, then crouched and nearly fell, but still managed to stay upright. Just then, an invisible battering ram slammed me with a mental blow.

The infernal beast had thrown a spear of horror but miscalculated: my dormant *illustrious talent* absorbed the fear to the last drop, like a dry sponge absorbing water. I didn't even lurch.

I smelled burned wire and the Gauss caster misfired, but electricity overcame magic yet again. After a second's pause, the weapon stopped sparking and spat out another portion of bullets at my pursuer.

The otherworldly creature jumped to the side with unexpected agility and hid among the dense bushes; I didn't rashly chase after him, instead grabbing the second carbine from the earth and beginning to distribute reserve magazines in my coat pockets. As soon as I straightened up, I heard the piercing trill of a police whistle somewhere very nearby.

It was time to make haste out of here.

I turned around and raced down the narrow passage between the sheds, contorting and pulling my head into my shoulders as not to hit my forehead on the edges of their roofs. The carbine made it harder to run, but I had to hold it at the ready, because the unknown sniper could shoot again at any moment.

Sure, he had saved my life before, but who could say what he had in mind? Life had taught me not to trust the nobility of other peoples' intentions. After all, those guys were going to kill me! Shoot me down after I blew up Duke Logrin.

And there couldn't be the slightest doubt in their identity. I recognized the boys in the rain slickers – they were the very same two who came to the poet's house with William Grace. All that remained unknown was whether the gunmen had been acting her Highness's orders, or the lieutenant's.

In the side passage, someone shouted in surprise; I softly pushed the decrepit old man with the stock of my gun, weighed down by the electric jar, and walked further. I turned once or twice, jumped over an overturned barrel with rusted rims and, leaving the sheds behind me, hopped into a silent passage.

And a steam carriage immediately rolled out from the gates of the neighboring yard!

I practically stitched through its side with a burst of the carbine but recognized the familiar Ford Model-T just in time and led the gun aside. Thomas Eliot Smith, sitting at the wheel with his cap pulled down to his very eyes, threw open the door and shouted:

"Hop in!"

I sped up, caught the carriage and jumped into the passenger seat. The investigator immediately increased his speed, and the Model-T raced away, bouncing on the potholes and mounds of the uneven road.

AT FIRST, we drove in silence. Thomas Smith was turning the wheel in agitation; I was looking all around in a similar state. But we got away. We just managed to leave the area before anyone found out about the attack on the mint and closed off the surrounding streets.

"What brought you to Riverfort?" I asked, when the self-propelled carriage came to a stop at the cart-worn Ritterstraße.

"I wanted to ask you the same thing," the investigator snorted and removed his left hand from the wheel. It was wrapped in a blood-soaked bandage.

"Was this somehow connected with the Aztecs?" I hazarded.

"Was it?" Thomas looked at me sharply in response.

I pulled off my overcoat and threw it at my feet atop the carbine already laying there and smiled carelessly.

"Thanks for the cover!"

"I hope I chose the right target," the investigator grumbled, steering the Ford Model-T around the carts blocking the road.

After passing the cause of the jam, the self-propelled carriage dashed quickly down the road; I looked at him and shrugged my shoulders nervously.

"You made the right choice. Don't you doubt

it."

But Smith didn't find that a convincing statement.

"Well, I do doubt it," he declared and turned off the road down what seemed to be a random alley. But it wasn't. Just fifty meters later, Thomas got out of the self-propelled carriage and started fussing with the lock on a carriage-house door. It was built between a two-story house on the one side and the high fence of a neighboring building on the other.

"Lev, help!" the investigator requested.

Together, we threw open the gates, then Smith drove the Ford Model-T inside and started closing the gates, leaving us inside.

"Are we staying here?" I didn't understand.

Without an answer, the investigator blocked the gates with iron bars and turned to me.

"Tell me!" he demanded, lighting a kerosene lamp. "Who do you work for?"

I looked around and took a fated sigh. Even in the dim light of the hanging lamp, I could make out a thick layer of dust covering everything. I had to get up on the self-propelled carriage's seat; my legs plainly were too wobbly to stand on.

"Who do you work for?" Thomas Smith repeated his question.

He was standing with his side to me, his bandaged left hand held out. Remembering his *talent* of fast movement, though, I didn't try to take advantage of his defenseless position. He'd manage to turn around and shoot before I raised the carbine under my feet.

But as for the pistol on my belt, that was another matter entirely...

Anyhow, I didn't even consider grabbing the gun. In fact, I answered as honestly as possible:

"I'm working for the Imperial Guard."

"And what were you doing at the mint?"

"No!" I held my hand out before me. "My turn to ask questions!"

But Smith just laughed.

"Drop it, Lev! I saved your life! Am I asking for a lot in return? Just answer the question, and we'll be even! Alright?" And, not waiting for my agreement, he asked again: "So, what were you doing at the mint?"

I considered what to keep quiet on, but there wasn't much room for maneuvering: Smith had doubtlessly seen me throw that bomb.

"Alright," I sighed. "Alright. I was given the mission of blowing up a self-propelled carriage that would arrive to the mint at noon."

"Why?"

"I was not told such details."

"And that was enough for you?"

"The order came from the very top."

Thomas Smith rubbed the bridge of his nose and suddenly asked:

"Were you tasked with blowing up the carriage as it entered Riverfort, or exited?"

"They just wanted me to blow it up."

"Are you sure? Try to remember. It's very important!"

"I would remember if an emphasis was made to that effect."

"Curious," Smith snorted, walking up to the self-propelled carriage and pulling a Gauss caster out. "Any idea why they ordered to get rid of you?"

"Where'd you get that?"

Instead of an answer, Thomas pulled out a magazine and showed me the bullets, elongated like steel acorns.

"A titanium jacket with an iron core," he said.

"And what of it?"

"The mere fact that this precise Gauss-cannon model was a joint production of Dupre Electrical Machines and Vickers, sons and Maxim. It is only to be found in the Imperial Guard armory. Lev, the men who tried to shoot you were Imperial Guards."

I nodded. The story was coming together just perfectly. An illegitimate descendant of late Emperor's brother blew up the regent, intending to declare his ambition for the throne, but the guards killed him as he fled from the scene of the crime.

I hadn't the slightest basis to doubt the substance of that story, yet still I allowed myself a skeptical question:

"How'd you find out about the carbine?"

"Remember that rifle you gave me at Montecalida?"

I nodded.

"It was made by the *Colt Company* together with *Edison Electric Light*. It was thought that the contract with the Imperial Guard was in their pocket, but at the very last moment, it was scooped up by Hiram Maxim. He and Thomas Edison have been at swords since the New World."

"First I'm hearing of it."

"Doesn't matter," Smith waved it off. "All that matters is whether you were ordered to blow up the carriage as it came or left."

"I was not given any instructions on that account." I shot out. "And let's talk about you! What were you doing there?"

Thomas Smith sighed heavily, placed the carbine on the driver's seat and called me after him.

"Let's go!"

He walked up to the ladder against the wall, went up it and threw back a hatch leading to the roof. I came after him, not understanding the need for such complications, but we didn't have to go down to the ground. The investigator went right down from the garage onto the eave of a neighboring building and climbed into a window that had been left open. There was nothing left to do but join him.

The cramped kitchen was extremely messy, and it was obvious that most of the trash was left here by the previous residents. All that belonged to Thomas, clearly, was a battery of vials on the bedside table. They were too clean and free of dust.

"Make yourself at home," Smith said, pointing at a crooked stool and pulling off his jacket. On his belt, there was a holster with a semi-automatic pistol, the very same government model Colt.

I closed the window frame and sat down on the

stool, but before I managed to start interrogating, the investigator asked:

"How do you mean 'from the very top?' Her Highness is in a coma. Did the order come from the regent?"

"I don't know the details. Better tell me what you were doing there, Thomas. Your turn to answer questions."

The investigator winced in pain and started unbandaging his left hand but didn't keep mum.

"I was expecting Aztecs," he said. Then he exclaimed: "Curses! They led me there!"

I remembered the darkness filling Riverfort and shivered.

"Did the priests perform some kind of ritual there?"

"Do you have any other theories?"

"Wait!" I shuddered. "But you knew about this in advance! You told me about this yesterday! Why didn't you inform Department Three then?!"

Thomas Smith threw the bloodied bandages in the waste bin and turned to me with his fingers splayed. His bloodied pinky was missing a segment, and his ring finger was missing two.

"I did," the investigator declared and pulled back his shirt collar, showing a bandage on his neck. "And I very nearly lost my life after that. I don't think the attack was random."

"Did Aztecs do that?"

"No, some local expert. He was waiting in the back yard of my hotel with a knife."

"Start from the beginning," I suggested. "Alright?"

Smith removed a grimy pot from the sink and uncorked one of the bottles, pouring transparent liquid on the stumps of his fingers. The smell of spirits dispersed through the kitchen.

"What do you know about the Reaper?" he asked, beginning to place a fresh bandage on his hand. "He's a hardened killer who cuts out peoples' hearts."

"Only what's written in the papers. At our last meeting, you said it was Aztec related."

"And it is," Thomas confirmed, unbuttoning his shirt and starting to change the bandage on his neck. The cut looked deep and inflamed.

"You sure you don't wanna go to a doctor?" I suggested.

"I'll live."

"What if it gets infected?"

"It was a clean cut," Smith assured me. "I knew all along that it was Aztecs behind the murders, but I couldn't prove it."

I nodded in silence, not wanting to interrupt him.

"Only after the fourth murder did I notice a strange pattern," Thomas continued and pointed at the table. "Open the map-holder."

Inside, I found a map and a tour guide of New Babylon.

"I don't know the city well, so I marked the locations of the crimes on the map," he

— The Dormant —

explained. "Yesterday, when I was planning my route for the next day, I realized all the murders could be plotted on a circle."

I turned over the well-thumbed map and studied the even circle drawn, not by hand, but with a compass. The needle point of the measuring tool was around Palace Square, and the circle encompassed practically the whole old city. The crime scenes were not placed on the pencil line at random; all five of the dots were equidistant from one another.

"A pentacle?" I forwarded a theory of how the investigator had managed to determine the location of the last murder.

"The very same."

"But why did you decide to wait for killers at the gate to the mint?"

"Tell me, Lev, how could I have gotten inside?" Thomas snorted.

"No!" I waved it off. "Why Riverfort exactly? After all, the murder might have happened somewhere nearby? The scale of the map is insufficient for such accurate calculations!"

Smith put the trash bin under the sink and left the kitchen.

"Let's go, Lev." he called me after him.

The narrow dark corridor led us to a room with a curtained window. The investigator laid down on a sagging couch, and I unbuttoned my jacket and sat down on the inflated bed.

Thomas splashed some bourbon from the open bottle into a dirty glass, drank it and poured some more right away.

"Pain killer," he explained, sitting back in the couch.

"Get yourself to a doctor."

"Nonsense!" the investigator shot out. But he immediately calmed down and begged forgiveness: "Sorry, Lev. I haven't been in my right mind the last few days."

"Let's get to business," I suggested. "So, why Riverfort precisely?"

Thomas took a sip of bourbon and furrowed his brow.

"There were two aspects that drew my attention from the beginning," he said after that. "Only women were being killed..."

"The papers said they were all prostitutes."

"So they said," the investigator nodded. "All the victims had their eyes pulled out after death."

"Excuse me?" I asked in confusion, not really fully understanding. "So what does that mean?"

"For Aztec rituals, the eyes have no significance," Smith assured me. He took a sip of the bourbon and continued his story: "And that caught my interest. I thought: why pull out a dead body's eyes? What is that meant to hide? I didn't believe the killer was some mere madman, after all..."

"They're *illustrious!*" I suddenly guessed, and stinging shivers ran up my spine. "All the victims were *illustrious!*"

"As it turned out, yes," the investigator confirmed my theory. "With some weak *talents* and hereditary diseases, but *illustrious* nevertheless. At first, that didn't tell me anything, but the fourth victim was found in the middle of Piazza Galileo, and the body wasn't simply thrown there. No – the heart was outlined for all to see. So, I understood that it wasn't only the identity of the victims that held significance, but the location of the ritual as well!"

"And then you drew the circle?"

"Indeed," Thomas Smith laughed and drank his bourbon. "And also bought the travel guide."

"And?"

"And it turned out that the guesthouse they discovered the first body in on Faraday Boulevard was built on a former wasteland. And, on the Night of the Titanium Blades one of *the fallen* was killed there. And so on for all the crime scenes increasingly. One, two, three. On Piazza Galileo, four *fallen* were executed and in Riverfort..."

I remembered Princess Anna's words. I remembered where my grandfather was that night.

"Their blood flowed like a river," I said, sensing everything freeze up inside me.

Thomas Smith took a half-empty bottle off the nightstand and looked at it in thought. He didn't fill his glass again, though, and placed it back.

"I drew the circle, calculated the approximate location of the next crime and very quickly discovered it. Riverfort."

"And the time?"

"There was a month between the first and second murders. The third was just two weeks after that, and the second was another week later. Calculating the approximate time was not difficult. I knew where and when, so I went to the police. I didn't tell them the details over the phone, I said only that I had found the trail of the killer and agreed to a meeting. On the evening of the same day, someone tried to cut my throat."

"Who in the police did you work with?"

"Senior Inspector Moran," said Smith, noting how my eyelid twitched as he said it. Like an experienced poker player, he got on guard. "Ever met him?" he asked.

"I've had the pleasure, yes," I admitted.

"Now, I'm not gonna say he was mixed up in all that," the investigator warned. "The leak could have come from one of his subordinates. I spoke with an assistant."

I nodded. That really may have been.

"The Aztecs couldn't get into Riverfort. I supposed that they would perform the sacrifice on the bridge and took a position on the roof of a nearby building." Thomas Smith stood to his feet with a pained grimace and looked at me. "But instead of the Aztecs, you showed up. How did that happen, Lev?"

"Hardly a simple coincidence, Thomas."

"Exactly! The circle was closed, the ritual completed. Someone very important brought the priests to the mint. We don't know who, it all comes down to your order. When were you meant to blow the bomb: as they entered the fort, or as they left? Were you supposed to prevent the ritual or get rid of the

Aztecs afterward? That's the question!"

I didn't share the investigator's conviction at all, because I knew the intended victim of the explosion. But I found myself giving into doubts nevertheless.

What if I had been used, lied to, and that wasn't an attempt on the regent? Or maybe I was supposed to kill two birds with one stone?

Thomas Smith went into the kitchen and returned with a jacket in his hands.

"Where are you going?" I started worrying.

"I'm going out to hear what people are saying. It's probably best for you not to show yourself outside. Close the door behind me."

I shut the lock, returned to the room and sat on the sofa. I had to think my unfortunate situation over, but my head was filled with fog, and it was as if I was being pushed down into the couch. Sleep flooded over me with unbearable weight. My eyes started sagging, and I began to yawn. Then I forced myself on my feet and started pacing from wall to wall.

The door of the dress cabinet flew open with a creak, but I didn't even shudder. I was expecting something like this. With plain malice in his eyes, the Beast was staring at me with his toothy countenance. His pale skin was glowing from the inside with the luster of an otherworldly power.

"Bugger, Leo!" The albino melted into a wide smile. "Congratulations, you goofed up again! Now your cousin will certainly order your head cut off!"

"My head will be cut off, but we'll both go to

hell," I reminded him calmly.

"My boy, that is wonderful! After all, I'm the embodiment of your drive for self-destruction, or did you forget?" the Beast snorted and lit his cigar. Then he thoughtfully stroked behind his ear with a clawed finger and added: "Although, it must be said that you're doing a great job of self-destruction without me."

"None of that is right!"

"Everything is going according to plan, Leo. You just aren't aware of it. A pawn is not told it will be exchanged for a queen. It just gets moved forward."

"I'm no pawn," I shook my head. "I'm at the very least a rook."

"Bugger!" the albino laughed hard, narrowing his eyes, glowing with an otherworldly luster. "You're right about the most important bit!"

"I'm right."

My imaginary friend's word about another person's plan burned my soul with unexpected power.

The murders of *illustrious*, all women, a circle on the map around the Old City, human sacrifice in the place where the blood of *the fallen* was spilled, that was all part of something incomparably larger. I was also reminded of my cousin's fears, and somehow all at once, the prattle about a creature dormant in her blood stopped seeming funny. The center of the circle was on Palace Square, and that could not have been a simple coincidence.

Someone was playing a game with devilishly high stakes.

"Bugger! Boy, your head is just bursting with bad ideas right now!" the Beast grinned. "Splosh! And there go your brains!"

"Shut up!" I demanded. "Don't bother me!"

The albino came out of the cabinet, which was too small for him. He took the half empty bottle of bourbon from the nightstand, tossed his cigar butt in the glass as if in revenge, and went back.

"I'll shut up," he groaned after that, "but, boy, what are you gonna do when a police detachment comes to visit?"

Leaving deep scratches with his claws, the Beast slammed the door shut from inside and went silent. I walked over to the cabinet, opened it and discovered without particular surprise that there was no one inside.

"A magician, bugger!" tore itself from me.

I patted on my lips, took the glass with butt and walked over to the window, but I couldn't open the dried-out frame, and headed for the kitchen. Tossing the cigar and the rest of the brandy outside, I looked at the empty yard carefully, then stood at the entrance and listened. Silence.

A wave of sleepiness rolled over me again. I started digging through shelves in search of something to perk me up, but didn't find coffee or tea, or anything edible. Thomas clearly hadn't planned on needing a secret apartment, and hadn't had time to look for something more suitable after that man slit his throat.

What could I say? Trying to work with the

metropolitan police could lead to quite frightening surprises!

I laughed quietly to myself, and immediately heard a knock at the door.

I didn't look through the peep hole, just stood to the side and cocked my pistol.

"Lev, it's me!" I heard from the corridor.

My imaginary friend's warning had scratched my stretched nerves, but I decided to believe the investigator and undid the lock. Thomas walked over the threshold, quickly locked the door and extended me a paper.

"You've got big problems, buddy," he said, extending a fresh edition of the Capital Times with a grainy photograph of me.

However, it wasn't all so bad – the note didn't refer to any involvement in the attack on Riverfort, they were searching for me based on some cockamamie accusation that I was a threat to state security. What was more, they used a photo taken on my last visit to the Newton-Markt and a person who didn't know me well would find it extremely difficult to recognize me now.

"Department Three!" I frowned in disgust.

"You aren't surprised?" Thomas squinted.

"I was expecting something like this," I admitted, crumpling the paper in annoyance and throwing it into the trash can. "Do you think I linked up with the Imperial Guard because my life was going well?"

"Is that how they convinced you to help?"

"Well sure."

"Very interesting!" The investigator shook his head, walked into the room and looked around for the bottle. "Lev, where's the bourbon?"

"Enough drinking!" I rebuffed the investigator. "What'd you hear about Riverfort?"

"Everyone is talking about a gas attack, but they haven't decided yet if it was anarchists or someone else," Thomas answered. "The neighborhood has been blocked off, and no one can get in or out."

"Gas attack?" I considered it. "Not a bad explanation."

Smith collapsed on the sofa and frowned, rocking his wounded hand.

"Complete nonsense!" he shouted out angrily. "It won't fool anyone! It smells of the otherworldly no matter what! The Aztecs were on the rise, they were gathering strength gradually. At first, the place where one *fallen* died, then two, three and so forth. Such power cannot be kept under control for long, so they had to increase their tempo. But they got what they wanted. They took Riverfort, the most impenetrable fortress of the Empire."

"I don't think it has to do with the mint," I shook my head. "The gold was lefft in the safe."

"The Aztecs have plenty of gold," Thomas snorted. "What matters is the very fact of the successful attack! It's spitting in the face of the Empire, public humiliation!"

I shook my head.

"Remember what you said about the placement

of dots on the circle. Five points at even distances. Doesn't that remind you of something?"

"The Aztecs drew a pentacle? And what of it?"

"A pentagram," I said. "Pythagoras, Luca Pacioli and Leonardo da Vinci. The golden ratio. Harmony."

"Oh devil!" Thomas Smith gasped, hopping to his feet and walking from the window to the door and back. "Every pentagram can contain another pentagram. If the Aztecs harnessed the power of the ritual not with a circle, but in accordance with the golden ratio..."

He ran to the kitchen, returned with the map and stuck his finger in the center of the Old City.

"The final ritual should take place at Palace Square!" the investigator announced, glancing at the watch and biting his lip. "And its power will be truly colossal..."

"One cannot cut out the heart of a person in the middle of Palace Square," I doubted. "No magic can allow them to force the police to look the other way. That is impossible!"

"But they got Aztecs into the Imperial Mint!" Thomas parried easily.

I was already captivated by the new story, though, and didn't let that knock me off course.

"It isn't all so simple. The creature that burst out of Riverfort will not stay in the city long, it can only go one place – into the catacombs."

"I don't get it." Thomas Smith shuddered. "What creature?"

"Didn't you see it?"

"What creature, Lev?!"

I gathered my thoughts and briefly described the infernal creature I'd seen earlier:

"A person with flayed skin and a stone knife in his hands. Seemingly obsidian."

"Devil!" the investigator went pale. "They summoned Itztli!"

"Who?" I didn't understand.

"Itztlacoliuhqui, the deity of obsidian knives and human sacrifice," Thomas Smith explained. "If you're right, that will increase the power of the subsequent ritual by ten times! We must tell the authorities!"

"The authorities?" I snorted. "Which authorities exactly? After talking with Moran, you nearly lost your life!"

"But there must be someone above him!"

"He's the current deputy head of the metropolitan police. Above him are only the minister of justice and the regent. Whose carriage do you think was used to transport the Aztecs into the mint?"

"The minister of justice's?"

"The regent's!"

"Oh devil..." Smith groaned, sitting on the couch and pressing his face in his hands. "But we have to do something! Have them close off Palace Square!"

"The ritual will take place underground."

"Why?"

"New Babylon is defended against infernal beings," I assured the investigator, not telling him the story of the electromagnetic radiation devices. "But these beasts can hide in the catacombs as long as they like. This Itztli will certainly be taking shelter there."

"The ritual will take place in the next few hours. We must stop it!" Thomas Smith declared and suddenly shuddered: "Wait, Lev, did you say the avatar of Itztli had no skin?"

"It was a beastly spectacle," I shivered.

"Was it bleeding?"

"Yes, and what of it?"

"I can track him!" the investigator lit up and stood from the couch. "Let's go!"

But I blocked Thomas's path and shook my head skeptically.

"I won't ask how, but alright, we'll track the beast. But what then? We need something more serious than a Gauss caster. And even more powerful than the portable Hotchkiss, if you still have the machine gun with you."

"I do," the investigator confirmed. "And what do you mean by 'more powerful?' Grenades?"

"Something like that," I nodded. "I need to make a call. Where is the easiest place to do that around here?"

"The pharmacy on the corner. But you'd better not show yourself on the street."

"Drop it!" I laughed. "No one is gonna care about me today. The attack on Riverfort – that's what they're concerned with."

"Let's hope so," Thomas Smith sighed and

clipped his cap on my head. "Yeah, this is much better..."

6

THE INVESTIGATOR'S WORRYING was utterly in vain: the city-dwellers were just discussing the attack on the mint and the majority of patrolling police had been moved out to reinforce Riverfort.

Thomas ordered a mug of beer in a cafe on the corner and stayed on the street. I meanwhile bought two packs of aspirin in the pharmacy and used the telephone, but the first conversation, to my utmost pity, ended without result. Alexander Dyak could not create a portable electromagnetic radiation transmitter in one day, nor even a week, and his present device, as he said, was completely impossible to lift.

I had to call Ramon Miro's office. No, I wasn't planning to rent his armored vehicle to transport Dyak's new equipment. It wasn't a bad idea, but the self-propelled carriage would certainly not be able to drive through the catacombs. I was interested in the incendiary grenades he had offered me this morning. White phosphorus explosives had proven to have a high worth in conflicts with supernatural creatures; a flamethrower would help as well, but Ramon didn't have a flamethrower.

My former partner and I agreed to meet at

Euler Bridge in two hours. I left the pharmacy and threw a box of aspirin on the table Thomas Smith was sitting at. The hectic flush of his sunken face was not at all to my liking.

"Take some!" I demanded.

The investigator smoothed out the wire brush of his black mustache, but didn't argue, tearing open one of the paper packages and sticking the contents into his mouth. After that, he finished his beer and smiled.

"Happy?"

"Completely," I nodded, although Smith's smile looked more like a scowl. "In two hours, we have to be at Euler Bridge. Do you know where that is?"

"Approximately," Thomas answered none too certainly and looked at the sky. Wisps of gray clouds were quickly drifting across it. "It's getting dark, that's good..."

I didn't ask exactly why that was good, and followed the investigator to the carriage-house, where we were awaited by the Model-T. To my utmost relief, Thomas didn't seem drunk at all and walked straight without stumbling.

He was also not taken by a particular desire to speak and fired up the steam engine in silence, thinking over something in agitation. I decided not to interrupt his thinking. All told, we exchanged just a couple words the whole way. We were doing more looking from side to side. By evening, there were obviously more police on the streets, but the traffic flow was not being limited. We managed to reach the meeting place without particular difficulty an hour before the scheduled time.

The square on the Yarden embankment was unusually crowded: gathered in groups of five to ten people, the esteemed public was discussing recent news vivaciously; there were two constables on horseback maintaining order.

After parking the Model-T down an alley with a view of the bridge, Thomas raised the carbine from his legs and popped a new magazine into it.

"Is your contact a reliable guy?" he asked, checking the charge of the electric jar.

"More than," I answered and prepared the second Gauss caster for battle.

The investigator nodded, touching the bandage on his neck with a pained grimace, but not saying anything.

The usual sounds were mixed up into the evening silence of the city: the clapping of powder engines, the clacking of horseshoes on the causeway, the drawn-out honking of steam trams and the cries of street hawkers. But very soon, the silence started sitting heavy on me and I asked:

"How'd you guess the victims were *illustrious*? Having the eyes cut out doesn't make that obvious at all."

Thomas took out his pocket watch, glanced at it and put it back.

"Six fingers," he said finally. "One of the victims had six fingers on her hand."

"And what of it?" I asked, dumbfounded.

"The power of *the fallen* changes peoples' bodies. *Illustrious* people have children with physical deformities somewhat more often than common folk."

"First I'm hearing of it."

"Well, here in New Babylon, the blood of *the illustrious* is strong. It maims the conscious mind, but not the body," the investigator chuckled unhappily. "In the New World, there were many less *illustrious* from the start. The blood grew weak long ago, and freaks started being born."

"I didn't know."

"Anyway, as for the first two victims, I had no certainty. But when it came to light that the third victim worked in a three-ring circus..."

"In the papers, it said all the victims were prostitutes."

"Carnie or whore, is the difference so great for the esteemed public?" the investigator cringed. "The third victim worked in a three-ring circus. She even had her own trick, she could breathe underwater."

"Useful *talent*."

"It is," Smith nodded distantly. "She would get locked in a glass cube and they would fill it with water. She would choke for show, then the water would be pumped out and she was brought back to life. And so on, performance after performance. That's trash, not life."

"But better that then losing one's heart," I decided, mechanically rubbing my chest on the left side. "Much better."

"No one can argue that," Thomas frowned. The

conversation was putting him into an obviously bad frame of mind.

Fortunately, just then, a familiar armored car drove onto the bridge. I got out of the self-propelled carriage and counted the money as I walked across the road. Ramon Miro accepted four hundred francs from me, threw open the side door and pulled an unadorned wooden box from the back.

"As we agreed, one dozen incendiary devices and the same number of fragmentation grenades," he said.

"Has Professor Berliger turned up?" I asked, accepting the box.

"Vanished without a trace."

"Find him," I asked and returned to the Model-T.

A beat cop, his interest caught by the strange fussing around, headed in our direction. But before he managed to get close, the armored vehicle drove off in one direction, and we rolled off in the other. The constable didn't whistle after us.

ON OUR WAY to Riverfort, Thomas Smith dropped into a telegraph office.

"Lev, I'm not a lone hero," he explained, catching my confused gaze. "I work for Pinkerton. The agency must know what is happening."

"What if they're against it?" I asked, throwing up my hands. When the investigator returned, I asked: "And how are you preparing to find this... Itztli?"

"I'm going to track the bloody footprints."

"And the police?"

"They won't get anything done," Thomas answered confidently. "They have no idea what they're up against."

"And you? You can do it? What makes you so sure?"

Smith chuckled.

"I ran away from home at fifteen and joined the army. I spent two years in an infantry corps, and another four in army recon. I've seen everything."

The appearance of a gaunt dandy with well-manicured hands, trimmed mustache and fashionable hair didn't quite connect with his army service. But appearances are often deceiving, and I didn't place the investigator's words in doubt. As I didn't ask why he decided to run away from home; everyone has skeletons in their closet.

WHEN WE ARRIVED at the Imperial Mint, there was already dense twilight outside. The police had the whole embankment and several neighboring streets under surveillance. That caused a massive traffic jam, and it became impossible to get where we wanted to go. The traffic cops at the intersections were overwhelmed by the transport collapse and were just tearing their voices and threatening the especially slow-witted cabbies for nothing.

While the Model-T crawled at a turtle's pace in the flow of carts, I quickly leafed through the investigator's tour guide. I didn't find any mention of ways down into the catacombs in the vicinity. However, I didn't doubt they did exist: in its two-thousand-year history, New Babylon had grown not only outward, but also upward, leaving whole streets under the earth. And there were innumerable ways down there.

It was surprisingly easy to get through the first line of the police barricade. There was a huge hullaballoo on the streets, and Thomas just calmly handed the sergeant his private detective card and a paper from the Ministry of Colonial Affairs.

"My assistant and I are expected by Senior Inspector Moran," Smith said confidently, overcoming possible interrogations about the reason for his visit.

"Let them through!" ordered the cop, caught up in his duties and waving a hand to his subordinate.

After passing the barricade, Thomas Smith drove the self-propelled carriage into the first alley he came across, got out from behind the wheel and threw open the baggage trunk.

"Take this, Lev!" he extended me a traveling bag. "You light the way."

"What do you mean?" I didn't understand.

"Take out the lamp," the investigator asked and again brought the Model-T onto the embankment.

Attracting police attention with additional lighting didn't seem like the best idea to me. But when I took an electric torch from the traveling bag, with great surprise, I discovered that the bulb was covered by a lens of black glass.

"What the heck is this?" I asked when the

switched-off torch lit up with a barely noticeable purple glow.

"A Wood's lamp," Thomas explained. "The human gaze practically cannot detect light at this spectrum, but blood spots, unlike wine or juice will start to shine with a velvety glow. You won't confuse it with simple dirt."

"Fascinating," I chuckled and pointed the light at the street.

And we drove on like that. Due to the break in the power lines, the electric lights weren't working, and the street was immersed in darkness. There were just spotlight beams coming from a dirigible hovering over Riverfort and sharp blasts of magnesium sparks coming from the river. Some newspapermen had rented boats and were competing to see who could take the best shot. Meanwhile, a constable in a steam-powered shuttle boat was coursing along the island informing them not to get too close to the mint.

The turn onto the bridge was blocked with temporary barricades, but we didn't have to drive there. The Model-T drove past it, quietly rattling its steam engine. When I saw the velvety purple footprints under the self-propelled carriage, though, I pulled air through my tightly clenched teeth with a whistle.

"Do you see that?" Thomas Smith shuddered. "Where should we go?"

"Straight!" I ordered. "Straight for now!"

We drove past the constables, who were surprised at the violet glow and rolled on, gradually getting farther from the mint. At the next intersection, Thomas Smith turned off the embankment and soon the Model-T drove past a police barricade. Then we dropped our speed and started roving the neighborhood, using the Wood's lamp to seek out the glowing black-velvet drips dotting the earth.

Itztli had run through courtyards, but his blood showed the way better than the thread of Ariadne. To our great fortune, the weather today was clear, and the rain hadn't managed to wash away his tracks.

"Where to now?" Thomas asked me at the next intersection.

"He took the shortest way, straight," I said. "Let's go left!"

The investigator did just that, then turned another few times, driving around the block, but other than the first trail of drops, we did not manage to see any tracks.

"He's in here!" Smith exhaled loudly. "Here, Lev! He must be in here!"

"Wait," I ordered and, with the Wood's lamp in one hand and a pistol in the other, I walked into the public thoroughfare.

The bright glow of the blood prints on the earth led very quickly to a dilapidated building. Its stone masonry was unlike the neighboring houses. It had a monumentality that made it stand out. The empty window frames of the ruin were filled with impenetrable darkness. I quickly looked from side to side and returned to the investigator.

"It seems I found a way down."

"Excellent!" Thomas said, joyful. Then he commanded: "Let's go!"

"Excuse me?" I asked in surprise.

"How long can a carriage stay here without attracting any attention?" Thomas noted reasonably.

And in fact, the boys smoking at the neighboring intersection were watching us with unhidden interest. The area just seemed to be asleep; in fact, our arrival attracted lively attention from the locals.

"Alright, let's go," I said, deciding not to track the Aztec god of obsidian blades on my own. Our last encounter had forced me to think of him with a wary respect.

To be perfectly honest, now, I didn't so much want to stop the Aztecs as I wanted to figure out what was happening before sleep wore me down. I expected that, whatever talk I would be having with my cousin, it wouldn't be an easy one...

WE LEFT the Model-T in one of the neighboring yards, after agreeing with a night guard to look after our self-propelled carriage. I picked up the overcoat sitting at my feet, shook it out and put it on.

"Help, Lev!" the investigator asked, opening the box I'd gotten from Ramon.

Working together, we screwed the fuses into the grenades, placed them and the incendiary bombs in our bags and started checking the Gauss casters. They were in perfect order. Then Thomas Smith placed long electric torch tubes over the barrels.

"What the heck is that?" I was blown away.

"Look!" said the investigator and jerked up his carbine in a sharp movement.

The torch lit up all on its own. It illuminated the neighboring fence and, in the middle of the bright spot, there was an easily visible green dot in the darkness.

"That's a target mark," Smith hinted. "Use it as a base, but remember the weapon isn't sighted. The torches turn on automatically and can be switched to constant mode if necessary."

"Not bad," I whistled, looking over the torch on my own carbine.

According to the markings, it was made by the Berlin firm Wespi. The color of the aiming dot was produced by a green crystal inside the lens.

With the weapons under our cloaks, we left the yard and headed off to the ruins. By then, it had grown completely dark outside The only light was the odd spot of bright windows and the cigarettes at the neighboring intersection. I could hear loud shouts and laughter over there.

Under the cover of darkness, we reached the stone ruins and crawled into the empty window frame. Inside, it smelled strongly of piss. The torch revealed a trash-strewn floor. Thomas Smith immediately took the Wood's lamp from me and decisively pointed it deeper in the room, where it stopped on a broken wood hatch.

When I saw the path down into the catacombs,

I felt plainly beside myself. It seemed like my subconscious fear of basements had long ago retreated, but much to my surprise, I realized I was grinding my teeth in fear of walking onto the narrow stairs leading down into the darkness.

"Lev?" the investigator turned to me.

"I'm coming," I forced a smile, but didn't move.

"This is not a cellar," I mentally told myself and repeated: "This is not that cellar at all."

The panicking fear retreated somewhat and, overcoming my fear, I went off after Smith. The stairs brought us to an empty room with dirty stone walls. In the far corner, there was a gnawed-at rat skeleton next to a sewer pipe. The vaulted brick ceiling was low, and I had to triple over not to hit the top of my head on its slippery surface.

For Thomas, who was short, it was easy to get through the tube, so he walked first and lit the way. Anyhow, the smell of filth and stink of decay caused the investigator no less agony than me. Luckily, the bloody prints quickly led down a side passage that didn't stink so bad. We walked down it until we discovered a dilapidated stairwell leading down one level lower.

"I don't like the look of this," I couldn't hold back.

"Tss!" Thomas hissed and walked on.

The stairway held the weight of the investigator, so I also stepped onto it.

The rectangular room we soon found ourselves in was in some way reminiscent of a sewage collector.

From it, there were four corridors heading in different directions. But it was no work to find our way. We were guided as before by the blood glowing in the light of the Wood's lamp.

Yet, the further we walked, the weaker its luster became. In places, dirty water ran from the ceiling, and full brooks streamed underfoot. At every intersection, the subterranean paths needed to be looked over for a long time to catch the light reflection of blood drops that stretched on after the Aztec deity.

"We didn't give a single thought to how we'd get back," I muttered at the investigator's back.

"We'll make it out somehow!" he waved it off carelessly.

I didn't share his confidence on that. We had descended into the catacombs no less than a half hour ago and had managed to leg it a decent distance. What was more, the subterranean paths were defined by confusion, and at times we met collapses, holes in the floor and rusted grates, while some passages were just narrow cracks or dark holes. It was a near certainty that we'd turn down the wrong path at some point on our way back.

"Oh no!" I groaned when the trail of dried footprints led us further down.

The steep narrow stairs led into the darkness and, under it, there was dangerously sagging uneven stone cladding. Thomas Smith managed to get through the steps sideways, while I had to get down on my haunches.

On the next level, the ceilings were sufficiently

high, the walls impressed with their solid stone masonry. Sometimes, I saw collapsed doorways. Meanwhile, at the intersection of two passages, I got the sensation that this was a now buried street of the ancient city.

"Well, where to now?" I asked softly, looking from side to side.

I seemed to hear falling water down one of the passages and, there was a slight waft of fresh air that way as well, but the investigator expectedly headed in the opposite direction. Soon, the ground was fully covered in cloudy dirty slime, and it had to be crossed on boards thrown from stone to stone, rotten and slippery. My mood was improved by that one bit.

Anyway, why did I care about dirt? I remembered the ghastly flayed body with black holes for eyes and shivered. I had no desire at all for a reunion with the earthly incarnation of the Aztec god.

"It's here," Thomas whispered suddenly, hurriedly turning his torch down.

I looked closely and made out a door bound with iron strips. However, the mortar around the doorframe was dried out, so the masonry wasn't too resilient.

Smith pressed himself to the door, listened, sniffed, took a step back toward me and said:

"There's someone inside. It's heaving with tobacco."

"The tracks lead right here?"

"Yes, there's blood on the doorstep."

"Then let's go in," I decided, holding the carbine

at the ready. Due to the magazine inside the pistol handle and the heavy electric jar in the stock, the gun was balanced toward the back, and the wires on the barrel only partially rectified the situation. When shooting bursts, kickback flung the bullets quite high up.

Thomas leaned against the door, cautiously touched the handle and turned to me.

"Locked," he said. "What are we gonna do?"

I chuckled and took a hand grenade from my bag.

"What do you think?"

The grenade fit perfectly in the gap between the stones; I carefully removed the pin barbell and turned the investigator.

"You follow me," he warned.

Remembering his *talent* of quick movement, I nodded, removed the pin and ran behind a stone ledge. A moment later, the explosion blew away the unstable masonry, and the door flew off its hinges collapsing to the ground. Streams of dust and small stones came down from the ceiling, but the thick dome of the underground bore the blow, and it didn't collapse.

"Lucky," flickered in my head, then I hopped out from the cover and headed out after the investigator to the smashed doorway.

Naturally, at a slower pace. It was as if Thomas dissolved into a stripe of fog and was gone in an instant. And immediately, shooting!

As soon as I jumped into the spacious room, I

jerked up my carbine in a sharp motion. The bright beam of the torch lit up a bullet-riddled body on the floor, then slid over the writhing wounded man at the wall, and immediately hit upon someone's bare back. My green dot was blinking between the stranger's shoulder blades, and I quickly pulled down on the trigger. A short burst trilled out, and the boy was knocked off its feet before he managed to shoot at the investigator, who was running for a far door.

Thomas Smith slipped into the next room, and I heard many frequent shots. Meanwhile, a side passage caught my eye. As I ran, I took down the wounded bird reaching for his shotgun, and jumped into the next room, blinding an enemy I had caught off guard. He was firing blind and trying to cover his eye with a hand but didn't manage to do anything more. Not losing an instant to aim, I shot him with a couple short bursts. Coughing up blood, the boy slid down the wall to the floor; his shirt, marked with a green dot, instantly changed from white to crimson.

Done.

And immediately, a grenade blew up nearby. I hopped out of the room headlong, but the investigator didn't need my help.

"Clear!" he shouted, leaving the far corridor.

"Me too!" I answered, shining my light on the dead bodies and cursing vexingly: "Devil! Those were no Aztecs!"

And in fact, the boys we shot didn't look one bit like red-skinned natives of the New World. One of them was a fully blue-eyed blond.

"Perhaps the Aztecs hired bandits," Thomas Smith suggested none-too-confidently and asked: "Keep watch, I'll walk through the rooms."

The investigator hid in the far corridor for a few minutes, then returned with a wooden box and threw it forcefully at the wall.

"Do you know what that is?" he asked, picking up a bag of white powder from the broken box. Then, cutting it open with his pen knife, he said: 'Cocaine!"

"So maybe we did find the right place?" My spirits perked up, because all of this contraband narcotic came from lands under the control of Tenochtitlan. "But what if it's just drug dealers?"

Smith shrugged his shoulders and started searching more carefully. I stood watch for some time, then couldn't hold back and joined him.

"What have you found, Thomas?"

"There are a few more people living here than we just caught," the investigator said and threw me a jar filled with leaves. "And here, look!"

"What is that?" I asked in surprise, catching the glass container with my left hand.

"Coca leaves. Aztec priests chew them to increase their concentration and reduce fatigue."

I removed the tightened lid with difficulty, pulled one of the leaves out and wanted to stick it in my mouth, but Thomas stopped me:

"Come off it, Lev. It's a ghastly filth."

"I'm trying not to fall asleep."

"Then you need quinoa ash, it's from some local plant," the investigator warned me, digging around and pulling out an envelope of some kind. "Here. And don't chew the leaves, just set them between your teeth and cheek."

I did just that and very quickly felt numbing like from an injection of anesthetic. The quinoa ash smelled strongly of anise, and it had little bits of cane sugar in it, which at least somewhat mitigated the bitterness of the leaves.

"Lev!" Thomas suddenly called out to me, not stopping his digging through the room. "Help!"

Together, we dragged a wooden shield from a room small room and discovered a hatch under it with powerful iron latches. We didn't have to break it: the padlock was sitting next to it, unattached.

"Open it!" Smith ordered, then stood to the side with the carbine in his hands.

I threw back the massive lid with strain and immediately took a step to the side, pulling a fragmentation grenade from my bag. But there was no one alive in the small rectangular basement, just a body lying on a stone slab with its rib cage split open. Its heart was sitting in a ritual goblet; the improvised sacrifice and floor was dotted with dried blood. The smell of death and damp turned my stomach.

I do not know for certain if the deceased was an Aztec, but he was certainly a native of the New World. His pitch-black hair and swarthy reddish skin tone bore clear witness of that.

"Cover me!" the investigator ordered, going down the wooden ladder propped against the wall.

He didn't spend long in the cellar and came

back out looking gloomier than a stormcloud.

"Bad news," he told me. "There are women's things in the cage. They were keeping a sixth prisoner."

"They kidnapped someone in advance!" I realized.

"We have to stop them!" Thomas announced and walked decisively toward the exit. "Let's go, Lev!"

I stayed back to bring the jar of coca leaves with me and caught up to Smith, who was now in the doorway we'd blasted open with a grenade.

"Wait, Thomas! What are you going to do?"

"We know the place – the catacombs under Palace Square. We know the time as well – right now. We need to hurry!"

I spit a wad of the softened leaves angrily underfoot and stopped the investigator, grabbing him by the shoulder.

"Are you joking?!" I inquired, looking him grimly from top to bottom. "Do you have any idea how long it will take us to get from here to the Imperial Palace? Underground? Not knowing the way?"

"I have a great sense of direction!" Thomas Smith answered, turning his hand and confidently stepping down the passage. But he immediately turned back. "Alright, let's get up top and catch a cab. Sound good?"

"Sure."

"Then let's go, we don't have much time!"

But if the investigator had a great sense of direction, I had a good nose for trouble; in particular, for the horrors of the supernatural.

So, when a wave of chill ran over my back, I didn't curse at the breeze, I sharply turned and threw up my carbine. The Aztec with exposed ribcage jumped out of the dark and ran on the attack. But the Gauss caster instantly spat a half a dozen bullets at him, and his head spattered with brains. He took a few more wobbly steps after that, pulled out an obsidian blade and fell to the floor.

At that very moment, the emanation of an infernal spirit burned my soul with an unseen fire, and it was as if I could physically feel an otherworldly creature quickly approaching.

"We're too late!" Thomas Smith gasped, not in the mood to talk.

The underground passage filled with fog. The haze started to sting with cold and drain my energy. My legs and arms were bound by an incomprehensible dread. In flickers, I saw the bodies of the bandits come back from the dead, but I couldn't make anything out properly. The electric light of the torches was drowned out in the impenetrable whiteness, not having the power to fight back its unnatural essence.

I shot a few short bursts at random and stepped back, my left hand pulling at the flap of my bag.

"Thomas, cover me!" I shouted to the investigator, feeling for an incendiary grenade.

With a quiet clank, the pin leapt out, the aluminum cylinder flew into the fog and, a moment later, splashed out a burning flame of white phosphorus. Their magical defense was burned through in an instant, and the walking dead fell, embraced by the fire. But there were other beasts stealing up behind them. Agile, leaping and fanged, they were reminiscent of a dog and a monkey at the same time. Demons with jaws full of sharp fangs.

We opened fire on them from the Gauss casters, and the titanium-jacketed bullets started piercing their hoary semi-transparent bodies, leaving ghastly wounds. The demons didn't have time to fully acquire flesh, but it wasn't a lack of imagination on the part of the malefic who had brought this nightmare to life. The infernal beasts required human blood and flesh.

Our flesh and our blood!

"Let's get out of here!" Thomas commanded, and as soon as I stepped back, the investigator tossed a fragmentation grenade at the horde of pursuers.

I added another incendiary bomb to that, and we ran away as fast as we could. With a flash and a clap, the chemical flame hissed to life and wafted a fierce rage that could dissolve human flesh like concentrated acid.

Another demon jumped out from the side, but Thomas's torch caught it, and our heavy bullets sent the beast back.

"Here!" Smith shouted, hopping over the melting body of a demon and ducking into a side passage.

I turned after him. A moment later, a dense

cloud of fog raced with the speed of a cannonball down the corridor. The wave of cold came unraveled on the walls like a stinging sleet. The investigator had to throw an incendiary grenade behind his back, blocking the fog with its chemical flame.

Slipping with our shrapnel-sprayed feet, we ran up the stairs and turned around, riddling the demons chasing us with a few long bursts. After that, we ran further, but in the next room, Thomas stumbled on some rubble and rolled over the earth. That little bit was enough for our infernal pursuers to catch us and throw themselves on the attack from two corridors at once. Without torches, this would have been the end of us, but the beams of the electric bulbs didn't only blind the demons, they allowed us to shoot without wasting time on aiming.

Burst! Burst! Another!

The whitish semitransparent beasts fell dead at our feet. The green spot of the target marker jumped from one hairless creature to another, freezing for a moment on their fanged jaws or between their red eyes and immediately jumping onward as soon as a quiet shot rang out.

On my carbine, the electric jar low-charge light started blinking treacherously, but I kept pushing down ceaselessly on the trigger. Thomas Smith, meanwhile, used his buttstock to break the lock off a rusty grate in the corner the demons had backed us into.

A ghastly cold was drifting up from a hole in the floor. I threw one of the last incendiary bombs down, and Thomas Smith immediately yanked me after him. He didn't have time to deal with the lock, though he did manage to break two iron bars out of the masonry. And we slipped through that gap.

The passage went down at a slope. The ceiling gradually lowered, filth flowed in the gutters underfoot and it became clear that we had managed to turn up in the storm drain system. All that remained was to hope it didn't lead to a waste collector...

"The fresh air is drawing me!" the investigator exhaled hoarsely and threw an incendiary grenade back to meet the demons. The electric jars in our carbines had already nearly died once and for all by that time, and the weapon ceased to fire bursts. They could only get off single shots every other time, in fact.

A blinding white flame flickered behind us. It devoured the transparent flesh of the demons, and they were caught in soundless writhing, melting and dissolving, not powerful enough to resist the fury of the chemical flame.

Thomas and I were rushing, using up the last of our energy. Then the investigator suddenly threw up his hands and fell out of the tube. Not having managed to stop, I jumped after him into the darkness. But, fortunately, there was a stone ledge a meter and a half under the tube where my partner had fallen, his strength now drained. We were actually lucky – from there, I could see the leaden surface of the Yarden.

Standing to my feet, I ripped the bag from Thomas, pulled out the pin of the first grenade I came upon and threw it as hard as I could into the drainage hole together with one of my own.

"Let's run!"

We hurried away. Behind us came a dull clap, and a long pillar of white smoke shot outside. Another somewhat more powerful explosion followed; a burning flame spit out of the pipe as if from the top of a volcano, and fragments of stone flew. A moment later, the sewage pipe was totally blocked by collapsed masonry.

We got out!

7

WE RAN DOWN a narrow projection off the granite facing of the embankment until we reached a jetty and threw both carbines far into the river, having removed their torches in advance.

The investigator stopped a cabby. He looked at us with unhidden doubt but, for double the pay, still agreed to take us to the port. There, I got myself more or less in order in the washroom of a small café. Thomas Smith, meanwhile went to send another telegram to the Pinkerton Detective Agency. I ordered a mug of strong black coffee and stood on the terrace watching the brightly illuminated decks of the ocean liners.

I heard echoes of music and frequent bursts of laughter coming from them. I wanted unbearably to forget about all my problems, steal Lily from her parents' house and set off with her on a round-the-world cruise. Or at least go to the continent.

Now, something that small was all I needed to be happy. Too bad it wasn't my fate.

I even got the idea to call Liliana. But before I managed, the disheveled Thomas Smith returned. The investigator ordered a mug of light beer, paid up and stood next to me.

"Lev, are you certain the ritual has already been performed?" he asked, taking a few greedy gulps of beer.

"Did the demons not convince you of that? I answered with a question. "Really?"

The investigator sighed and wiped some foam from his mustache.

"Well, what now?"

"I have no idea."

"And your contacts in the Imperial Guard?"

I chuckled.

"After today's fiasco?"

"Any other suggestions?"

I finished the coffee and placed the empty mug on the nearest table, then sighed heavily.

"I need to have a talk with Moran."

Thomas frowned and raised his hand with the bandaged finger stubs.

"Are you sure? What if he's somehow connected with all this?"

"Well, this way we'll know for sure." I shivered from a piercing gust of wind blowing off the water and called the investigator after me: "Let's go, there's nothing else to do anyhow."

Smith hesitated for a bit, then gave in and walked after me. But it was obvious that I wouldn't be able to convince him once and for all. While the cabby took us to the self-propelled carriage we'd left near Riverfort, the investigator sat in agitated silence, then started nervously walking from side to side as he waited for the powder engine to warm up.

"Are you sure this is a good idea?" he couldn't hold back.

"I'm not," I admitted, putting on my jacket. "But what options do we have? If we can come to an agreement, Moran will solve all our problems."

"And if we cannot?"

I just smiled. Such an outcome was much less to my liking, but I was ready for it as well.

"Devil!" Thomas Smith had his own interpretation of my smile. "I don't want to know!"

"Don't you worry, I'll do it all by myself."

"And the demons? What will happen if they get out of the catacombs?"

"Their path into the city is closed," I assured the investigator. "No matter what ritual the Aztecs performed, they have to stay underground."

New Babylon, like the majority of the Empire, was protected against the otherworldly by a series of powerful electromagnetic transmitters. I had no reason to doubt that they were still functioning.

Science is stronger than magic.

"Alright, Lev!" Thomas sighed, rubbing the bandage on his neck. "Alright! How will we do it?"

I shrugged my shoulders.

"We shouldn't visit Moran at work. We have to figure out where he lives and... have a heart to heart. I'm sure I can manage."

Thomas Smith shot me a sour look in reply and suddenly said:

"I know where he lives."

"Is that so?" I asked in astonishment.

"Yes!" the investigator confessed. "Yeah, I also thought to talk with him eye to eye." He touched the bandage on his neck again. "You know, I don't like having a razor stuck into my neck!"

ON THE WAY, we went to retrieve the Irish killer's case. While Thomas kept watch, I wandered with a torch in the tall grass. I found the case, checked if the suppressor was well attached to the pistol barrel, and dry fired the gun several times. I then chambered a round and stashed the Webley-Scott under my jacket.

The investigator wasn't too inspired by my manipulations but didn't refuse my plan. We simply had no other way to figure out what was happening here.

BASTIAN MORAN lived in a quiet part of town near the Embassy Quarter. There was an unnamed canal between his house and the Old City. Its cloudy waters served as a kind of boundary between the austerity of the historical buildings and the pretentiousness of the modern architecture.

In order not to alert the private guard of this complex of three five-story buildings, Thomas Smith decided to rely on luck and leave the self-propelled carriage in a neighboring alley. He then led me through a small, somewhat gloomy-looking square up against the common fence of the grounds.

"Fifth floor, third and fourth windows from the corner," he said, pointing me to the inspector general's apartment. "He doesn't have a family, and if he does keep a lover, it is somewhere else. His servants all go home for the night, as well. The concierge is armed, so you cannot go through the main door."

"And I wasn't planning to," I snorted, throwing a coil of strong rope from the Model-T over my shoulder.

The investigator gave me a lift onto the wall. I laid down on it and looked around the property from its two-and-a-half-meter height. There were gas lamps near the canal and main entrances, but the depths of the complex were obscured by thick shadows.

"Alright then, I'm off," I exhaled and slid down.

Taking cover behind the neatly trimmed bushes, I walked along them to the building. I carefully glanced around a corner and immediately realized that getting over to the senior inspector's dwelling unnoticed would not merely be quite difficult, but simply impossible, except perhaps for the legendary Japanese Ninjas.

So, I didn't take a risk. I walked over the neatly manicured lawn and took a jump, grabbing the lower rung of the fire escape and easily climbing up onto the roof with its carved stovepipes. Trying not to stomp on the rooftop, I walked to the opposite edge and quietly looked down under my nose: my accurate eye did not let me down. The distance between neighboring buildings was in fact over a meter and a half.

Not short? Sure, but not long either.

I looked quickly down and made sure there was no one in the yard, then crouched and straightened up sharply like a spring after being compressed. That moment of flight, twenty meters off the ground, ended in me slamming into the neighboring roof. My boots gave an echoing strike on the iron sheet, and I had to somersault and lay out flat on my stomach to burn off the inertia.

I spent a few seconds lying like that and listening in agitation to the silence, but no one had raised a shout or blown a whistle. It was quiet, but I could still hear a record spinning in an apartment on one of the upper floors. It was the recent Billy Murray tune *Any Little Girl.*

Making sure there was no danger, I got to my feet and immediately hissed in pain at my thigh, which was still not healed. Fortunately, I didn't fall into spasms, and the wound didn't have any effect on my mobility.

Mechanically shaking off my jacket and pants, I walked over to the edge of the roof and froze in the shade of a stovepipe. There was a wonderful view from up here: the dark line of the canal and the austere architecture of the Embassy Quarter beyond it, raised spires with signal lights and dim starlight in the sky with a gray haze stretching up into it.

I had always liked looking at the city at night. Ever since I was a child.

I was reminded of my family manor on the slope of Calvary, and my heart ached in dull sorrow. And I immediately heard a fluttering behind my back.

"Beautiful, bugger!" the Beast declared, coming out from behind the smokestack. "Say, Leo, why don't people live on roofs?"

"Devil!" I exhaled. "You scared me!"

"And why's that? Dirty conscience?" the albino grinned, demonstrating a full jaw of fangs as he took out a cigar. "Let's sit and have a smoke, eh?"

"Put that away!" I demanded, although the eyes of my imaginary friend were glowing no less brightly than his cigar cherry.

The Beast obediently stashed the cigar, sat on the roof and suggested:

"Let's just be quiet like in the good old days."

"I haven't got time," I refused.

"Moran isn't home yet. He's wrapped up in business, all awash in concerns. That's what they call a promotion! It's a joke! Let's just have a sit, Leo."

"Another time."

"What will happen?" the albino doubted, walking to the edge of the roof and looking down. "What if you slip right now and get flattened like a pancake, what then? What then, boy?"

"I won't slip!" I looked angrily in reply, tying my rope around a stovepipe, carefully knotting it then running the free end under my armpit.

The Beast watched me with doubt, then held his right hand out in front and thoughtfully waved his clawed fingers.

"Are you sure, boy?"

"Make yourself scarce!" I cursed and walked off the roof, bracing my legs on the wall. The rope stretched, but it held my weight, allowing me to successfully lower down onto the small balcony with a guard rail made of bent metal bars.

I nearly twisted my neck right away, stepping on a chair which Bastian Moran most likely enjoyed sitting in as he admired the view of his neighborhood. My heart was still pulling me back down.

The Beast leaned over the edge of the roof and asked:

"You gonna kill him like Marlini?"

When he mentioned the hypnotist, shivers ran down my spine, but I stayed silent and crouched down by the balcony door with a crowbar in my hand. I didn't even have to break the lock – the catch was not down.

Then I armed myself with my silenced pistol and carefully slipped into the small kitchen. I didn't stick around there for long, turned on my torch and headed into the bedroom. But the senior inspector was really not home.

Deciding to prepare for my meeting with Moran, I removed the pillow case from a pillow and hunkered down in a secluded pigeonhole next to the coat cabinet in the entryway. I stood there for ten minutes, but soon my eyes started sagging, pulling me to sleep.

I didn't like that one bit and headed off to search the apartment.

I was most impressed by the collection of porcelain miniatures that completely occupied one of the rooms. All the rest was a wide assortment of gramophone records in the guest room, expensive wine in the bar, pictures on the walls and even a rich library with a stack of unread popular-science magazines, mostly from the medical field. I was left with the impression this was all a simple attempt to fit in with his peer group. I did not manage to look into just the gun safe: it was locked behind several complicated mechanisms.

I sat down at the desk in the senior inspector's office and started pulling each drawer open one after the next but couldn't find keys or any other work-related documents. But at that, I hit upon a pocket Browning with a round in the chamber. I though it fit to pull the magazine from the handle and uncock it.

Just then, I heard the clapping of a powder engine outside, and I quickly returned the magazine to its place, closed the drawer and ran into the entryway with the pillowcase in my hands. Soon, I heard steps on the stairwell, then a key clanked into the lock and the door flew open.

Bastian Moran walked into the entryway, turned on the light and headed for the guest room, but suddenly froze in place and lowered his hand to his belt holster. In an instant, I was at his back, throwing the pillowcase over his head. Without especially holding back, I laid into the back of his head with my pistol butt.

The senior inspector collapsed like he was thrown under a bus, and I barely managed to keep him from hitting the ground. It wasn't a sense of benevolence, I simply didn't want to make any noise and alert his downstairs neighbor.

I disarmed Moran and dragged him into the office, sat him on a chair and laid his chest down on the tabletop. I then left through a side door into the guest room and brought two knives from the kitchen, a silver table knife and a common butcher knife.

I returned just in time: he had already begun to move his arms, but still unconsciously, just barely coming to his senses.

"Don't move a muscle, Bastian!" I warned him, drawing the Webley-Scott I had tucked in my belt with a silencer on the barrel. "Just remove the pillowcase and return your hands to the table."

The senior inspector obeyed, looked at me with hatred and cursed:

"You stinking bastard!"

His hair was disheveled, his lip was swollen and there was fresh blood on his cheek, but his eyes were looking firmly and sharply, without the slightest bit of fear.

"Let's refrain from insults," I suggested.

"That's a matter of fact! You reek of piss!"

"Would you like me to shoot you in the foot? In light of recent events, that would give me untold satisfaction!"

"Shoot yourself in the head!"

I just snorted, continuing to hold the man in my pistol sights.

"Why did you hire Lynch to kill me?"

Despite my expectations, Bastian Moran seemed neither surprised nor alarmed by my question.

"Why did I hire him?" he arched a steep brow. "You need to be stopped, that's why!"

"And what did I ever do to you?"

"You're not a person, but a bloodthirsty animal. And your death would be doing humanity a huge favor."

"Nonsense!" I snapped "The tests..."

The senior inspector shot forward and bared his teeth.

"I don't know what was wrong with the tests, but you are a werebeast!"

"You're biased!"

"I have enough clues!"

"Clues?" I couldn't hold back. "That damned Irishman stuffed me full of silver, but here I am standing before you. And you still speak of clues?!"

Bastian Moran shot me a sullen look in response and shook his head.

"That cretin must have used the wrong rounds."

"Alright," I smiled. "Are you prepared to believe

your own eyes? Are you prepared to hear me out, if I prove that I am not a werebeast?"

"And how are you planning to do that?"

I shifted my pistol to my left hand and picked up the butcher knife from the table.

"You are most likely aware, senior inspector, that the body of a werebeast is defined by fast regeneration. Their wounds heal extremely fast. That is a well-known fact."

"It is," Moran confirmed.

I led the knife over my wrist, and the sharp blade easily split my skin. Blood flowed.

"It isn't healing," I chuckled.

"Some kind of trick..."

I was prepared for the senior inspector's skepticism and replaced the kitchen knife with a silver one.

"Your very own table silver, isn't that right?" I asked, clenching my teeth and cutting my wrist, splitting the skin with the fairly dull knife. It bled again.

"You're ruining my Persian rug!" Bastian Moran noted sullenly.

I returned my pistol to my right hand and extended my left to the senior inspector.

"Steel and silver, see the difference?"

"I can't see anything at all!" Moran answered.

"Then turn on the light!"

The senior inspector followed my advice, looked closer and was forced to admit I was right.

"That means you're not a werebeast after

all..." he muttered under his nose. "Strange. I was certain..." He threw himself into the back of his chair, continuing to hold his hands against the tabletop. "So then, Leopold, what do you want from me? Is the criminal investigation bothering you?"

"It is," I confirmed and demanded: "Call off the accusations! Now you know I'm not guilty!"

The senior inspector looked at me with unhidden doubt, then sighed.

"Well, I think that can be arranged. I'll have to sign some papers and remove the evidence again, but it's all solvable. Anything else?"

"Yes," I nodded, lowering my pistol. "Seeing as we've come to a mutual understanding, there's one more aspect of this issue I'd like to discuss with you..."

I got distracted looking out the window for just a moment, but that short instant was enough for Moran to throw open the upper drawer of his desk and point the Browning at me.

"Drop your weapon!" the senior inspector demanded. "At once!"

"Hmm, now what do we have here?" I frowned, not even considering fulfilling his order. "Are you going to accuse me of breaking and entering or attacking a government figure? A bit over the top, don't you think?"

Bastian Moran's face turned to stone. He got up from the table, slightly wobbled and grabbed the pistol in both hands. I suppose it was all the fault of the vertigo after being struck on the back of the head.

"Nothing personal, Leopold," the senior inspector said in a cold tone, "you just had bad luck with your family."

"How do you mean?"

"The problem is your cousin," Bastian Moran explained. "Her Highness Crown Princess Anna, our future Empress. If you think about it, I'm actually doing you a favor..."

"What are you on about?!"

"Her Highness is ill. She has a congenital heart disease. She doesn't have long to live. But there are stubborn rumors about a heart transplant, and the greatest chances for a successful operation, if the donor is a close relative. The only close relative of the Princess is you."

I chuckled due to the unexpected sensation of *déjà vu* creeping up on me.

"You'd put me under the knife for the sake of the Empire?"

Bastian Moran cringed.

"Not at all! For the sake of the Empire, you must die!"

"What?!"

"The Empire needs a strong hand!" the senior inspector declared. "The constantly ailing girl, hovering between life and death, is not capable of running a government. If we leave everything how it is, it won't be three years before the country collapses to different provinces and a war of everyone against everyone begins. Millions will die! And they will die entirely in vain, just for that wretched blood, poisoned by the curse of *the fallen*!"

"Sedition!"

"Truth! I have never hidden my reductionist inclinations! You and those like you are just a vestige of a bygone era. You're halting progress, perverting its entire essence! The Second Empire is one of normal people, and *the illustrious* have no place in it!"

I nodded, but not in a sign of agreement, just to show that I understood his motives.

"So the accusation of murdering the Hindoos was just a pretext?"

"Naturally! Everything was spoiled by von Nalz. That senior dolt rejected all the clues I gathered!"

"So, a conspiracy?" I couldn't hold back the contemptuous smirk. "Now I see how you got your new rank. You just had to close your eyes to some ritual murders. Who cares about whores cut up by Aztecs? All the more so given they were tainted with *illustrious* blood. You mean to say *the illustrious* have no place in the Empire, isn't that right?"

Bastian Moran squinted, and immediately cracked the firing pin of the Browning drily.

I was expecting this outcome from the very beginning of the conversation, and still turned to stone for an instant in surprise. And that fleeting moment decided everything. The senior inspector didn't try to cock it or load another round, but instead made a blistering jump through the side door.

And I was too late. The silencer-dulled shot clapped out on his heels and slammed into an empty doorframe. A moment later, the Browning thundered out boomingly and I dashed off on my heels. I ran out through the second door into the dark corridor, raced into the kitchen and jumped out onto the little balcony. There I stuck the pistol handle into the side pocket of my jacket, grabbed the rope and, bracing my legs on the wall, started up onto the roof. As soon as I came over its edge, a belated shot came after me.

"Choked again!" the Beast chuckled offensively as he sat next to a stovepipe. He'd also managed to pilfer a bottle of expensive cognac from God knows where.

Without answering, I ran like hell and hopped onto the neighboring building. I raced to the fire escape, went down it and jumped onto the lawn. In the courtyard, I heard a loud blast of the doorman's whistle, but no one managed to guess my escape route, and I got over the wall before the night guards ran up to the corner.

I fell into a thorny bush and immediately jumped to my feet then dashed across the square to the self-propelled carriage that had just flickered on its headlights. The Model-T started off and I jumped into the moving vehicle through an open door, then we raced away.

"What happened?" Thomas Smith demanded explanations, turning the wheel in agitation.

"Moran is with the conspirators!"

"Did you kill him?"

"No. I didn't manage."

The investigator cursed in vexation, but I didn't try and justify myself.

I had an excellent opportunity to shoot Bastian Moran, because I knew for certain that his pistol was not loaded. I could have, but I didn't.

Moran was supposed to cock the gun! He was supposed to cock the gun and die! Then I would have shot him without the slightest hesitation or moral anguish.

But the clever fox sniffed out my game, and it turned out how it turned out.

I uttered a silent curse. Then, the silence of the city at night was broken by a peal of deafening thunder. A blasting wind bent the trees, and I heard the clink of breaking glass.

"What the devil?" Thomas cursed, slamming on the breaks.

The Model-T started skidding and nearly turned over, but I didn't even notice. All my attention was wrapped up in a ghostly glow over the Old City. The low clouds there were devoured by a hellish flame, and that was no illusion. Dirigibles were going up in flame and collapsing on the roofs of buildings one after the next.

"What is happening, Lev?!" Thomas Smith poked me on the arm, watching in horror as the ominous purple sunk its teeth higher and higher into the sky.

"Hell has broken loose," I answered, not able to turn away from the horrifying spectacle.

The sky was blazing brightest of all over the Imperial Palace. I didn't have the slightest doubt that this was the ghastly aftermath of the Aztec priests' final ritual. It seemed the electromagnetic radiation was unable to hold the otherworldly power inside the catacombs.

The underworld tore out onto the streets of New Babylon, and I was afraid to even imagine how much effort would be required to cleanse the city of this filth. What was more, I didn't know if it would be possible at all...

PART SIX

ANGEL

Cursed Blood And Nightmares Incarnate

1

THERE ARE SITUATIONS when the conscious mind simply refuses to perceive what is going on and one simply cannot shake the sensation of a bad dream. In those times, it seems enough to simply close one's eyes and open them again, then everything will change for the better all on its own.

It will not change, believe you me. I know that for a fact...

NEW BABYLON, bulwark of the scientific world and the heart of the most powerful Empire, upon testing turned out to be a rotten apple. The cursed blood of *the fallen* had eaten it away from the inside like an infernal worm and became the skeleton key that opened the door for the otherworldly. And though the mad gunfire was only coming from the Old City for now, we had no reason to doubt that the hastily erected barricades would not be able to hold the demons for long.

The only hope that remained was for electromagnetic waves and, as strange as it may have sounded, the laws of magic. According to all rules of ritual, the circle around the Old City along which the sacrifices took place should hold the otherworldly creatures inside. Maybe not forever, and just for some time, but it would hold them.

The lights over the city went out slowly but didn't completely disappear. Meanwhile, the burning purple spot right over the Imperial Palace was gathering into a giant diabolic eye. The city dwellers that spilled out onto the streets were watching the sky with horror; some were screaming hysterically about the end of the world, some were maintaining their presence of mind and expounding on the Earth colliding with a giant comet. Simpletons lamented the untimely end of Her Highness, cynics whispered about a coup d'état. The smartest left town when they saw army divisions enter the city, taking their hurriedly packed suitcases right to port. But there were very few such people.

The turmoil on the streets was outrageous. In the end, it took us more than two hours to reach Leonardo-da-Vinci-Platz where Thomas Smith decided to take me. From time to time, we had to honk the horn to clear the road of alarmed gapers. At other times, we had to pull over to let endless columns of armored vehicles and steam trucks with recoilless rifles and powerful Howitzers on trailers roll past to the center.

After letting me out, the investigator headed to the central telegraph office, intending to send news to the Pinkerton Detective Agency, while I headed over the fence into the yard of the shop Mechanisms and Rarities and knocked on the back door.

Alexander Dyak opened up almost immediately; like the majority of city dwellers, he was not sleeping tonight.

"What is happening, Leopold Borisovich?!" the old inventor asked in agitation.

While the shop owner treated me to some tea, I quickly brought him up to speed.

"It's much worse than that," Dyak said after hearing my tale of the events of today. "Much, much worse, Leopold Borisovich!"

"What are you talking about?"

"Follow me, I'll show you!" the inventor called me after him into the back room.

I finished the tea, filling the glass again and went after him. There was fog in my head. I wanted unbearably to sleep, and only the strong bitter drink did anything to mitigate my exhaustion.

In the far corner of the workshop, there was a device swishing a slate pencil measuredly on a ribbon of paper. Dyak stood next to it and explained:

"This is a lightning sensor. It doesn't emit any rays, just registers electromagnetic disturbances. I set it to the proper wavelength, and here, look..." Dyak extended me a fragment of the paper ribbon, marked with an unbroken kinked line. "This device was recording before yesterday. But yesterday, the picture changed in the most cardinal fashion!"

The difference between the old drawing and the line the lightning detector was sketching out now was apparent to the naked eye. The extreme points were the same, but the middle of the range was now mush.

"They changed the signal," I whispered. "That's why the demons made it out of the catacombs! When did that happen?"

Alexander Dyak started to dig in his papers, then slapped his forehead and got out a notepad.

"Two hours before midnight," he said, looking at his work notes.

"Just after the ritual!" I gasped and walked from corner to corner, then returned to the inventor. "This is no mere coincidence! This is treachery! I don't know who in the Sublime Electricity movement is responsible for the transmission of the signal, but we have to force them to restore the proper settings!"

Alexander Dyak just shook his head.

"I'm afraid it won't be so easy."

"What are you talking about?" I asked, baffled. I then left my glass of tea on the workbench and asked: "What do you mean, Alexander?"

The inventor took a heavy sigh and explained his words:

"I'm afraid I'm talking about another signal on the very same wavelength. If we align the sheets, elements of the original signal become visible. Last night, a new transmitter was turned on! It broadcasts on the same frequency as the Sublime Electricity ones, and the signals stack on one another. That breaks the defense in some way..."

I shook my head.

"I don't believe in such coincidences."

"I'm not saying this is a coincidence!" Dyak assured me. "Look for yourself: the new device transmits an extremely similar signal, and thus dulls the old one."

"That's too complicated for me!"

"Remember, you asked me to translate the Pater Noster into Morse code and transmit it? Now imagine someone is sending the same signal at the same time, but in reverse, as is done at black masses! It's just an analogy, but the principle..."

"Oh devil! Alexander, who did you send your research to, Edison and Tesla? Is that right?"

"I am not accusing anyone!" Alexander Dyak reacted with hostility to my suspicions. "It has happened many times that different scientists made the very same discovery independent of one another and practically at the same time!"

"Edison and Tesla," I repeated, reminding him of the recent conspiracy, when the criminals were armed with electric casters made in a partnership between Colt and Edison Electric Lights and sighed: "Edison..."

"I ask you to refrain from unfounded accusations!" Dyak objected. "That is just monstrous!"

"Drop it, Alexander!" I interrupted the inventor. "We are not in a court of law! Tell me about the new transmitter. Could you calculate its position?"

Dyak sighed and beckoned me to the back door. He threw it open and pointed at the purple clouds over the palace.

"The transmitter is there!" the old man announced confidently.

"What makes you think that?"

"The glow of the clouds is caused by an elevated concentration of otherworldly energy," the inventor explained, closing the door. "Based on the diameter of the luster, the power of the transmitter is quite low, and it is covering only the central part of the Old City, while my lightning sensor is only picking up echoes of its signal."

"So the very epicenter is..." I muttered out, "in the palace..."

"I can make you up a bed on the couch," Alexander Dyak suggested and, shambling on the floor with his slippers, went out into the pantry. "I'll go to the Sublime Electricity lyceum in the morning. They should know what's happening. And don't try to talk me out of it, Leopold Borisovich. It won't work! My mind is made up!"

I didn't even try.

By now, the infernal effect had touched just the area of the Imperial Palace, but the rest of the city would remain safe while the mysterious transmitter was turned on. What if it was not running at full capacity, or wasn't the only one of its kind?

The grave thoughts made my head hurt. It started feeling cramped and stuffy, as if I were the fairy-tale Alice, and had suddenly increased in size.

"Alexander!" I hailed the inventor. "Can I take your cloak?"

"Going somewhere?" the old man asked in surprise.

"For a walk."

"Take it, of course!" Alexander allowed and immediately started worrying: "Will you be gone long?"

"Wait for me," I asked him. "We'll go to the lyceum together."

"Agreed!" the old man lit up, invigorated by my support.

Regretting that I had forgotten my raglan overcoat somewhere, I crammed myself into on the short tight cloak, popped on a dark blue felt hat and went outside.

THERE WAS A FINE cold drizzle coming down from the sky: I went out of the back yard of the shop and hurried to the sound of gunfire. The artillery cannonade near the Imperial Palace didn't quiet down for even a moment. The cannons were mirrored by gunfire. Rifles clapped, and machine guns chattered frequently. Rarely, building windows would shudder from far-away bomb explosions. In the sky, there were army dirigibles, but they didn't risk getting near the demon-controlled neighborhoods.

There were noticeably less city-dwellers on the streets by that time. Some had been convinced to disperse by police, and others were scared off by the rain. And there really wasn't much to see: the purple flame in the sky was pulsing measuredly over the palace like a ghostly heart, and there wasn't anything else interesting.

Anyhow, there were still plenty of people that hadn't given in to the constables and remained on the bridges and sidewalks to see the glow in the night sky. I heard wailing over the death of the heiress to the throne and cursing at the weak government. The seditious talk would instantly die down, though, when a police squadron walked nearby.

I was not the only one that wanted to get closer to the Old City, and although the sentries posted on the intersections were turning curious onlookers back, the stubborn could easily find ways around them.

The sound of gunfire and explosions was gradually getting closer, and army patrols started being seen on the street, turning back the gapers and not making exceptions for newspapermen, or those who worked for local councils. I decided not to risk it and went up a fire escape onto the roof of a four-story building, hoping to get a better look from up high. This place had already been chosen by a group of local boys and two photojournalists. The view over the old town was surprisingly decent from up here, while the purple spot in the sky was now pulsing seemingly right over our heads.

Further down the street, the darkness of the night occasionally exploded with sparks of rifle fire, but we couldn't make out who the soldiers were firing on from here. Even an old man pressed up to a pair of nautical binoculars, who began cursing dirtily every time one of the boys came to him with questions, couldn't see.

Unexpectedly, the building shuddered and seemingly swayed. An instant later, a heap of broken brick rained off the corner manor on the neighboring intersection. A steam-powered backhoe on treads rolled up to it with a bass roar, lowered its shovel and began to scoop the rubble onto the road, forming a second line of defense.

Desperately wailing its siren, an armored vehicle drove around it, dragging a recoilless rifle behind on a trailer. A booming Howitzer clap came from somewhere to the side, and the Old City was suddenly lit up by the explosion of an incendiary bomb. Wisps of smoke started curling up into the already gray sky. No fewer than a dozen buildings were on fire, but the cannons quieted down only after shooting another three or four phosphorus rounds.

"Tesla generators!" the boys on the other edge of the roof suddenly said, startled. "They're on cars! They've got Tesla generators on cars!"

I ran over and saw a column of armored vehicles. On their towers were metal steam rods with copper balls on the end. Between the spheres, electric shocks sparked from time to time.

"Well, that'll give 'em the old what for!" the rugged boy chuckled with zest, but we didn't have time to see. Suddenly, the attic doors loudly flew open and the constables that came out onto the roof chased us all down.

2

WHEN I RETURNED to Mechanisms and Rarities in the early morning, Alexander Dyak, despite the early hour, had already unlocked the shop. What was more, it was packed to the brim with visitors. But no one was buying anything. They were all academy teachers drinking coffee and discussing last night's events, occasionally running out to the street for a smoke. It was a visiting session of the discussion club.

"Leopold Borisovich!" the inventor grew joyful, letting me in through the back door. "At midday, there will be a speech by Nikola Tesla in the Sublime Electricity lyceum, and I will try to visit with him!"

"Tesla?" I asked in surprise. "How will he get to New Babylon? He's in Paris right now, after all!"

"But it's Tesla!" Alexander Dyak declared with a look that seemed to explain positively everything.

And it really did. There were all kinds of wild stories about Nicola Tesla.

"They say Edison is coming as well," the inventor added.

"Well, Edison certainly isn't going to cross the Atlantic!"

"They say Edison came to New Babylon incognito just a week ago. He's allegedly intending to lure the New Babylon chapter of the Sublime Electricity to his side."

"I very much doubt he'll succeed."

"As do I, Leopold Borisovich. And now, forgive me, but I have to leave you," Dyak said. "I need to take care of my guests and find a temporary sales clerk. I won't have the time to man the shop for the next few days."

The upcoming meeting with Nicola Tesla had inspired the old inventor in an unbelievable fashion. It was as if he had grown fifteen years younger, and my tongue couldn't turn to disappoint him. However, he had a low chance to reach one of the highest hierarchs of the Sublime Electricity through his many secretaries and assistants.

Instead, I put on some coffee, as strong as I could make it.

BY ELEVEN O'CLOCK, I had such unrestrained bitterness in my mouth, the flavor of coca leaves seemed pleasant by comparison. It was as if someone had poured half-handfuls of fine sand into my eyes, and I wanted just one thing – to lie down and doze off. But I had no time to sleep. And I couldn't...

"How do I look?" Alexander Dyak asked, walking into the back room in his best morning coat and striped pants.

"Very respectable," I yawned and asked: "Is it time already?"

"Yes, there's a cab waiting for us."

Leaving the shop to the student Dyak had hired to keep watch, we went outside and told the cabby to take us to the Sublime Electricity lyceum. But, to be honest, we would have gotten there on foot much quicker. The streets were so crowded with carts, coaches, and self-propelled carriages there was no getting through. Also, there were police occasionally stopping traffic to let columns of army vehicles pass.

The city-dwellers didn't seem too panicked, either. All that was located near the Imperial Palace were government administration buildings, so the number of missing was relatively low. Many lamented the death of the heiress to the throne, but not too strongly: the rumors about the Princess's weak health had been a constant since her very birth and even the most incurable optimists had no expectation that she would rule for long.

The gloomy light in the sky was extinguished with the coming of dawn and no longer frightened people with its ominous purple. But the echoes of far-away gunfire kept the locals from considering last night's events just a simple bad dream, so the square around the lyceum was flooded with city-dwellers. The pandemonium there was such that a camera man had gotten up on the pedestal of the Ampère, Ohm and Volt memorial, and the cabby let us out a full two blocks before our destination.

I suppose many came here not out of a desire to see the famous Tesla but to restore their faltering mental balance. The Sublime Electricity lyceum's two steel masts tearing into the heavens served as obvious confirmation of the infinite power of science. Around the huge copper balls that capped the elegant structures, there were crackling crowns of electricity. The air there regularly lit up with blinding sparks filling the square with sharp cracks. Today, they didn't scare anyone; in fact, they delighted people and were anticipated with plain impatience.

Electricity is power!

Even I wanted to believe in it just as unreservedly as before...

HOLDING ALEXANDER by the hand, I stood on my tip-toes, looked over the square and came to the dismal conclusion that we couldn't get into the lyceum through the central entrance. There was such a sizable line before the gates that there couldn't possibly be enough room inside, even if people decided to stand on each other's heads. The constables had already begun to wedge into the crowd, cutting most of it off from the lyceum.

"In such circumstances, members of the movement must be let in through the service entrance," the inventor guessed, and we hurried around the building.

My head was spinning in weariness; other peoples' emotions rolled over me from all sides, striking me with an unseen wave of feverish agitation and nearly knocking me off my feet. My *talent* was dormant as before, but the sensitivity to others' phobias hadn't gone anywhere. The mental hurricane was driving me mad. After a hundred meters, I was so burned out it seemed I wasn't walking around the square but climbing up a sheer wall.

Fortunately, on the other side of the lyceum, there were somewhat less people. My heartbeat gradually returned to normal, and my head stopped spinning. But the sharp echoes of others' fears continued to pierce me, even when we had already escaped the crowd.

"That way!" Alexander Dyak announced confidently and pulled me to the back gate, which guarded by two constables armed with revolvers and clubs. Another six police with semiautomatic carbines were spread out over the property.

I had no desire to talk with former colleagues and stayed back from the inventor, having decided to await his return on the street. I didn't have to fear attracting the attention of the constables with aimless wandering, though. It wasn't so crowded on this side but, there were still plenty of gapers here too. One rapscallion newspaperman even used spurs to climb a telephone pole.

I took out my handkerchief and wiped the perspiration from my face, then suddenly saw Alexander Dyak turn away from the gate and walk straight toward me.

"No, no!" I had my own interpretation of the situation. "Go alone! I'll wait for you out here, it will be ghastly sultry inside."

"Leopold Borisovich! They didn't allow me in, can you imagine?!" the inventor objected. "They said entry was restricted to those on a special list and only through the front door! We have to go back!"

"Go, Alexander," I sighed. "Go. I need to wet my whistle, though."

The inventor headed off back with a fated sigh, and I stood in a line to the street tent, but at the very last moment changed my mind and didn't buy carbonated water with syrup. Instead, I walked into a street cafe and asked for home-made lemonade. After the bitter coffee, the drink seemed like a divine ambrosia; I couldn't hold back and drank a second glass, then paid up and went back to the square.

There, I walked along the outer wall of the lyceum and unexpectedly realized I was hungry as a wolf. That surprised me a bit. I hadn't been able to boast of a good appetite for some time. I felt I hadn't even drunk lemonade in a hundred years. But now, starvation was rolling over me.

"I should have just ordered a whole pitcher," I chuckled and tried to delve into the emotions of people around me but could only sense a vague nervousness; my *talent* hadn't yet awoken, and others' fears slipped past me like water through my fingers.

That annoyed me.

A motorcade of three self-propelled carriages drove out onto the square, and the newspapermen sitting at the tables of street cafes jumped up in an instant, their camera's sparkling with flashes.

"Tesla! Tesla has arrived!" sounded out from all sides.

The lyceum workers quickly threw open the back gates, and the constables that came to help them squeezed out the gapers blocking off the passage. The reporters ran off after the self-propelled carriages, nearly falling under their wheels, shouting out questions, and banging on the side windows and doors. But the motorcade drove through the gates without slowing down.

Contrary to his habit, Tesla didn't want to talk with any newsmen.

Maybe his guards had something to do with that?

The disappointed newspapermen began to disperse, getting into arguments and cursing each other out. The reporter that had climbed up the pole kept watching the lyceum grounds, not even thinking of coming down.

My interest was drawn by the unusual camera in his hands, and I headed for the post. But I couldn't make out the journalist. The dim autumn sun was shining through the clouds right into my eyes. I placed my hand to my forehead, noticed the edge of a reddish beard and suddenly realized I had met this reporter before.

But who was he? I had never before rubbed shoulders with journalists.

And suddenly I recognized him and gaped in surprise.

The man who'd climbed the pole was Ivan Sokolov, the Russian society observer!

Ramon Miro had mentioned a Russian looking to buy explosives in Foundry-Town, and another random acquaintance had once introduced me to Sokolov as a person with anarchist convictions. And although Krasin, the smiling fat man who had let that slip, turned out to be a bastard and a hired killer, I had no reason not to believe his judgement about Sokolov.

Taking a step back from the pole, I glanced at the constables at the gates and hesitated, not knowing if I should draw their attention. Then, something hard poked into my side.

"No stupid stuff!" The man behind me warned.

"Speak of the devil..." I gasped, because I knew this voice perfectly well.

The man holding the pistol was none other than Yemelyan Krasin!

"Leopold Borisovich! Aren't you happy to see me?" The fat man aped well-intentioned surprise.

"I pictured our reunion going... somewhat differently," I smiled in strain.

"Oh, I can imagine!" Krasin chuckled good-heartedly.

After Yemelyan Nikiforovich had gassed me, I intuited that he had been hired by the mad architect Tacini. But now everything was cast in a somewhat different light.

"What have you cooked up now?" I asked, looking askance at the fat man at the very edge of my vision, but I could only see the blurred silhouette of a stout man in a dark cloak and bowler.

"Why the devil ask questions you already know the answer to?"

"You're going to blow up the lyceum? But why?! The *haut monde* of scientific thought is gathered there!"

Krasin just furrowed his brow.

"The *haut monde* of scientific thought?! They're nothing but a collection of retrogrades and pencil-pushers, infinitely far from the interests of the common man! Bourgeois servants of big capital, that's who they are! These men can only benefit the working class by dying! Our action will be the spark to ignite the flame, then the fire of world-wide revolution will spread!"

"Now is not the time!" I tried to bring him to

reason. "Otherworldly powers have infiltrated the city. We need to do everything in our power to burn out the infection!"

"Do we?" Yemelyan Nikiforovich doubted. "If New Babylon falls under the earth, if all Atlantis sinks beneath the waves, the rest of humanity only stands to gain. The Second Empire is the prison of peoples! The quicker it falls, the better! New Babylon must be destroyed!"

And yet I couldn't shake the feeling that the Russian Anarchists had come here not out of a desire to commit an act of terror, which would certainly make the front page of even the smallest notable publications. Or, at the very least, not only for that...

"Who do you work for?" I asked. "Who ordered you to blow up the lyceum right now?"

"We're fighting for the rights of the common people..."

"Empty words!" I cut him off. "As you were attached to Malone and Tacini, this mission must have also been sent from above. You are no ideological strugglers, but mere paid provocateurs!"

"You have too loose a tongue, Lev Borisovich!" Krasin said with unhidden threat. "For a person in your position, that is fraught with serious problems!"

"What are you saying?" I smirked and asked: "Are you working for Duke Logrin? Or still for the New World? Or maybe for big capital itself?"

I wasn't even remotely interested in the answer to my provocative question. I was just trying to knock

Krasin off track and, based on the trembling of the revolver barrel against my ribs, my last guesses had hit their mark.

Not missing my chance, I twisted my body, simultaneously moving away from the gun. Just then, a shot rang out, and a man standing in front of us in an elegant slicker threw up his hands and fell onto the causeway. My side just burned.

Grabbing Krasin's gun hand, I twisted it and stuck it under his other armpit, then sharply stood up, lifting his body onto my back. My lower back cracked, but the sharp pain in my ligaments didn't stop me from the wrestling move, and I threw the corpulent anarchist over me.

The fat man collapsed onto the paving stone with such a force that the earth shook under our feet. Or so it seemed for the first moment. Then the shockwave from an explosion of horrifying power struck me in the chest, threw me onto my back and sent me in a somersault. My ears were blasted by a horrifying thunder, and the lyceum building of the Sublime Electricity collapsed like a flimsy house of cards. The masts with copper balls lurched and fell to the square, and a true cloud of dust shot up to the sky.

When I managed to get myself off the causeway and look around, people thrown about by the shockwave were lying everywhere. But only the guards standing beyond the fence were seriously hurt. I myself got a contusion, and my ears were ringing. The skin on my side meanwhile, burned by the gunpowder fumes, felt like it was on fire. In the same place, I discovered a long narrow hole in my jacket.

I tried to stand from the paving stone, but immediately had an attack of vertigo. My vision turned gray, and I had to stay on the cold stones. The sounds hadn't yet returned. All colors were faded also, and everything happening looked like just a stupid black and white movie. Some city-dwellers were getting off the ground with the drunken stumbling of knocked-out boxers, others were running off the square in a panic, wanting to run from the danger as quickly as possible. A few stayed behind to help those wounded in the explosion, and a horrible squeeze was formed instantly on the alleyways leading away from the lyceum.

Shock. It was just a shock.

"Krasin!" that thought struck like lightning in my head. I returned and watched the fat man getting up heavily on all fours. Blood was coming from his ears, but that was the only wound he'd taken in the explosion.

I pointed the Cerberus from my pocket at him but I was seeing double, and my arm was shaking, so I couldn't aim. The anarchist noticed me and bared his teeth strangely; with one hand, he leaned on the paving stone, and with the other he reached for his fallen pistol.

The Cerberus gave three spits of fire, totally silent, and I felt the handle kick back in my hands. Krasin shuddered and slammed his face into the causeway. The first two bullets hit him in the side and shoulder, while the last had gone through his temple, and a spot of blood started spreading on the rocks around his head.

Totally mechanically, I changed the pistol magazine for a new one and stood to my feet. But by then, the trail of the second anarchist had already gone cold. Sokolov had escaped.

"Scoundrel!' I cursed, hiding my pistol hand in my jacket's side pocket. Then, stumbling like a drunk, I walked around the lyceum's outer wall, which was leaning and, in places, totally collapsed.

Not many people had been seriously hurt on the square in front of the collapsed building: most of the concussed city-dwellers there dispersed throughout the area on their own. There were an unlucky few that needed urgent care though, those who had been hit by bits of glass flying from the windows. But nearer the main entrance, where the shockwave had torn out of the building, the paving stone was soaked in blood. There were broken bodies and torn-off appendages lying everywhere. Due to the collapsed basement, the right wing of the lyceum was totally underground, and it was hard to even imagine how many people had fallen into the hole in the causeway.

Pushing aside the fortunate, who had not yet managed to get into the lyceum, I started making my way for the central gates and suddenly noticed Alexander Dyak, who was walking up to meet me, squeezing his bloodied forehead with his hand.

"Alexander!" I shouted, but the inventor didn't hear me.

I walked over to the old man and braced him, helping him stay on his feet. There were already volunteers rushing from the neighboring buildings to help, but I led Dyak not to one of the surrounding cafes, which had become improvised first aid points, but right to an ambulance carriage that had driven onto the square. Orderlies ran after the heavily wounded with gurneys, and a doctor remained at the carriage to admit the injured. They didn't think Alexander Dyak was seriously hurt, but I took a couple hundred-franc notes from my wallet and slipped the rumpled bills into the doctor's chest pocket.

"Don't make me convince you by other means," I said after that, not able to hear my own voice.

The doctor shivered and decided to place Dyak in one of the free spots.

The carriage rolled off to the hospital five minutes later, and another few came to replace it. I stuck my hands in my pockets and walked away, hurrying off the square before the police closed the neighboring streets and began a total document check.

I had no doubt that a roundup would follow, so when someone grabbed me by the hand from behind, I spun in place excessively abruptly and only at the last moment managed to hold back from striking with my already raised elbow. But it wasn't some mettlesome constable behind me, it was Elizabeth-Maria, the succubus.

"What are you doing here?" I asked,

thunderstruck.

Elizabeth-Maria started saying something quickly but to me, she may as well have just been opening and closing her mouth. My hearing still hadn't come back, and all I could detect was ringing.

"I can't hear!" I said to her and quickly got a heavy slap.

"Is that better?" the succubus asked.

Then I could hear her perfectly. After the trenchant slap, something clicked in my head and I was surrounded instantly by a horrible cacophony. Some were screaming, some were crying their eyes out, howling and whining. Not far away, the bell of a fire brigade rang out, and I heard a piercing police whistle. A street loudspeaker began indiscriminately squealing, and reality immediately stopped seeming like a ghastly film.

All this was happening here and now. It was happening to me!

I quickly grabbed Elizabeth-Maria by the hand and dragged her off the square.

"Just you wait!" The succubus boiled over. Her nostrils were flaring with zest, and the tip of her tongue was running along her thin pale lips from time to time. Human suffering had drawn her demonic spirit here and that made for an unpleasant spectacle.

So, I didn't listen and just dragged the succubus after me. She had once again dressed in a way that was none too appropriate for a lady of good taste. I mean, the blouse and bicycle pants didn't deserve reprimand, but the red kerchief and orange leather jacket were extremely provocative.

"Where are you dragging me?!" Elizabeth-Maria objected when we'd reached the intersection. "I left the carriage on the other side of the square!"

"Don't scream!" I demanded. "I already lost my hearing once today!"

"I can see that!"

"How did you find me?"

"It wasn't hard. After all, we're connected. Did you forget?"

I took a few heavy sighs, walked off the sidewalk along which frightened city dwellers passed from time to time, to the wall of a building and asked.

"What do you need?"

"Liliana was taken away by the police!" Elizabeth-Maria announced, and my heart stopped in horror.

Just up and stopped. My soul was pierced with fear, and all sounds went quiet again while the world turned gray. For a moment it seemed I had died, and perhaps I really had. But my heart started beating again after an instant that lasted a whole eternity, now more distinctly, sharply and angrily.

My pulse started pounding in my temples with angry beats, and an unbearable splitting seared behind my eyes. I raised my gaze to Elizabeth-Maria, and she took an involuntary step back.

"When?" I rasped out. "When did that happen?"

"Around an hour ago," Elizabeth-Maria said. "She had just gotten back from her parents'."

Devil!

I smacked my fist into my palm with all my might.

Devil! Devil! Devil!

What would it have cost me to call and warn her? Why didn't I even think of doing it?

"Leo!" the succubus pulled me by the sleeves. "Leo, calm down!"

But I couldn't calm down. Now, I could only think about Liliana. I wouldn't get her out of the Newton-Markt, but the detention had certainly been arranged by Bastian Moran, he could bring her wherever he wanted. Maybe I still had a chance...

"Leo!" snapped the raging Elizabeth-Maria. "A note came for you!"

"What?"

"The police left you a note! Here, look!"

With my shaking hands, I unfolded the rumpled sheet. It had a telephone number written on it. A telephone number and nothing more.

I looked around and saw a teeming pharmacy. I didn't even try there, but instead ran into a small hotel where I told the porter I needed their phone for a police emergency.

I didn't have to tell the police emergency lie more than once. All the lines were overloaded with urgent calls and the porter didn't know when it might be my turn, until he saw the Newton-Markt number on the paper.

Bastian Moran picked up the phone.

"Speak!" he barked, not bothering himself with the rules of decent conduct.

Anyhow, it was surprising that he even found the time to answer phone calls right now.

"This is Leopold..."

"No names!" the senior inspector threw out abruptly.

"If anything happens to her..."

"Shut up and listen!" Moran interrupted me again. "We will meet at the place you found the muse. At exactly three. Don't be late and come alone. And don't try anything stupid!"

I tried to get in at least a word, but the senior inspector hung up immediately. I couldn't reach him again.

"What did you step in this time?" Elizabeth-Maria asked me when we'd gone outside and were walking around the square to her self-propelled carriage.

"Same as before," I sighed, looking at the succubus and warning: "I'm going to need your help."

"A service for a service."

"It's not me who needs help, but Liliana. Aren't you and her friends?"

"A service for a service," Elizabeth-Maria repeated.

"Just think about her..."

"Leo, you don't understand!" the succubus glanced unkindly at me. "Altruism is foreign to my nature. You scratch my back, I scratch yours. Or find someone else."

I had such a disdain for the idea of making another deal with the infernal creature that I was gritting my teeth, and I started mentally flipping through other possible candidates. But no one I knew could help me avoid the bloody slaughter; quite the opposite – if any of them helped me, a bloodbath would be inevitable.

"Alright!" I gave in with a fated sigh. "What do you want?"

"Powers, naturally!" Elizabeth-Maria laughed. "When you gifted me with the power of a *fallen one* for just a few minutes, you only annoyed me! True might, now that's what I want. And you be sure – I will not miss my second chance."

"I cannot give that to you. And you know I cannot!"

"You cannot now, but don't worry, I'll wait. As soon as you get the ability, you'll imbue me with power. Swear it."

"You could wait forever. I'll never be able."

"As you once said yourself: forever is a very long time. I believe in you, Leo. Swear it or get lost."

I took out my pocket watch, glanced at it and hid it back.

"If I promise to imbue you with power, you will help me free Liliana and cover me in a conversation with Moran?"

"I could even tear off his head," the succubus said with an unpleasant smile.

"No one's head needs to be torn off!"

"Why not? It's been a long time since I felt such an upwelling of power!"

"Well, will you help me or not?"

"Free Liliana. Cover you. I'll do it."

"Alright!" I exhaled hoarsely. "In exchange, I swear to imbue you with power as soon as I get the chance."

The instant I pronounced these words, I was overcome with an unpleasant pressure. It was as if the oath had taken on a certain materiality and now hung like another load on my soul, which was already ruined by one deal with this underworld native.

"Excellent!" Elizabeth-Maria said, melting into a bloodthirsty smile. "What do you need done?"

"Let's go to the Greek Quarter," I ordered.

"Is that where the meeting was scheduled?"

"Yes, not far from the cabaret where you met Albert."

The succubus nodded thoughtfully and then gave an abrupt soft laugh.

"What is it?" I asked, getting on guard.

"Surprising!" Elizabeth-Maria shook her head. "They say that tragedy tends to repeat itself as a farce, but for us it's the other way around. First the farce, then the tragedy."

"No need for tragedies!" I shot out, although I understood the succubus's point perfectly. My former boss Inspector White had once kidnapped her from me, hoping to obtain my assent to a madly dangerous if not to say entirely insane affair.

And is it not the most extreme absurdity to kidnap a succubus?

But now, everything was exactly the opposite. My life and that of Liliana were riding on this horse, and that was already no farce at all, but the most authentic drama.

I couldn't hold back and exhaled quietly to myself:

"Tragedy, bugger..."

3

I EASILY CAME TO AN AGREEMENT with the nephew of the owner of the Charming Bacchante cabaret, where Albert Brandt had once rented an apartment. I'm sure that, even if I hadn't slipped the boy five francs for his trouble, he would have sat at the wheel as soon as we got out of view, and just stayed there until we got back.

Complications arose where I was not expecting them. Parking the carriage on the quiet embankment of a narrow little canal, Elizabeth-Maria threw open the baggage trunk and removed my grandfather's saber.

"What the devil are you doing?!" I objected. "How are you going to walk down the street? Everyone is watching you already, the last thing we need is for some beat cops to ask questions!"

"You want me to help you or not?" her cold reply followed.

"I'd prefer to avoid firefights with the police!"

The succubus sighed loudly but didn't argue and put the saber back.

"It'll be your fault if something goes wrong."

"I'm sure you'll manage!" I parried and led Elizabeth-Maria down the narrow alleys of the Greek Quarter to the place I'd be meeting the senior inspector.

On any other day, all the neighborhood lades would run to see the emancipated bimbo in pants and a leather jacket but, today, it was as if the neighborhood had died out. Most of the shops were not working. Their blinds were closed, and their doors were locked. There were no matrons hurrying to the market with small children, or old men sitting on chairs up against the building walls. And the few city dwellers who did meet the eye usually quickened their pace and walked to the other side of the street when they saw us.

Fear had come to New Babylon. I could sense it just as clearly as mint leaves thrown into a pitcher of lemonade.

"Are you not going to wear your glasses?" Elizabeth-Maria asked suddenly. "People will give you a wide berth!"

"Drop it!" I waved it off.

Then the succubus pulled out her powder box, opened it and let me look in the little circular mirror. I glanced at my own reflection and whistled quizzically. The former transparency of my eyes had been replaced with a clear glow, as if there was a light bulb of twenty or forty candlepower inside my head.

But how could such a thing have happened? Could Liliana's fear have been the catalyst that restored my electroshock-weakened *talent* to life?

Not busting my brains over it, I quickly took my dark glasses from my pocket, one of their lenses marred by a long crack, and clipped them onto my nose.

"Is that better?"

"You look so..." Elizabeth-Maria frowned, but immediately waved her hand. "Anyhow, it'll do!"

By then, the Greek Quarter was behind us, and boarded-up windows or broken doors became more of a rarity. There were plenty of frameworks of once sturdy and well-maintained manors, while a wrecking ball crane loomed in the distance over the rooftops. Some sly wheeler-dealer must have decided to buy part of the abandoned neighborhood and build apartments. There were even temporary poles here with aerial telephone lines. So, the building where I had once found the muse tormenting Albert had seemingly changed a bit recently.

I stopped at the nearest intersection, and Elizabeth-Maria climbed swiftly over the leaning fence, heading through the yard to scope it out.

She soon came back and got my attention from behind the fence.

"Yes?" I called back.

"Two on the first floor. Smoking," the succubus said. "Maybe there's someone in the basement, but I'm, not sure. This building is... strange. I practically couldn't feel anything."

I looked at my watch, it was two thirty. I decided not to draw out time, unclipped my pistol holster and asked:

"Can you cover me?"

"Give me five minutes. I'll get from the next building into the attic. From there, I can go down into the building."

"Just don't make any noise. Don't do anything until I call you."

"I hope you don't get your throat cut at the entrance," Elizabeth-Maria chuckled and hid from view.

I waited for the scheduled time and walked over to the abandoned manor in the middle of the road no longer trying to hide. It felt like a lump of ice had frozen in my stomach, and all I could do was encourage myself with the thought I had the succubus at my back. Elizabeth-Maria had a blood interest my well-being, she would tear through them all with her bare hands just to get the power I promised her. And still this was strange. Very strange.

But I walked forward. There was just nothing left to do.

Dumb as it may have been, I needed to rescue Liliana in the worst way, no matter what. I was obliged to take care of my girlfriend! Otherwise...

I didn't even want to think about what might happen otherwise.

Horror was pounding inside me, but it didn't drive me into a stupor, instead nudging me in the back and whispering into my ear: "Kill, kill, kill!" Few recognize that fear doesn't always force a person to retreat. Not even close. Often, fear pushes a person to such foolish actions that afterward, standing in the middle of a blood-soaked room with a knife in hand, they themselves don't understand how they managed to fly off the handle and land themselves in such a bind.

I had no doubt that this would end in blood. If Bastian Moran wanted to get me to confess, he would have forced me to come to the Newton-Markt. But now, he had scheduled a meeting at the end of the world. And clearly not for no reason...

As I walked through the wide-open gate into the courtyard of the abandoned manor, my nerves stretched to the limit. Touch them and they wouldn't even ring, your finger would get a bleeding cut.

And so, when a trim boy came out of the house in a low-key gray suit and felt hat, my hand just about tore my Steyr-Han from the holster all on its own.

I cannot say what helped me avoid doing anything dumb: the senior inspector's underling's surprising calm for such a serious situation, or the four-barreled lupara in the hands of his partner, a strong man of middling age.

"Weapon!" the young boy pointed at the dried-out wooden table, most likely pulled out here for that express purpose.

I tried to use my reborn *talent* to catch the echoes of any fears, but I didn't have any success. Moran's subordinates were entirely calm, as if they were on duty, and that fact surprised me greatly because it didn't fit with my interpretation. But my surprise didn't stop me from setting out first my Steyr-Han then the Cerberus on the table.

"Turn around!" the boy demanded after that. "Hands to the side and legs at shoulder width."

I obeyed, and was carefully patted down from ankle to collar, which is where neck knives are usually hidden. The young man acted so calculatedly that he never once covered his senior partner's line of lupara fire.

"What's in your pockets?" he asked after feeling my jacket sleeves. "Everything on the table!"

I unloaded the pen knife, wallet, extra Cerberus cassettes and loaded Steyr-Han clips.

"Leave it!" the boy ordered.

"Are you serious?"

The boy let my rhetorical question go in one ear and out the other, then pointed to the door.

"Go inside. You're expected in the basement."

I tilted my head to the side in incomprehension.

"And what about the honor guard?"

"Go inside and get down into the basement," he repeated.

With a bewildered snort, I got up on the porch waiting for the older man with the lupara to come after me, but he just stepped aside and let me in.

Totally alone, to the creak of the dried-out boards, I walked to the stairs to the basement. Over the year and a half since I'd last visited this manor, it had become totally abandoned. The floor was covered by a crust of dirt, the dirty wallpaper was peeling off the walls and hanging down in ratty strips. It seemed as if the building had been striving to evict the otherworldly infection that had made this place its lair, but the poison had penetrated too deeply. Instead of purifying, it had self-destructed.

Standing on the upper step of the basement staircase, I looked down and shivered nervously. I didn't want to go down. Ever since I was a child, I couldn't bear basements. Every time I entered one, it seemed like I would never come back up. And now my expectation of death was stronger than ever.

"Come down, Leopold! Come down!" I suddenly heard Bastian Moran's voice. "Enough milling about and creaking boards! I have a very busy schedule today!"

Rage helped me overcome my doubts, and I went decisively down the rotten boards of the rickety staircase. The altar of the creature that had fancied itself an Ancient Greek muse was no longer in the basement. Instead, there were two stools. Bastian Moran was sitting on one of them with his legs crossed. The second was unoccupied.

"Where is Liliana?" I immediately asked the senior inspector.

"Take a seat," he pointed at the free stool with his pistol.

"If anything happens to her..."

"Shut up and sit down!" Bastian Moran raised his voice. After I obeyed, he continued: "Now, I want to tell you that nothing bad will happen to your sweetheart. She will simply be interrogated and brought back home. But as for what will become of you, Leopold, that depends exclusively on whether or not we can find a common tongue."

"Are you serious?"

"Enough playing the fool!" the senior inspector came unhinged. "Devil knows what is afoot in the city, and I'm wasting my time on you! Either start talking or get buried!"

People need hope, even if it contradicts common sense. Skilled manipulators can get a person stuck on it like a fish hook. And police investigators were some of the most skilled operators around; I knew that perfectly, but still decided to grab onto the straw he'd extended.

"What do you need?" I asked the senior inspector directly.

"Whores, Aztecs and some kind of conspiracy – what were you on about yesterday? What do you know about the ritual murders?"

I glanced at the man with unhidden surprise.

"Are you serious? You want to talk about that?"

"You're wasting my time!" Bastian Moran said in an icy tone. "Your company does not provide me with any joy, so just answer my question! The sooner we finish this, the better!"

There was no reason to draw out time, so I told the senior inspector a condensed version of everything I'd discovered about the Aztec plot from Thomas Smith. Near the end, after brief hesitation, I shared my own conclusions on the matter. Something in Moran's behavior led me to believe pains had not been taken to tell him the details of the conspiracy.

"You believe that Duke Logrin is behind this upwelling of the infernal?" the senior inspector asked thoughtfully after he heard my story. "What makes you so sure?"

"Is fecit, qui prodest[1]," I replied, showing off my knowledge of Latin.

"Balderdash!" Bastian Moran shot out. "Putting the Empire on the edge of collapse is not in the regent's interest! He could have gotten rid of the Crown Princess in hundreds of less destructive ways!"

"He tried," I told him. "But he failed. And it might well be that, this time, his New World allies didn't tell him all the details. That doesn't matter! What does matter is that the Duke brought the Aztecs to Riverfort. I was there! I saw it!"

"What were you doing there, Leopold?"

"Carrying out an order from her Highness... or people from her circle."

Moran stood to his feet, looked thoughtfully at the pistol in his hand and asked:

"That Pinkerton agent, why didn't he come to me?"

"He called and set up a meeting. That same evening, he was nearly cut down. That can hardly have been a simple coincidence!"

The senior inspector frowned and led his gaze away, but immediately overcame himself and, as if justifying, said:

"When Department Three was tasked with

---

[1] For whom the crime advances, he has done it (Lat.).

finding the Reaper, Duke Logrin came to me with an unofficial request to keep him up to date on the investigation and immediately inform him of any progress. It didn't seem suspicious to me. The series of murders caused a large societal resonance, while the position of the regent in the Imperial council left better to be desired. Any minor issue could be critical to him. It never occurred to me he may have been somehow connected with these murders!"

Moran spoke as if by the book, but I was in no rush to take his words for the genuine article.

"On our last meeting, you made a very different claim."

"Are you referring to my thoughts on her Highness?" the senior inspector snorted. "I said it yesterday and I'll say it again: the death of the Crown Princess would only be to the Empire's benefit. I am sincerely convinced that someone else should be elevated to the throne. Someone... more human."

"So, everything comes together for you in the best conceivable way, isn't that so?"

"First of all, her Highness is still alive and, no more than an hour ago, emerged from her coma," Bastian Moran blindsided me with the unexpected announcement.

"How do you know?"

"The palace defenders are still holding out. The Imperial Guard is in telephone contact with us."

"I see," I drew out my words in thought. "And second?"

"And second, I want a change of dynasty, not

the collapse of the government!" the senior inspector practically shouted in response. "He should have waited for the Crown Princess to die of natural causes or set up a palace coup. What is happening now..." Moran looked at me in concentration. "This is the end of the Empire. Don't you understand that?"

"I'm not sure I follow..."

Bastian Moran snorted scornfully.

"The unity of the Empire was based on two things," he said in a mentoring tone. "The metropole provides the provinces defense against infernal creatures and guarantees the inviolability of their borders. But what talk can there be of defense with such devilry afoot in the capital? The Imperial Palace is under siege, but we cannot do anything!"

I nodded. What had happened was a clear demonstration of the weakness of the central authorities. If the situation was not resolved very soon, there would be no avoiding unrest.

"And it isn't all fine with the borders either," Moran sighed and went gloomy, loosening his neckerchief. "Alexandria and Teheran have concluded a military alliance and made a joint ultimatum saying that we must completely withdraw our armed forces from the Island of Arabia and cede Gibraltar to Great Egypt and Constantinople to Persia. The closing of the Persian and Red Gulfs would block the short path to India, while the loss of the Bosporus and the Pillars of Hercules would be an unmitigated catastrophe!"

"What, is that the first such ultimatum?"

"It is the first ultimatum the cabinet of

ministers is seriously considering! The regent doesn't want war, he insists on negotiation. He believes a compromise is possible!"

"I see Duke Logrin is no longer your hero," I chuckled, not understanding the purpose of this whole conversation.

"Duke Logrin is doing everything so improperly, that whether I like it or not, doubts in his true motives are stealing up on me!" the senior inspector shot out. "This goes beyond criminal negligence. It looks like intentional sabotage!"

"And what do you want from me?"

"From you?" Bastian Moran snorted and suddenly returned the pistol to its holster. "Nothing. I've found out everything I wanted to know."

"And Liliana?" I jumped up from the stool.

"She'll be brought here in a quarter hour," the senior inspector promised. "I'll call off the search order. And I suggest you leave Atlantis at once, while you still have the chance."

Bastian Moran started walking over to the stairs, but I called out to him:

"Wait! What are you planning to do?"

"Me?" the senior inspector asked in surprise. "I'm planning to do what I do best. Ask questions, nothing more."

"You're not afraid to share von Nalz's fate?"

"The fate of the Empire is at stake. If the government falls, civilization will be thrown back half a century. And that's in the best case!"

I hesitated, but still decided to believe the

senior inspector and asked:

"And if the Crown Princess manages to get out of the palace?"

"No more than half a dozen people even know that her Highness is alive. There will be no rescue operation."

"And still? If the Crown Princess does leave the Old City, what then?"

The senior inspector frowned.

"As infuriating as it may be to admit, a miraculous rescue of the heiress to the throne could bring the negative situation to an abrupt end. I do not have warm feelings for her Highness, but the Empire is above all else. The coronation of the *illustrious* girl is not the highest price that can be paid for the salvation of the country. Anna wants compromise less than anyone. The Duke will have to retreat."

"After the coronation, there will be no more need for a regent."

"That is true." Moran nodded. "As long as her Highness survives until the coronation. Oh, that sick heart of hers..."

"Will you shoot me for preventative purposes?" I squinted.

Moran shook his head.

"That doesn't make any sense now. The Princess will not get out of the Old City. She is only alive due to the reserve batteries feeding the palace defense. But they only have enough power for a few days."

I cursed.

"Can you provide me passage to the combat zone?"

"Why all this self-sacrifice?"

"I have my own reasons," I said, not telling him about the hook my cousin had in my lip. Devil take that poorly-considered oath!

Bastian Moran thought briefly, then shrugged his shoulders.

"My people are keeping watch near Kelvin tunnel. If you want to risk it, you'll be let through."

After saying that, the senior inspector went back upstairs. I scampered up after him and asked:

"Do you want to pressure the regent?"

Moran turned and arched a brow.

"Is there something you didn't mention?"

"Today's explosion at the Sublime Electricity lyceum – I'm sure that the Duke or his allies are behind it."

"According to the preliminary investigation, the Tesla generator blew up."

"The detonation was caused by an explosive charge. The signal that set it off, most likely, was transferred via telephone wire. On the square, you will find the body of a Yemelyan Krasin, a Russian anarchist. His partner was Ivan Sokolov, a man from Petrograd who claims to be a society observer."

"Where did you obtain this information?"

"I was there."

"I should lock you up in the Newton-Markt..." Bastian Moran frowned, but shook a hand and went outside. "Call a carriage!" he commanded a young guardsman in the yard, then took out a pack of Chesterfields and lit one up, taking one long drag after the other.

The senior inspector's subordinate was not in the least bit surprised by his order. He ran out to the intersection with a small case, threw back its lid and pulled out a pair of telescoping rods with hooks on the end. The policeman skillfully clipped them onto the wire of the aerial telephone line, placed a call with the portable device, then packed up the equipment and returned to the courtyard.

"The carriage is on its way!" he said to the senior inspector. "It'll be here in fifteen minutes."

Bastian Moran nodded and lit another cigarette.

"Is Liliana being brought here?" I started worrying.

"Yes," the senior inspector confirmed and went outside, ordering the investigator with the lupara to keep tabs on me.

4

BASTIAN MORAN kept his word. Not ten minutes later, a self-propelled carriage stopped at the intersection with a metropolitan police crest on the radiator grill. The driver in a new uniform got out of the cabin first and threw open the back door, allowing Liliana Montague to come out.

My heart skipped a beat.

My girlfriend looked around in alarm, noticed me and ran across the street. Bastian Moran exchanged bows with her with a considerate smile and got into the passenger's seat next to the driver. His subordinates sat in the back and the carriage rolled on, leaving Liliana and I alone.

"Leo!" she shouted in alarm. "What is happening?"

I embraced Lily, pressed her to me and calmed her down:

"Nothing. Everything is fine."

"Leo, don't take me for a fool!" Liliana objected, freeing herself from my embrace. "I was detained in the Newton-Markt then, without asking me a single question, I was brought here! What does that all mean?!"

"The senior inspector thought it would be the simplest method of getting me in for a meeting."

"You gave yourself up for me?" she guessed and threw herself on my chest. "Oh, Leo!"

"Like I'm saying, it's a simple misunderstanding. And It's already solved Everything will be fine. I promise."

Liliana suddenly looked over my shoulder and said in surprise:

"Mary? What are you doing here?!"

"Oh, I don't have the slightest bit to do with this!" the succubus assured her friend. "Leopold just needed a driver."

"So where is your carriage?"

"We had to park it nearby," I said, walking into the courtyard, taking the pistols off the table and stashing them in my pockets before my girlfriend saw them.

"And what is in that building?" Liliana asked, looking from side to side. "It's looks strange..."

"It's a house for Department Three's secret meetings. You know how paranoid they are!" I lied with my heart at ease and extended a hand to Lily. "Well, let's go?"

Elizabeth-Maria snorted behind me, attracting attention.

"Do I need to bring you somewhere again, Leopold?" she asked when I had come back.

"Yes, Leonardo-da-Vinci-Platz."

"And what's there?" Liliana asked in surprise.

"I need to pay a visit to an acquaintance," I answered and asked: "Lily, have you got your passport with you?"

"Yes. Why does that matter?"

"I'll explain later," I dodged a direct answer. "Well! Let's go, on the double!"

ELIZABETH-MARIA took us to Mechanisms and Rarities at the speed of the wind. Either she could detect empty streets with some otherworldly ability, or the city-dwellers were all hidden in their houses, but the drive took just fifteen minutes. And that was great – otherwise, I'd have fallen asleep right in the passenger's seat where I sat in embrace with Liliana.

"I'll be right back!" I warned the girls, running

into the shop.

"Has something happened to Mr. Dyak?" the student shop-minder asked, shooting up from the counter at once. "The only thing anyone's talking about is the explosion in the lyceum!"

"Alexander got a concussion," I said, walking into the back room. There, I threw my underwear into the first bag I came across, set a clean vest, pants and a jacket over them, left back into the front room and handed the things to the student. "I don't know what hospital he was brought to, start with the ones nearest the Sublime Electricity lyceum."

"But..." the student stammered.

I didn't listen though, digging a few rumpled fivers and tenners from the cash register and slipping them to the boy, then pushing him out the door.

"Run! I'll look after the shop!"

The student looked around timidly, but didn't argue, throwing the strap of the bag over his shoulder and dashing across the intersection at a skip. I immediately hung a "Closed" sign on the door, entered the code of the massive combination safe in the back room and pulled out the traveling bag I had given to Alexander a few days earlier.

The money was all there. I put one bundle into my jacket pocket and went outside. Liliana was talking with Elizabeth-Maria, discussing the succubus's enticing getup; I lead my girlfriend aside and handed her the traveling bag.

"What is that?" Lily asked in surprise.

"Ninety-five thousand francs," I said. With my

heart seizing, I told her: "You need to leave New Babylon at once!"

"What are you talking about, Leo? But why?!"

"Staying in the city is too dangerous."

"But I cannot just pick up and leave! What will I tell my parents?"

"Send them a telegram from the continent. And it would better for them to not sit around in the capital, either. It's going to be pretty wild here for the next few days."

"Leo! I don't understand this at all!" My girlfriend was upset, and tears glistened in her colorless gray eyes. "What is happening?!"

"Lily, everything will be alright," I assured her. "Just go to Switzerland, to Geneva. I'll finish my business and find you there. I'll either come straight to your place or send you a letter of demand to the main post office. I have to stay here for just a few days."

"I'm not going anywhere until you explain what is going on!" Liliana shot out.

"You heard what happened last night in the Old City?"

"Yes, but what does that have..."

"The same thing could happen in any other neighborhood! Any one, you get it?"

"And you?"

"I have obligations. I cannot simply drop everything and leave." I embraced Lily and whispered into her ear: "Everything will be alright. I'll find you in Geneva and we'll head on our honeymoon to Zuid-

India. Just believe in me. Alright?"

"I believe in you, Leo." Liliana took a step away, kissed me and added: "I believe in you, but I don't believe you. I'd just get in the way, right? Achilles heel, weak spot. You're afraid that someone will use me against you, right?"

Her suspicions were not far from the truth, but I didn't confirm them. Instead, I told her as convincingly as possible:

"I'm afraid Atlantis will share the fate of its mythical predecessor! As soon as possible, send a telegram to your parents, have them drive to the continent."

"And the others? Albert, Mary?"

"I'll talk with them, but I doubt they'll consider my fears well-founded. They don't know what you know."

Liliana sighed and suddenly patted me on the cheek.

"Geneva?" she asked and smiled. "Why not Paris? I always wanted to walk down the Champs-Élysées. They have such fine stores and ateliers there..."

I laughed unwillingly.

"Alright, you can stop in Paris on your way to Geneva. But you need to leave right now. Elizabeth-Maria will take you to port."

"Take the money," Lily extended me the traveling bag. "It feels like you're paying me off!"

"I need you to keep it safe. I'm not sure I'll be able to retain access to my accounts. It may happen that the last of my fortune is in your hands."

Liliana went gloomy and warned:

"If this is a trick and you don't come, I'll chase you to the ends of the earth, Leopold! Know that!"

"Just believe in me."

"I believe in you, Leo. I believe!"

They weren't empty words at all, such was Liliana's *talent*. With her faith, she could add a little push to reality. When I was next to her, my heart beat without its usual anguish.

Simple autosuggestion? Maybe that was so.

In any case, I was intending to find Lily in Switzerland as soon as I got the chance. And though I didn't know for certain whether my feelings for Lily were sincere or had been foisted on me by the dead hypnotist, I was positive that that no longer had any meaning. I needed this relationship, needed this love.

More than forgivable weakness for a person in my position.

More than, yes...

"Take her to the port and make sure she gets on the ferry to Lisbon," I asked the succubus after sitting Lily in the self-propelled carriage.

Elizabeth-Maria rolled her eyes ostentatiously, but didn't protest, got behind the wheel and the steam carriage rolled abruptly away.

Immediately, such weariness rolled over me my arms just sank. My heart seized, the back of my head was splitting, and I was also yawning so much my jaw nearly fell off.

I wanted madly to leave the city with Liliana,

but such an unreasonable outburst could not lead to anything good. As it was, if I played my part properly, there was a small chance of escaping alive. A miserable chance, but human nature is such that a man will grasp at any straw.

I locked the door, walked into the back room of the shop and collapsed on a sagging couch. I fell back in it, stretched out my legs and fell asleep as soon as I closed my eyes.

FIRE. What awaited me in this dream was fire. A sulfur rain was pouring down from the heavens from horizon to horizon. A sharp gust of wind rolled over me from head to toe like a liquid flame and my burned flesh immediately cried out with a ghastly pain.

The pain forced me to wake up; I crawled off the sofa to the floor and writhed, burning unbearably from inside. I was torn apart by the fire. It flew from the carpet to the wall, and the room was filled with a thick black smoke. I don't even know if I burned to death or suffocated.

That death was the beginning of a new nightmare. Uncountable times, I had to die in those fierce flame before the final awakening cast me out into the back room of Mechanisms and Rarities.

My whole body was aching unbearably. The smell of sulfur and burned flesh caused waves of nausea to roll over me. I had no idea that I had awoken until I saw the figure of a person standing next to me. To be more accurate, I saw his boots right before my face lacquered to a shine.

"Don't touch him, Willy!" a derisive voice came through the vexing ringing in my ears. "Can't you see the boy isn't well?"

But the weakness had already left me; I braced my arms on the floor, raised my head and, without any surprise, met gazes with the barrel of my very own Steyr-Han.

"Now this is funny," I muttered, getting to my feet. After that, I calmly pulled a mug from the workbench, scooped some water into it from a bucket in the corner and took a drink.

All that time, William Grace was holding me in the sights of his gun.

"Willy, drop the weapon," the lady-in-waiting asked, her feet up on the little sofa. "It looks like the boy has something to say."

William didn't twitch, just squinted his left eye, then the oracle raised her voice:

"Lieutenant! Lower your weapon! Now!"

Grace frowned and lowered his pistol hand, but didn't stop aiming at me, just prevented the lady-in-waiting from seeing the Steyr-Han.

"I suppose her Highness is not pleased with me," I chuckled.

"Her Highness thirsts for blood," the lady-in-waiting confirmed, mechanically stroking the large pearl on her neck with her left hand.

"Her Highness is in no position to throw her weight around with those loyal to her."

"Loyal?" the lieutenant hissed and threw up the

pistol again. "I should shoot you through the head right now! You were supposed to blow up the regent's carriage!"

"And I would have," I smiled calmly in reply. "But her Highness forgot to mention that the regent needed to be blown up before he visited the mint."

"What does that have to do with anything?" William Grace didn't understand.

"So, you don't know?" I suddenly guessed. "You really don't know? That must be it!"

The lieutenant's face turned to stone and, holding back intently as not to burst into a scream, asked:

"What do we not know?"

I looked at the very comfortable sofa with doubt, but I didn't get near the lady-in-waiting and sat on the wooden stool.

"What do we not know?!" the lieutenant growled out again, finally having lost his patience. So, I had to tell the story of the regent's conspiracy for the second time today.

Near the end, William Grace swore to shoot the traitor with his own hands, while the lady-in-waiting didn't lose her calm demeanor.

"Get out of here Willy, stop gadding about!" she demanded and smiled. "This is all very interesting, Leopold, but how can you be of use to her Highness now? You don't have any proof of the Duke's betrayal."

"I suggest her Highness be evacuated from the

palace."

"Complete nonsense!" Grace exploded. "The Old City is covered. The soldiers can at will, and even I couldn't get permission to enter. I was told it was too dangerous! It's a conspiracy! The conspirators will not allow us to save the Princess!"

I sighed and extended a mug to the lieutenant.

"Drink some water and cool down. And as for getting to the Old City, I can arrange it."

"You?" William cringed in mistrust.

"Me."

"Even if that is so, what does it give us?" the lady-in-waiting inquired with unhidden skepticism. "Last night, half a dozen army dirigibles were lost, and a countless number of armored vehicles. None of them even got near the palace! Observers are saying that a ring of magical energy has formed, which has fully encased the Imperial Palace and the area around it. There's no way through. It s certain death."

To me, that news came as an unpleasant surprise, but I didn't lose my presence of mind, and suggested:

"We'll have to concern ourselves with defense against infernal effects."

"As if that's so easy! The electric grid in the Old City is totally shut off!" the lieutenant declared. Then, he suddenly froze in place after hearing a knock from the front room.

"Calm down!" I whispered out. "That, most likely, is the shop owner returning."

And that was true, I heard Dyak's voice shortly: "Leopold Borisovich, are you here?"

"Not a word!" the lieutenant warned me and started aiming at the door into the main room just in case. But he miscalculated.

"Drop your weapon!" sounded out from the back entrance.

William Grace froze, and the lady-in-waiting reacted to the unexpected turn of events with an unexpectedly calculated calm. While all Thomas Smith's attention was wrapped up in the Imperial Guard lieutenant, she pulled a nickel-plated lady's pistol from her reticule and aimed it at the private investigator.

"Be so kind, mysterious stranger," she smiled, "as to not move or even breath. I wouldn't like to put a hole in such a handsome man."

"Leopold?" Alexander Dyak called me again. "Can I come in?"

"Just a minute!" I called back and tried to take the situation under control: "Allow me to introduce Thomas Eliot Smith, an investigator from the Pinkerton Detective Agency. He has been looking into the ritual murders and helped me get a handle on everything. Thomas, these are the gentlepeople of her Highness's inner circle. And now, if you promise not to kill one another, I'll leave you for a moment. I need to have a talk with the shop owner, he's an elderly person and was injured in today's explosion."

Before anyone managed to object, I went out into the main room.

— The Dormant —

To my significant relief, Alexander Dyak didn't look that bad. His split head hadn't even been bandaged, just some scratch on his forehead had been given a crisscross of adhesive plaster.

"Leopold Borisovich!" the inventor lit up and caught his breath with relief. "I'm glad you're doing fine! Your friend Thomas thought the self-propelled carriage in front of the shop was suspicious. He was looking for you, as it were..."

"Don't worry, I invited my friends here to discuss a very delicate matter. But I never could have hoped you might join us. How are you feeling?"

"My head is spinning a bit," Alexander said, leaning heavily on the counter. "But what is happening in the city... It's a pure nightmare! Everyone is certain that one of Tesla's experimental devices blew up for some reason, and Nikola hadn't even make it into the lyceum!"

"So, Tesla survived?" I lit up.

"Yes, he was just badly concussed. He's already flown back to Paris."

I winced. The conspirators managed to take the famed inventor out of the game.

"And what problem were you discussing?" Alexander Dyak inquired.

"Just a minute!" I walked up to the door and warned: "Ladies and gentlemen, we're coming in!"

There was a decent chance I would find myself in the sights of a pistol as soon as I stepped over the threshold but no, I got by without it. The investigator was sitting on the workbench and looking at the bandage on the fingers of his left hand. The lieutenant was leaning on the wall with a glum look. And the lady-in-waiting was smiling charmingly up at us from the couch. Although the tension in the room could be cut with a knife, no one had their weapons out.

"Allow me to present our host Alexander Dyak, a leading researcher in the field of electromagnetic radiation."

"Come now, Leopold Borisovich, I don't know about 'leading...'" the inventor got embarrassed and walked over to the lightning sensor in the corner. He started up the device and watched the movement of the pencil on the paper ribbon. After some time, hesnorted in confusion and told us: "As I feared, the disturbances are still at their former level, while the intensity of the original signal has fallen by approximately a third."

"What are you talking about?" William Grace got on guard.

I just waved the lieutenant off and asked the inventor:

"Alexander, does that mean that one of the three transmitters covering New Babylon was located in the Sublime Electricity lyceum?"

"That would be a logical conclusion," Dyak confirmed, stroking his gray beard. "But most likely there are two transmitters. Radiation does not drop in a strictly linear fashion. What's more, some electromagnetic waves may be reaching us from the continent."

"So if the conspirators destroy the second

transmitter, the capital will be left defenseless?"

"That is correct," Alexander sighed. "And I cannot help in any way. Any device I would be able to construct would not be sufficiently powerful to overcome the disturbances. It is simply impossible."

"And your new work? You cannot apply that somehow?" I enquired, not turning my attention to the confused gazes of the unfortunate bewildered onlookers.

"It's a totally different frequency," Alexander Dyak shook his head and suddenly snapped his fingers. "That's it! A different frequency! The disturbances wouldn't be effected, but microwaves can destroy the physical shells of demons! I warn you, though, it's effective radius would be no more than twenty or thirty meters."

"Wait!" Lieutenant Grace cut into the conversation. "Do you mean to say that this device provides defense against demons and we can take her Highness out of the palace?"

"Theoretically that is correct," the inventor confirmed, "but we'll need a powerful source of energy. And the device is quite heavy. A usual self-propelled carriage will not suffice to transport it."

"We need an armored vehicle!" I realized. "William, have you got an armored vehicle?"

The lieutenant's face went sour as if he'd just taken a bite of a lemon.

"No. All I have is five soldiers, two light self-propelled carriages, a few hand-held machine guns and Gauss casters."

"Not even grenades?"

Grace remained silent.

I shook my head, went into the front room and called Ramon Miro's office from the telephone on the counter.

"Still moving to the Caribbean?" I asked when he picked up the phone.

"Why do you ask?"

"Have you found a buyer for the armored vehicle, yet?"

Ramon sighed loudly and asked after a brief pause:

"You looking to buy?"

"I'll give you twenty thousand."

"By check?"

"By check."

"Make it twenty-five. And there's no place for negotiating."

I chuckled.

"Alright, but I need it right now."

That was perfectly fine with Ramon. I explained where to bring the armored vehicle, then returned to William Grace.

"Well, I've solved the transportation problem."

"Just wonderful, but how far can we trust this old man's ideas?" the lieutenant responded with a gloomy look. "He's like a mad inventor off the pages of some pulp novel!"

"I've trusted him with my life more than once," I assured him and extended a hand: "And now, if you'd be so kind, give me back my pistols."

William Grace hesitated. Then, a smoldering mew came from behind him:

"Don't be stubborn, my sweet. The shop owner is so old. It would be hard for him to wash blood out of this room...'

The lieutenant swallowed fitfully and extended me the Steyr-Han, handle first.

"And the Cerberus," I reminded him, collecting the pistol and looking at Elizabeth-Maria in disapproval. "What are you still doing here?"

"I feel obligated to you, and I cannot bear it. It's contrary to my nature," the succubus answered, lowering the saber.

I frowned and turned to the lieutenant:

"William, be so kind and leave us for a few minutes."

Grace slowly stepped back from the succubus, looked her over and asked:

"Who is this, Leopold?"

"A friend. And yes, she can be trusted."

"Well, look..." William Grace snorted and stumbled into the back room. Elizabeth-Maria appeared behind me silently, making an indelible impression on him. As, it should be said, did the bared saber and her delicate arms.

I grabbed the succubus by the shoulder and pulled her to the entrance.

"Where is Lily? Did you put her on the ferry?"

"As promised!"

"And she left?"

"Of course she left! She asked me to say she

believes in you."

I felt a stone fall off my soul. I caught my breath with relief and asked:

"What do you need? After all, you don't do anything just because!"

"I do not," Elizabeth-Maria confirmed, setting her saber on the window sill. She then looked into the mirror and began putting her short red hair up into a kerchief. "But you were planning to rescue the Princess. Meanwhile, I can feel an upwelling of diabolic power near the palace even from here. I'm certain that you could pinch off a bit for me."

"Listen..."

"No, you listen to me, Leopold!" Elizabeth-Maria grumbled. "I'm going with you! Period!"

The succubus grabbed the saber and walked decisively into the back room, while all I could do was exhale a soundless curse after her.

With a rescue team like this, we could only guess who would be rescuing us from one another...

5

WE REACHED THE OLD CITY only at dawn of the next day. We spent all evening and most of the night setting up Alexander Dyak's transmitter. I even had to take all the armor plates off the tower of the armored vehicle, otherwise there was no way for the microwave transmitter to fit up there. We had to entirely remove the side doors as well, just to get the clunky device and generator inside. As a result, there was only room for six people. Another two could fit in the cabin.

"Good luck, Leo!" Ramon Miro squeezed my hand farewell. He had been helping us refit the armored vehicle all night, but didn't ask a single question, nor express any interest in our venture. "I hope we see each other again!"

"Until next time!" I slapped him on the shoulder, and the hulking man left the yard.

I watched him go, sighing heavily as he saw William Grace's subordinates unload the Lewis guns and their loaded disks from the self-propelled carriage. A hand-held mortar with a five-round drum had already been transferred into the back of the armored vehicle and a pneumatic cable gun that fired a fairly large two-pronged spear. The spear was connected to a weighty electric jar in an over-the-shoulder pack by a spool of wire that looked like it belonged on a spinning wheel. According to the boastful lieutenant, the electric charge of the batteries could lay low any of the dukes of the underworld. I myself had no desire to test that assertion.

But I had somewhat more hope in Dyak's transmitter. Started in test mode, it exploded a nearby bottle of beer and the spilled liquid went up in a cloud of white steam.

While the guardsmen moved the machine guns into the armored car – mounting two to side windows and a third in the front – I threw the strap of the small bag over my shoulder and started to fill it with incendiary grenades, which Ramon had brought more of. William Grace and Thomas Smith followed my example.

I heard occasional rumbling blasts from the Old City. The sky there was stretched over with black smoke, but even that didn't obstruct the view of the scarlet glow over the palace.

"Nothing changed overnight," Lieutenant Grace told us. "But there is also some good news."

"And what might that be?" Thomas Smith expressed curiosity.

"Last evening, a bomb was thrown from a building window into the regent's carriage. The Duke survived but lost an arm and is now in critical condition," William said and chuckled. "As you see, sometimes anarchists are useful. The most important thing now is to get her Highness out of the palace."

I looked carefully at the lieutenant, but he was totally serious about the anarchists.

"Are you sure it was anarchists?" I then asked.

"Yeah, some screwball Russian," Grace confirmed. "Department Three spooks shot him during the arrest."

"Ah, so there it is!" I drew out my words in thought, guessing the regent's coconspirators had tried to get rid of him, or that it was Bastian Moran's attempt to influence events.

"We need to go," the investigator hurried us.

"Yes, it is time," the lieutenant nodded.

He sat two guardsmen at the wheel and machine gun and took another two subordinates with him into the back. The lady-in-waiting and Elizabeth-

Maria sat on bullet boxes opposite one another, and Thomas Smith sat right on the floor, while I had to get up on the rack to the microwave transmitter. It was remarkably uncomfortable to ride on the tower with no armor.

However, I wanted to be in the company of the oracle and succubus little enough to bear it. Although both ladies had seemingly swallowed their tongues, the tension between them was nearly throwing off sparks.

The armored vehicle very quickly left the area of the Imperial Academy, crossing Euler Bridge to the other side of the Yarden. Once there we made a hook and turned toward the entrance into the Kelvin tunnel. This passageway, which had been laid under the river a few years back, led right into the Old City but, was distant enough from the quarantine zone not to be patrolled by army divisions. Here instead there were metropolitan police.

When the armored vehicle drove down a nearby alleyway and stopped, I got down from my perch, threw open the side door and called the investigator after me:

"Thomas, let's go!"

"Is everything in order?" Lieutenant Grace got on guard.

"Completely," I waved it off and asked Smith: "Thomas, find out who is in charge. If need be, refer to Senior Inspector Moran. Say we need to speak with him."

Smith nodded and walked to the police

barricade, came back a few minutes later and said:

"The senior inspector is on his way."

Shivers crawled up my spine. If Moran had suddenly changed his mind about working with us, we'd never get out of here alive.

Anyway, I wasn't the only one feeling agitated. Thomas suddenly pulled the glass lenses from his eyes, set them in a jar of fluid and said:

"An order has come from the agency to just observe the situation and not take action."

"What the devil?" I turned to him. "Why do they want that?"

The investigator shrugged his shoulders.

"For justice, perhaps?"

"Balderdash!"

"Indeed," Thomas confirmed, furrowed his brow, dried his tears and looked somewhere aside. "My little sister had six fingers on her hand. She was beaten to death on her way home from the store. The locals said *the illustrious* are the spawn of the devil. They believe in the primacy of science and spoke of the devil. Tell me, how is this possible?"

"Did they find the killers?"

"And no one was looking."

"And you?"

"Well, I signed up to the army a month before that. And now I'm thinking maybe I was meant to die then, but I just ran away."

I just shrugged my shoulders. We all have our skeletons in the closet, and some of them are best left forgotten.

"Look, he's coming over," Thomas Smith nodded at a stocky investigator in uniform walking up the road, the very same who had been holding me in the sights of his lupara yesterday. Now, instead of a weapon he was holding a little bucket of bleach with his hand in it.

"Where's your vehicle?" Moran's subordinate asked as he walked, not wasting time on a greeting.

"In the alley."

"Show me."

We led the policeman to the armored vehicle, and he drew a big white letter M on the sheet covering the transmitter.

"Don't erase it. Without the mark we'll blow it up," he warned, standing on the running boards and commanding: "Let's go!"

Thomas and I quickly got into the back. The armored vehicle burst from place and rolled off toward the tunnel. At the entrance there were sandbag defensive positions. At them, alongside a few machine guns and recoilless rifles, there were two stationary flamethrowers. On the side, a little vehicle-mounted Tesla generator tower peeked out from behind a high caponier.

Before the barricade, the driver lowered his speed. But as soon as the police cleared a lane, the armored vehicle picked up the pace and went under the stone entrance of the tunnel. The electric streetlights weren't working, but our powerful headlights did a perfect job lighting the way anyhow.

At the first sign of danger, I was prepared to

fire up the microwave emitter, but I didn't have to. We didn't come across anything on our way through the tunnel. In the Old City though, the situation was profoundly different. There was a sheet of smoke hanging over the streets. There were constant machine gun bursts crackling out nearby, and powerful explosions boomed and echoed with frightening regularity.

The magic in the air could be felt almost physically. For a moment, it seemed that some phantasmagoric force had returned me to the past and I was surrounded by my cursed family mansion. But no – now the whole Old City was cursed. Dead grass blackened the lawns, barren trees stood frozen, strange and frightening affronts to nature. There was broken glass all down the sidewalks, and smoking buildings loomed with the empty gaps of their windows. Holes left by explosive rounds gaped in the upper floors.

Suddenly, a ghostly silhouette appeared in the smoke, and a demon dove out at the armored vehicle. It looked most of all like a flying stingray of unbelievable size.

I could hear the mounted machine gun start chirring madly. The infernal creature slipped down from the heights of the fourth floor to the very earth and raced in our direction. Pulling down on the activation handle, I started up the device and strained to turn its iron shield toward the demon. When I finally did, it shuddered and dispersed into a ball of lightning, leaving just a charred spot on the causeway.

But it was too early to celebrate: from the neighboring alley there came a trio of possessed people, covered in blood from head to toe. One, based on the shredded uniform and revolver, was a policeman. I got on guard, turning the emitter shield in their direction. The skin of the walking corpses instantly started bubbling and smoking. I heard a few revolver claps, but the bullets whistled off the armor, ricocheting. Then, the side machine gun started up, sending the possessed to the ground in one long burst.

The armored vehicle rolled onward, and I soon saw another group of walking corpses down a side alley. But this time, they were wearing wreathes of hand grenades. Fortunately, though, the carriage had picked up a decent amount of speed by then, so we raced past before they reached the road.

At full speed, we flew into the smoke over the road, and visibility fell to a minimum. Then a titanic four-armed figure wove itself out of the gray haze before us. Electromagnetic radiation from the microwave cut the demon into a hundred invisible copies and scattered them, dashing their physical substance.

A moment later, a booming explosion thundered out up above, and I barely managed to dive into the vehicle before tile fragments drummed out on the armor!

"What was that?" Lieutenant Grace turned to me. Just then, another blast rang out, but behind us.

The back shuddered in the hail of shrapnel, but our armor held out.

"A howitzer!" I realized.

"They're firing from the air!" William Grace announced, banging on the grate separating the back from the cabin and shouted: "Turn around! Turn around right now!"

The armored vehicle turned sharply to the side, nearly cutting the corner off a building, and the subsequent explosion threw paving stones from the causeway right where we would have been if we had kept going forward.

The side street led us to a collapsed building, where nearly the entire road was covered with shards of the hard body of a crashed dirigible. The crest of the Imperial Air Fleet could be seen on one of the crumpled stabilizers.

"Turn toward the palace! The palace!" the lieutenant shouted to the driver and turned to me: "Leopold, get up there, step to!"

I climbed up into my rack and immediately felt a sweltering heat coming off the emitter plate, but I couldn't turn the device off – there was an impenetrable haze of dark clouds crawling in front of us. In the depths of it, I could see the twinkling of ominous sparks and flashes of dark shadows.

The armored vehicle flew into it at full speed, and the invisible microwaves bored a tunnel right before us. And still, such a fierce cold swept over us that the armor was snaked with lines of hoarfrost. Not able to bear the icy wind, I hid in the back and the armored vehicle was immediately shaken by a severe blow. Something scraped along the left side, as if some beast was trying to break through the steel sheets with its claws. Then I heard a hum, a thud, and the stench of the grave wafted over us. But the heavy self-propelled carriage stayed on the road. An instant later, there was cloudy sky above us once again.

After flying past the next two intersections, our armored vehicle was right near the palace. But instead of turning onto the street that led to the back gates, the driver headed straight for Palace Square.

"What the devil?!" I cursed out when the wheels jumped onto the tall curb and I was shaken to the point my teeth chattered.

The heavy armored vehicle barreled through an accurately groomed row of acacias, plowed through a dead lawn, turned a corner and made it to the edge of the square.

In the very center, there was a towering pedestal with half a dozen Aztec priests. With confident slashes, the pagans were opening the rib cages of their sacrifices with obsidian knives, cutting out their hearts and throwing them into a ritual basin. There were haphazard heaps of dead bodies all around, but there were still plenty of victims left. Hundreds of possessed people were crowded on the square, unaware of anything. Without any forcing, they walked up the blood-soaked steps, humbly giving their lives to the diabolic ritual. And in the depths of the gaping whirlpool above us, I saw the purple luster of the underworld glow stronger and stronger.

The air on the square was simply permeated with magic, and it flowed in a ghostly stream from the pedestal to the palace fence. Just past that, electric wires spit sparks, and most of the otherworldly power was turned back. That was where the icy fog that had nearly overwhelmed us was coming from. And still, the palace complex was not totally untouched. The main gates had been blown away, and there were plenty of gaps in the fence.

And then, all the armored vehicle's machine guns started up at once. Long bursts stitched through the crowd and swept the priests off the pedestal, adding a bit more blood to the already red granite tiles.

Only then did William Grace's plan become clear to me. The lieutenant had decided not only to rescue the heiress to the throne, but also to cut off the pagan ritual.

"Damned idiot!" I cursed out, having noticed some possessed people rolling an artillery cannon out of the gates.

I slipped off my perch into the back, pulled the lieutenant off the side machine gun and shouted in his ear.

"They've got a cannon!"

William Grace found himself instantly. He pressed up against the cabin window and shouted:

"Full speed reverse!"

The armored vehicle's engine barked and started backing off the square into an alley but, at that very instant, a highly explosive bomb hit us. A deafening thunder rang out. The self-propelled carriage shook strongly, and everyone in the back was knocked off their feet. Thick black smoke started pouring out of something.

"Reverse!" the lieutenant shouted out again. "Full speed reverse!"

It was no use. Although the bomb had hit the transmitter, which covered in a steel sheet, the guardsmen in the cabin were riddled with the shrapnel that got through the defense.

I grabbed the hand mortar, leaned out the side door and sent an explosive round at the artillery cannon. But it landed five meters from the target, and all the shrapnel was absorbed by the cannon shield, shuddering from the strike. Then I jerked the barrel higher and totally emptied the drum in a few seconds.

A successful shot threw the possessed in all directions before they managed to get a second shot off. But then, bullets started clicking off the paving stones, and I had to hurriedly take shelter behind the fountain.

William Grace joined me with the machine gun, extended the bipod of the Lewis gun on the marble parapet and let out a ceaseless string of bullets toward the possessed coming down from the pedestal in our direction.

"Let's get to the palace!" he barked, straining to overcome the thundering gunfire. "On my command!"

We really didn't have any other options left. More and more smoke was pouring out of the wide-open doors of the armored vehicle, and the engine could blow at any moment.

"I'll cover you!" I shouted, placing new rounds into the mortar drum with shaking hands.

"Me too!" Thomas Smith called out to help.

The lieutenant gave him the machine gun, threw the cable gun electric-jar pack over his shoulder, grabbed the pneumatic gun and dashed to the corner of the palace fence.

"After me!" he shouted to the others as he ran.

The guardsmen and lady-in-waiting tore off in pursuit, but Thomas Smith had loaded another disk into the machine gun and was now knocking down the possessed running toward us with short bursts.

I reloaded the hand mortar and shot a few rounds into the crowd, practically without aiming. The explosions threw steel fragments and bits of stone in all directions. And although that couldn't fully stop the possessed, their agility had taken a noticeable hit.

At that moment, the guardsmen had reached their position around the corner and started giving us supporting fire. Elizabeth-Maria jerked me by the arm.

"Leo!" she shouted. "Let's get out of here!"

I threw the mortar on my shoulder and dashed from the fountain to the fence, and the succubus raced after me. Smith, meanwhile, stayed behind to finish the Lewis gun disk, then retreated. Elizabeth-Maria and I had already crossed the open space when, just some ten meters from the fence, the investigator rolled along the paving stone, his ankle shot through.

He splayed out on the ground with a moan and tried to stand but was unable. He started to crawl along the causeway. I threw down my mortar and raced to his aid. Another of Grace's boys ran after me. We grabbed Thomas under the arms and started dragging him after us. We had almost reached shelter when an explosion blasted out with such power that the earth underfoot shook.

The armored vehicle was blown to smithereens. A stray iron fragment split open the head of the guardsman helping me, and he collapsed dead on the sidewalk.

"Devil!" William Grace cursed out heatedly. "May you all blow up!"

"Curses!" I swore, tearing the pants of the investigator and beginning to bandage the wound.

"What happened to the leg?" Thomas asked, leaning up on his elbows.

"The bullet went clean through," said Elizabeth-Maria, who was helping me. "The bone was not damaged."

By then, the machine-gun disk was empty, and the guardsman started away from the corner. Then William Grace tossed two grenades at the possessed at once and commanded:

"Let's get out of here!"

The incendiary bombs hammered out together, and under cover of the wall of fire and toxic white smoke, we ran along the stone fence to a gap left by a steam car ramming it at full speed. The many-ton monster hadn't managed to enter the grounds of the palace complex, but one of the sections had collapsed, opening a path inside.

Elizabeth-Maria and I had to drag Thomas on our backs, otherwise the investigator risked being left hopelessly far behind. A trail of his blood stretched out behind us on the paving stone.

"Careful, don't touch the wires! They're live!" William Grace warned after clambering up a heap of stones.

The lady-in-waiting, her skirt rolled up, was scrambling after us, while a guardsman had thrown the Lewis gun over his shoulder, waiting for us. At that moment, something abruptly whistled past above us, and the ribcage of the soldier exploded in crimson fragments of lungs and ribcage.

The boy, ripped in two, flew five meters back and collapsed on the sidewalk. Then, a blurry human figure in a long cloak weaved together from the fog of the neighboring street. A ghostly luster glowed from under the deep hood, and another magical bomb raced toward us.

The succubus and I dragged Thomas behind the back of the armored vehicle lodged in the fence, and the spell tore up one of its sides, casting it about the palace complex.

"Faster!" the lieutenant shouted, extending us a hand from atop a heap of rubble.

He pulled the wounded investigator after him, and Elizabeth-Maria and I got over the heap on our own. At that very instant, the ghost tore off after us.

The damaged electric defense couldn't hold the infernal beast back, but, slipping between the sparking wire fragments, it lost a large part of its physical nature. Elizabeth-Maria spun in place and easily split the otherworldly creature in half with a wave of the saber. The blade cleaved the ghost into a cloud of dust and it dissolved into tiny burning particles in the air. Just that and it was no more.

"Faster!" William Grace cried.

I grabbed Thomas and dragged him after the lieutenant along the lawn with black brittle grass. All the trees in the garden were dead, and there were only green leaves near the far-away castle with its neat towers. But in that direction, we could hear an intense exchange of gunfire, which was covered up from time to time by exploding grenades and artillery rounds. Although the defense kept the demons at bay, the possessed people they made managed to fortify positions on the palace grounds and were now sieging the building.

Fortunately, William Grace was not intending to fight his way through. Saddling the cable gun on his shoulder, he hurried through the dead garden to a granite-tiled square bordered by the wide-open gates of empty carriage houses. A long administrative building stretched along the fence from there, which is where we were headed.

The lieutenant ran up on the side porch first, opening the mortice lock with his own key and racing through the barricade. Immediately, a burst from inside thundered open the front door. Two possessed people spilled out, their eyes burning with the gloomy fire of the underworld and their faces covered in blood. They ran down the stairs with unexpected speed, but I met them with a long burst from the Gauss caster, aiming at their legs. Elizabeth-Maria then came from the side and beheaded the now immobilized dead with two confident slashes.

She was simply soaked in blood to her ears, but she was happy as a kid in a candy store. The lady-in-waiting was looking at her with uncomprehending astonishment and even some fear. Oracles are extremely perceptive of the otherworldly, and all that remained was to pray that she had not recognized Elizabeth-Maria's true essence.

William Grace saved the situation.

"After me!" the lieutenant commanded and went first to take shelter in the building.

The lady-in-waiting ran after him, and the succubus tailed the procession with the saber in her hand, so I had to drag the wounded investigator on my back all alone. It was quite a challenge to get him up to the third story. Near the end, I was fully soaked through with sweat and nearly collapsing in exhaustion.

The stairs took us to a long hallway, which stretched down the whole building. Right at the exit from the stairway, we ran into a disfigured body, prostrate on the blood-painted floor. The dead man was *illustrious*. I could make out the colorless gray of his wide-open eyes perfectly.

The lady-in-waiting walked around the dead

body and suddenly shouted and squeezed her head in her hands.

"There's something there!" she groaned, pointing to a ghostly white glow at the far end of the corridor. An instant later, the infernal spirit, bending space itself with its unnatural presence, ran on the attack!

Doors swung open and flew off the hinges. Light bulbs exploded under the ceiling, stucco was torn from the walls, and the parquet floor stood on end in a forest of splinters. The demon, indistinct in the semi-gloom of the corridor, started gaining more and more speed. I pulled an incendiary grenade from my bag but was too late. William Grace stepped out forward, aimed the cable gun and fired.

Its two-pronged spear raced down the corridor, and the spool started humming in rage, letting the wire out. An instant later, the lance hit something invisible and hovered in the air. It began to be pulled back but, after a second of delay, a blinding arc of electricity flashed between the prongs. With that, the demonic spirit dissolved without a trace, leaving just a gust of musty air racing down the corridor at us. Electricity had proven stronger than magic yet again.

"Run!" William shouted, reeling in the wire.

"Drop it!" I advised him.

"It's still got plenty of charge!" the lieutenant answered. "Run! I'll catch up!"

And we ran and ran through the whole building. At the end, we found a long, covered gallery leading to the neighboring building, the castle with towers from earlier, the lesser Imperial Palace. There were almost no full windows in the gallery and, in places, I saw gaps going through the walls. There was a battle raging below, rifle shots clacked and grenade explosions thundered.

William Grace caught up to us and walked in front, shouting:

"This is Lieutenant Grace! Don't shoot!"

"Let them through!" came an instant command behind the barricade blocking the passage. "William, faster!"

The guardsmen defending the palace moved aside a combination safe that was lying on its side and slid a high-caliber Gatling gun out of the way, allowing us to slip through the crack.

"Any wounded?!" the totally gray gaunt gentleman in an Imperial Guard captain's uniform got on guard with his non-uniform unbuttoned collar. "Stretchers, now!"

Thomas Smith was instantly laid on a stretcher, which Grace and I had to carry. The captain wouldn't allow any of his guardsmen to leave their post.

"Her highness said you'd arrived," he told us, looking at our company, "but she was talking about some kind of transport..."

"Ugh," the lieutenant went gloomy, "our armored vehicle got bunged up on Palace Square."

The captain just croaked out in annoyance, not grieving pointlessly about the lost possibility of leaving the palace.

I guessed he must have gone gray quite recently...

THE PALACE looked more like a besieged fortress from inside. There were guardsmen armed with electric dischargers and Gauss casters standing watch at the windows. The servants who were still alive were hard at work. Some were loading machine-gun belts, while others were moving massive furniture, setting up additional barricades. There was something for everyone, though perhaps only to avoid a panic.

Soon, the corridor led us to a central stairway where guardsmen were manning several firing positions at once. And not for nothing. The main entrance was without a doubt the weakest defense point. The stone walls, one and a half or two meters thick, couldn't be penetrated by the possessed, but they could remove doors.

My eye was met by a lower hall filled with dead bodies. It even seemed that some of the possessed were still moving, but I didn't look particularly closely. I was already nauseous enough.

We went two stories higher up the central staircase and carried the stretcher into a guest room with terrified ladies-in-waiting. Three Imperial medics immediately ran up to the wounded investigator, and I left Thomas to their care with an easy heart. Elizabeth-Maria was also taken for wounded at first, and the *illustrious* oracle led her into the washroom to wash the dried blood off her face and hands.

"Her Highness is expecting you, lieutenant!" the

gray-haired captain declared, buttoning up his collar and turning his gaze to me, as if mentally comparing me with a description. "And you as well..."

"Just a minute!" the lieutenant tarried, throwing the pneumatic caster and electric-jar backpack against the wall. Then, standing at the mirror, he started feverishly smoothing out his disheveled hair.

"Lieutenant!" the Imperial Guard captain raised his voice. "Her Highness expects you immediately!"

"Yes, yes! I'm on my way!"

We surrendered our weapons to the guardsmen standing at the door to the Princess's personal chambers and walked into the spacious room. We stopped at the threshold in respect, though, waiting for the heiress to the throne to deign to pay us attention. As it was, she was frozen at the window with a pair of binoculars in her hands.

Short, pale and with a frail boyish figure and dark bags under her starry eyes, the Princess gave the impression of a very ill person. There was no reason to expect anything else from someone who had spent the last month in a coma, but she simply got lost in the spacious room with elevated ceilings.

"Captain, check the posts!" Crown Princess Anna ordered, and her voice was unexpectedly authoritative and strong, as if it wasn't coming from such a sickly body.

The gray-haired captain pursed his lips but obeyed and left the room. And quickly I heard the lieutenant's pistol being cocked behind me with a click.

"What is this, William?" the Princess demanded explanations.

"We don't need him anymore," Grace answered with so much ease it was as if he were talking about a broken tool.

I didn't turn around, just raised my right hand and laughed:

"Did you really believe that tall tale about the werebeast heart, lieutenant? I mean, come on, you cannot seriously be so naive!"

As soon as I'd crossed the threshold of the medicine-stinking room, I started hearing the vexing beating of a heart. It had once been mine but was now beating in the chest of the Princess, and it was extremely simple to imagine fingers grasping it and giving a slight squeeze.

I clenched my fist. Princess Anna gasped and grabbed the table with the battery of variously colored flasks but still couldn't stay on her feet and slid down to the floor. William Grace threw himself on the heiress to the throne, lifted her head from the carpet and pointed the pistol at me.

"Stop it!" he shouted. "Stop it this instant!"

I unclenched my fingers and the Princess started breathing hoarsely.

"That is low!" she reproached me, when she had gotten onto the bed with the lieutenant's help and laid her head on the pillow.

"What's low is cutting out your cousin's heart!" I parried, placing a hand behind my back and walking over the luxurious Persian rug, looking at the landscape paintings of famous painters hanging on the walls, mostly depicting endless steppe. Some of them were made in such detail that they seemed to be windows into another world. But, unfortunately, they were not. Simple pictures, nothing more.

"I had not made a decision!" the Princess answered after a second's pause.

"So, it wasn't you that ordered the guardsmen to shoot me then? It isn't your fault? Your circle just filled up with these moral abominations all on its own?"

The Princess glanced at the lieutenant, who was still holding me in the sights of his pistol, and very quietly and calmly, but just so as to make shivers run over my skin, asked:

"Is that true, William?"

"It was necessary!" he answered calmly.

I didn't barge into their conversation, took the binoculars from the table and walked over to the window, wanting to see what had caught the Princess's interest. The windows of the heiress to the throne's chambers looked out over the Old City and Calvary looming over it. I could even see the iron tower on top of the hill. But no matter where I looked, my gaze returned unfailingly to Palace Square or, to be more accurate, to the sky above it. The clouds there, as before, were spinning into an inverted crater. In the depths of it, the ominous luster of the underworld continued to glisten. Shooting the priests hadn't changed anything.

My heart was clenched by fear, and I hurried to walk back from the window deeper into the room.

"Well, your Highness," I turned to the Princess, the pallor slowly retreating from her face, "have you decided who is at fault here and what must be done with him?"

"More respect!" William Grace growled. He hadn't yet put his pistol back in the holster but was no longer poking me with it.

"Cousin, we are in the same snare!" the Princess reminded me, burning me through with the gaze of her *illustrious* eyes. "And what was that ghastly trick you just performed?"

"My heart... let's just say you're only leasing it and put a pin in that topic. We can return to it in better times."

"No, allow..." the lieutenant began to boil over again, but the Princess immediately cut him off.

"We're leaving this topic for now!" she ordered, heavily standing from the bed and walking to the table to drink some medicine.

I delicately turned away but continued to follow the lieutenant with the corner of my eye. After long hesitation, he had returned his pistol to the holster.

"Cousin, what can you say about our position?" Crown Princess Anna asked, having swallowed a pill with a few gulps of mineral water.

"In decent society, it is not accepted to say such things," I joked unhappily and shuddered when a nearby machine-gun burst knocked with a frequent thrum.

The disordered firing continued for a few seconds and the glass echoed from grenade explosions. All that time, the electric nightlight flickered. As soon as the firefight quieted down, it again glowed with an even and sharp light.

"Don't be afraid, cousin," the Princess smiled. "The defense can hold out another few days, and the possessed will be held back by the guardsmen."

I could say that I was not afraid, but I didn't deny the obvious. I was afraid and didn't see any reason to hide that. To me, fear was not something to be ashamed of. From my very birth, it was a part of me.

"There's no way back out into the city," the lieutenant said, looking down at his feet. "We only got through the magical fog by a miracle. The hand-held dischargers do not have enough power for us to make it back."

I could have said whose bone-headed decision it was that had lost us the armored vehicle, but I didn't, just asked:

"Is the telephone still working?"

"With outages," Crown Princess Anna answered. "And what of it?"

"A bomb was thrown at the regent, he's wounded. Maybe..."

"No," my cousin shook her head. "Nothing changed. I was promised they'd prepare me a special dirigible, but they cannot say when it will arrive. I don't believe them."

"I'm certain that, in the nearest time, your death will be officially announced," William Grace poured oil on the fire.

I couldn't see a reason to make such guesses and got right to the heart of the issue:

"Your Highness, how long exactly will the palace's reserve batteries last?"

"Two or three days," the Princess forwarded. "And what of it?"

"We cannot run, our defenses won't last long, and we cannot not count on help," I enumerated and chuckled. "Did I miss something?"

"Get to the point!" William Grace demanded, looking at me like a wolf.

I didn't engage him in a skirmish and asked the Princess:

"What do you know about our defenses against the underworld, your Highness? Not just the palace's but the whole Empire's?"

Crown Princess Anna shivered cold-bloodedly and forwarded:

"Is it somehow connected with electromagnetic radiation? I haven't probed into such details."

"It is, that's exactly it," I confirmed. "And somewhere in the palace, there is a transmitter creating disturbances, depriving these defenses of effectiveness. Most likely, it was installed by an order from the regent. We cannot find it. The only way out is to totally disactivate the power grid."

"Then the palace will be left without power!" the Princess shot out.

"As soon as the disturbances stop, the radiation from the Sublime Electricity transmitters will drive off the demons and dispel the magic. We'll just have to fight off the possessed."

"But wait!" my cousin frowned. "As soon as the battery loses charge, the other transmitter will stop giving off disturbances! We can simply wait!"

"I suspect the transmitter doesn't need as much power to work normally as the palace defenses do," I sighed. "They will turn off much sooner."

"William, what do you say?" Crown Princess Anna then turned to the lieutenant.

Grace faltered for an instant, but overcame himself and answered with military directness:

"We shouldn't underestimate the conspirators. They could easily reach the remaining Sublime Electricity transmitters and destroy them. Then, there will be nothing to save us."

The Princess shook her head.

"I cannot give an order to turn off the reserve batteries. They'll simply think I've gone mad!" she declared, her fists clenched in anxiety. "That is our only defense against hostile magic. We cannot deprive our people of hope!"

"Then we'll do it ourselves!" William Grace declared.

"The two of us?"

The lieutenant looked at me in doubt and cringed.

"I could manage alone."

"No!" Crown Princess Anna shot out. "It's too

dangerous. You'll have to go down into the basement, and we have no information about what is happening there right now. You'll both go!"

"If you say so, your Highness," William Grace gave in facilely.

"Cousin?"

"You can count on me."

"Then go at once!" the Princess ordered. "And invite your companions to my room. I'd like to get to know them."

We left the heiress to the throne's chambers and, while William Grace lied to the captain about inspecting the reserve power source, I had time to look around. I was most surprised that there were no *illustrious* among the ladies-in-waiting or the guardsmen.

Was it really true that all *illustrious* had been purged from the palace?

"Let's go," Grace called me, throwing the strap of his Gauss caster over his shoulder.

"And what about the cable gun?" I kicked the backpack with the electric battery that was lying against the wall with the tip of my boot.

"I don't think we'll need it. The protection is still working for now."

"It is," I nodded, but still brought the grenade pouch with me.

6

WE HAD TO GO DOWN into the basement through the elevator shaft. It was dark, gloomy and seemingly bottomless. The stairwells had been mined, so there simply was no other way.

Clacking my boot soles on the iron rungs, I went down first, jumped onto the stone floor and lit up the room with my torch, revealing many dark corridors.

"Another basement!" I muttered quietly to myself, looking around, but William Grace still heard me.

"What?" he got on guard.

"Nothing. Where to now?"

"Follow me," the lieutenant said confidently, as if he had been here many times, and we walked down the underground passage, following rubberized wires snaking under the ceiling.

The presence of the otherworldly could not be felt one bit in the basement and there was good reason. The air down here was so electrified that our every movement was accompanied by an electric rustling. This was no place for demons.

But our opponents were such low beasts that they let the underworld have a hundred-point advantage. My hands were just itching to shoot the lieutenant in the back of the head – just for preventative purposes! – and I had to shake myself and talk myself out of doing anything stupid.

"It's here!" William Grace said a bit later and

started unlocking the door, which was no less monumental than that of a bank vault.

As soon as we walked into the long basement, my skin was pinched by the huge amount of static charge in the air. My head started spinning. In the depths of the room, lit by the uneven glow of electric bulbs, there were rows of electric cabinets all along the walls. Each of them had a breaker painted red.

"You take the left row, I take the right!" William pointed and lowered the first lever, severing the sealed wires.

I followed his example, and we walked down the basement, disabling one cabinet after the next. And the farther we walked, the more the static electricity receded in favor of the icy presence of the otherworldly.

"Faster!" I shouted, now at a run.

The lieutenant was not far behind.

When the line of electric cabinets finally ended, and the emergency lighting turned off, I turned to the exit. But a bright torch beam sharply cut into my face.

"I suppose we'll have to sort everything out here and now." William Grace had picked a bad time to have it out.

The stone floor shook underfoot, and cold shivers of incertitude ran down my back. But I didn't lose my presence of mind and gave an arrogant sniffle, hiding the Cerberus I had snuck down here behind my back.

"You'd shoot an unarmed man?" I asked,

masking my fear behind a crooked smirk. "How noble!"

"Tell me, by what diabolic means did you deprive her Highness of consciousness!" the lieutenant demanded. "And don't get a mind to lie or wheedle! I can easily sniff out a lie!"

"And what does it matter to you?" I snorted and, in an intentionally provocative tone, enquired: "Were you appointed to be her Highness's keeper? Or is it personal?"

To be perfectly honest, I was intending to shoot him as soon as he moved. My teeth were grinding due to my fear of basements, and dying – again or once and for all? – in a basement made me doubly fearful. And I was not going to waste valuable time, nor allow myself to get shot.

I wanted to get out of here right away and was watching the lieutenant closely. His face had gone purple in rage, but before he managed to do anything, the already impenetrable black shadows of the underground behind him grew denser.

"People...!"

The quiet whisper sounded out right in my head and passed over my bare nerves like an emery board. William Grace turned sharply and pointed his electric torch at the skinless, crimson flesh of Itztli.

"Pitiful little souls!" the deity of obsidian blades exhaled and sharply jerked his bloodied arm, as if tearing our little souls right out of our bodies.

William Grace collapsed dead on the stone floor. An instant later, the unknown power sharply knocked me forward as well. An unbearable pain flashed in my chest, and before my eyes everything started swimming. But just then, my tattoos scorched my skin with a burning fire, and that burning helped me stay on my feet in the most astonishing way. Not paying any mind to the smell of burned flesh, I straightened up, spread my shoulders and laughed through the pain:

"Is that the best you can do?"

The deity of obsidian blades was still wafting with the otherworldly, but the Cerberus was renowned for its reliability against wizardly charms, and I could count on three shots no matter how this played out. Most important was not to miss.

"I'll cut out your heart!" Itztli growled.

"It's already been cut out," I answered calmly and added with an acrid smile: "Twice!"

Itztli raised the obsidian knife, intending to run on the attack, and immediately a nasty metallic squeal rang out behind his back.

"Who's the snappy dresser?" asked the Beast, coming out of the darkness. The tip of the kitchen knife squeezed in his paw had left a long scratch on the door of an iron cabinet.

The Aztec god turned to the new opponent and unleashed a long tirade in an unfamiliar language. The echoes of his voice cut into my head like the clinking of a smith's hammer, while the Beast just contemptuously spit on the floor under him.

"Carrion, bugger!" he cringed. "Made of dead meat, and also full of bluster! Frankenstein's monster, bugger!"

Itztli threw himself on the attack in a movement not visible to the naked eye, but the Beast gracefully slipped away from the obsidian blade and split the side of his skinless rival in a return blow, as if making an incision on an anatomical mannequin.

I didn't join their skirmish, just shot all three rounds of the Cerberus into Itztli's back and took to my heels. The otherworldly presence of something immeasurably greater than this minor deity of blood rituals was warping the surrounding reality more and more, and just one word was pounding in my head: "Run! Run! Run!"

Sensing the fierce breath of the underworld behind me, I turned and saw a wave of icy fog racing down the corridor. I tossed an incendiary grenade as I ran, then another and ran on with all my might. The phosphorus flame allowed me to gain a few seconds, and that time was just enough for me to reach the elevator and start up the rungs immured into the shaft walls.

The wave of frost struck the stone wall and froze everything below, but I was already too high up. Just a blurred echo of the fierce evil reached me.

I got away!

While I climbed the brackets, I heard a frequent thunder of shots and grenade explosions from above. But before I managed to crawl out of the wide-open elevator doors, I heard the guardsmen shout out elated cries.

I couldn't hold back and cursed aloud.

It worked! It actually worked!

Bugger, how wonderful!

I laughed and laid out powerless on the cold marble floor, feeling like the true savior of the Empire.

But then, the sunken countenance of the gray-haired colonel loomed over me.

"Where is William?" he asked, looking me gloomily from top to bottom.

"Dead," I answered shortly, heavily standing to my feet. In my turn, I enquired: "I heard shouts, did something happen?"

"Her Highness ordered you brought right to her after inspecting the batteries," the colonel told me, leaving my question unanswered.

That worried me, but not too much. No matter how I spun it, despite the death of Lieutenant Grace our undertaking had culminated in unspeakable success. As soon as the conspirators' transmitter had stopped generating disturbances, the Sublime Electricity's signal had cast all the demons out of our reality. The possessed, though, who were less sensitive to radiation had just been forced to retreat into the catacombs. The black-magic fog quickly dispersed, and even the ghastly pit in the heavens started to fade and lose its dimensions. The purple flame in it faded.

When I, accompanied by the colonel and a few of his subordinates, walked into the guest room of her Highness's apartments, an untamable joy reigned. The ladies-in-waiting, the Imperial medics and guards were plainly overjoyed, as if they had been condemned to death but been pardoned at the last moment.

As for the Princess, though, she garbled her celebratory speech half word when I entered, drily congratulated the courtiers on the miraculous rescue and quickly hid in her chambers.

I handed in my weapon and headed off after her without any desire.

As soon as I closed the door behind me, my cousin walked away from the window sill she had been leaning on, and dismissed the lady-in-waiting oracle with an annoyed wave of the hand.

"Leopold! I'm waiting!" the heiress to the throne then called me by name.

Thomas Smith, sitting on the divan, was too occupied by his wounded leg to notice the annoyance that came through in her voice. But as for Elizabeth-Maria, she immediately turned away from the picture of poppies and sized me up with her stubborn gaze but, fortunately, didn't do anything.

Overcoming my indecision, I walked over and stood next to the Princess.

"What happened to Lieutenant Grace?" Anna asked whispering so no one else would hear.

"Electromagnetic waves don't make it underground. We were caught by a demon. The lieutenant died."

"How did you escape?"

Instead of answering, I pulled back my unbuttoned shirt collar, letting my cousin look at the tattoos inflamed on my neck by the burn. The designs on my shoulders, back and chest burned my skin no less.

Crown Princess Anna sighed fitfully, and the elevated beat of her heart began echoing painfully in my temples. My cousin was silent for a long time, gathering her thoughts, and was about to ask another question when a bright spark flashed somewhere in the city.

"What the devil?!" I cursed out and grabbed the binoculars. A few seconds later the powerful explosion's shockwave made it to us and the windowpanes rattled in their frames.

I watched the iron tower on top of Calvary careen to the side, torn out of the ground, then the pulse of an unseen battering ram knocked me away from the window. I tripped over an ottoman behind me and fell to the floor, while my cousin fell on top of me, having lost her balance. Thomas Smith was thrown off the divan, and the lady-in-waiting oracle fell senseless on the carpet. Only Elizabeth-Maria was still on her feet. But she too was turning her head and heavily leaning her hand on the wall like a boxer who had just taken a knockout punch.

"Curses!" I rasped out, lifting the heiress to the throne to her feet. "What now?!"

"It's in the castle!" my cousin exhaled. "It's here! Lock the room now!"

Finally knocked off course by the unexpected order, I ran over to the front door and, with horror, saw the servants and guardsmen in the entryway dead, as if the otherworldly creature rushing through the castle had drawn all the lifeforce from the people in one swipe. Only the *illustrious* had survived. The Princess, Thomas Smith, the lady-in-waiting and I could not be harmed by the diabolic curse. Elizabeth-Maria all the more.

"Door, cousin!" the Princess shouted again. "Lock it!"

The bodies of the servants began to stir, but it was not life that returned to them. Some incorporeal infernal creatures had entered their corpses.

"Curses..." I whispered, locking the bolt. Then the Princess gave a thin shout behind me.

I was next to her in an instant. I looked out the window and nearly shouted in surprise myself when I saw a giant figure on Palace Square with a bare skull.

The conspirators had fallen back on their reserve plan. After losing their electromagnetic disturbance device, they had rolled the dice and destroyed the last transmitter protecting New Babylon from the underworld. That risked wiping the whole city off the face of the earth and ending millions of lives but, in the struggle to determine the new world order, anything was allowed. To some, human blood is just the grease of the gears of history.

I wondered if Mr. Edison had a hand in all this.

I wanted to believe he didn't.

"We're dead!" The Princess whispered out as the door shuddered after a strong blow.

"Is there a secret passage here?" I asked.

Before my cousin managed to answer, the room was filled by a prolonged wail from the lady-in-waiting. Kneeling, the oracle was pressing her face in her hands. There were streams of dark blood running between her thin fingers with bright red nails. After that, she stood imperceptibly to her feet, moving brokenly and unevenly like a marionette. She pulled her hands from her face and led a frightening gaze over us, her eyes filled with an impenetrable blackness. In her bloodied hand, as if by magic, there appeared a ladies' pistol she'd snuck past the guards.

"Bow before the power of Mictlantecuhtli, lord of the dead!" the oracle said in another's voice and suddenly started laughing a mad, elusive and barking laughter. "Pitiful worms, who of you is ready for a meeting with the lord? Maybe you, beanpole?"

The muzzle stopped between my eyes, and I froze motionless, trying not to breathe.

"Or you, limpy?" the oracle whispered out, taking Smith in her sights. "Or you, red vixen? Oh no, what about our little sleepyhead?"

The lady-in-waiting, having fallen under the influence of the powerful otherworldly creature due to her *talent*, acquired an unbelievable sharpness of motion and turned her pistol from one to the next so rapidly that no one managed to even move. The blood covering her eyes did nothing to worsen her aim.

"So, who wants to meet the lord first?" the oracle asked. "No one knows but the lord! And me! I know! I know, oh yes!"

I was prepared to throw myself at the possessed lady if a chance presented itself, but I had no way of guessing her next move, so I just waited. The last thing I wanted was to catch a bullet.

"Skin to the right! Brains to the left!" the lady-in-waiting started to suddenly recite some ghastly rhyme, spinning ceaselessly in place like a Persian dervish. "Meat on ice! And eyeballs cleft!"

With every phrase, the pistol pointed at someone else, but not in a circle, without any obvious order.

"The bones they go for hellhound treats!" The lady-in-waiting turned her barrel from the succubus and aimed it at the princess. "And souls alone we do not keep!" she said after that and whispered out: "Oh poor Anna, I'm so sorry..."

Thomas Smith jumped off the divan just an instant before the oracle pulled down on the trigger. The investigator threw his arms in front of him, but his wounded leg left had less power than he wanted. He made it and was too late at the same time.

The bullet intended for the Princess pierced straight through his pistol hand and slammed into the investigator's left eye. Before Thomas hit the ground, Elizabeth-Maria had struck the lady-in-waiting with the lamp she grabbed off the nightstand. The bronze base easily split the skull of the possessed lady, and the oracle fell dead onto the ground. A single bloodied pearl rolled along the carpet.

"Curses!" Elizabeth-Maria exhaled, wiping the streaks of blood off her face. "Leo, we really put our foot in it this time!"

And I couldn't argue with that. The figure of the Aztec god of death was becoming more and more physical, and the evil emanating from it rolled over me in waves, bending reality with its power, intoxicating the conscience.

Our *illustrious* blood had protected us, but that couldn't last long.

"It was all in vain!" the Princess groaned, and the crystalline purity of her fear shook me no less than an electric shock.

In the fireplace chimney, I suddenly heard a rustling, and the Beast fell into the room in a cloud of soot. In his clawed paw, the albino was clenching a heart, pulsating with a ghostly luster. The air around was warped by the power of a *fallen one*.

The Princess shrieked in surprise and flattened herself against the wall, while my imaginary friend calmly threw back his head, clenched his claws and squeezed the rest of the blood from Itztli's heart into his mouth.

"Bugger, rotten meat!" he cursed, throwing the heart into the far corner of the room and taking the jar of coca leaves I'd lost in the catacombs from under his blood-soaked cloak.

"You're the last thing we needed here!" Elizabeth-Maria cringed.

"What beast is this?" the Princess asked, her teeth chattering in fear as the albino started packing his mouth with the juicy foliage.

"Where are your manners, cousin?" the Beast growled, working his jaws quickly. Then, he pulled out the kitchen knife he had tucked into his belt. "Bugger! Leo, don't yawn! I'll be blown up!"

"What is happening?!" Anna cried when the

albino walking toward her slit his meaty palm with the knife.

"I need your nightmare!" I answered in an attack of sudden illumination. "Let me bring that rain of fire into reality! Let me burn the impurity out once and for all!"

The Princess hesitated.

"Believe me!" I begged. "It's our only chance to escape!"

"But how?!"

"Just accept the power and give me your fear!"

Anna bit her lip and decisively extended her right hand. The Beast split the heiress to the throne's skin unceremoniously and squeezed her fragile girlish hand hard with his big paw. The glow filling the albino ran out into the Princess, and he started to quickly flicker and become incorporeal.

Without delay, I clenched my cousin's free hand and stretched out with my *illustrious talent* to the horror beating desperately inside her. I scrambled further and deeper, past it to her nightly nightmares of fiery rain, the vile stench of burned flesh and the fierce luster of a new star in the black stormy heavens over New Babylon.

The power pouring out of the Beast lashed me with a stormy flow and ran into the desolate dead-ends of her consciousness. I didn't resist its pressure. Quite the opposite. I sped it up and drove it on, stoking the flame of her fear of the end of the world further and further, manifesting it with my *illustrious talent*.

— The Dormant —

But before I finished, the flow of power suddenly ran dry.

The Beast dissolved without a trace and the old kitchen knife fell with a metallic clang to the floor, while I was flung away from my cousin onto the bed. I did a somersault over it and rolled onto the rug.

Princess Anna, though, didn't even flinch. With her arms spread wide, she was frozen in the middle of the room. The statue-like immobility combined in a surprising way with the marble whiteness of her skin. Crimson blood continued to streak down the split skin of her palm. In all other ways, though the Princess remained fully motionless, not blinking and, seemingly, not even breathing.

Or was she really not breathing?

I overcame the weakness that had captivated me, and stood to my feet, walked over to the window and looked outside with hope. But the ghostly black crater was still spinning in the heavens as before. No firestorm, none of the furor of a star falling to earth.

The angel had not appeared to save us. I had failed.

But then, the otherworldly dread from Palace Square wafted stronger and stronger, the emanation of evil piercing my soul and tearing it to bits. Reality withered and was destroyed, not able to bear the unnatural presence of Mictlantecuhtli. The light of day went dark, the purple fires in the empty eyeholes of the Aztec god's skull blazed brighter than the sun.

"It was all pointless," I rasped out, spitting a clot of blood on the floor. "Pointless..."

The electromagnetic radiation was no longer protecting New Babylon, and the power of *the fallen* had flowed between my fingers and evaporated without a trace. Nothing could stop the Aztec divinity of death from throwing open the gates of his underworldly kingdom now.

I prayed for the Creator to come to our aid!

The light on the square finally went dark. I stumbled back from the window and unexpectedly realized that this had nothing to do with the sun going out. No, it was all to do with the luster behind my back!

I turned sharply and covered my eyes with my hand, not having the strength to bear the glow emanating from the Princess. My cousin was hovering a half meter off the floor with her arms spread wide. Blinding beams were blasting out of her wide-open eyes, and her dress had burned to ash. The fiery threads of tendons burned under her skin, filling the room with an unnaturally bright glow as if from thousands and thousands of bulbs.

The silhouette of the Princess lit up and she began to become incorporeal, at the same time increasing in size and turning into a living luster. Then – in an instant! – with a taught clap, blindingly white wings spread out behind her back.

A burst of thickened air threw me to the wall, but even the dizziness of the strong blow to the back of my head didn't stop me from recognizing the blinding figure. It was exactly what the angelic embodiment of the Princess looked like in the dream!

Only then did I realize what a mistake I'd made. My cousin was not afraid of the retaliation of *the fallen*, nor the end of the world. She was horrified that she might lose her human essence and become something else once and for all!

Cretin! Damned cretin!

The beating of the angelic heart echoed in my head with an unbearable pain. All the color in the room dimmed and faded, while the pictures turned into gray panels, as if the Princess had taken every last drop of their beauty.

I do not know how long I would have been able to withstand the horrifying presence of this supernatural creature, but a light flap of her blindingly white wings made the stone wall of the palace shudder and with a deafening creak, she fell outside.

The angel was pushed out of the castle and started falling to the ground. She her wings just above the earth and rose up to the very heavens with a fiery flourish.

The clouds, cloven by this rapid motion, burned with the luster of red-hot steel, and a sulfur rain began lashing down on the Old City.

Chaos raced over the city with a destructive tsunami of fire. Fragments of glass exploded, and the doors flew out. Tile flew off roofs and some whole buildings just collapsed. Towers were demolished, and trees were pulled up by the roots. Everywhere and everything was flickering with the purifying flame of the heavens.

I hurriedly retreated deeper inside, but still could sense the burning echoes of fire, which torched the otherworldly power, not leaving the Aztec god of the dead the slightest chance. The supernatural fire even burned and dissolved the granite tiles of Palace Square. It seemed the air itself was burning outside.

And it was.

The gates to the kingdom of the dead dispersed without a trace, and their ghastly creator went with them.

And suddenly, the ferocity of the fiery rain falling onto the capital started diminishing, while the blinding star hovering over the square shot up into the heavens like a roman candle. But the angel didn't disappear from this world, nothing of the sort. I could still sense the echo of her measured heartbeat in my head.

"Damn it..." I whispered, not having the power to think over what had happened.

Something suddenly rustled under the Princess's bed and a disheveled Elizabeth-Maria crawled out.

"Just what was that?" she demanded an explanation. "Leo, what have you done now?!"

"It wasn't me," I answered, shaken by a nervous shiver. "It was all fear."

"Did you bring a *fallen one* back to life?" Elizabeth-Maria squinted. "You decided to manifest a nightmare?!"

"It was not a *fallen one*, but an angel," I corrected the succubus. "I turned my cousin into an angel. That was her fear."

"Yet another image in your head?" Elizabeth-Maria cringed and licked a drop of blood off the back of her hand.

"You might say that," I confirmed, undoing the lock.

The front door took some effort to open due to the heap of bodies on the other side but, overcoming my disgust, I walked over them into the guest room then out into the corridor.

It was simply unbearable to remain in the palace.

Elizabeth-Maria followed me and suddenly asked:

"And where'd you get the power, Leo?" but she immediately waved it off. "No, don't answer. It doesn't matter now."

"What do you mean?" I turned.

"It doesn't matter where you got the power. It matters that you didn't give it to me. You violated your oath, Leo."

Sensing an incomprehensible consternation, I took a step back from the succubus, and held my open hand out in front of me in an awkward defensive gesture, then sped up:

"Wait! But I saved us! I saved everyone, this whole cursed city!"

"I don't give a damn about this city!" Elizabeth-Maria raised her voice. An instant later, she was next to me. "You broke an oath!"

Her long fingers clenched my shoulder. Her

nails had become claws and pierced my jacket through to the flesh, stopping me from pushing her away.

"What are you doing?" I rasped out, nearly losing consciousness from the piercing pain.

"I'm taking what is rightfully mine!"

"But what about my soul?"

"Keep it! I no longer need it!" the succubus laughed, clenching something invisible in the fingers of her free hand and pulling it to her.

She pulled out my *talent.*

Everything started swimming before my eyes. The world became a blur.

Red hair became black, facial features grew more defined, and a sickly angularity took shape. I suddenly realized that before me was no longer Elizabeth-Maria, but Crown Princess Anna. The succubus had become her infernal twin, a doppelganger.

"You've got a wonderful talent, cousin!" Elizabeth-Maria said in another's voice and shrugged her narrow shoulders, allowing her leather jacket to slide off. "Just astonishing! And now, it's mine!"

"And what about me?" I murmured with a lifeless rustle. "What about me?"

"You're long dead, my boy. You just cannot make peace with that. But you'll have to..."

Elizabeth-Maria stepped back abruptly, as if breaking the thread that bound us, and my chest was pierced with a sharp pain. Something squelched and blood flowed from a gaping wound. In a soundless plea, I extended a hand to the succubus, but the beast threw my hand back with a laugh. I had already started to get corpse spots.

"Make peace with it, Leo. Make your peace and die already!"

A sharp jab pushed me onto my back. I fell face up on the cold stones, broke through them and fell into the very underworld. But only my soul went into the abyss, my body remained, looking with glassy eyes at the ceiling.

I died.

7

DEATH IS FALLING into an abyss, fast and unending. There are no devils with pitchforks, one's soul simply flies into a black hole, passing old memories and breaking into bits on the sharp edges of insults and disenchantments. Then it grows back just in time to slam full speed into another betrayal or treachery. And so on, without end.

The cold of the icy basement, the dim light of a kerosene lamp, the steely reflection of a butcher's knife – a carefully forgotten memory had just begun to pull and swallow my mind when a certain power burst into my soul with a ghostly harpoon and drew it back into my body with a sharp burst.

I squirmed, coughed and started breathing.

I cursed.

I was reborn.

Not feeling capable of believing the miracle, I yanked the shirt off my chest and gasped in amazement, not seeing any open wounds, or even old scars. What was more, even my tattoos had disappeared. I had become the person I was born as, and there could only be one explanation for that.

"Liliana!" I whispered, feeling the subtle support of her faith.

That could not save me from a banal knife blow or bullet to the back of the head, but my girlfriend believed, and her sincere faith had managed to replace my absent *talent*.

Stumbling and faltering at every step, I walked over to the first set of mirrors. The succubus had left her old clothing next to them, but I just stared at my new reflection. I had calm gray eyes and a round face, no longer so sharp and angular.

I had become the very person Lily imagined me to be. I had changed somewhat, but I was alive again. I could easily leave everything as it was, quietly sneak out of the palace, go to Switzerland and never regret my decision.

What was more, that was exactly what I should have done.

Liliana had given me the chance to start everything again, and it would have been deeply ungrateful to not make use of that chance.

Become a normal person and not sense fears, not touch them and not manifest them. Use my imagination only when reading books. Get married, have children, live the calm and quiet life of a rentier with my beloved wife and die on the same day as her.

I was supposed to accept Liliana's gift, but I could not do so.

After all, I no longer heard the beating of my second heart so I was doomed to see a dead angel in my dreams, full of hopeless sorrow, hovering in the black wasteland of space until the end of days. And every night, I would die together with it in the midst of that limitless waste.

Every cursed night...

I didn't want that for myself.

Anyhow, who was I trying to fool?

In fact, my teeth were grinding with desire to square up with the succubus!

It was my thirst for revenge that forced me to act; the noble will to rid the Empire of the power of a bloodthirsty monster, capable of outdoing Caligula and Nero together in her madness was just an excuse for my own unreasonable act.

I returned to the guest room of the heiress to the throne's chambers, picked up the cable gun Lieutenant Grace had left on the floor and looked thievishly into the room with a missing wall.

The succubus was standing there, her naked female figure enshrouded in wisps of ghostly smoke, the remnants of the otherworldly power that had yet to fully burn away. Elizabeth-Maria was feeding on these particles greedily. Slowly but surely, the gloomy luster of the black nimbus of a *fallen one* was forming around her head.

Then the succubus suddenly threw her hands over her head and shouted out in rage, shaking her frail fists:

"I'm on top of the world! Forever!"

Then I caught her feminine back in my sights and plunked down on the trigger of the pneumatic gun. It clapped and the spool unwound with a shriek, unwinding the wire. An imperceptible instant later, the lance went straight through the succubus and stuck out of her chest with two bloodied points.

Elizabeth-Maria stayed on her feet and fitfully grabbed the steel prongs with her hands, hurrying to pull them out, but then the shock flickered up. Electricity started lacerating the succubus, changing her body and returning it to its initial appearance. But the transformation from ungainly heiress to the throne into a seductive creature with a high chest, waspish waist and long legs was not her final one. Soon, the pale skin of the succubus was covered with slippery scales, and sharp fangs sprouted from the mouth. Her back warped into a disgusting hump with two long scars, seemingly left by lost wings.

The demonic being turned and stumbled, but stayed on its feet and walked toward me, burning with desire to tear me to shreds. The electric jar in the backpack had already begun sparking and smoking, so I threw the cable gun away and took a step back, feverishly looking around for another weapon, but then the electric power finally overcame the succubus. Her deformed body fell onto the floor and began twitching in endless convulsions.

Electricity is stronger than magic. That was for certain.

"I should have done that from the very beginning," I gasped out hoarsely, picking up the kitchen knife from the rug and, standing over the motionless succubus, gave a crooked smile. "Anyhow, some things are better done late than never..."

A QUARTER HOUR LATER, I left the palace, covered head to toe in vile sticky blood and holding a glass jar under my armpit. It had once housed the coca leaves, but now there was a muscular chunk of demonic heart in it, beating measuredly. I hadn't taken it out of some desire to consume it, it was just too dangerous to leave the receptacle of dark power in the broken body of the succubus.

The light of day seemed unexpectedly sharp and bright. My eyes burned unbearably. I had to pull my dark glasses with cracked lenses from my wide-open shirt and clip them on my nose.

My eyes were no longer gray. My *illustrious talent* had returned after the death of the succubus and my body had also returned to normal.

The scars, tattoos and sores all came back.

But I didn't regret a thing.

Curses! I was happy.

I had become myself again!

I heard the sonorous clacking of iron heels on the stones, turned and saw the leprechaun in his rumpled accordioned top hat, dirty green camisole and boots with no toe jumping from one granite tile of the square to the next.

"You have to remember not to step on the cracks!" he shouted, continuing his simple game. "Remember, boy! If you step on a crack, you'll have to marry a witch!"

I just shook my head and walked away.

And I didn't even turn when the tapping behind me suddenly cut off and I heard an annoyed: "Bugger!"

In the sky over the haze of clouds, there was the faintly glowing luster of a second sun. At the same time, I could hear the sharp echoes of another's heart stronger and stronger in my head.

Because of that, I was not going stay in New Babylon for an hour, even or a minute longer than I had to.

I had no desire to figure out whether her angelic majesty the Queen Empress Anna intended to begin her rule with retribution against the apostates for their sins or would suppress her righteous anger and not turn her subjects into pillars of salt left and right.

I knew perfectly well already what I would do and sticking around had no place in my plans.

I was intending to cross to the continent on the first ferry, find Liliana and take her as far away as I could.

To Siberia or even Zuid-India. Even to the edge of the world, or past it! Anywhere, as long as it was far from New Babylon.

This cursed city had drunk enough of my blood, and it would be stupid to give it another chance to put me in the grave. In the end, there were plenty of places on earth where Leopold Orso, the *illustrious* Viscount Cruce hadn't fallen into scrapes...

End of Book Four

Want to be the first to know about our latest LitRPG, sci fi and fantasy titles from your favorite authors?

Subscribe to our NEW RELEASES newsletter:
http://eepurl.com/b7niIL

Thank you for reading *The Dormant!*
If you like what you ve read, check out other LitRPG
books and series published by Magic Dome Books:

Dark Paladin LitRPG series by Vasily Mahanenko:
The Beginning
The Quest

**The Dark Herbalist LitRPG series
by Michael Atamanov:**
Video Game Plotline Tester
Stay on the Wing
A Trap for the Potentate

The Neuro LitRPG series by Andrei Livadny:
The Crystal Sphere
The Curse of Rion Castle
The Reapers

**The Way of the Shaman LitRPG series
by Vasily Mahanenko:**
Survival Quest
The Kartoss Gambit
The Secret of the Dark Forest
The Phantom Castle
The Karmadont Chess Set
Shaman's Revenge
Clans War
The Hour of Pain (a bonus short story)

Galactogon LitRPG series by Vasily Mahanenko:
Start the Game!

Phantom Server LitRPG series by Andrei Livadny:
Edge of Reality
The Outlaw
Black Sun

**Perimeter Defense LitRPG series by Michael
Atamanov:**
Sector Eight
Beyond Death
New Contract
A Game with No Rules